KING ARTHUR AND HER KNIGHTS BOXSET- BOOKS 4, 5, AND 6

EMBARK, ENLIGHTEN, AND ENDEAVOR

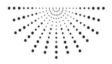

K. M. SHEA

KING ARTHUR AND HER KNIGHTS BOXSET- BOOKS 4, 5, and 6

Copyright © 2017 by K. M. Shea

Cover design by Myrrhlynn

www.kmshea.com

ISBN-10: 0692979905

ISBN-13: 978-0692979907

❀ Created with Vellum

CHARACTERS

Adelind: Wife of King Pellinore—Queen of Anglesey

Agravain: The second son of King Lot and Queen Morgause of Orkney.

Ban: One of two kings who marched with Britt against Lot and his allies. He is from France, is well groomed, and is said to have a son who is an impressive knight.

Bedivere: A knight Britt met in London when she was crowned King. Britt chose him as her marshal on an impulse, without any input from Merlin.

Bodwain: Britt's constable and one of Merlin's Minions.

Bors: One of two kings who marched with Britt against Lot and his allies. He is from France, although he appears to be half bear. His two sons are said to be gallivanting around with King Ban's son.

Ector: The man who was selected to be Arthur's foster father. He has taken a similar role in Britt's life.

Gaheris: The third son of King Lot and Queen Morgause of Orkney.

Gareth: The youngest son of King Lot and Queen Morgause of Orkney.

Gawain: The eldest son of King Lot and Queen Morgause of Orkney.

Griflet: A young, ignorant knight who is related to Sir Bedivere and is close friends with Ywain.

Guinevere: The daughter of King Leodegrance whom Britt dislikes thanks to modern King Arthur stories and legends.

Igraine: Mother of the real Arthur. Uther Pendragon was her second husband.

Kay: Britt's seneschal and supposed foster brother. He takes Britt's safety seriously and is often seen writing in a log book.

Lancelot: The only son of King Bors whom Britt despises thanks to modern King Arthur stories and legends.

Leodegrance: King of Camelgrance, one of Britt's first allies.

Lot: King of Orkney and Britt's worst enemy. He rallied kings and knights and led them to battle before Britt and her allies overthrew him.

Maleagant: A duke and friend of King Ryence.

Merlin: Britt's chief counselor who is also responsible for yanking Britt back through time. He openly uses Britt to accomplish his dream of uniting Britain.

Morgause: Daughter of Igraine and Arthur's half-sister. She is married to King Lot of Orkney and has four sons: Gawain, Agravain, Gaheris, and Gareth.

Morgan le Fay: Daughter of Igraine, Arthur's half-sister and full sister to Queen Morgause and Queen Elaine. She is known to have magical powers.

Nymue: The beautiful Lady of the Lake who "gave" Excalibur to Britt.

Pellinore: A noble-looking king who attacked Britt with King Lot, King Urien, and King Ryence.

Percival: A Knight of the Round Table and the son of King Pellinore.

Ryence: A cowardly king who attacked Britt with King Lot, King Urien, and King Pellinore.

Tor: The son of a cowherd who is made a knight by Britt. He has a squire named Lem.

Ulfius: An older knight who once served Uther Pendragon and now serves Britt as her chamberlain. He is one of Merlin's Minions.

Urien: The brother-in-law of King Lot and a king in his own right, Urien fought with Lot, Pellinore, and Ryence against Britt but has since become Britt's vassal because he believes she holds his son, Ywain, hostage in Camelot.

Uther Pendragon: Considered to be one of the greatest kings of England. He is the real Arthur's father and died some years ago —leaving all of his lands and money to Arthur.

Ywain: The only son of King Urien. He swore loyalty to Britt after being captured by her men and has revered her ever since. Morgause is his aunt.

EMBARK:

KING ARTHUR AND HER KNIGHTS BOOK 4

GUINEVERE'S ARRIVAL

Britt was wearing her best set of armor when Guinevere arrived. Not her gold armor, but the silver set that was emblazoned with the red dragon—her personal insignia, the symbol of King Arthur.

"They've arrived?" Britt asked, emerging from the castle keep with bright, blue eyes. Cavall, her apricot-colored mastiff, snuffled as Britt laid her hand on the dog's head.

Sir Kay eyed her with apprehension. "The watchmen confirmed that Lady Guinevere and her escort have passed the outer gates of Camelot and are approaching the inner palace gates," he said.

"Excellent! Thanks, Kay. You're the best." Britt left her foster-brother and made a beeline for a pavilion raised above the court-yard for such occasions.

"Is it time, My Lord?" Gawain—Sir Gawain now, as Britt had knighted him a little over a week ago—asked as he joined Britt at the base of the pavilion.

"Finally, yes," Britt said, self-consciously checking her gold hair to make certain it was pulled back in a "manly" half ponytail. "I nearly forgot. Has Gaheris mended yet?"

Sir Gawain bowed. "I expect in a day or two he shall demand another go at riding a charger. Indeed, I don't think the spill did much besides rattle his bones."

"I'm glad to hear that." Britt stretched her mind to see if she could remember any Arthurian lore about Gaheris. For what felt like the hundredth time since she arrived in medieval England, she wished she knew more about the mythical King Arthur. That would make her job as the stand-in, counterfeit Arthur, easier.

Britt was an American girl from the twenty-first century. When touring England with friends, an ancient magic pulled her through time, plopping her in medieval London where Merlin explained that the real Arthur had run off with a shepherdess, and Britt was going to be the replacement.

"My Lord, you must be anxious to once again set your eyes on the delightful pinnacle of femininity that is Lady Guinevere," another knight said, joining Sir Gawain at the base of the stairs.

Britt managed not to groan, but she couldn't help the sneer that spread across her lips. "For the last time, Lancelot, Guinevere is *not* my lady-love," she said. "She is staying in Camelot as a visitor—as many noble ladies do. I shall be her guardian of sorts —*not* her lover."

As King Arthur, she made the unfortunate acquaintance of Sir Lancelot du Lac—the legendary figure Britt had despised from childhood thanks to his unscrupulous affair with Queen Guinevere, whom Britt had scarcely kinder feelings for.

Britt had reluctantly come to tolerate the idea of Lady Guinevere—or perhaps it was better to say she felt sorry for the girl since her father tried to use her as a bargaining chip to gather more money—but Britt's hatred for Lancelot the swine still burned brightly.

"As you say, My Lord. But I have seen you trounce an evil duke for her. Indeed, your generous love knows no bounds. A knight such as I—who has traveled near and far to save fair damsels—would understand that," Lancelot said with a winning smile before he bowed to a passing lady.

To Britt's irritation, the lady giggled before hurrying on her way. Lancelot's coal black hair and dreamy green eyes often had that effect on the women of Camelot, much to Britt's disgust.

"It seems most of your knights are present, My Lord," Sir Gawain said, recapturing Britt's attention.

"Yes," Britt agreed, her eyes sweeping over the hoards of men eagerly lining the courtyard. "Although I'm afraid I don't understand why."

"It's no secret you've been looking forward to this day since we returned to Camelot weeks ago, My Lord," Sir Gawain said, his lips creasing in a subdued smile.

Britt gave the younger knight a returning grin. "Perhaps."

Lancelot looked back and forth between the two and, for quite possibly the first time since Britt met the self-inflated knight, said nothing. Instead, Britt and her two knights watched the servants scurry about, finishing last-minute preparations as heralds gathered at the base of the keep and knights assembled, making the courtyard a lake of glittering chainmail and armor.

When Lady Guinevere—daughter of King Leodegrance of Camelgrance—and her escort entered the courtyard, it was packed with all the typical signs of pomp and joy. Flags and standards flapped in the wind; the knights were dressed in their best armor; and several notes were sounded on horns and beaten on drums.

Guinevere dismounted her palfrey, a small, sweet-tempered mare. She stuck out even when her serving ladies joined her, her reddish-blonde hair gleaming in the afternoon sun. Behind her were dozens of knights guarding numerous carts—some of which contained Guinevere's belongs; the rest held a gift from the penny-pinching King Leodegrance.

Those from Camelot grew quiet when Britt swept down the stairs of the pavilion, a soft smile filled with longing twitching across her lips. Like a man in a dream, Britt walked down the pathway that opened up in front of her as her knights edged out of her way. She broke through the crowd, her smile growing wider and her footsteps quicker. Knights looked knowingly to each other and ladies tittered as they watched Britt—King Arthur —approach Guinevere and...pass her.

Those from Camelot stopped talking altogether as Britt approached a cart and twitched off an animal hide that was wrapped around what appeared to be a curved section of a rather scratched-up table.

"Finally, the Round Table has arrived," Britt said, her voice filled with awe as she placed a hand on the table top.

"Are you *crying?*" Merlin asked, his sudden appearance at Britt's side causing exclamations and startled yips.

"So what if I am? This is it, Merlin. The Round Table! It's finally here—the legend can *finally* begin," Britt said.

Merlin frowned. "You are too concerned with the legends of the future. A square table would serve you just as well."

"No. It has to be the Round Table," Britt said, pulling another hide off a different section of the Round Table—which was donut-shaped since it was so large it had to be pieced together like a toy train-track.

"That may be so. But you have neglected to welcome your guest," Merlin dryly said.

"What?" Britt said.

Merlin tipped his head in Guinevere's direction.

"Oh," Britt said. "Right. Sorry."

"By the Bells of Heaven—it's a good thing you're charismatic and charming when you choose to be," Merlin said, his voice dripping with disapproval.

Britt reluctantly parted from the table, giving it one last look of longing before she pasted her King Arthur smile on. "Welcome, Lady Guinevere—daughter of King Leodegrance—and Knights of Camelgrance. May you be at peace here in Camelot and find your stay to be filled with rest and all things that are good as you wander from your home."

"What is that supposed to mean?" Merlin asked through his teeth that were clenched in an uncomfortable-looking smile.

"It means they're not staying here forever," Britt muttered. Her words were also hidden behind a smile.

"I thank you, King Arthur, for your generous invitation that allows me to visit Camelot," Guinevere said. Britt wondered at her sincerity, but after studying Guinevere's bright eyes that were widened with curiosity, she grudgingly accepted them.

"My father sends his best wishes and the table of King Uther as a token of his respect and esteem. He has also sent several dozen knights to serve in your courts."

Britt and Merlin exchanged looks. King Leodegrance was a known coward. His knights were most likely of the same mold, which meant they would be little more than a decoration and a drain on the treasury.

"Oh," Merlin said. "He shouldn't have."

Britt shrugged. "We already have Lancelot and his piggy cousins staying with us. What's a few more mouths?" she whispered to Merlin before giving Guinevere a politician's smile. "Your father is too kind to part with such stout knights. I hope you all find Camelot agreeable in your stay. If you wish to be directed to your quarters, please see Sir Ulfius. He is my chamberlain and will see to your needs. Tonight, we will have a welcome feast in honor of your arrival."

Before Britt could continue, the Knights of Camelot broke into cheers at such a ringing volume, she could feel it in her chest. She waited for the roars of approval to subside before she said, "Furthermore, all day tomorrow we will celebrate, finishing with the establishment of the Round Table. Prepare yourselves, my knights. Tomorrow, you will be challenged."

The Knights of Camelot cheered even louder at this, making the ground buzz with their energy.

"You're lucky you have a bunch of warmongers in your court," Merlin said as he and Britt pushed their way back into the crowd and Sir Ulfius, an older knight with a genteel air to him, took their place.

"We'll see. I'm not sure how they will accept their oaths," Britt grimly said.

"They'll take them—out of sheer loyalty to you if for no other reason. The Round Table is a good plan," Merlin admitted.

Caught off guard by Merlin's rare praise, Britt blinked in surprise before she offered him a smile—not a King Arthur smile —but *her* smile—sweet and unguarded.

Merlin uncomfortably shrugged. "You best lead the way inside, lest all your knights stand here and gawk at Guinevere and her ladies like swine herders at a festival."

"Right. I'll do that." Britt altered her direction to push towards the keep. Sir Gawain and Sir Kay popped up on either side of her as the keep doors opened in front of her. Several of Britt's closest knights—Sir Bedivere, Sir Bodwain, Sir Ywain, and Sir Griflet among them—followed after her, starting the stream of knights who trickled into the keep, clearing enough room for servants to begin unpacking Britt's precious table.

Sir Lancelot du Lac watched them go, his green eyes sharp as he leaned against the inner walls of Camelot, cloaked by shadows.

"You were right. Lady Guinevere is a pretty little thing," Sir Lionel—Lancelot's cousin—said, folding his arms across his broad chest. "Though she looks hen-witted."

"Lionel," Sir Bors said, frowning at his brother.

Sir Lionel shrugged. "You can't tell me she's as sharp as the Lady of the Lake."

"No female is as conniving as the Lady of the Lake, with the exception of the wretched trio of Queen Igraine's daughters," Lancelot said, watching Guinevere giggle with her ladies.

Sir Bors shifted. "You mean Queen Morgause of Orkney, Queen Elaine, and Morgan—"

"Yes, them." Lancelot fixed his gaze on the doors through which King Arthur had disappeared scant minutes ago. "I find I am growing tired of him."

"Of Arthur? Why?" Sir Lionel asked, leaning against a horse hitching post. His giant hulk made the wooden post groan.

Lancelot narrowed his eyes. "He is too perfect."

"I should think so. With Merlin holding his chain, I don't think the wizard would let him be anything *but* perfect," Sir Lionel said.

"That's not it," Lancelot snapped. "It's the way everyone fawns over him. The mindless devotion his knights hold for him is sickening, and his unshakeable faith in them is even worse."

"What is *their* devotion to you?" Sir Bors asked. "Who cares what his men think?"

Lancelot rested his hands on his sword belt and was silent.

Sir Lionel and Sir Bors exchanged looks. Sir Lionel shrugged and stretched. "Must mean it's about time to head out then? We swore allegiance to him, but he has not officially recognized us like he did Gawain and Ywain. Even if we're supposed to be his knights, we could go questing some more—perhaps stop in and see if the Lady of the Lake will house us again."

"No," Lancelot said, the word as unyielding as iron.

"Then what do you want?" Sir Bors prompted.

"I want to shake Arthur's wretched faith. I want to rouse his suspicion and curdle some of that *fondness* he has," Lancelot sneered.

"What do you have planned?" Sir Lionel asked, his eyes lighting with interest.

Lancelot smiled darkly.

~

WHEN GUINEVERE WAS SUMMONED to Merlin's study—for a "private" welcome from Britt and the wizard—Guinevere shrieked with joy.

"Thank you, Arthur! It's so wonderful here!" she said, launching herself at Britt before Merlin closed the door behind her.

"Right. You're welcome," Britt said, trying to wrench Guinevere off, but the young lady held on with the grip of a bear. The pair nearly backed into one of Merlin's workbenches before the wizard peeled her off.

"See here, lady," Merlin said, holding Guinevere away from him as if she were a dead mouse. "You cannot act this way in public."

"Oh, I know! It's a big secret, right?" Guinevere said, her eyes wide as she looked back and forth between Britt and Merlin. "No one is to know that Arthur is really a girl. What is your name? Your girl name, I mean. Surely Arthur isn't your Christian name?"

"It's—"

"You will never find out!" Merlin said, shaking a finger at Guinevere. "I can barely trust your father to hang onto his own kingdom. I *certainly* don't trust you with such information as *that*. Heaven knows you'll go spilling it everywhere through sheer dimwittedness," the wizard grouched.

"Yes, sir," Guinevere said, nodding her head emphatically. She wasn't even offended by Merlin's insult but hung onto his words like they were gems.

"None of this touchy-feely-female-camaraderie either," Merlin went on.

Britt watched with an amused smirk—happy to see the wizard dominate someone besides herself so thoroughly. She had been entirely against ever speaking to Guinevere—much less bringing her to Camelot—because she didn't want to give any leeway to the King Arthur legends she knew, particularly the ones that blamed the downfall of Arthur and Camelot on Queen Guinevere and Sir Lancelot.

But when Britt visited Camelgrance in the previous months and witnessed for herself the way King Leodegrance used Guinevere as a bargaining chip, Britt found enough strength in her heart to begrudgingly offer Guinevere the chance to visit her in Camelot. It helped that the empty-headed girl had learned that Britt—King Arthur—was really a girl.

"You are to remain dignified and elegant when you dine with Arthur. Arthur is a *male* King. You must act accordingly in public," Merlin continued with his rant.

"But in private, I can speak my mind, yes?" Guinevere asked, almost bouncing with excitement.

What would we *have to talk about?* Britt wondered. Just because she was allowing Guinevere to stay didn't mean she liked the girl.

Merlin must have similar thoughts, for he furrowed his eyebrows. "This is not a wedding party, Lady Guinevere. You are free to fill your days as you please, but Arthur will not be available at your beck and call. She has a *kingdom* to run."

"I suppose that's true," Guinevere said, jutting her lower lip out in a pout.

Merlin folded his hands together and squeezed them until his knuckles turned white.

"Does the Lady of the Lake know your secret, too?" Guinevere asked Britt.

"She does," Britt confirmed. "But what Merlin is trying to emphasize, Lady Guinevere, is that secrecy is absolutely critical. You cannot allow anyone to even ponder the truth of my identity, and if you make a mistake, we will send you back to Camelgrance, immediately. Do you understand?"

"Of course," Guinevere scoffed.

"In that case, will you excuse us? I'm sure you want to prepare for the feast," Britt said.

"I really should. I have this delightful new dress. It's a shade of blue that's just so *perfect*—"

"Thank you, Lady Guinevere," Britt said, offering the young lady a flat smile before she opened the door.

"We will see you when we dine—you sit with Arthur as a guest of honor," Merlin said.

Guinevere clapped her hands in excitement. "Until then," she bid before she disappeared through the doorway.

"I'm surprised," Britt said, closing the door. "Usually, you are odiously kind to foreign dignitaries."

"Since visiting Leodegrance, I realized I over-estimated his importance. Frankly, I don't care a fig for him. It would be our good fortune if we were not his ally. Someone else can defend his lands for all I care," Merlin drawled. "I would still be kind to the girl—ill-treatment of her would reflect badly on Camelot, after all—but my biggest concern is to make sure she doesn't spill your secret. I will do whatever it takes to wedge that concept into her head."

"She isn't the brightest," Britt said.

"She's worse than your menagerie of animals…and your greenest knight," Merlin said. "I have absolutely no faith in her. If she doesn't share your secret with someone before the week is out, I'll be impressed."

"What will we do if she does?" Britt asked.

"It depends whom she tells. I might be able to cover it up with a bit of magic, but we shall see," Merlin said. "If she tells too many people, it will be beyond my powers. But we need not worry about it until it happens."

"I can't believe *I'm* the one saying this, but she may not tell anyone. She really wanted to get out of Camelgrance—so much so that she might remember to keep her mouth shut," Britt said.

"We shall see," Merlin grimly said. "Are you ready for tomorrow?"

"It's just feasting, isn't it?"

"Of course…not."

"Dang it."

"Pull up a chair, lass, and I will outline your day."

"I hate it when royalty visits," Britt grumbled before doing as the wizard directed.

2

THE ORDER OF THE ROUND TABLE

The following day's celebration was deemed a marvelous success. However, Britt was more than a little off put that everyone seemed to be under the impression that the reason for the celebration was *Guinevere* and not the Round Table.

"They'll understand eventually, My Lord," Sir Kay said, standing with Cavall next to Britt's throne.

"I hope so." Britt sighed and looked out at the throne room that was filled with standards, knights, and peasant folk. Merlin proclaimed that Britt had to spend the day granting boons to the peasants of the area to further good will. As such, Britt was stuck on the throne, listening to people who had come to complain to her. Sir Kay was her appointed babysitter as she was less likely to squirm away under his watchful eye than under any of Merlin's minions. "Next petitioner," she said.

One of her guards (the burly one who talked with a Scottish accent) led a tall, mountain of a boy forward. He looked like he was in his late teens—perhaps 18—but was built like an ox. He was taller than Britt—taller than Sir Kay, in fact—and had the shoulder breadth of a defensive lineman in the NFL. He also, Britt noticed with interest, held an empty scabbard.

"What is your name?" Britt asked.

"Tor, My Lord," the mountain of a boy said. "I am the youngest son of Aries the cowherd."

"And what is your request, Tor?" Britt asked.

"I would like to be made a knight of Camelot," Tor said.

The constant murmur of conversation that prevailed the throne room faded at his declaration, but Britt propped her arms on her knees and leaned forward in interest. "And why would you want that?"

"I love the sword, and I want to fight for the helpless. Everyone says you're the best in Britain, and if I could be a knight, I should like to serve a King who is known to be just. Also, I make a horrid cowherd," Tor admitted.

"Do you have your father's blessing?" Britt asked, curious.

Tor nodded. "He said my head is daft from fairies, and I'll be lucky if I'm not thrown out, but I might ask you anyway."

"I see. You said you love the sword, but have you used it before?"

"I practiced whenever I could, though I don't know if I'm any good," Tor said, holding up his empty scabbard. "I have a sword, but the guards took it when I entered the keep."

As Britt studied Tor, the whispers were renewed with vigor.

"Sir Gawain, Sir Bedivere," Britt finally said.

The two knights emerged at the base of the dais on which Britt's throne was placed.

"My Lord," Sir Bedivere said with a sweeping bow. Gawain mimicked him.

"I want you to test young Tor. I would like you, Gawain, to engage him in a sword fight at the practice grounds while Sir Bedivere watches and judges his skill," Britt said.

"Yes, My Lord," Sir Bedivere and Sir Gawain chorused.

"Will you agree to this test, Tor?" Britt asked.

"Of course, My Lord," Tor said, bending forward in a deep bow before he hurried after Sir Bedivere and Sir Gawain.

Britt shifted her attention back to the petitioners. "Next," she called.

Although Britt focused on the new requests and petitions, the knights and ladies whispered amongst themselves. Several knights motioned in the direction Tor and the testing knights had gone as they spoke, all while giving Britt speculative looks.

Britt settled a dispute over a cow, granted a chicken keeper a new bag of corn, and blessed three babies before Sir Gawain, Sir Bedivere, and Tor returned.

"Well? What did you find?" Britt asked, hefting her long frame out of her throne so she could stand on the top stair, Sir Kay at her side.

"He lacks the grace of a knight, My Lord, but he was no sapling," Sir Bedivere said. "Some time spent with a trained master could fix the worst of his stance, although he has the strength of an ox. Should he ever learn to use a lance, I think he would be a worthy opponent."

"I see. Sir Gawain?" Britt asked.

"His blows were powerful," Sir Gawain admitted. "I would not like to face him with a shield. He could crush one's arm through sheer force."

"Hmm. Call for Merlin," Britt said, twisting to look for a page boy.

"No need; I am already here," Merlin boomed, appearing mysteriously behind Britt. The ladies and knights of the room gasped in surprise, although it was obvious he had popped out of the small room—the entrance of which was hidden by a thick tapestry—located behind Britt's throne.

Merlin's Gandalf-rip-off-cloak swirled around him, making his dazzling blue eyes look stormy as he swept up to Britt's side. "I know what you are thinking," he murmured. "And I agree. It was one of *my* people who sought Tor out to tell him you were granting boons."

"Great. I'll knight him now?" Britt asked, reaching for Excalibur—which was leaning against her throne.

"My Lord, you can't possibly be considering this," a knight said. He approached the dais with a scowl, the colors of his armor marking him as one of Leodegrance's flunkies. "He is the son of a *cowherd*. The position of knight is an *honor* given to noblemen."

"Perhaps it was in Camelgrance, but that is not how it is in Camelot," Britt said, unsheathing Excalibur. "I value things like integrity, honor, and just actions. I care little for pedigrees and bloodlines."

"Pedigrees?" Leodegrance's knight asked.

Merlin discreetly—and sharply—elbowed Britt for the mistake.

Britt hastily continued, "Sometimes those of great character come from the least of places. I will knight Tor, but let it be known that any knight who obstinately acts without honor and without remorse will *lose* his shield and be exiled from my courts."

"Lass," Merlin warned as the crowd gasped. "*That* I did not agree to."

Britt walked down the steps to get out of elbowing-range. "Kneel, Tor," she said to the boy, who was so overcome with joy his shoulders shook.

"Tor, son of Aries the cowherd, you are to be the first knight who swears the oath of the Round Table. Never murder, and flee treason. Don't be cruel, but give mercy to those who ask for it. Always give aid to ladies—"

"My Lord, you forgot part of the oath," Merlin said, eyeing Britt as he joined her in front of Tor.

"So I have," Britt reluctantly said. She had worked out the oath with Merlin weeks ago, but she still didn't agree with all the parts he insisted that she add. "Don't be cruel, but give mercy to those who ask for it upon pain of forfeiting their lordship to me, King Arthur, forevermore. Always give aid to ladies, damsels, and gentlewomen, and let no man do battle in a wrongful quarrel for no law, or for any worldly object or tradable good. You are charged to ride abroad redressing wrongs, to speak no slander nor to listen to it, to honor God, and finally, to love one maiden only and to worship her through the years by noble deeds until she has been won. Do you swear to do all of these things?"

"I do," Tor reverently said. Britt got the feeling that he was more misty-eyed over being made a knight than over the idea of serving her, but, as she touched his shoulders with Excalibur's blade, she could see kindness in his face and decided he would probably be one of the most just knights in her service.

"Then rise, Sir Tor. Welcome to the service of Camelot," Britt said.

She was grateful when Sir Gawain and his younger brother, Agravain, started cheering. "Sir Tor!"

Tor grinned shyly as several of Britt's closer knights took pains to give the cowherd's son a warm welcome, in spite of the frosty looks Leodegrance's knights were giving him.

"I wish Leodegrance hadn't sent knights with the table," Britt said to Sir Kay and Merlin as they retreated back up the stairs, heading for Britt's throne.

"You'll never please everyone, lass. It's better to learn that now," Merlin advised.

"Yeah, I know," Britt sighed as she crouched in front of Cavall, smiling when he pressed his wet nose to her cheek.

"Cheer up, My Lord. Tonight, all your knights will take such an oath," Sir Kay said.

"Yes," Britt agreed. "Finally."

WHEN EVENING CAME, Britt assembled all of her knights in the grand hall where the Round Table of King Uther was assembled in a ring. The ladies of the court and any noblemen who were not knights directly under Britt's charge were not present, but were at a separate celebration for Guinevere.

There was no food, although drinks were already placed on the scratched table. Plain, wooden chairs with undyed, linen cushions were crowded around the table perimeter. There was one chair that was a little more ornate, having flourishes carved into its surface. The back was emblazed with what Merlin *claimed* to be letters that spelled out "King Arthur." Britt couldn't be sure, though, as she couldn't read the terrible spelling and letter formation of old English.

Britt stood behind her chair and allowed Merlin to sift through the knights, deciding where they sat. She was a little disappointed. The Round Table was the ultimate symbol of King Arthur's court. It stood for chivalry and good deeds. Most of Britt's career as the false King Arthur had been steeped in secret political agendas. She had hoped to make the Round Table the one fair place in her life by leveling the playing-field—which was what inspired the oath and the Order of the Round Table.

Merlin had crushed that dream by demanding to draw up the seating arrangement for the table. ("I will not undermine your rosy picture of chivalry, lass. The truth is, everyone is going to fight to sit closest to you, and you might accidentally put together men who can't stand each other. There will be nothing political beyond that. I promise.")

Britt didn't trust his vow. Things were *always* political with Merlin.

Britt watched with true pleasure as Sir Ector—her supposed foster-father—Sir Kay, Sir Bedivere, Sir Bodwain, and Sir Gawain were given chairs near her. Sir Ywain and Sir Ulfius were not much farther down, as were—unfortunately so—Sir Lancelot and his cousins: Sir Lionel and Sir Bors. Britt was surprised to see an empty chair that was only one seat away from her. She was about to call attention to it when King Pellinore busted into the hall with a noble smile and quick pace.

"I apologize, King Arthur. For once it was not the questing beast that caused my late arrival, but my wife. She wanted to be certain she had an appropriate gift for Lady Guinevere. I am glad I arrived before you started," King Pellinore said, giving a slight bow to Britt.

"King Pellinore," Britt said, at something of a loss.

"I thought we agreed you would call me Pellinore?" the tall, noble man said.

"Indeed, we did. But only if you agreed to call me Arthur," Britt said with a sly smile. King Pellinore had, at one time, been one of her loudest nay-sayers. Now, Britt was glad to call him her friend.

King Pellinore chuckled. "As you say, Arthur."

"King Pellinore, I am so glad you could make it," Merlin said, swooping between them.

"Indeed, I would not miss it. It is my pleasure to declare loyalty to Arthur," King Pellinore said, bowing in Britt's direction.

"What?" Britt said, a smile stuck on her face.

"Your presence at the Round Table will be celebrated. Here is your chair," Merlin said, indicating to the empty chair.

"Thank you," Pellinore said, taking his seat with grave honor.

Britt grabbed Merlin by the throatlatch of his cloak and dragged him to the side. "Nothing political besides the seating arrangement, you said. You *liar*!"

"What? You *like* Pellinore," Merlin snorted.

"Yes, but he's a *king*. He's not my *knight*. The whole point of the Round Table and the order and oath are to teach knights how to act as my vassals! I can't make him swear an oath of fealty to me!"

"He already has."

"*When?*"

"When you were officially made allies in early summer."

"He did no such thing. He only acknowledged me as King of

Britain!" Britt hissed, glancing over her shoulder to make sure no one could hear them. Thankfully, the knights were too involved in inspecting their new positions around the Round Table to take notice of her conversation with Merlin.

"Yes, that was when he swore fealty," Merlin said, speaking slowly, as if Britt were stupid. "By acknowledging you as *King* of *Britain* he acknowledged that you are sovereign above him. It's perfectly reasonable that you should call him one of your knights."

"Then why didn't you tell me?"

"Because I knew you wouldn't like it. You're too aware of what you perceive to be his honor to see that he's not making himself a lesser. Besides, is your Round Table not about equality and making the least on the same level as the greatest? Hmmm?" Merlin asked.

Britt groaned. "You are unbearable."

"If it helps, I was anxious to get Pellinore in your order for more logical reasons. He's a seasoned warrior, and you need him on this table of greenhorns. Your older knights—like Sir Ulfius and even Sir Bodwain—aren't likely to go out on these quests you dream of. They must stay close to Camelot due to their positions. And the last thing you need to do is release a hoard of young idiots on the country, right?" Merlin asked.

"I guess," Britt said.

"Good, now sit down and begin your grand speech," Merlin said, nudging Britt to her chair.

Britt gave the blonde-haired man a dirty look but did as she was told. When she sat, the knights—everyone from the newly knighted Sir Tor to the seasoned knights like Sir Bedivere, and even King Leodegrance's knights—fell silent.

Britt took a moment to appreciate the silence...and the event. For a long time, she had asked after the Round Table. At first it was because she knew it was part of the legend, but as time passed, Britt realized that she wanted to use it to give the knights a guide for their behavior. That was why she and Merlin had spent weeks making the oath, because it wasn't just a piece of the legend but a code of conduct. And now, after weeks of waiting, Britt would finally have a way to hold her knights—and herself—accountable.

"Men, tonight I am establishing the Order of the Round Table," Britt said. "The Round Table is symbolic. It has no corners, no place that is higher than another. Here, everyone has equal value, and everyone has equal say. At this table, there are princes, lords, and kings among the knights—and all of you may have the same authority...even cowherds," she nodded to Tor. "I am still your King. But here, I am of the same worth as you," Britt said. She waited, looking around the table to gauge reactions. Some knights were grinning; others looked thoughtful.

"However, to be part of the Order of the Round Table, one must prove to be a knight of excellent character. It is an honor, *not* an expectation, to sit here. You must take the oath I presented to Sir Tor earlier today," she continued. "Anyone who chooses not to take the oath of this Order may leave now, and I will not think less of him."

Everyone remained sitting.

"In that case, I require all present to take this oath: Never murder, and flee treason. Don't be cruel, but give mercy to those who ask for it upon pain of forfeiting their lordship to me, King Arthur, forevermore. Always give aid to ladies, damsels, and gentlewomen, and let no man do battle in a wrongful quarrel for no law, or for any worldly object or tradable good. You are charged to ride abroad redressing wrongs, to speak no slander nor to listen to it, to honor God, and finally, to love one maiden only and to worship her through the years by noble deeds until she has been won," Britt paused to catch her breath. "Will you swear it?"

Sir Bedivere was the first to stand. "I will never murder, and will flee treason," he started.

Sir Ywain leaped to his feet. "I will not be cruel, but give mercy to those who ask for it—"

"Upon pain of forfeiting their lordship to King Arthur, forevermore!" Sir Griflet said, almost knocking his chair over in his glee.

Sir Kay, Sir Gawain, Sir Bodwain, King Pellinore, and Sir Ulfius joined them, as did Sir Lancelot, Sir Lionel, and Sir Bors.

The hall throbbed as the knights—just a few short of 120 or so—raised their voices and declared the oath.

Britt smiled as she also stood and repeated the oath. When they finished, they sat back down—the sound of chairs scraping the ground drowning out most words.

"All for one and one for all," Britt declared.

"I beg your pardon, My Lord?" Sir Kay asked.

"Nothing," Britt said, placing her arms on the table in front of her. "The first order of business: questing."

"Questing, what a joyous occupation of time. Doing good deeds is a worthy and just cause," Lancelot said.

"Yes. Thanks for that," Britt said, eyeing the knight. "As a member of the Round Table, you will be asked to ride out for a part of the spring and summer season to go questing," Britt said before she leaned back in her chair and waited for the buzz of conversation to die down.

Sir Kay smoothed his moustache in great joy. As Britt's seneschal, the knights' feeding and upkeep had caused a constant drain on her coffers that he didn't appreciate. He had heartily approved of the plan to send knights out when Britt and Merlin first discussed it.

"You see? I told you the young ones would like the idea," Merlin murmured to Britt.

"Leodegrance's knights aren't thrilled," Britt whispered.

"Of course they aren't. This will require them to risk their lives. Forget those old swine. It appeals to your younger knights —the rowdy ones who *need* to be aired out to play," Merlin said before he raised his voice to speak to the crowd. "Arthur asks this because I have foreseen the great things you will do. Ladies will be saved; mythical creatures will be slain, and kingdoms shall be won!" he boomed, lying through his teeth.

The crash course on the order of the Round Table went on until late in the evening. When even Merlin could hear Sir Ywain's stomach growling, he released them to a celebration feast in the main hall.

There, they joined Guinevere and the ladies and knights who would not be in the Order of the Round Table.

3

THE QUEST OF THE WHITE HART

As usual, Britt was seated at the head table in the feasting hall. Only Merlin and Guinevere sat with her, although a steady flow of knights passed by the table to give their compliments to Guinevere and make eyes at her, or to ask Britt (and Merlin) a question about the Round Table.

"I hope you have found your first day at Camelot to be pleasant, Lady Guinevere," Merlin said in one of the few lulls.

"There are so many great knights," Guinevere giggled.

"Yes," Merlin cautiously agreed, giving Britt the evil eye as she leaned back in her chair, feeding Cavall bits of meat. Britt ignored the look, leaving him with the job of speaking. "Have you made friends?" Merlin asked.

"Certainly. Lady Blancheflor and Lady Clarine first greeted me when I arrived. They were very kind and complimented me on my dress," Guinevere said, rattling off the other ladies who greeted her as Merlin grew a vacant expression.

Britt hid her amusement—*Merlin*, entering in girl talk!—behind her wine cup before she took a mouthful of a beef pasty.

"Have you met King Pellinore's wife, Queen Adelind?" Britt asked, nodding to the table directly in front of the dais, where

King Pellinore and his lovely—and brilliant—wife sat with Sir Kay, Sir Ector, and a number of Britt's closest knights.

"No. Is that bad?" Guinevere asked, quickly turning away from Merlin to stare wide-eyed at Britt. "I'll go introduce myself right now," she said, standing so fast she stepped on the hem of her dress.

"Guinevere, it's fine," Britt said, catching her by the wrist.

Guinevere shifted and looked ill. "Are you certain?"

"Yes, I'll introduce you in a bit," Britt said, cocking her head as she took in the younger girl's worry. "You don't have to worry about offending me, you know."

Britt knew she guessed correctly when Guinevere shivered.

"Look," Britt said, glancing at Merlin for assurance. "I'm not a jerk. I know we warned you about...*talking*, but I'm not going to kick you back home just because you haven't met everyone yet."

"Indeed," Merlin said. "As long as you don't make too much work for the servants or cause rebellion among the knights, you may stay as long as you please."

Britt was not fooled. She could see the cranks of his mind working behind Merlin's innocent expression. Already he was pondering ways to use Guinevere's presence for their advantage.

"But the *moment* I find you taking liberties—claiming to be my lady or love or something else equally as stupid—you're going back to Camelgrance. If you never do that, we're good," Britt said. "Although I want my table back to myself in a few days."

"Hear, hear," Merlin grumbled.

Britt noticed, with a stormy countenance, that Lancelot seemed to be working his way in their direction. He probably intended to spill more poetry at Guinevere—who was all too easily impressed.

Fortunately, the entire banquet was interrupted when the doors to the hallway banged open. A white stag ran into the room, his antlers gleaming like ivory as he jumped tables and knocked over two servants and a knight. A white hound, baying like a beagle, nearly skid out as it too ran into the room, chasing after the deer.

Britt watched the crazed parade with narrowed eyes before she studied her wine glass. "We should ask Sir Ulfius who brewed this stuff. It's potent," she said.

"You are not seeing visions, Arthur. The hart and hound are real," Merlin said, standing with a thoughtful look.

"Seriously? What's a hart?" Britt asked, rising out of her chair.

"The deer," Merlin said, watching as the hound almost caught the stag but missed—its jaws snapping shut on air. The hart pranced out of the room, and the dog followed, colliding with a foreign knight at the door. The knight picked the dog up—quite the feat as it wasn't a small canine—and hurried from the room.

The room was silent for several moments, until Britt broke it with the unkingly observation of, "What just happened?"

No sooner were the words out of her mouth than a beautiful lady *riding* a white palfrey—a *horse*—indoors, entered the room. "My Lord, be merciful and address my grievance! The hound that was just stolen from here is mine. Please send someone to retrieve it—no!" the lady shrieked when another unknown knight—*also* riding a horse, but his was a courser, a warhorse— stormed the room and grabbed the lady off her horse. He tossed her over the front of his saddle and urged his steed from the room. "No! My Lord, help me! Please," the lady called as she fell out of hearing range.

No one moved—except for Britt. She climbed down the dais steps and picked up the reins of the abandoned, white horse. "How did they get a horse in the keep, and why didn't anybody *do* anything?" Britt said, eyeing her tables and tables of knights.

The knights sheepishly looked at each other as Britt patted the horse on the neck.

"'Tis a quest!" Merlin declared.

"How?" Britt frowned, handing the horse off to a page boy.

"The signs are unmistakable. The hart and the hound—even

the lady's horse are all white—the color of holiness," Merlin said. "The damsel is now in distress and must be rescued—as should her dog."

"And the hart?" Britt asked, approaching the dais again.

"And the hart," Merlin agreed. "It is obvious. This is a quest the heavens have delivered to glorify the Order of the Round Table, that a select few knights may be honored."

"Right." Britt looked at him quizzically. He eyed her back. "So, who volunteers to go out on this quest?" Britt asked, turning to face her men.

"I will," Sir Tor said, standing by his seat in the back of the room. He was stationed near the door that the unusual party-crashers had used. "If you will give me your leave, My Lord," he added.

"Of course, Sir Tor," Britt acknowledged. "You shall pursue…"

"The hound," Merlin whispered.

"The hound," Britt repeated, her voice loud enough for Sir Tor to hear.

"I will go forth as well, should you wish it, My Lord," Sir Gawain said.

"Me, too!" Sir Ywain was quick to add.

"Gawain is the best choice for the deer—the hart. You will use the two tracking hounds I gave you at Christmas?" Britt asked.

Sir Gawain bowed. "It will be my pleasure, My Lord."

"As for Ywain," Britt hesitated. Sir Ywain was young and eager to please, but Britt wasn't sure he was the best choice to send after a kidnapped lady. He was brash and tended to take large risks—a trait that wouldn't mix well with the task of rescuing someone.

"I would be honored to go—either with Sir Ywain or alone," King Pellinore said, standing.

"Really? I mean…" Britt snapped her mouth shut to hold her words in as she looked to King Pellinore's wife.

Queen Adelind was famous for running Pellinore's lands

whenever he was off chasing after the questing beast—which was often. She was even more famous, though, for sending Pellinore scathing notes for being absent for so long.

Queen Adelind, who was beautiful in a soft, subdued way, tucked the elaborate braid her long, brown hair was coiled in over her shoulder. "It would be an honor to Anglesey if my husband would take up this quest and refrain from running off, should he happen to see the questing beast," she said with a smile that was beautiful but as firm as a shield of stone.

"I don't want to send Ywain alone, but do he and King Pellinore get along well?" Britt whispered to Merlin.

"Well enough, but I doubt he could keep Pellinore's pace," Merlin said.

"Ah," Britt said before raising her voice. "Of course. In that case, I ask that King Pellinore would retrieve the genteel lady who was taken before our very eyes."

"My Lord," Sir Ywain objected as Sir Griflet patted his shoulder in commiseration.

"You're still too bad at jousting to go questing, Ywain," Sir Griflet said.

"You aren't any better than I am," Sir Ywain scoffed.

"Yes, but I wasn't fool enough to ask to go out on a quest, as terrible as I am," Griflet pointed out.

"No, I suppose you learned your lesson the first time," Sir Ywain grunted.

"What did you say?" Griflet demanded.

Britt ignored their scuffle and addressed the three knights. "I imagine you wish to start your quest tonight, lest the trail becomes cold—or lost?"

"It would be for the best, My Lord," King Pellinore said, his hands clasped and his lips folded in a smile. He was looking forward to the chase.

"Very well. Let us end the festivities for tonight. It seems there is some clean-up to be done. Knights, I wish you well in your endeavor. Good evening," Britt said to all those present.

"I have words of wisdom to share," Merlin said, approaching the three knights. "Especially to you, Sir Tor."

When Britt was assured the young wizard was fully distracted, she slipped from the feasting hall—making her apologies to Guinevere—and made a beeline for her room, Cavall padding faithfully behind her.

"Send for Roen—have him saddled. For a long ride," Britt said to a servant girl she found finishing the preparations in a visitor's room.

"Yes, My Lord," the girl said, curtseying before she ran away.

Britt hurried to her room, shutting the doors behind her.

"This time, you're coming with," Britt said to Cavall as she dug out two saddle bags. One saddle bag was already filled with all the things she would need for camping outside for a day or two. (On one occasion, Merlin had spirited her out to the forest to give her a much-needed break from her kingly duties. Since then, Britt made it a habit to have a bag prepared. Just in case.) Britt shoved a leather leash for Cavall and a spare collar in the second bag. She slung the packs over her shoulder—intending to fill the second bag with food for her dog—and walked for the door. She tripped on her backpack—one of the few items she had left from her life in the twenty first century—sending the contents of the bag sprawling across the floor.

"Dang it," Britt breathed.

"And where do you think you're going?" Merlin said from the doorway.

Britt looked up and set her packs aside, scooping items—clothes and a travel book—back in her backpack. "Nowhere. I just have a few items I want to give to Gawain, Tor, and King Pellinore."

Merlin looked unconvinced. "A likely story," he said.

"Whatever. Could you grab my iPod?" Britt asked, nodding at

the iPod touch that had flown from the bag and was now a foot or two away from Merlin.

"Your *what?*"

"The white and black thing," Britt said, pointing as she zipped up her backpack.

"I see. Arthur, we need to talk," Merlin said, glancing at the door that was barely cracked.

"About?"

"Earlier today I received word from one of my men. He's heard rumors," he said, grunting when he stooped over to pick up Britt's iPod.

"About?" Britt repeated.

Merlin pursed his lips. "An attempt against your life."

Britt blinked. "Oh," she said, her muscles going slack for a moment. "From whom? King Ryence? King Lot?"

Merlin shook his head. "No names, only a whisper that someone from the north seeks to harm you."

Britt snorted. "That isn't a surprise. Someone is *always* out to get me."

"Perhaps, but one should never take spoken rumors lightly," Merlin said.

"You told me I should never take rumors seriously either," Britt said.

"That, too," Merlin agreed. "Either way, it is best to be paranoid at all times and in all things. Are you paranoid in all things?"

"Maybe it's Lancelot. If Lancelot tried harming me, could we exile him?" Britt asked with a dreamy smile.

"It's not Lancelot," Merlin sourly said before he looked down at the device he held in his hands. "I say, what *is* this?"

"It's an iPod. It plays music. Or, it used to play music. The batteries were drained ages ago, and it's not like you have an electrical socket I can plug it into."

"Is it some sort of thin music box?" Merlin asked.

"Yes, only this can play hundreds of songs instead of one," Britt said. "Wait, they *have* music boxes already?"

"Good heavens, *no*," Merlin said, turning the iPod over in his hands. "But I've heard from other wise men about that—men who can see the future. Like Blaise, my master. This is a marvel," Merlin said, studying the mp3 player—even though the screen remained blank.

"I thought you didn't approve of knowing about the future. You said you were more concerned with the present," Britt said.

"I am. I care not about future *events*. But the advances in tools and industry can be fascinating," Merlin said.

"Mmm. Did you need anything else?" Britt asked.

"No, but something should be done about the death threat. It is against *you*, so we must take some kind of action. We would be fools not to," Merlin said frowning and glancing at the door. "Did you hear that?"

"Hear what?"

"Nothing," Merlin said.

"Have you told Sir Kay?" Britt asked.

"And the rest of our core group, yes. Sir Ector suggested we march north and sweep across the entire country," Merlin dryly said.

"Then do what Kay recommended and tighten up the castle defenses," Britt said.

Merlin eyed Britt. "How do you know he said that?"

"It's Kay. He's quite predictable," Britt said.

"Perhaps," Merlin agreed. "What are the packs for?"

"Gawain and Tor."

"Oh?" Merlin suspiciously asked, holding out the iPod.

"You can keep it, if you want," Britt said.

"It is a keepsake from your home," Merlin said.

"Yeah, but…not quite. It's not working—it won't play music ever again unless I can get it hooked up to a power source. You may as well have it."

"I...thank you," Merlin said, surprisingly pleased with the gift.

"You're welcome," Britt said, smiling fondly at the wizard's excited look. She shifted in irritation when Merlin gave Britt a smile, making her heart thump oddly.

"I'm going to my study. Don't wander too far," Merlin said, weighing the small machine in his hands as he left the room.

"Of course," Britt cheerfully replied. She waited until his footsteps retreated down the hallway before hurrying from her room, Cavall padding after her. She needed to make herself scarce before Kay started looking for her. Merlin always knew when Britt was thinking of something that might remotely affect one of his King plans, but *Kay* seemed to have a built in radar that activated only when Britt was about to put herself in a position that did not have her swaddled and coddled like a baby. Granted, he was growing more understanding—provided that she tell him of her schemes and plans and allow him to come with her. But what Britt had planned for tonight? There was no way Kay was going to allow it.

Britt wove her way to the back hallways—stealing her way down the wing that housed the pages and squires. She stopped in a room that contained only a cot and a set of white, unadorned armor. Moving quickly, she slipped on a hauberk, essentially a tunic made of chainmail, and grabbed the base pieces of the white armor set—the cuirass, which was a chestplate; the plackart, which reinforced the cuirass around her belly; faulds, the flaps of armor that covered her thighs; and a gorget, which covered her throat. For Britt, these pieces of armor were not only the most important as they covered her vitals, they were also the pieces that made her appear bulkier and hid her lack of male development.

Britt slipped on her leather, knee-high boots—the first of their kind. Britt had worked for *weeks* with the royal cobblers to get them made, as boots weren't really a thing yet—and grabbed her packs. She hooked the lighter pack on Cavall and carried the other, as well as her necessary pieces of armor, before she left the room and slipped out a side entrance that dumped her near the dimly lit stables.

Britt sighed in relief when she saw King Pellinore on his horse, studying the plump, nice-looking horse Sir Tor was to ride. Sir Gawain was nowhere to be seen.

"Didn't Kay and Sir Ulfius get you properly geared up as a knight, Sir Tor?" Britt called as she made her way across the stable yard, Cavall on her heels.

"Good evening, My Lord," Sir Tor said with a pleasant voice and an unassuming bow. "They did. They gave me new weapons and an armor set, My Lord."

"That is kind of you, Arthur. Most Kings make their knights pay for their equipment. *I* make my knights pay for their equipment—meaning no disrespect to you, Sir Tor," King Pellinore said.

"No offense taken," Sir Tor said with an easy-going smile. "Sir Kay said as much and informed me I better be worth the cost."

"It isn't normal for me to hand out armor, but I would hate to send you off on a quest with improper gear, like the horse. They didn't get you a charger?" Britt asked, dumping her packs on the ground and nodding her thanks to a stable boy who led Roen— Britt's black-as-night destrier. The big gelding nickered when he saw her and lipped her palm before sniffing Cavall.

"I told them I already had one. Father said I could keep Mud if Camelot would have me—though I'm not sure he really expected it to happen," Tor added.

Britt whistled and caught the attention of a stable boy. "Saddle up one of the spare chargers for Sir Tor, please."

"Yes, My Lord," the stable boy said, plucking the reins of Sir Tor's horse from his hands.

"It's unnecessary," Sir Tor started to say.

"Nay, you'll kill that little mare if you ride her for days like you'll need to on this quest," King Pellinore said.

"More than likely, you'll trounce a recreant knight while you're out and win his armor and horse. Then you can return all of your gear, and no one will lose. Except the blackguard knight," Britt said as she started securing her bags to Roen.

"Are there many recreant knights, then?" Sir Tor asked.

"I haven't seen many, but Pellinore has a regular collection of shields from knights he has trounced," Britt said.

Pellinore grinned widely. "I use them to decorate my weapons hall. Adelind won't let me hang them in the keep."

"I should think not," Britt grunted, unhooking the mostly empty pack from Cavall.

"Need provisions for the dog, My Lord?" a hostler asked.

"I do."

"I will handle it, My Lord," the man said, taking the pack and heading past the stables to the kennels.

King Pellinore leaned back in his saddle and rested his hands on his sword. "I am reluctant to enquire, Arthur, but what are you doing?"

"I'm coming with you," Britt said. She briefly considered tying Excalibur to her saddle before tossing the idea aside. It was better to have it attached directly to her side as Excalibur's scabbard was magical and would keep a person from bleeding out.

"Oh, I see," King Pellinore said, easily accepting the answer.

Sir Tor's new horse—a chestnut gelding that was not as fine as Roen or King Pellinore's horse, but would suit the new knight well—arrived just as Gawain, mounted on his steed, entered the stable-yard with three leashed dogs.

"Good evening My Lord, King Pellinore, Sir Tor," Gawain said, his armor twinkling in the torchlight.

"Hello there, Gawain," Britt said, stopping to pet the large scent hounds. "You're borrowing Agravain's dog as well?" Britt asked.

"Yes, My Lord."

"Just as well. I imagine three hounds are better than two—

thank you," Britt said to the man who gave her back her pack—
now filled with provisions for Cavall, as well. "We're all assembled. Shall we go—er, depart?" Britt asked, swinging onto Roen's
back.

"You are coming with us?" Sir Gawain asked.

"Yes," Britt said, patting her hose.

"Do you need to secure your dog, My Lord?" Sir Tor politely
asked.

"No, he'll stay with me," Britt said, smiling at her pet from
her perch.

"Then I think it is time we leave. The trail grows cold," King
Pellinore said.

"Right. This way," Britt said, leading the way.

4

TRAVELING WITH SIR TOR

When they passed through the inner walls of the palace and then the outer walls of Camelot, the guards stationed there stared hard at Britt—who had no doubts that Sir Kay would hear of her adventure as soon as she was out of sight —but did nothing to stop her from leaving.

"Anyone know how to track our objectives?" Britt asked.

"Our what?" Sir Tor asked.

"Our quarry," Britt said.

"I took one of my hounds to the feasting hall to get the hart's scent. She should be able to pick up the trail out here," Sir Gawain said, nodding to one of the hounds—who had her nose planted on the ground.

"We may as well follow you for a time," King Pellinore said—holding above his head a torch he had swiped from the last set of guards. "I imagine whatever the story is behind the hart, it will also involve the kidnapped lady and her hound."

"Seems logical," Sir Tor said.

"I would like to keep her leashed. If she runs off, she'll be hard to track down again," Sir Gawain said, letting the hound lead him into the meadow surrounding Camelot, taking a path that would lead to the Forest of Arroy—which hemmed around Camelot in an arc.

"It's just as well. If we go galloping off into the darkness, who knows what footing our horses will encounter," Britt said.

"It is true," King Pellinore acknowledged as he moved his horse to the head of the line so it walked side by side with Gawain's leashed hound. Sir Tor took up the rear, leaving Britt and Sir Gawain to ride together.

"My Lord," Gawain said, his words hesitant, "If I may inquire…"

"Yes?" Britt asked, patting Roen's thick neck. She had missed the warhorse—Kay rarely let her ride him, preferring that she would ride Llamrei, her white mare that was trained to flee rather than fight.

"Why have you come with us?" Gawain finally asked.

Britt was quiet as Roen's sauntering walk rocked her back and forth. "I wished to be free of my courts," she finally said.

Behind her Sir Tor snorted. "You'll have to do better than that, My Lord," he said, his voice just as cheerful and open as she expected.

Britt grinned and glanced at Sir Gawain. His expression was thoughtful, but he said nothing more.

"That's a reason I can sympathize with," King Pellinore said from the front of their small party as they entered the forest. "There's nothing worse than being cooped up with a bunch of goat-footed knights hemming and hawing at your every move."

Britt laughed. "I rather like my knights. Most of them, anyway," she amended, thinking of Lancelot.

"We'll see. Now that King Leodegrance's fools have come to your halls, you might think differently," King Pellinore said.

"That's a harsh judgment," Britt said.

"It is the truth," King Pellinore said. "Didn't it ever occur to you how dishonorable it is that King Leodegrance has so many knights in his territory, and not one of them would ride to Lady

Guinevere's defense when Duke Maleagant attacked? There's a reason why you had to be her champion, Arthur."

"I had forgotten about that," Britt said, her lips twisting in a frown.

"So, what's your real reason for wanting to come with us?" King Pellinore asked.

Britt was silent for an even longer time as she tried to find a way to phrase her deep-rooted desire.

In the twenty-first century, Britt never had much time for King Arthur stories. One of her closest friends was a King Arthur fanatic, but Britt had been turned off from the legend at a young age by her disgust with Lancelot and Guinevere. Still, she couldn't completely avoid contact with the famous legends. Besides the memory of King Arthur's terrible wife (Guinevere) and dishonorable best friend (Lancelot), Britt most remembered the Round Table and that knights went out questing after its establishment.

She also remembered (because she pointed it out quite often to her Arthur-crazy friend) that after the knights started questing, King Arthur's role began to diminish. His courts were great because he was a king that his knights loved, and his knights took this love to the country by righting wrongs and performing good deeds. But after the Round Table...Arthur accomplished very few great deeds.

Britt feared this. She didn't want to be a King in name only. She wanted to hold herself to the same code of conduct to which she held her knights. She wanted to make a difference, too.

"I want to set an example...and I want to remind myself what ruling is about," Britt said, speaking slowly. "Holed up in Camelot, it's easy to think that everything is peaceful and prosperous. I need the reality check."

To Britt's surprise, no one questioned her odd word choice, and they rode on in silence.

"We should make camp soon," King Pellinore said after what felt like an hour or two of riding in the darkness.

"I won't argue that," Britt said, stretching before she dismounted. She went to work, unhooking her packs and removing Roen's tack and gear.

"I'll get a fire started. The torch will burn out soon. It will be easier to use it to start a fire than by thumping around in this darkness. I'll be back shortly—I need to find some decent-sized branches," Pellinore said.

"Would you like me to hold your horse, King Pellinore?" Sir Tor asked.

"You needn't bother. This old boy and I have camped together under a hundred different skies. He knows the pattern," King Pellinore said, fondly patting his horse before walking off, taking his torch with him.

Britt fumbled with her packs in dark night, setting them aside. She managed to blindly slip Roen's saddle and bridle off before King Pellinore returned with an armload of branches.

"This will get us started," the older king grunted. He arranged the branches and prepped tinder before starting the wood on fire with his torch, casting a bright light on the knights.

"Thank you," Britt said as she hunkered down to hobble Roen before setting him loose. The horse sniffed around the forest, nibbling a few weeds as Britt prepped her bed with unease. Sleeping on the ground wasn't a problem—she had done it before. The real issue was Britt's hauberk. Britt knew from experience that sleeping in the chainmail would make her achy the following day, but shimmying out of it in front of the knights would give Merlin a heart-attack, even if he wasn't present.

"Is there a water source nearby?" Britt asked.

"I saw a faerie pond. It's past your horse. Just keep walking, and you will not miss it," King Pellinore said.

"A faerie pond?" Sir Tor asked.

"It had no scum or lily pads on its surface and was as clear as a cloudless sky. It could only be a faerie's work," King Pellinore said.

"I see," Sir Tor said.

Britt set off before she heard more of the conversation, carefully shuffling through the dark. She almost walked straight into the pond before she noticed the wisps of moonlight and starlight that made it down through the trees were reflecting on the ground.

She drank, gratefully pulled off her hauberk, and slipped on a much lighter—but still disguise-worthy—leather doublet.

When she rejoined the men, she gave Cavall a snack of some kind of dried meat before curling up to sleep with her dog and equipment mounded around her, and the knights softly talking.

~

"DO YOU NEED HELP, MY LORD?" Sir Gawain asked, his gaze hinged on one of the armor straps Britt was struggling to tighten the following morning.

"If you wouldn't mind, thank you," Britt said, holding her arm up so Sir Gawain could make the adjustment.

"Good news," King Pellinore boomed as he made his way into their camp, making Britt and Sir Gawain jump like startled fawns.

"Young Sir Tor and I scouted ahead. It seems two horses carrying loads followed the hart's trail—which is quite obvious now that we can see its tracks—and split off not a short ride from here," King Pellinore said, smacking Sir Tor on his broad shoulders.

"So we haven't lost any time by following the hart's trail?" Britt asked, flexing her shoulders when Gawain finished helping her.

"Indeed, we have not," King Pellinore said, heading for his horse—which was already saddled and munching on undergrowth. "We can bridle our steeds and water them at the faerie pond before we split up," he said. Clearly, he was excited to be on a quest again.

"With whom shall you ride, My Lord?" Gawain asked.

Britt checked Cavall's collar to make sure it wasn't too tight. "Sir Tor, I think. I would like to observe you in action—if you don't mind," Britt asked the ex-cowherd.

"Not at all. I should enjoy the company, My Lord," Sir Tor said, just as chipper in the morning as he was the previous night.

"Then it's settled. Let us begin our journey!" King Pellinore boomed.

In less time than Britt thought possible, she and Sir Tor found themselves alone—excluding Cavall and their mounts—following the hoof-prints of the horse King Pellinore and Sir Tor thought to be carrying the man who kidnapped the hound.

"How did you surmise this is the hound-napper?" Britt asked, watching Sir Tor as he kept his eyes on the trail.

"The hoof-prints, My Lord. The knight who came for the lady was much bigger and—according to the guards I spoke to before receiving my gear—rode a horse that was larger as well. Not only are the horse's hooves bigger, but because he carried a heavier load, they sank deeper into the ground," Sir Tor explained.

"Ah," Britt said, afraid to betray her lack of knowledge.

"Do you go hunting much, My Lord?" Sir Tor asked.

"No, I can't say I do. I sadly haven't the time for it," Britt said, offering out the lie Merlin had come up with. The first and only time Britt had ever gone hunting, she was nearly killed by some of King Lot's men, not to mention she was terrible with a bow and stood no chance of hitting anything. "Have you?"

"Only small game—rabbits and such. I was thankful to King Pellinore for teaching me about tracking horses," the new knight said.

"I can imagine," Britt said, glancing down at Cavall when silence fell. Sir Tor—as cheerful and good tempered as ever—

seemed to have no trouble with it, so Britt kept quiet and allowed the younger man to follow the trail.

The two rode for maybe an hour when they found...Britt knew he had to be just a short man but he looked much like, well, like a dwarf from a fantasy movie. He had thick, braided hair, carried several hand axes, and was wielding a stout staff.

"Excuse us, good sir," Sir Tor said, moving to steer his horse around the dwarf.

"You shall not pass!" the dwarf shouted, jumping in front of Sir Tor's horse.

Britt laughed so hard at the unintentional *Lord of the Rings* reference she almost fell from Roen's back.

"Are you finished?" the dwarf asked when Britt's mirth finally subsided.

"I don't know. If you say that again, then no, I don't think I am," Britt said, flicking a tear of laughter from her eye.

"Why can't we pass?" Sir Tor asked the dwarf.

"I won't let you," the dwarf said, eyeing Britt when she hid a gurgle of laughter behind a cough.

"And why won't you let us?" Sir Tor patiently asked.

"Because I serve one of those yonder knights, and he has instructed me to send all traveling knights to fight him," the dwarf wearily said, pointing at two knights who were hammering at each other with maces just outside two brightly colored tents. "You could always turn around and go back the direction from which you came," the dwarf helpfully added.

"That won't work. We're following a trail. We must go forward," Sir Tor said.

"Sorry, I can't let you pass. My master will flay me should I let you continue unmolested."

Britt had another suspicious coughing fit.

"What do you recommend, My Lord?" Sir Tor asked Britt when she recovered.

"Normally, it's best to avoid unnecessary conflicts, but in this case, I see only good in fighting those knights—provided we can trounce them," Britt said.

"Neither of them are very good," the dwarf wryly said.

"Then why are you with your master?" Sir Tor asked.

"He didn't give me much of a choice when he slew my previous master," the dwarf said, crossing himself.

"That's unfortunate," Sir Tor commiserated.

"Right, let's go rattle some knights. Come on, Sir Tor," Britt said, directing Roen in the knights' direction, Cavall trailing behind with a wet snuffle.

The squabbling knights saw them coming. They stopped beating on each other and instead ran at Britt and Sir Tor.

Roen lashed out before the knight aiming for Britt could reach them. He knocked the knight down, tossing him straight into a mud puddle.

"Thanks, Roen," Britt said, patting her horse before she carefully dismounted and unsheathed Excalibur.

She saw Sir Tor throw himself from his mount, flattening his opponent like a pancake when he landed on top of him.

Britt adjusted her grip on Excalibur as she approached her challenger—who was on his feet and unsheathing his sword, having tossed his mace away.

"You are cowardly with the gizzard of a chicken," the knight declared.

Britt ignored the taunt and exhaled, sinking into an offensive stance as years of training as a medieval mixed martial artist took over.

The two things that most greatly extended her lifespan in this crazy time period was her desire to wear a riding helmet and her mastery with the sword. Even though Britt had yet to be beaten at swordplay since she arrived in ancient England, she approached every fight with a gravity and fierceness that kept her clear-headed and observant.

Even as Britt took in the knight's sword stance with disgust—

he had holes in his defense *everywhere!*—she planned for the best attack that would end the fight as swiftly as possible.

"You are a recreant knight, smeared with pig dung!" the knight said.

Cavall growled, the fur on his spine standing on end.

"Cavall, stand down," Britt whispered to the fierce dog.

The knight opened his mouth to speak another insult, but Britt lunged forward, striking like a viper. She hit with such speed that the knight, not expecting it, found his sword swatted aside before Britt ground her elbow into his gut. The chainmail he wore did nothing to soften the blow, and as he gasped for breath, Britt threw him over her leg, sliding Excalibur next to his throat as he sat, pinned like a bug.

The knight gurgled and tried to suck in air, his eyes wide and chest heaving as Cavall stiffly approached Britt, his lips pulled back in a silent snarl.

Britt risked a glance at Sir Tor, who peeled the flatten knight off the ground and shook him like a terrier with a rat.

Sir Tor set the man on his knees and shook a stern finger in his face. "Treat your squires with more respect!" he said.

The knight exhaled and fell over, thoroughly rattled.

"Well done," Britt said, planting a foot on her opponent's chest when the knight squealed at Cavall.

"I thank you!" Sir Tor said with a shining smile. "Though I had hoped my first fight would be with a sword," Sir Tor said, looking regretfully to the sword that was still sheathed at his side. "This is the knight that is your master, yes?" Sir Tor asked, calling to the dwarf who was making his way towards them.

"It is," the dwarf said. "A recreant knight if there ever was one. Are you going to slay him?"

"Mercy," Sir Tor's rattled knight said.

"M-m-mercy," Britt's pinned knight said. He struggled to speak under the weight of her leg—which she was leaning on.

"Sorry," Britt said, removing her foot and petting Cavall.

45

"I will grant you mercy, if you will give up all your posses-
sions here and go to the courts of Camelot to throw yourself at
the feet of King Arthur and pledge loyalty to him. Oh—and if you
have any land, it will go to King Arthur. If I find out you haven't
done this, I will find you," Sir Tor said.

Oh, yeah, I nearly forgot about that, Britt thought, turning to her
captive. "I will spare your life if you forfeit all your land and trea-
sures to King Arthur and travel to Camelot to swear loyalty to
him. Should you fail to do this, I will hunt you until you drop
from exhaustion."

"Agreed," Britt's opponent wheezed.

Within minutes, the two recreant knights—divulged of their
armor, horses, and equipment—walked away, heading in the
direction of Camelot with wide eyes.

"That was well done, Sir Tor," Britt said.

"Thank you, My Lord," Sir Tor smiled. "I'm glad. Being a
knight is just as fun as I thought it would be."

"You two belong to King Arthur's courts?" the dwarf squire
asked.

"I do," Sir Tor said before he grimaced and looked to Britt. "I
suppose if I had been thinking, I could have made that knight
swear loyalty to you right now."

"No; it's better if they don't know who I am," Britt said.

"*You're* King Arthur?" the dwarf squire said, raising a bushy
eyebrow at Britt.

"I am," Britt said with her King Arthur smile.

"Hmph. You are just as pretty as they say—though you still
don't look a day over sixteen…My Lord," the dwarf squire said.

Britt frowned at the observation as the dwarf turned all of his
attention to Sir Tor.

"You have helped me, Sir. Thank you," the dwarf said. "I
would like to enter your services as your squire."

"There's no need for that, good sir. I freed you so you may do
whatever you please—not so you would serve me," Sir Tor said.

"I thought as much, but I would still like to enter your services. Though you lack finesse, you have the bearings and the character of a true knight."

"I couldn't—I mean, you really don't want to serve me," Sir Tor protested.

"You may as well take him on," Britt said. "Believe me; it is really hard to get all your armor on alone. If you go questing a lot, you'll be thankful for the help."

"Yes, but...My Lord," Sir Tor frowned. "The...expense may be more than I can handle."

"Look at it this way. In the first morning of your first quest, you have already acquired a warhorse, at least one set of armor—"

"Two," the dwarf piped in. "He had battle armor and armor he used to go court ladies in."

"Two sets of armor—which even if they do not fit you, you could sell for a pretty price—the horse's equipment, and a tent," Britt said, pointing to one of the bright tents. "Even if you do not defeat another knight, I do not think you will be overburdened by the addition of a squire."

"I have my own mount already," the dwarf helpfully added.

"Alright," Sir Tor caved. "I thank you for your service, good sir. Though I should be upfront and tell you I am but a new knight. Before yesterday, I was nothing but a cowherd until King Arthur granted me the boon of becoming a knight."

"Believe me, it's obvious," the dwarf said.

5
CAUGHT

I t took Brit, Sir Tor, and the dwarf—whose name was Lem—
the better part of an hour to pack up the tents and equipment
and get it loaded on the animals.

With the petty knights gone, Cavall was back to his pleasant
self and trotted after Britt like a lamb—seemingly to Lem's
disgust.

By the time all the animals were secured, it was late morning.

"I fear we will be well behind our quarry," Sir Tor said,
squinting at the tracks.

"What are you chasing?" Lem asked, mounted on his mule.

"A knight, carrying a stolen white hound," Britt said.

"Him? No, you don't need to worry about losing him. His lady
is camped not far from here, and I have no doubts it was to her
that he carried the hound," Lem said.

"You've seen the hound, then?" Britt asked.

"Yes. He carried it through here late last evening. My master
would have stopped him to fight, but he ran his horse as if the
hounds of Hades were chasing him. He is another recreant
knight—although I suspect it is more that he is in love with a
selfish troll of a girl," the dwarf said.

"At least the hound isn't much farther," Sir Tor said.

"I suppose. This way to the lady's camp," Lem said, kicking his long-eared mule.

They had taken less than five steps when a horn was sounded, and at least a dozen men mounted on swift horses swept through the clearing.

"It seems we may be taken captive," Lem said with a tight face.

"Hardly," Sir Tor said, just as cheerful as ever.

"It is just my nursemaids. They have finally caught up," Britt dryly said.

"*ARTHUR*," Merlin called from the center of the force. Most of them were guards—specifically Britt's guards—who were no doubt there to take Britt back. Two knights, however, had accompanied the party: Kay, who was no surprise; and Lancelot, who had probably come just to be annoying.

"Hello Merlin, Kay, guards...Lancelot," Britt said, spitting the last name out with a frown.

"*ARTHUR*," Merlin repeated, his voice loud and forbidding.

"Oh, I'm sorry. Forgive my manners, this is Lem—Sir Tor's new squire," Britt said, swinging Roen aside so her guards could see the dwarf on his mule.

"I think what Merlin means to say, sir, but finds his words failing, is where have you been?" one of the guard captains asked.

"I've been questing with young Tor here. You missed it. Together, we beat two recreant knights and sent them to Camelot," Britt said.

"Arthur," Kay frowned. "Just a few months ago, you promised you would tell me if you planned to do something stupid, like this."

"Would you have agreed I should go?"

Sir Kay shifted in his saddle and said nothing.

"Well, there you have it. Besides—I didn't go alone. When we set out, King Pellinore and Sir Gawain were with us as well," Britt said.

"A merry traveling company!" Lancelot proclaimed.

"Of all the stupid things you've done, *ARTHUR*, this is near the top," Merlin said, drawing closer on his spindly horse.

Britt twisted in the saddle to look at Tor. "I apologize, Sir Tor. It seems you shall have to continue on without me."

"Very well, My Lord. Safe travels home," Sir Tor said, gathering up his reins.

"Thank you. Good luck with your quest."

"Indeed, with luck we will see you soon in Camelot. Lead on, Lem," Sir Tor said, turning to his new squire.

Lem eyed Britt and her company, but kicked his mule forward, leading Sir Tor deeper into the Forest of Arroy.

"Well?" Merlin asked.

"Well, what?" Britt said when the knight and squire were out of sight.

"What do you have to say for yourself?"

Britt thought for a moment. "I thought you would catch up sooner," she said.

"*ARTHUR!*" Merlin shouted.

"To be honest, I was surprised I even made it out of the castle. You used to be sharper. What's happening to you, Merlin?" Britt innocently asked, widening her blue eyes and looking at Merlin with sympathy.

"*You*," Merlin glowered. "I will have you tarred, and stretched, and *tied to your throne, you silly—*" Merlin cut himself off and glared at Britt.

"We may as well head for home. But good news—I won another horse," Britt said.

"The last thing you need is another *horse*," Merlin spat before riding to the front of the guard formation to speak with the captain.

Britt frowned as Roen and Cavall joined the procession, surrounded on all sides by guards. "He seems especially bothered," Britt said, tilting her head in Merlin's direction when Sir Kay joined her.

"He was upset to discover you left without leaving any kind of notice. I must admit that I am upset as well."

"What?" Britt blinked.

"We have discussed this before. You said you would tell me next time you left."

"I know. I should have thought it through better, I guess. I'm sorry—"

"You said you were sorry last time!" Sir Kay said, his voice as close to a shout as Britt had ever heard. "You claimed you wouldn't do it again. We cannot trust you, Arthur. *I* cannot trust you. It is my job to make sure you are safe, and your careless actions make you the biggest threat to your own wellbeing!"

Britt could feel herself shrink in the saddle. The guards riding around Britt were stone-faced, though Britt didn't doubt they wished they were anywhere but here, listening to Sir Kay scold her.

"I asked you to tell me—I thought you trusted me. But it seems you do not," Sir Kay said before he cued his horse forward and joined Merlin at the front of the line.

Britt almost groaned when Lancelot cleared his throat as he drew his horse alongside hers. "I found your absence worrisome, as well," Lancelot said.

Britt gave him a withering glare.

"It's true," Lancelot said, looking injured.

Britt ignored the knight and stared straight ahead.

"All of Camelot was in an uproar when it was discovered you had left with the questing knights last night," Lancelot said. "Your nephew, Sir Ywain, almost roused a search party of fifty knights before Merlin and Sir Ector decided it would be best to track you in daylight."

They rode in silence for a bit, Britt unwilling to force herself to converse with a man she despised.

"Sometimes I think, My Lord, that you are more of a wizard than Merlin is," Lancelot said.

"What?" Britt frowned at the handsome knight.

Lancelot shrugged. "You have your men grasped so tightly. They are so deeply invested and involved in you, that all action stops if you go missing or run off on an adventure. You have some knights who would do anything to be in your inner circle, and you purposely keep them at arm's length."

Britt studied Lancelot, not sure how to interpret his unusually deep observation.

"Anything, My Lord," Lancelot remarked, highlighting his previous statement.

Britt opened her mouth to speak, but no words came to her mind.

"Of course, that may also be because you have such wonderful knights in your court," Lancelot said, sounding silly and pompous again. "I know Sir Gawain, Sir Kay, and Sir Bodwain are widely celebrated, but I flatter myself by including my name amongst the greatest. Did I ever tell you that I killed a dragon before I joined your company? It was a great and mighty leezard."

Britt's shoulders heaved in relief. She could safely tune Lancelot out once again. The young knight had, unintentionally of course, given Britt great deal to think about. Was it selfish that she ran off, not telling anyone of her goals? The guards let her go, yes, but wasn't it because she was king rather than she had an actual right to leave?

Britt pondered Kay's words and Lancelot's accidental observations, as the fashionable knight jabbered the whole way home.

"...Of course there I smote it, and the fair damsel was so relieved she all but collapsed. I sought to carry her across the river, but Lionel insisted—which was just as well, for I was forced to fight off a sea serpent along the way..."

~

THE FOLLOWING DAY, Britt sat on a wooden fence and watched some of her knights joust, compete in archery, and duel with swords. What was meant to be a day of practice in arms—which Britt had declared in the morning after sitting through an uncomfortable/icy meeting regarding the castle's defenses with Merlin and Sir Kay—was becoming more of a small, informal tournament. Knights who won paraded themselves before the court ladies—who were all aflutter in their bright dresses.

Britt—standing on the edge of the practice ring—twisted to look at Sir Kay, who was speaking to a guard not twenty feet behind her, a swarm of ladies standing nearby.

Britt sighed and drummed her fingers on the fence. After contemplating her actions for the past day, Britt was forced to admit that she was wrong, or at least she had gone about addressing her worry of inactivity all wrong. She owed Sir Kay and Merlin—all of her men, really—an apology.

"Might as well start with Kay," Britt said, kicking her legs over the fence. She waited to approach Sir Kay until the guard left.

"My Lord," Sir Kay stiffly said, bowing when she drew close.

"Sir Kay," Britt said, standing next to the stone-faced knight.

After a few minutes of silence, Sir Kay bowed again and moved to walk away.

"Wait, please," Brit said, catching him by the arm.

"My Lord?" Sir Kay said, squaring his shoulders.

"I know...saying I am sorry or deeply regretting my actions isn't enough. I knew why you wouldn't want me to go, but I—" Britt broke off in a sigh. "What I mean is, I was being stupid, and I'm willing to do anything to make up for my actions."

"Anything?" Sir Kay asked.

Britt swallowed. "Anything."

Sir Kay said nothing for a few moments. "I am glad you see the error in your ways, My Lord. My greatest wish is that you would not do it again, but I do not think that wish will be realized."

"Then I'll work to see that it is, and I will regain your trust," Britt said.

Sir Kay sighed. "I'm afraid the true problem is the reverse, My Lord. *You* do not trust me."

"No, that's not it," Britt said, shaking her head. "I trust you a lot, Kay. I trust you with my life, and, even more important, I trust you to be my friend. I guess...sometimes I forget why it's *important* that I trust you with my life, and I become..."

"Blinded by your goals," Sir Kay said.

"Yes," Britt said.

"It's good that you're passionate, My Lord. But blindness leads to folly."

Britt had nothing to say to such an astute observation, so she nervously shifted in the silence. "Am I forgiven?" she asked when she couldn't stand it anymore.

"Of course, My Lord."

"Great," Britt said, sagging with relief.

Sir Kay said nothing.

"So we're...siblings, again?" Britt asked.

One end of Sir Kay's lips curled in a reluctant smile. "Siblings," he said. To the quiet knight's shock, Britt reached out and clasped him in a hug.

"Thanks, Kay," Britt whispered before she released him. She glanced at the practice ring and scowled when Lancelot bowed at some of the spectators, having disarmed his third opponent.

"If you'll excuse me, I have a twit of a knight to defeat," Britt said. "Wish me luck?"

"You have no need of luck, My Lord."

Britt laughed. "I'm certainly glad you think so," she said, making her way to the practice ring. She smiled at the ladies who clambered to her side. "Good afternoon, gentle ladies," she said.

"My Lord, are you going to fight?"

"Wear this sprig of ivy if I find favor with you, My Lord."

"Would you like a token of affection to carry into battle?"

Britt slipped over the fence—and out of their grasp—as quickly as she could. "You are too kind, ladies. But I would like to challenge Sir Lancelot before someone else does," Britt said, offering them a wink before she trotted off.

Behind her, the ladies sighed like love-sick schoolgirls, and Britt congratulated herself on her success at evading them, and making up with Sir Kay.

"That's one down and one to go," Britt said, jumping a second fence to get to the area where knights were practicing their swordsmanship. She smiled and nodded to Guinevere when the young girl caught her eye—causing a storm of giggles—before she approached Lancelot.

"Are you here to fight, My Lord?" the handsome knight asked, tilting his head.

Britt checked to make certain her cuirass and plackart were securely fastened. "I am," Britt said.

"Oh, no. I fear I am about to lose, my ladies. Will you comfort me after our round is finished?" Lancelot asked his adoring audience.

"Oh, Sir Lancelot, don't say that!"

"You can win, Sir Lancelot!"

"Nay! None can beat King Arthur," Guinevere said, joining the conversation with a smile and a blush.

"Thank you for your defense, Lady Guinevere. I hope you are correct, in this case at least," Britt laughed as she unsheathed Excalibur. "Arm yourself, Lancelot."

The handsome knight looked curiously to Guinevere before he detached himself from his fans. "At least it will be my honor to face my King," Lancelot said with an elegant bow to the ladies before he faced Britt.

Britt had fought—and beaten—Lancelot multiple times, but she still respected him the way she respected a snake if she didn't know if it was poisonous or not. Although Lancelot was undoubtedly an idiot, he and his cousins were the only knights in

Britt's court that had spent a significant portion of their time questing. As such, Britt somewhat suspected Lancelot was holding out during their matches.

Britt crouched, adjusting her stance as she watched Lancelot grow quiet, the smile smoothing off his face as he stared Britt down like a wolf.

Britt feinted a jump to his right before rolling her weight to her opposite leg and attacking his left. Their swords met with a clash of metal—Excalibur singing in a unique pitch.

Lancelot drew backwards, nimbly avoiding the knee Britt tried to thrust into his unprotected side. Britt followed her action forward, sinking low to try and shove a shoulder into Lancelot's gut. She made contact and heard his breath hitch, but the knight didn't move.

That was bad. Being "underneath" Lancelot so to speak, was a serious disadvantage. She had to move! Cursing under her breath, Britt pitched forward in an awkward roll—thankful she didn't wear all of her usual armor and only her regular pieces used to disguise her body. She rocked forward on her feet and had just enough time to spin and bring Excalibur up to block a blow from Lancelot.

The sheer force the knight used made Britt grunt and clench her teeth—she couldn't take many of those kinds of strikes without sapping her strength. She needed to get back into an offensive stance as quickly as possible.

Britt tried slamming her booted heel on top of Lancelot's toe, but he was wearing the metal shoes of his armor, so it did nothing but make Britt's heel vibrate in her boot.

Lancelot chuckled, and Britt met his gaze long enough to see the shadows in his green eyes. He drew back and extended his sword in a sweeping arc. Britt deflected it, although it forced her to plant her weight, leaving her unable to counter attack.

A crowd of knights and ladies had gathered around the ring

by now. Shouts filled the air, and ladies cheered. Some servants had even stopped to watch their sovereign fight Lancelot.

Unfortunately, Britt had a sinking suspicion she was going to lose.

"Do you give up, My Lord?" Lancelot asked, raining two blows on Brit as quick as lightning. Britt had barely enough time to defend.

"To you? Not ever," Britt said, her teeth gritted and expression stubborn. Lancelot would get cocky—it was his style. She just had to wait for it…

Lancelot chopped downward, forcing Britt to rest the flat of Excalibur on her arm to hold it steady.

"Are you sure?" Lancelot asked, drawing closer to put more of his weight into his blade as he made Britt hold their swords aloft. He was so close, Britt could practically taste the salt of his sweat.

"Gotcha," Britt growled into his ear.

"What?" Lancelot blinked. Holding her sword and Lancelot's sword aloft with her forearm, Britt let go of Excalibur with her other hand and chopped the back of his neck. Lancelot stumbled, his sword shrieking as it scraped down the length of Exalibur's blade. Britt flung her arm holding Excalibur aloft and wide— pushing Lancelot's sword away—before hooking her foot behind his knee and shoving him down. When he fell to his knees, Britt tightened her grip on Excalibur and swung it down, landing a blow on Lancelot's armored chest that sent him sprawling backwards. Britt was on him in an instant, stabbing Excalibur near his exposed armpit.

Her shoulders heaved, and she breathed heavily in the sudden silence.

It took two moments before the audience reacted in wild applause.

"My Lord!"

"King Arthur!"

"—picture of knighthood!"

Britt was so weak her knees shook, and she held herself upright only through the stiffness of her muscles.

"I say, well done, My Lord. You certainly trounced me that time," Lancelot said with a beautiful smile before he turned to the cheering crowd. "Our just and honorable lord: King Arthur!" he said, gesturing to Britt.

Britt panted and eyed Lancelot as the knight slid his sword back into its scabbard. "You certainly are the best swordsman in all of Christendom," Lancelot said with a bow before he turned away. "Gentle ladies, though I lost to such a skilled opponent, did I not put up a worthy fight?"

"Immeasurably so, Sir Lancelot."

"You were the breathing illustration of skill!"

Britt looked away from the knight and his adoring fans. She raised a hand in acknowledgement as she finally regained control over her muscles. She slid Excalibur in its scabbard and slowly made her way to the ring's fence.

The crowds scattered, drawn to the jousting practice field, where Sir Bodwain—who was cleaning the clock of everyone who dared to go against him—was preparing to face down Sir Bedivere.

Britt made a face as she eased herself over the fence. "That was much harder than I would have liked," she muttered, replaying the fight in her mind.

She could have sworn that for a split second, just when Lancelot realized he had been beaten as Britt moved to stab Excalibur into the ground next to him, that his eyes darkened, and he looked...*frightening.*

Britt glanced over her shoulder at the flighty knight, who was accepting a cloth from a pretty girl to wipe away his sweat.

Were my eyes wrong? Is there more to him?

"My Lord, you fought so well," a brown-haired, teenage girl in an emerald green dress said, pushing close to Britt. "You looked so handsome with your golden hair shining."

"Thank you," Britt said, trying to side-step the girl so she wouldn't be so close. "It was a close fight."

"Never! Everyone in Britain knows you cannot be beaten," another teenage girl said, clasping one of Britt's hands in hers.

"Did you fight the battle, thinking of any particular maiden, My Lord?" a young lady—who was pretending to be shy—asked as she threaded her hands through her blonde hair.

"I can't say I did. I was mostly trying to not get stabbed," Britt laughed, pulling her hand from the over-familiar female.

When girls first started blushing and fluttering their eyes at Britt, she had been amused. She would have been fine to let things continue as they were, but as no one seemed to be "winning" the race for Britt's affection—much less make any kind of headway with her—the girls were growing increasingly more affectionate and grabby.

For the sake of her disguise, this was not good.

Britt was wondering if the best escape would be to duck back in the practice ring, when Guinevere shoved her way through the crowd of maidens.

"My Lord, well done!" Guinevere said.

"Ah, thank you," Britt said. After a moment's hesitation, she offered her arm to the younger girl.

Guinevere thoughtlessly took it and chattered away. "At first I didn't think you were going to win, even though I know you're good. The knights from father's castle told me you had to be among the best to defeat Duke Maleagant, but it really did look like Lancelot was going to beat you. He's so noble—Lancelot, I mean. Not Maleagant."

Britt led them away from the pool of girls, her shoulders heaving when they were out of hearing range. "I find myself in the rare position of being the one to thank you."

Guinevere blinked. "For what?" she asked, completely oblivious to the exit she had just provided.

"Nothing," Britt sighed.

"It's a shame Sir Gawain is not here. He is nearly as handsome as Sir Lancelot. It would be a pretty thing to watch him fight," Guinevere said.

"I see. Enjoy the rest of the matches," Britt said, nudging her arm in a hint to make Guinevere let go.

"Of course. Thank you," Guinevere said. She curtseyed and reluctantly went on her way.

Britt groaned and pinched the back of her neck.

"Tough fight?"

"Merlin!" Britt groaned. "More like *hellish* fight. He nearly had me there." Britt uncomfortably rubbed her arm and frowned. "How likely is it that there is more to Lancelot than what we see?"

"I would say there's a good chance. Aren't you always spouting off as much?" Merlin asked, his wizard-cloak flapping in a breeze.

"I am…but…he might be worse than what I thought," Britt said.

Merlin snorted. "Now you sound like Kay. Speaking of which, you have made amends with him?"

"I have. Merlin, I'm sorry about yesterday. I—"

Merlin cut Britt off with a raised hand. "I expect your actions had something to do with one of your infernal King Arthur legends from the future?"

"Sort of. I wanted to make sure I stay…relevant, I suppose," Britt said.

Merlin raised his eyes to the heavens. "Why am I not surprised? I would like to speak of Guinevere."

"Wait, aren't you going to further scold me?" Britt asked.

"I would, but that has proven to be an ineffective tool in the past," Merlin dryly said. "It seems I would experience more success if I guilted you into submission."

"I always love it when you learn new tricks," Britt dryly said.

"More importantly!" Merlin waggled a finger at Britt before indicating to the ladies. "Watching that gave me an idea."

"Oh?" Britt asked.

"Indeed. Guinevere is here, feeding off us like a pest, and she already knows about...that. She may as well be useful to us. She could pretend to be your intended," Merlin said.

"Absolutely *not*," Britt said.

"I know you dislike the girl—I would be remiss if I did not admit that I find her less than tolerable—but you are supposed to be a young man. Sooner or later, knights will wonder why you never shower affection on a single female, particularly when you instruct *them* to do so," Merlin said.

"Kay doesn't have a lady either," Britt said.

"That you know of," Merlin said.

"What?" Britt frowned.

"Forget Kay. It would be better for your image, anyway."

"No. If you're so eager for me to have a cover-up, I'll ask Nymue, but not Guinevere."

Britt had a rather tumultuous relationship with the mythical Lady of the Lake. When she first met Nymue, she forcibly took Excalibur from the faerie lady, but since that rocky start, the two seemed to get along better—exchanging sharp-mouthed insults like compliments. Britt would even say they were friends...sort of.

"The *Lady of the Lake* is far too important to play make-believe with you," Merlin scoffed. "Guinevere is your best choice. Why are you so reluctant?"

"*WHY?*" Britt hissed, stabbing her finger in Guinevere's direction. "I already told you all the legends of King Arthur point to Guinevere and Lancelot as Camelot's ruin! They—" Britt stopped speaking when she realized that Lancelot was standing with Guinevere.

The handsome knight was smiling down at Guinevere, who was blushing and knitting her hands together.

"So you are still obsessed with that, hmm? We must talk sometime about these legends—they seem to drive every stupid move you make. If it upsets you that much, we can scrap the plan. Perhaps we should instead cultivate the image that you love all women and will not tie yourself down because you are too passionate," Merlin said, adjusting his cloak. "Britt?" he said when she didn't respond.

"What?" Britt asked, looking at the couple with unease. She forced a smile when she noticed Sir Ywain and Sir Griflet standing a short distance away, watching her with great intent.

Merlin sighed and draped an arm across her shoulders. "Stop worrying. We won't use the useless pest," he said, poking Britt's furrowed brow to smooth it out.

"Thanks," Britt said, sagging. "It's just—it's been a tough day, and I *really* hate Lancelot."

Merlin patted her shoulder. "There, there. What would you say to a day trip...two days hence?"

"A day-trip?" Britt perked.

"Yes. I was going to visit my mentor—Blaise. You could come with. You would enjoy making his acquaintance, and you *have* been forced to put up with Lancelot and his antics recently. I suppose you deserve a break," Merlin said.

"Really?" Britt said, her stance growing a little awkward when she realized just how close she and Merlin were standing with his arm affectionately draped over her. She was thankful for the heat of the day, which masked her self-conscious blush.

Merlin—oblivious as ever that she was a woman—chattered on. "I believe I've told you about him before. He's a hermit, and he lives in a chapel that is only a few hours ride from here. We'll have to set out early in the morning and warn the core of your knights—Sir Ulfius, Sir Bodwain and the like."

"Okay," Britt said, her heart beating erratically in her chest. This was getting worse.

Merlin nodded in satisfaction. "It is settled. Perhaps Blaise will have some words of wisdom to share with you regarding your worries," Merlin said, patting Britt in a brotherly way once more before stepping away—to her regret.

"I've always been curious about the man who raised you. I will look forward to it," Britt said.

"Wonderful. I may as well prepare Sir Kay, or it will be a traumatic experience for him," Merlin winked.

Britt laughed. "He'll insist on sending guards with us."

"Unnecessary. You're the best swordsman we have, and I'm a *wizard*!" Merlin scoffed.

"That's sure to impress him," Britt said.

Merlin grinned and said, "Be sure you are ready for your session in court later this afternoon. If you show up sweaty and in your practice armor, I'll have you dunked in a horse-trough."

Britt rolled her eyes. "Yes, Merlin."

"Enjoy the matches, lass," Merlin said quietly. He winked and strode away, humming a song under his breath.

Britt watched the wizard go with a wry smile. She knew her attraction—she *refused* to call it love—for Merlin was horribly one-sided. The wizard had told her he didn't even really *think* of her as a girl, and even if he was vaguely aware of it, he would never enter into a relationship that could jeopardize his precious plan for King Arthur's rule. Britt doubted Merlin would ever really *love* a woman anyway. He was too focused on his goal and too driven.

She sighed. "Still, it's disappointing."

As an adult—in her early twenties—Britt was satisfied to say that her crush on Merlin was not the all-consuming, dramatic passion of a teenager, which meant she could live with it. Britt was content to act as King Arthur, spend time with Merlin, and live with her new friends and adopted family.

Britt slapped dust off her thighs and looked to the jousting field. "If Sir Bodwain is still jousting, I should watch the match," she said, craning her neck.

Behind Britt, there was a sharp, whistling noise and a thud.

"*MY LORD!*" someone shouted, and Britt was hit by what felt like a train.

Britt groaned and coughed, the air knocked out of her.

"Sorry, My Lord, are you unhurt?" Sir Ywain asked, peering dolefully down at Britt, even as he held her pinned to the ground.

"Ywain," Britt coughed. "*What* are you doing?" she asked, barely audible over the womanly screams of shock and the hoarse shouts of several knights ringing around her.

Ywain didn't answer and looked over his shoulder.

"Arthur!" Sir Ector said, using his jolly belly to bulldoze his way through the crowd. "Are you alright, boy? Are you injured?"

"I've been flattened," Britt said, wincing as she tried propping herself up on her elbows. "What happened?"

"Arthur," Merlin said, his faced lined with worry as he and Sir Ulfius joined Sir Ector and Ywain. "It missed you—thank God."

"*What* missed me?" Britt asked, starting to grow irritated.

"A stray shot," Sir Ywain said, finally moving aside so Britt could see the arrow that was embedded in the ground a few feet away.

"It was a near miss," Sir Ector said, his face white.

"We should have taken the threat more seriously. Can you stand?" Merlin grimly asked.

"I'm fine. Are you alright, Ywain?" Britt asked, rolling to her feet when Ywain moved aside.

"Move!" Sir Kay snapped before he—trailed by a panicked Sir Griflet—broke through the crowd that encircled Britt.

Lancelot was only a few paces behind him. "My Lord!" he said, his voice dramatic.

"I'm fine," Britt repeated for her incoming foster-brother's sake. "I wasn't hit, just a little jarred. There's no harm done," Britt said, brushing grass off her thighs.

"I apologize. I didn't get to you until after the arrow was shot, but I was worried there would be more," Sir Ywain blushed.

Britt slapped Ywain on the shoulder. "There's nothing to

apologize for. Instead I should be thanking you. It was a smart move."

"Aye," Sir Kay echoed.

"It is a lucky thing it missed you," Lancelot said. "To think, it came so close!" The knight shook his head—the image of horror —and could only be consoled by several ladies who gathered around him.

"It's one of the practice arrows from the archery range," Sir Ector said, plucking the arrow out of the ground. "I don't think it's poison-tipped. What do you say, Merlin?" Sir Ector asked, passing the arrow to Merlin.

"I'll have to take it to my study to be certain, but it does not seem that it is," Merlin said, gravely studying the dirty arrowhead.

"What should we do, Sir Kay?" Sir Ywain asked, looking to the stormy seneschal.

"Get Arthur inside. I'll have a squadron of guards meet you in the keep," Sir Kay said, his voice tight.

"Don't you all think you are over-reacting?" Britt asked. "Someone at the archery range probably just misfired."

"My Lord, the archery range faces the *opposite direction*," Sir Ulfius said.

"Oh," Britt said.

"Whatever black knight that did this shall be caught! He will pay for his misdeed against King Arthur," Lancelot declared and was generally ignored by those closest to Britt.

Kay was already talking to a guard—who nodded as the knight gestured at the crowd. Merlin and Sir Ulfius were hunched over the arrow, carefully studying it.

"Better do as Kay says and go inside, Arthur," Sir Ector suggested.

"But—" Britt started.

"Yes, Sir," Sir Ywain and Sir Griflet said.

To Britt's shock, the two knights grabbed her by each arm and dragged her back to the keep—their grasp light but surprisingly *strong*. "You don't have to tote me like a doll," Britt said, trying to yank herself from their grasp without any success.

"We do, or you would never go with us, My Lord," Sir Griflet cheerfully said.

A smile broke through Britt's stormy countenance, and she looked at the two knights and realized—with a start—that they had both grown and now had broader shoulders and wider chests. Britt was still taller than they—just barely so—but they escorted her as if she had the strength of a helpless kitten.

"Thank you, you two," Britt said when they left the practice grounds behind. She glanced over her shoulder—Merlin was shouting at all the knights who had been at the archery range—and shivered.

"You're safe now, My Lord," Sir Ywain said as they stomped through Camelot's gates.

"Indeed," Sir Griflet said. "No one will reach you in Camelot."

6

BLAISE THE HERMIT

The marksman of the stray arrow was not found.

The episode nearly put Britt's day-trip with Merlin in jeopardy, until Merlin reasoned that it might be safer for Britt to leave Camelot and the public eye for a day, which was how, a week later, Britt found herself in a charming cottage owned by Blaise—Merlin's mentor, and a renown hermit.

"You've recorded everything Merlin's ever done in these books?" Britt asked, paging through the crude, leather books with awe.

"I have," Blaise smiled. As Merlin's mentor, Britt should have known Blaise would also scorn most concepts of hermits and wise men. Blaise wore a bright green tunic and had well-combed, bark-brown hair. His beard was trimmed and orderly, and he was built more like a knight than a holy man.

"So, this is like a baby book," Britt said in delight.

"A what?" Merlin frowned.

"A baby book? I love it," Blaise said, his laughter was loud and booming. "The future has such wonderful ideas," he said. (As Merlin's mentor, the wizard had naturally told the hermit everything, so Blaise was aware of Britt's gender *and* her origins.)

Britt tilted her head and studied an illustration. "…Is that Stonehenge?"

"Merlin knocked one of the formations over when playing with magic. We had to get a giant from France to set it right again," Blaise said.

"Wait, so it's here? It's already been built?" Britt asked.

Blaise nodded. "Indeed. I believe those responsible for keeping it breathed a sigh of relief when Merlin finally grew old enough to control his magic."

"They did not," Merlin scoffed.

"I want to visit it," Britt said. "In my time, it is considered a marvel of the world. Merlin, we have to go see it."

Merlin rolled his eyes to his mentor. "Do you see what you have done?"

"I won't apologize," Blaise laughed. "Flip a few pages forward, Britt. You'll find the time Merlin was practicing shape-shifting and accidentally got stuck in the form of an old woman."

"You can shape-shift?" Britt asked, eagerly flipping pages to look at the colored illustrations.

Merlin made a face like a puckered lemon. "I *used* to. It is a practice I avoid at all costs."

"Wise choice," Blaise said, standing to lift a pot of boiling water off the fire. "Would either of you like blueberry tea? I use fruit and mint leaves for flavoring."

"Yes, please," Britt eagerly said, looking up from the book.

"Tell me, Britt. How do you like being King of England?" Blaise asked, pouring the hot water into three mugs.

"I can't say it was ever a personal aspiration, but I'm getting used to it." She thoughtfully leaned back in her chair. "I've been very lucky. I've made so many friends, and Sir Ector and Sir Kay welcome me like I am a real member of their family."

"You do the role justice. Better, I am forced to admit, than the real Arthur would," Merlin said.

"You just mean I listen to you. The real Arthur probably wouldn't," Britt said.

"No, he would, he was merely too impulsive to make a well-thought-out decision—as made obvious by his choice to run off with a shepherdess," Merlin said.

Blaise winked. "I would take the compliment, Britt. Merlin doesn't dole them out often—it's as if he's afraid someone might think him a nice person or something equally as horrid."

Merlin sniffed in distaste. "What I meant is Britt is the best possible person for this job. Obviously, as it was *my* spell on the sword in the stone that selected her," he said, accenting his words with a smile.

"You copied most of that spell from a faerie magic book," Blaise said.

Merlin shot his mentor a look. "How quickly I remember why I don't visit you very often."

"I apologize, lad," Blaise said, solving Britt's puzzlement over Merlin's use of lad and lass in medieval England. "It is merely that I don't often meet someone who can rile you as much as I can," Blaise said before turning to Britt. "Merlin was an awkward child. He was too smart and found it difficult to get along with others his age. I'm glad he has found you—even if he had to look through centuries to find someone who could stand on equal ground with him."

"Blaise!" Merlin said.

"Thank you," Britt said, leaning her elbows on the table. She took the mug Blaise gave her, sniffing the mint-scented steam that rose from it.

"Our partnership works only because Britt acts more like a man than a woman," Merlin said. "She has never displayed any of the usual symptoms of an irrational woman—for which I am thankful."

Britt eyed Merlin. "If you don't stop talking, I will be forced to kick you on behalf of all the feminists in the twenty-first century."

"Careful—it's hot. You shouldn't drink it for a few minutes," Blaise warned, putting a mug in front of Merlin. "Did you put water in the horse trough when you arrived?"

"I did, but they could probably use a refill," Merlin said, groaning as he stood and brushed off his baggy cloak.

"Still wearing that thing, are you?" Blaise asked, shaking his head at the cloak.

"It's for the effect," Merlin said, "to make my role appear more authentic."

"Maybe it would have worked with young Arthur, but your current King has more of a refined look to her."

Merlin looked to Britt, his eyebrows furrowed. "I hadn't thought of that," he admitted. "She looks faerie enough to stand with the Lady of the Lake."

"It's something to think about," Blaise shrugged.

Merlin grunted. "I'll see to the horses," he said, making for the cottage door. He paused in the doorframe. "If you show her your illustrations about *you know what*, I will come back here at night and shave your beard off as you sleep," Merlin warned before ducking outside.

"What's *you know what*?" Britt asked when the young wizard was gone.

Blaise snickered, but he shook his head. "Even I'm not that cruel, lass. Now, tell me about you. In his last letter, Merlin mentioned there was a threat against your life. How are you coping?"

"Well enough," Britt shrugged. "It's not really anything new. Even if Merlin forgets, I always have it at the back of my mind that Camelot eventually splinters. What's an attempted murder or two next to that?"

"Ahh, yes, your knowledge of King Arthur comes into play," Blaise said, sipping his tea. "You do realize that as you are the king, it is *you* who creates the legends? That is to say, perhaps you could keep your kingdom from suffering."

"Merlin has told me as much, and he pointed out that the ending as I know it—where Camelot is split because of the love affair between Lancelot and Guinevere—doesn't have to happen to me. I mean, I'm a female, and I don't give two hoots about Guinevere. But…"

"It still bothers you," Blaise guessed.

"Yeah."

"Tell me, Britt. What do your legends of the future say about Merlin?" Blaise asked.

"Well…that he's a wise old wizard. He usually has a super long white beard and looks more like a mischievous grandpa. I think…at some point he's killed or something. I don't remember; I just know he wasn't with Arthur when Lancelot and Guinevere started their little escapade," Britt said.

Blaise nodded. "And is that true?"

"About him dying?"

"No, about who he is."

"No," Britt slowly admitted.

"Did Merlin ever tell you I'm something of a seer? I can see into the future—farther and with more clarity than most," Blaise said. "I've seen this America of yours."

"Really?" Britt asked, straightening in her chair.

Blaise took a sip of his tea and nodded. "It's also come to my attention that Britain and Europe—when compared to the Middle East and places like Greece or Egypt—are particularly *bad* at recording history. Our culture is more about oral tradition —right now, anyway," Blaise said.

"I could see that," Britt nodded. She took a sip of her blueberry tea, enjoying the natural flavors.

"So even if you *are* the same king all the King Arthur legends are about, don't you think your story would morph over the centuries?" Blaise asked.

"What do you mean?" Britt asked, her tone guarded.

"Say all of the stories you heard about Arthur are about you. Pieces of them might be true—like Sir Ector and Sir Kay adopting you. Other parts, the storytellers might change for the sake of their audience. Right now everyone knows of Merlin and respects him, in spite of his age. But a hundred years from now, will people still believe a young wizard and a time-traveling woman were responsible for the best kingdom in ancient England? I find it unlikely."

Britt was quiet as she thought.

"Stories—and history—are not unbiased. Each new generation will put their own thoughts and feelings into the past…so over the years, a fact that was inconsequential—like the age of a certain wizard—is changed. Perhaps a generation after you, storytellers will feel the need to reinvent King Arthur, and they will make Merlin old, or Sir Kay cruel to you."

"So you're saying I can't trust the legends I know because they have been changed," Britt said.

"In a way," Blaise said. "After all, have you ever even considered befriending Lancelot? The way Merlin says it, you win men for your cause like a faerie lady wins hearts."

Britt made a face. "Have you *met* Lancelot?"

Blaise laughed. "Then don't befriend him. All I am saying is rule with your gut, and use that sharp mind of yours. Your kingdom isn't the one you've heard of—at least, not in its entirety."

Britt was silent and drank her tea.

"Have I at all changed your thoughts on the subject?" Blaise asked.

Britt hesitated, something—like an inkling of hope—was forming in her mind. "If my story is changed to suit storytellers… does this mean…one day, I might go home?" Britt asked, raising her eyes to meet Blaise's gaze.

Blaise gave Britt a sad smile. "I don't know, lass. I can see the future of technologies and countries, but individuals slip past my eyes," he hesitated. "I doubt you will. Only a few of the faerie have such powerful magic, and they would have to be absolutely desperate before they would use it. Do you still want to leave that badly?"

"I don't know anymore," Britt admitted. "Sometimes I'm so happy here I could never picture being anywhere else. Other times…I want to be back in my time so badly it makes me sick."

"Such is the unfortunate burden of a time-traveler. You are blessed—and cursed—to stand between two times and two very different groups of people who love you. Yours is not an easy road."

Britt traced the rim of her mug with her thumb.

"But, cheer up. You are respected—and adored. Now, since Merlin seems to be taking his time, I shall tell you about *you know what.*"

"DON'T even dwell upon it!" Merlin barked, throwing open the door.

"I was starting to wonder if you had fallen in the trough," Blaise chuckled. "Sit, and we'll have some lunch."

"You cannot mollify me with offerings of food," Merlin said, ignoring Britt's thoughtful gaze as he sat down.

"He's right," Britt finally said, swapping her solemn expression for a grin. "If you want to sooth him, you'll have to compliment his magical powers."

"Merlin's powers are very great," Blaise said.

"Thank you," Merlin sniffed.

"Especially now that he has them under control. He came to me a toddler—those were dark times in my life as a result," Blaise said, winking at Britt.

Britt laughed, egging on Merlin to accuse the hermit of being nothing but a boring bachelor before his arrival—getting a larger laugh out of Britt.

The witty conversation continued well into lunch and ended only when Britt choked on her drink in her mirth.

~

IN THE MID-AFTERNOON, Britt and Merlin reluctantly admitted it was time to go. Britt saddled the horses while Merlin consulted with his mentor on several matters. By the time they were finished, Britt had already mounted Llamrei and was waiting for Merlin outside the cottage.

"Thank you for your help, Blaise," Merlin said, glancing at Britt—who was unaware of his scrutiny as she adjusted her stirrup. "She was happy about the Round Table, but since Lancelot's arrival, she looks more and more like a person shoved to the brink of an abyss."

"I am glad I could lighten her load. I only hope it helps," Blaise said.

"It will. She has not laughed half as much since she arrived in our time," Merlin said.

"I wanted to ask you about that," Blaise said. "She's been here over a year and a half, yes?"

"Yes."

"Has she changed at all? Physically I mean?"

"No. All her measurements are the same—or so the tailor and armor smiths tell me. Why?" Merlin asked, looking at his mentor with worry.

Blaise hesitated. "It only occurred to me, that as a person of the future stationed in the past…"

"Yes?"

"She might not age," Blaise finally said. "Whatever magic you used on her had to be powerful to pull her back through recorded history. It might have stunted her aging."

Merlin frowned as he studied Britt, his brilliant blue eyes swirling.

Blaise patted Merlin on the back. "Do not worry over it. It is just the musings of an old man. Be careful with her."

Merlin snorted. "You don't have to tell *me* that. Tell her! She is always going off on all sorts of fool's errands, nearly breaking her neck."

"I wasn't talking about her physical body. She has a gentle heart. Move carefully," Blaise said before slipping past Merlin to say farewell to Britt.

Merlin was frozen in the doorway for a moment. "What in the name of—what is that supposed to mean?" Merlin muttered before following him.

"Thank you for visiting, Britt. I hope to see you again someday soon," Blaise said, smiling up at Britt.

"Thank you. Me, too. I would still like to hear about whatever it is that embarrasses Merlin so badly," Britt said, patting her mare's neck.

"Someday," Blaise promised. "I wish you luck. You are a great King, Britt Arthurs."

"Thank you."

Blaise turned to Merlin. "Well, my greatest pupil, I wish you well in your endeavors. Come again when you have more stories to share so I might record them."

"Hmph," Merlin said before he boosted himself onto his horse's back. "Take care," he finally said.

"I will. Ride well—and try not to bring down Stonehenge."

"*Blaise*," Merlin groaned over Blaise's booming laughter as Britt and Merlin rode from the cottage.

"I like him," Britt said.

"I'm not surprised," Merlin groused.

7

SAD RETURNS

Britt and Merlin made good time on their ride home, and the sun was still high in the sky when they were less than half an hour—or so Britt estimated—away from Camelot.

"You've been quiet," Britt observed, tucking a strand of her gold-colored hair behind her ear.

Merlin squinted at the sky. "It's nothing. Just something Blaise said. I cannot fathom what he meant by it."

"What did he say?"

"That you have a gentle heart, and I should be careful with you."

Impressed that the hermit had caught on to her favorable feelings for Merlin, Britt raised her eyebrows. "That was...kind of him, I guess."

"I cannot make sense of it. It is almost like he thought..." Merlin cut himself off and dropped his panicked gaze to Britt. "You are not in love with one of your knights, are you? Was it Gawain or Tor? Is that why you rode off questing?

Britt burst into gusting laughing. "I am not in love with them, no."

"Good," Merlin said, settling back into the saddle. "That would have been worrisome."

"Give me some credit. I'm not going to fall for a boy still in his teenage years. My gosh, I'm at least five years older than most of them!"

"So, the older knights then? Sir Bedivere is about your age, I believe. It cannot be Kay—he is as comforting as a mountain bear."

"I'm not in love with Sir Bedivere, though he could be a model. And Kay is hardly a bear…"

"Then Sir Bodwain or Sir Ulfius?"

"Sir Ulfius could be my *dad*. No! I'm not in love with any of my knights!" Britt said.

"Good," Merlin repeated, falling silent again as Britt shook her head.

Britt steered Llamrei around a puddle and ducked a branch before Merlin spoke again. "Is it me?"

Britt felt her stomach turn cold—like it was sitting on ice. "What?" she said, trying to laugh.

"You never said you weren't in love; you just said you weren't in love with a *knight*. I'm older than you, and Blaise told *me* I needed to be careful with you."

Britt momentarily considered fessing up—before deciding that would make life incredibly awkward. "How big is your ego? I—"

"Tell the truth, lass," Merlin said, his voice tight.

Britt made a show of rolling her eyes. "Merlin. You—"

"Look at me," Merlin said, drawing Britt's gaze to him. "Look at me, and *promise* that you do not love me!"

Britt opened her mouth but couldn't say anything.

"Just say it, Britt!" Merlin said, clenching his horse's reins.

Britt swallowed and looked away.

Merlin groaned loudly and shouted something in a language Britt couldn't understand.

"What's your problem?" Britt frowned.

"What is my *problem*? My problem is that everything was going *so well*, and your stupid…" Merlin couldn't seem to find the right word as he gestured at Britt with a hand. "Your, your *feminine heart* has just ruined everything."

Britt frowned deeper. "You're being dramatic. Nothing has changed."

"But that's not true, is it? Everything has changed. You cannot love me, Britt. I forbid it!"

"Why? It's not like I was going to ever act on it," Britt said.

"Because this cannot happen. You will jeopardize everything we've worked for! You cannot start getting lovesick—you're King Arthur! You're supposed to be a man! Do you know what will happen if your knights that you love oh-so-much find out that you're a woman? They will rebel! I will lose everything I have worked for!" Merlin said.

"What part of my personality would *ever* make you think that I would be lovesick?" Britt demanded. "You didn't even figure it out until Blaise told you. Even then, it took you two hours."

"Don't play games. You are a female! You are a creature of passion and love. Sooner or later, you will get dreamy-eyed and start crying because I will never return your love."

Britt's tone was even and dark. "What."

"You will turn into a swooning girl, like every other female in this time, and your court will crumble when they see how weak you are."

"I resent that implication! What an—you are the most sexist jerk I have met in this century!" Britt shouted.

Merlin groaned. "I take it back. You are just as bad as the rest of your gender!"

"How can you even say such lies? I can be a woman and still be strong—you're scared stiff of Morgause and Nymue; don't try to deny it. And besides that, you didn't have a *clue* that I've had a crush on you, so I'm not obvious!"

"You're not. There is that saving grace," Merlin said, regaining some of his calmness. "Look, Britt. Whatever your *feelings* are for me, they must end. Now."

"Don't *worry*," Britt promised, her eyes flashing as she tightened up her reins. "From henceforth, I will hold you on the same level of affection and esteem that I hold *Lancelot*!" Britt said before heeling Llamrei.

"Britt," Merlin managed to say before the white mare took off, cantering down the road. When Merlin also cued his horse forward, Britt sank closer to Llamrei's neck and clung to her as the great mare threw herself into a gallop.

They popped out of the Forest of Arroy, booking it across the meadow in front of Camelot like a streak of lightning. They skid through the city gates and trotted up the busy road that led the way into the inner palace—into the keep.

By the time Britt reached the royal stables, Sir Kay and several guards were waiting for her.

"Arthur, is something wrong?" Sir Kay asked, his eyes tracing her for injuries.

Britt harshly laughed. "Why don't you ask *Merlin*? He seems to think the end is near." She savagely glared at the wizard, who clattered into the stable courtyard on his skinny horse.

"Arthur," Merlin said, sliding from his horse. "We need to talk."

"Enough!" Britt yelled, making several horses spook. "Whatever it is you fear, I can vow that it will *never happen*. Believe me, what little threat there was is entirely gone. But if you *dare* to speak to me like that again, you will find yourself without a king to manipulate," Britt said.

Sir Kay and the guards were frozen, like practice targets. Merlin shifted but said nothing in reply.

Scowling to keep back the tears, Britt swept from the stable, knocking into Lancelot on her way out.

"My Lord?" the vapid knight said, tipping his head like a curious dog.

"Sorry," Britt muttered, moving around him as she stormed to the keep, Sir Ywain and Sir Griflet trotted about twenty paces behind her.

Britt briefly turned back to look at the stable and saw some kind of messenger approach Merlin.

She wanted to scream. She wanted to push the wizard off Camelot's walls. He had done the most possible damage to her—not by being unable to return her feelings, but by entirely *rebuffing* her and acting as if it was the worst betrayal she could possibly commit.

Britt shook her head and entered the keep. "Never again," she vowed.

~

TWO DAYS LATER, Britt was admiring the gardens with Queen Adelind—Pellinore's lovely wife. The older woman was commenting on the blooming flowers when the two were interrupted.

"My Lord?"

Britt flashed a genuine smile of pleasure when she saw who greeted her. "Sir Gawain, Sir Tor—you have victoriously returned," Britt said.

Sir Tor—his arm in a cloth sling—smiled. "We did, My Lord. We completed our quests—although I might be a little worse for the wear," he admitted.

Sir Gawain looked down at the ground.

"Congratulations. I cannot wait to hear of your adventures," Britt said. "I planned to hold a feast when all three of you—King Pellinore included—returned, but in the meantime, I would love to hear what, er, befell you."

"If you forgive my frankness, My Lord, but there is no telling when my *dear* husband will return," Queen Adelind dryly said. "He has gone out on an inspection of our lands and disappeared for months on end. He many not return to Camelot until next week...or next year."

Britt hesitated. "Are you sure?"

"Hold the feast, My Lord. I'm sure your knights deserve it," Queen Adelind said, patting Britt's hand. She curtseyed to the knights and left.

"That settles it, then. I'll tell Sir Ulfius and Sir Kay we are celebrating your return immediately. Are you too tired to tell your stories to the Round Table tonight?" Britt asked.

"Not at all," Sir Tor said.

Britt hesitated when Sir Gawain still didn't look at her. "Are you alright, Gawain?" she asked, setting a hand on his shoulder.

"Yes, My Lord," Sir Gawain said.

"Excellent," Britt said, but she still eyed him warily. "In that case, let the preparations begin!"

BRITT SPARED no expense in hosting the young knights' feast. There were musicians, jugglers, a fire breather, trays and trays of food, and an endless supply of wine.

Spirits were high. The hall was filled with laughing ladies and well-humored knights.

Britt's table was in better spirits than it had been. Guinevere was still at the table—as was Merlin, but Britt wouldn't look at the wizard or speak to him unless it was for a court function. She was grateful that Tor and Gawain, as the honored guests, sat with her, giving her someone to happily talk to.

After most of the food had been served, Gawain and Tor told their tales.

"My story is rather silly," Sir Tor said, laughing good-naturedly. He glanced behind him, where Lem stood as his squire. "I rode forth with My Lord, that is to say King Arthur, in search of the white hound. While on the hound's trail, we ran across two recreant knights. They attacked us. I threw myself on one, and My Lord disarmed the other. We granted them their lives and instructed them to come back to Camelot to swear loyalty. I say—did they ever pledge loyalty to you, My Lord?" Sir Tor asked, momentarily distracted.

"They did," Britt nodded. Her chair was pushed back from the table and her hands were occupied petting Cavall's head—which the large mastiff had placed on her lap. "Mounted as I was, my party and I beat them back. I believe they are helping with the summer crops."

"Oh, Good," Sir Tor said before abruptly returning to his story. "The knight that I defeated had a great squire, Lem, who graciously offered to serve as my squire. I'm particularly happy about that." Sir Tor stepped aside so those not on the dais could get a glimpse of the new squire.

He then continued. "Some knights from Camelot came out about then and rode back to Camelot with My Lord, but Lem and I kept following the trail of the knight that kidnapped the hound. Lem knew him—by sight anyway—and led me to the campground of the lady to whom the knight paid homage. She—and her lady servants—were sleeping, with the white hound staked and tied up outside their tents with no food or water. T'was deplorable. The poor dog was so happy to see us, it started whining—which woke up the lady. She ordered me to leave it, but I told her I couldn't. T'was my quest from King Arthur. She warned me she would send her knight after me, but I paid her no heed, and Lem and I set out for Camelot."

"The hound," Lem hissed.

"Right, if you would bring out the hound, please," Sir Tor called.

The white hound—leashed by a servant—trotted into the feasting hall, wagging his tail and looking as jolly as Sir Tor.

"Well done, Sir Tor," Britt said as everyone admired the dog.

"Getting the dog was the easy part. Keeping it? That was a little more difficult. First, I accidentally got us lost trying to get back to Camelot, but then the knight that kidnapped the hound from these very halls found us and demanded that we give the dog back. I refused, so we fought. It was a close match—I was beaten quite soundly—but I managed to turn it around at the last minute. I regret to say the knight didn't ask for mercy—he didn't want it—and kept fighting back, so I had to kill him," Sir Tor said, looking sad for a moment. Lem shook his head sadly. "He injured me pretty badly, so Lem insisted that we stay at a small chapel we found until I could ride without falling off. That's it."

"That still is quite the tale," Britt said loud enough for all to hear as the hound was led from the room. "You have done well for yourself, Sir Tor. You have made me proud to have you within the ranks of the Round Table."

"Thank you, My Lord," Sir Tor said before sitting and attacking his food with relish.

Britt leaned closer and said to the young knight, "Did you keep the recreant knight's armor and horse?"

Sir Tor swallowed the wad of food in his mouth. "I did, My Lord. You were right. I didn't need to worry about money to keep my squire. T'was quite enjoyable to quest. I would like to do it again soon—though I think I need more training."

Behind Sir Tor, Lem grunted in agreement.

Britt grinned and leaned back in her chair, slipping a bit of her dinner to Cavall. "Well done, Sir Tor," she repeated in her announcer's voice. "Nephew, it's now your turn."

Sir Gawain sighed and stood up, as if it pained him. "My quest was to track the white hart and to bring it back to Camelot. It was a fiercely swift creature, and it took me days to catch up with it. During that time, I fought a rogue knight who was demanding compensation from peasants for so-called protection—while he offered no such thing. I defeated him. He asked for no mercy, so I gave him none."

"Well done, Sir Gawain," Britt said, although it was with sad eyes that she looked back and forth between Sir Gawain and Sir Tor. She didn't think questing would be so...bloody. "Although it seems there are more evil knights in the world than I thought," she added.

Sir Gawain nodded and squared his shoulders. "I eventually tracked the white hart to a castle, where I captured it and brought it home."

As Sir Gawain spoke, the white hart was led into the room by a man. The room buzzed with whispers and murmurs as they studied what Britt recognized to be an albino deer. It was a beautiful animal, and in spite of the huge amount of people present, it calmly looked about the room—much like a dog—and wore a scarlet red halter.

"I'm impressed. I wasn't sure you would be able to actually *bring* the deer back. Well done, Sir Gawain," Britt said.

Sir Gawain shook his head. "It is not so, My Lord."

"Why?" Britt asked.

"I did something most dishonorable—especially given the vows I swore at the Round Table," Sir Gawain said. "When I tracked the hart to the castle, a knight rode forth to match me in combat. I was...angered, and so I fought him with much hatred, first in a jousting match—in which I knocked him from his horse —and then in a sword fight. The knight—Sir Athmore—was... proud and did not wish to lose to me, though I was steadily winning. His lady was present and called for him to yield. As a knight of the Round Table, I should have known better. I should have offered him mercy even though he would not ask for it. Regardless, I was too angry and too eager to end his life."

Sir Gawain was silent.

Britt patiently waited.

"The lady could see as much," Sir Gawain finally continued.

"So when I disarmed him, and moved to smite him…she stepped between us. I-I could not stop the blow in time, and I slew her," Gawain said, swallowing with difficulty.

The hall was silent.

"I brought dishonor to you and dishonor to Camelot with my actions, My Lord. And I am sorry for it," Sir Gawain said.

For a while, Britt didn't know what to say. Gawain—the sweet, loyal knight—had killed a woman? "What happened to Sir Athmore?" she asked.

"He immediately regretted his actions—our actions—for he deeply loved his lady. He bid me to slay him, but I could not. It was he who led forth the white hart," Sir Gawain said.

Britt nodded. "And why did you fight him with such anger?"

Gawain lowered his eyes and could only whisper the words. "He killed one of the hounds you gave me, My Lord."

That made Britt feel a little better. She knew Gawain had a complex about pets—given to him by his pig of a father, King Lot. Still… "It is no excuse to kill an innocent, Gawain."

"I know," Sir Gawain said. He squared his shoulders and looked out at the feasters. "I am prepared to face the consequences of my terrible actions, My Lord. Should you choose to strip me of my knighthood and exile me from Camelot, I will understand. Now, at least, I will accept the consequences with honor."

Britt tapped her fingers on the chair.

What was she supposed to do?

Britt knew Gawain wasn't a killer. The boy was sick with guilt. It was clear he hadn't enjoyed the experience. But she was trying to hold her knights to a higher level of integrity. That was why she established the Round Table. What would the legends have her do?

Britt rolled her head as she thought. The legends would probably have her temporarily exile Gawain, but he wasn't even twenty yet, and he had gone through so much under his tyrant of a father before arriving at Camelot. It was incredible he had retained his gentleness.

"Arthur," Merlin whispered. Even though it was barely above a hushed utterance, it was loud in the silent hall.

Britt ignored him.

Blaise said to rule with my gut and my head. Very well, let's try it.

Britt slid Cavall's head off her lap and stood. The sound of her chair scraping on the ground was ominous in the oppressive quiet. Britt crossed the short distance between herself and Sir Gawain.

She stared at the young knight, who looked back at her with trust and despair.

"Sir Gawain, prince of Orkney," Britt started, drawing whispers from the crowd. "You have made a terrible choice and spilled the blood of an innocent. In accordance with your actions, I will place upon you a ruling as your King," Britt said.

"Yes, My Lord," Sir Gawain said, his eyes falling.

The hall fell silent when Britt smoothed Gawain's hair from his face and—in the most grave, elegant way she could—kissed his forehead. "I grant you a boon: a gift of mercy," Britt said, smiling fondly. "For I know you, Sir Gawain, and I know that you will not make this mistake again, and that you will spend the rest of your life struggling to make amends for it. I only strip knighthood from those who take delight in wrongdoings. That is not you," Britt said. "Instead, I dub you—evermore—the Ladies' Knight. You will be charged with fighting for those who have no one to speak for them. You will oversee their quarrels and act as the champion for any lady who requests it. Finally, I tell you to be known as the most merciful knight in my Kingdom. These things I charge you with, and I congratulate you on successfully retrieving the white hart. Well done, Sir Gawain."

The hall exploded into cheers. Sir Gawain, weak-kneed, dropped to Britt's feet. Britt crouched and hauled him upright, holding him aloft. "What do you say, ladies of Camelot. Do you accept your champion and agree to his charge?"

The ladies whispered and looked wide-eyed at each other—shocked, apparently, to be so openly addressed for their opinion.

"We accept," Queen Adelind said, standing to address the hall. "Arthur is wise beyond his years, for Sir Gawain is a good knight and will do us justice. But, let there be no more bloodshed of the innocent."

"Agreed!" Guinevere said, also standing, though she nervously licked her lips and looked to Britt.

"Then it is settled. Ladies, I give you your champion," Britt said, raising Gawain's arm in the air, inciting a new wave of cheers.

"You don't have to do this, My Lord. I don't deserve it," Sir Gawain said to Britt over the roar of the crowd.

Britt gave Sir Gawain her truest smile. "People usually don't deserve it; that's why it's called mercy. I hope you will remember this feeling and offer mercy to others as a result—even when they hurt you and cause you pain."

"Thank you, My Lord," Gawain said.

8

NORTHERN VISITOR

The following day, Britt, Sir Kay, and Sir Ector were in the stables, brushing out their horses after a short ride.

"You should let me ride Roen more often, Kay. He's getting jealous," Britt said, caressing the neck of her black gelding before taking a comb to Llamrei's mane.

"The bigger problem seems to be that he is growing fat from a lack of activity," Sir Ector said, peeking over the stall door to study the gelding.

"Llamrei is the superior riding horse, My Lord," Sir Kay said.

"Yeah, but isn't there a death threat against me? Riding a horse that will fight to protect me might be safer," Britt said.

"Who told you of a death threat, My Lord?" Sir Kay asked.

"Merlin," Britt said, tossing the wooden comb in a box.

"You two are talking again?" Sir Ector asked, scratching his beard.

"No, he told me before I left on the quest," Britt said.

Sir Ector sighed. "Oh. That's a shame."

"What made you come to blows?" Sir Kay asked.

"Let's just say Merlin has made it abundantly clear to me where we stand," Britt said.

"On the ground?" Sir Ector said.

"Merlin gave us a similar non-answer," Sir Kay said, wiping down his horse's bridle.

"Whatever the cause, I wish you two would end the quarrel," Sir Ector said. "It's not good for a King and his Chief Counselor to be at odds."

Before Britt could reply, a page hurried into the stables. "My Lord," he said, sketching a bow to Britt. "A guest has just arrived at Camelot. A *Royal* guest—a lady!" the young boy said, looking horrified.

Britt held back a groan but couldn't stop her expression of disdain. "Inform the lady I am busy with kingly affairs and send Merlin to greet her."

"Merlin already has greeted her," the page said, his eyes bulging. "She hit him with a club."

"Never mind. I shall meet this curious lady myself," Britt said, brushing horse hair from her clothes. "Do either of you wish to join me, Sir Ector, Sir Kay?"

Kay, shy and wary of women as he was, ducked behind his horse and kept brushing.

"I'll come with you, Arthur. Better to go in strong numbers lest this lady thinks to take something to your head, too," Sir Ector said, waddling past Britt and Llamrei. "Put away the horses, Kay, would you?" Sir Ector called over his shoulder as he led the way.

Britt looked down at her dirty leather jerkin and boots and grimaced, but she followed Sir Ector—and the page—out of the stables and into the open courtyard between the keep and inner walls.

There she saw Merlin—in his cliché gray cloak—sitting on the steps and holding a hand to his skull. Standing not far away from him—one hand planted on her hip, the other hefting a sturdy-looking staff—was a woman with silky brown hair pulled in an elaborate braid. She wore a wine-red overdress and a white kirtle and looked like she was roughly Britt's age. Her stance was elegant—if not forceful—and her expression was apathetic as she watched Merlin nurse his head.

When Britt entered the courtyard, the woman looked up. The smallest hint of a smile tugged at her lips. "Arthur?" she asked.

Britt tipped her head in a shallow bow. "I am. Welcome to Camelot, Lady."

"Thank you," the woman said, taking a few liquid steps in Britt's direction. "Brother," she added before hugging Britt.

Britt tried to puzzle through the implication and stiffened at the close contact. She was surprised Merlin was not swooning—in spite of their argument, keeping Britt's secret was his goal in life. But all of Britt's questions were answered when the beautiful woman pulled back and gave Britt her hint of a smile again.

"It is I—Morgan le Fay—your half-sister. Our sister, Morgause, wrote to me and told me *everything* about you," Morgan said.

Britt's worry cleared, and she smiled in real delight. "Morgan! Our sister…spoke of you. I'm so glad you have come to Camelot! Did Morgause send you?" she asked.

Queen Morgause was married to King Lot of Orkney and was mother to Gawain and his brothers: Agravain, Gareth, and Gaheris. Morgause was also aware of Britt's gender—although she didn't know Britt was from the future.

If Morgause told Morgan everything, that meant Morgan also knew Britt was female.

On the steps, Merlin moaned, but both of the women ignored him.

"Last year, she suggested that I visit you, but I'm afraid this was the first time I have found myself free of responsibilities and able to make the journey," Morgan said.

"I'm glad you could make it," Britt said, glancing at her foster-father when he shuffled. "Ah, excuse my gracelessness. Sister, this is Sir Ector of Bonmaison—my beloved foster-father."

"Lady," Sir Ector said with a grave bow.

"Sir Ector," Morgan said, curtsying. She looked to Britt—who was still smiling fondly at Sir Ector—before she added, "I have heard much about your courage and strength in the battle for Arthur's throne. Your support of my brother is truly a gift from Heaven."

It was the perfect thing to say to Sir Ector. The older knight beamed, and—in a gesture Kay had inherited—smoothed the upper lip of his beard. "You are too kind, lady."

"Many of our nephews are here—I am sure they'll be thrilled to hear you've arrived. Please, come inside," Britt said, leading the way to the keep. "Sir Ector, would you like to join us?" she asked when she realized Morgan was following but Sir Ector was not.

"Nay, Br—Boy. Enjoy yourself. I'll see to the horses with Kay and tell him he needn't...er...worry," Sir Ector said, glancing at Morgan before his face split in a grin again.

"Thank you, father," Britt said before entering the keep.

"You will not inquire after the wizard Merlin?" Morgan asked.

"Merlin can rot," Britt said.

Morgan chuckled—a low, husky sound.

"We should find Sir Ulfius—he'll get a room ready for you," Britt said, changing her plotted path and starting up a winding staircase. "What brings you to Camelot?"

"I was visiting faerie folk in the area and thought to seek you out. My sister's description of you piqued my interest. Morgause also asked me to visit for the sake of checking on Gareth and Gaheris," Morgan said.

"I hope you enjoy your stay here. I'm sorry, but you'll have to sit with me for meals."

"I am honored to be considered your guest."

Britt laughed. "Well, because of that, too. But I'm desperate for decent dinner conversation. I've been forced to sit with no one but Guinevere and Merlin at my table for days, and it's getting boring."

"Morgause told me you and Merlin got along quite well. Is this no longer true?" Morgan asked.

"As long as Merlin is acting like a mule, yes," Britt said, starting down a hall that branched off the stairs.

"I see."

"Morgause didn't get along with him. I take it you bear a grudge against Merlin as well?"

"I would not go so far as to say a grudge. I find Merlin... acceptable. However, it seems that whenever I first see him, I must always remind him that I am a powerful sorceress—not a petty hedge-witch."

"Nice," Britt said, glancing at the staff Morgan held with a newfound respect.

"It usually works quite nicely," Morgan humbly said.

"I'm glad someone is able to knock some sense into him," Britt said, stopping outside the chamber Sir Kay and Sir Ulfius shared to store their records and supplies. "Thank you for coming."

"It is my pleasure."

Britt rapped on the door. "Sir Ulfius? I have another guest I need you to prepare a room for."

IN THE LATE hours of the night, Britt sat in a garden, holding a red rope that was attached to the white hart's rope halter. She was alone—mostly. Sir Kay's required squadron of guards were with her, but since she was in a garden as opposed to walking the walls, they stuck to the shadows of the castle. It was unusual for Britt, in her insomnia—brought on by dreams and memories of her friends and family from the twenty-first century—to do anything besides walk the walls. But, for a change of pace, Britt decided to check in with her horses. When she slunk off to the stables—her guards shadowing her—she had found the deer housed in a horse stall and felt bad for it.

"So, Gawain tracked you down for his quest. Great. Now *what* am I supposed to do with you?" Britt asked the deer, watching it in the sputtering torchlight.

The buck wiggled its pink nose and stretched its head in her direction.

Britt passed it a cabbage leaf, which the buck delicately tugged from her hand. "There's absolutely no way you're becoming dinner, and I'm not going to have you slaughtered and stuffed."

The deer finished its cabbage leaf and inquisitively nosed Cavall, who was lying down at Britt's side.

"Oh no. I have enough pets already. I am not adding you to my menagerie," Britt said.

The buck ignored her and nibbled on grass.

Britt sighed propped her head up on her arm. "Dang it. Fine, but I'm naming you Rudolph."

Cavall sneezed.

"I don't care if it's silly! He's my stinking albino deer, and I'm sick of suppressing my twenty-first century knowledge. I can call him whatever I want!"

The newly named Rudolph stared at the pile of cabbage leaves mounded next to Britt.

"Greedy thing," Britt said, passing him another leaf. "No wonder no one wants to play any reindeer games with you. You —" Britt stopped talking when Cavall turned to look behind Britt.

Britt also turned around—hoping that, out of all people, it wouldn't be *Lancelot* who would find her talking to a quest animal in the middle of the night. Her good cheer sunk.

It was worse than Lancelot. It was Merlin.

Britt didn't say anything to acknowledge the wizard. Instead, she turned back to Rudolph and gave him another cabbage leaf.

Britt was silent until she heard his footsteps lead away from the small garden. Britt craned her neck to look for him, but he wasn't visible after leaving the light shed by the torches Britt's guards had posted. When he was gone, she sighed, her shoulders slumping. Her eyes stung, and Britt looked at Cavall and Rudolph before giving them a wet laugh.

"I miss him," Britt quietly admitted to the animals. "I miss him calling me lass and giving me the evil eye for doing something wrong. I *really* miss his smiles—those were *fine!*" Britt said with a grin. The grin faded, and she shook her head. "He could have just said no, but instead he stomped all over me. How are you supposed to come back from that? How can I ever look at him as a friend? As who I *thought* he was?"

Britt was silent for several heartbeats. "And why is it that I *still* harbor something for him?" When a few teardrops spilled over, Britt sighed in irritation. "And here I thought I was all grown up and not the least bit weepy. I guess that goes to show me," Britt said, wiping the tears from her eyes.

She cleared her throat and gave the deer another cabbage leaf. "So, Rudolph. Do you play fetch? What do deer even do? I only knew dogs were supposed to play fetch because I saw *Beethoven* a hundred times as a kid."

~

MERLIN STOOD on the walkway of Camelot's inner wall, scowling as he studied the guard formations posted on the outer walls—which were hued pink in the growing light of dawn. "Two threats in the span of a few weeks and a near miss with an arrow. I don't like it," Merlin said.

"I beg your pardon?" the guard standing with Merlin said.

"Nothing. Just musing on our odds," Merlin said. "The brush with the arrow happened roughly a week after I first received news that someone was out for Arthur. I received word of a second threat the day I returned from Blaise's hermitage. It's been a week since then. Kay has the king swaddled inside, so there is no risk of action now, but…"

"It's a lucky thing Morgan le Fay arrived when she did," said the guard—one of the regulars who stood with Britt during her nightly bouts of insomnia. "If King Arthur was not so busy entertaining her, I think he would be climbing the walls."

"Yes, that *is* a lucky thing," Merlin said. He folded his arms and frowned at the guard formation again. "Double the guards at the gate," he finally said. "If the guards do not recognize whoever is seeking entrance, ban them from entering until their identity can be confirmed."

"As you wish," the guard said, bowing.

"Merlin—you fiend. I've been looking all over for you," King Pellinore called as he climbed the last few steps, gaining admittance to the walkway.

"King Pellinore, you have returned. I trust your quest was victorious?" Merlin asked, his eyes sweeping King Pellinore's dusty clothes.

"It was. I found the maiden and brought her to Camelot. She is being reunited with her hound as we speak—though that wasn't what I wanted to talk to you about."

"Excellent. I'm sure Arthur will throw you a feast tonight—have you told him you've returned?" Merlin said, only half-listening.

"No, I *need* to speak to you," King Pellinore said.

Merlin tilted his head at the spark of worry he heard in the king's voice. "What is it?"

"While returning to Camelot, I spent a night in a glade not too far from here," King Pellinore said. "In the middle of the night, I found myself unable to rest, and I thought to get a drink from a nearby stream. It was there that I overheard a plot against King Arthur."

Merlin was silent as he fiercely concentrated on the king and waited for him to continue.

"The perpetrators were two men—though I would not know or recognize them again as I could not see them in the darkness of night. They spoke of how they had, under instructions from the north, smuggled a poison south."

Merlin's tension eased. "Poison is better news than I feared," Merlin said. "The staff at Camelot is without doubt loyal to Arthur. I will put them on alert. Thank you for the intelligence, King Pellinore," Merlin said.

With the kitchen staff keeping an eye on Britt's food, even if an enemy managed to sneak into Camelot, he would be unable to poison her. Merlin started to relax, until King Pellinore shook his head.

"One of the men explained to the other that he had successfully delivered it to Camelot," the king said. "Into the hands of a knight from the north whom King Arthur greatly cherishes and trusts. That knight will poison him."

Merlin heard church bells of alarm ring in his ears, and he stared unseeingly at Pellinore.

"I came as soon as I could for—though I am at loathe to say it —Arthur loves Sir Gawain—" Pellinore said.

Merlin interrupted him. "Guards—have any of you knowledge of where your sovereign is?"

"I believe he planned to break his fast with the lady Morgan le Fay and his nephews," a guard said.

9

FORGIVEN

Merlin ran down the walkways, his cloak grabbing at his legs like desperate hands. His heart pounded as he raced down the stairs that were pressed snug against the castle wall. He couldn't hear anything. He couldn't think. His sharp mind was incapable of anything besides absolute panic.

Britt!

"I'll kill her," Merlin said as he jumped the last few steps. "If she gets herself offed—I'll *KILL* her!"

Merlin tried to think of a strategy. He tried to think of a plan. Instead, all he could picture was Britt with her cursed-beautiful smile, grinning at Gawain as the knight fed her poison.

She would die.

Britt would die!

She was an idiot who would trust her life with anyone she was fond of. "*Stupid, stupid, stupid* girl!" Merlin muttered as he burst into the keep. "Where is Arthur?" He roared at the nearest guard.

"He called for food in the queen's garden," the guard said, naming a small, cheerful garden planted directly outside what was to be the queen's quarters.

Merlin darted back outside the keep, his heart squeezing painfully in his chest. He ran up a corridor, passing Sir Lancelot and a gaggle of knights.

He barreled around the corner, almost skidding out when he hit the green lawn of the queen's garden.

Britt was there, laughing and passing Morgause's two youngest brats a grubby beanbag—which they threw for Britt's mastiff.

Merlin relaxed for the barest moment, until he saw Britt reach out and take a goblet from Sir Gawain. She smiled at him and said something to Morgan le Fay as she raised the cup to her lips.

"BRITT!" Merlin shouted. "NO!"

$\sim$

"WE SHOULD HAVE THOUGHT of this ages ago," Britt said, patting Cavall as Morgan le Fay slathered butter on a piece of bread and passed it to Agravain. "This is much nicer than eating with everyone else."

"I never cared to break my fast with soup," Morgan acknowledged.

"My Lord, can we—did you bring Cavall's bag?" Gareth asked.

"Yes, thank you for reminding me. Here. Have fun," Britt chuckled, passing the spitty beanbag to Gaheris.

The two little boys ran a few paces away and threw the beanbag.

Cavall went and fetched it for them and was exuberantly rewarded with crusts of bread.

"My Lord, are you thirsty?" Sir Gawain asked, holding out a goblet of what looked like apple cider.

"Parched, thanks, though my teeth won't thank you for this," Britt said, taking the goblet. "I trust you slept well, Morgan?" she said, finally remembering her manners as a host before raising the goblet to her lips.

"BRITT! NO!"

Britt jumped and sloshed some of the juice. She owlishly blinked and looked up. "...Merlin?"

The wizard stormed towards them, his normally brilliant blue eyes were tumultuous—like hurricanes.

"He looks angry," Agravain observed.

"No kidding," Britt frowned.

"What did he mean—shouting Britt?" Gawain asked.

"Who knows, probably some strange, wizard thing," Britt said as the wizard drew closer. "Merlin—what's the matter with you? Normal people don't *shout* like that—hey!" Britt objected when Merlin plucked her goblet from her grasp.

Merlin rummaged around in his cloak for a moment before sprinkling herbs on top of the juice and swirling the cup.

"Great. Thanks for ruining my drink," Britt frowned as the cider went from a tangy, amber color to muck brown.

"Guards, arrest these fiends from Orkney!" Merlin shouted.

"What?" Agravain growled, leaping to his feet.

"Merlin. You've hit your head and have lost part of your mind. *What* are you doing?" Britt asked.

"Your drink has been *poisoned*," Merlin snapped.

"Check the jug, then. If my cider is bad, so is everyone else's," Britt said.

"Guards!" Merlin shouted. His cries brought guards and a number of knights meandering to the garden.

Britt growled in her throat as she saw Lancelot, his cousins, and a few of their lady friends whispering and watching.

"Stand down," Britt said to the guards before picking up a wooden tray and turning to the Orkney princes and Morgan le Fay. "I'm sorry for ruining our morning. You'll have to excuse me," Britt said, taking cups of cider from Agravain and Morgan. "Sorry, Gareth, Gaheris. Cavall, come," Britt said, her days of waitressing as a teenager coming back to her as she carried the tray in one hand and the jug of cider in the other. "Merlin, now!" Britt snapped in a much less pleasant tone.

Merlin tilted his head at Britt's supposed relatives before nodding to the guards and following Britt.

Britt and Merlin were quiet as they entered the keep through a side door and made their way to Merlin's study.

Britt kicked the door open and roughly slammed the jug and tray on one of his workbenches before she turned around and folded her arms across her chest. "Explain to me what just happened," she ordered.

"You were nearly poisoned by Gawain," Merlin said, setting down what was supposed to be Britt's goblet.

"No, I wasn't," Britt said shaking her head.

"You were. The reaction of these herbs prove your drink was tampered with," Merlin said, stabbing a finger at her cup.

"Fine, maybe the cider was spiked, but Gawain didn't do it. *None* of them did. They were drinking the same thing I was drinking! Check their cups," Britt said.

Merlin frowned but sprinkled herbs in the other cups. After he swirled the herbs around, the contents of each cup turned muck brown.

"SEE!" Britt shot.

Merlin didn't respond and instead poured out some of the cider in a spare cup from another workbench, testing it with the herbs.

Again, the cider turned muck brown.

Merlin sighed. "I have a man skilled with poisons. I'll get him up here to see if he can identify the type."

"Oh no. No, no, no. You are *not* just going to sweep your wrongful accusations under the rug without another word. That may be how dudes from medieval times do it, but that is *not* how I roll! We are going to talk this over, and you are going to apologize to Gawain if I have to hold a dagger to your back to make you utter it," Britt said.

Merlin rubbed his forehead as if he were tired. "I'm sorry. I don't know what came over me," he finally said.

Britt was silenced out of sheer shock. She didn't think it would be so easy to get him to admit he was wrong! "I'm not the one you should be apologizing to," she said stiffly.

"No, I meant I'm sorry for everything. For the words I said to you as we returned from Blaise's, for accusing Gawain of murder, all of it," Merlin said, swiping a hand through the air.

"*Why* are you sorry?" Britt asked.

"I should have known better with Gawain. He would sooner cut his own throat than hurt you—as would any of his brothers. And if Morgan wanted you dead, she has far more subtle ways to kill than a mass poisoning. Pellinore overheard a plot about a knight from the north you are well acquainted with who was going to poison you. The knight wasn't named, and I didn't think. I lost all common sense."

"A plot?" Britt frowned. "Are there any other knights close to me from the north?"

"No, now that I study it, I expect the threat was never from the north to begin with, but someone hoped to implicate the Orkney princes," Merlin said. "No conspirators would be stupid enough to trumpet the homeward location of their inside man—especially in a forest that is home to the faerie folk. Have you seen anyone you didn't recognize this morning? A new servant, perhaps?"

Britt shook her head. "We ran into Lancelot and his cronies when the servants were helping us carry our food and drink to the gardens. That was all."

The echo of a faint smile flashed across Merlin's lips. "It wasn't Lancelot, lass."

"One can hope," Britt grinned. Her smile faltered when she realized she and Merlin were joking—like they used to.

As if he could read her discomfort, Merlin said, "I meant what I said earlier. I'm sorry for my careless words. I know you, and I know that you are strong of heart and mind. I just…" he trailed off. "It cannot be," he finally said.

"I know," Britt said. She felt awkward and uncomfortable as her heart twisted in her chest, so she stared at the stuffed owl sitting on one of Merlin's bookshelves instead of watching the wizard himself.

"We're making real progress. You've established your code of chivalry and your courts. Questing was an excellent idea to spread word of Camelot near and far. In a year or two, we should think about facing the threat of Rome—they are still trying to dig their heels into Britain. Nothing can change, and I—"

"I know," Britt said, speaking quickly before Merlin could fill in the gap. She stared harder at the owl, as if she expected it to move.

Merlin would never see her as a romantic interest. She was his friend, his pawn, and his conspirator, but never his love.

Britt cleared her throat and stared harder. Nope, the owl still wasn't moving. "I've always known. That's why I never brought it up and never planned to."

"You hid it well," Merlin said. "I never guessed, which is why I was caught off guard and I…I acted like a donkey's colt, as Blaise would say," Merlin grimly said. "I apologize, Britt. My words were false, and you didn't deserve them. I have never thought you to be weak. Forgive me?" Merlin asked.

Britt dropped her gaze from the unmoving, stuffed owl. "In time," she said, offering Merlin a quick, lean smile before she looked past him at the cups. "You'll let me know what your poison-finder friend learns?"

"Of course," Merlin said. His tone said he was disappointed but understanding.

"Thanks," Brit said, moving for the door. "I'll go find out what the guards did to the Orkney princes."

"That would be wise," Merlin said, already looking to the cups.

Britt hesitated in the frame of the door. "Say, Merlin," she said, biting her lip. "Do you think, maybe, you could tell Sir Kay about this *after* I go out for a morning ride?"

Merlin laughed for several minutes.

"I didn't mean to be funny," Britt muttered.

"No, you just know your foster-brother. I doubt I can keep the news from him—Pellinore might have already found him. But if you leave shortly, you'll likely be able to get out of Camelot before he is able to place more severe restrictions on you," Merlin advised.

"Good idea. Thanks," Britt said before making her exit—her heart lighter than it had been since the fight.

∼

BRITT ARRIVED at the feasting hall early so she could arrange her table as she pleased. King Pellinore and Queen Adelind would be sitting with her, as would Morgan le Fay, Merlin, and Guinevere.

"Seat Morgan between Merlin and me, please," Britt said to Sir Ulfius as she nursed a cup of wine.

"I was under the impression you two had reconciled," Sir Ulfius said, pausing behind what was to be King Pellinore's chair.

"We have, but…just put Morgan there, please."

"As you wish, My Lord."

"Thanks, Sir Ulfius," Britt smiled.

"My Lord?"

Britt peered over her table to spy Sir Griflet waiting at the base of the raised platform.

"Griflet, what can I do for you?" Britt asked, gliding down the stairs.

"I was wondering, My Lord, if you would bless Sir Ywain and

I, and give us permission to go on a quest," Sir Griflet bowed. "Now that the threat has passed."

Britt blinked. "Threat?"

"Indeed—the threats against your life have ceased, have they not?" Sir Griflet brightly asked.

"They have, but how did *you* know about them?" Britt asked, narrowing her eyes as she studied her faithful knight.

"Ywain and I…er…that is to say, we, ah, overheard your discussion with Merlin in your room the night you left to follow the Quest of the White Hart," Griflet said.

"You what?" Britt said.

"We made it our personal, local quest to see that you were safe!" Griflet proudly said.

Britt tipped her head back and recalled the past few weeks. Ywain and Griflet had been skulking after her like a pair of terrible gumshoe detectives. They were there when the arrow almost hit her, just as they were there when she and Merlin came back from visiting Merlin's mentor. "Griflet," Britt said, unable to keep the amusement out of her voice. "I have guards to protect me. You didn't have to."

"No, but we wanted to! Indeed, Ywain does not think we should stop guarding you—which is why I approach you alone," Griflet said. "He does not know I am here."

"Do you have a goal in mind—for your quest, I mean," Britt said, sipping her drink.

Griflet nodded. "I have—or I hope—to secure the favor of a most wonderful lady. She is the pinnacle of all that is light and lovely. Her hair is like sprigs of flowers in the summer air. Her eyes shine forth like the white wool of little lambs!"

"What is the pinnacle of all that is light and lovely called?" Britt asked.

"Blancheflor," Griflet sighed in wonder.

"Blancheflor," Britt said, trying to bring the proper lady to her mind. The girl, while not one of Lancelot's ardent fans, often admired the knight. She seemed to be silly but sweet—a good match for Griflet's flair for drama. "You're going to try and steal her away from Lancelot?"

"Sir Lancelot is very noble indeed, and excluding a few, he has no peer among us knights. But I hope that with my devotion—and love—I can bring Blancheflor to love me," Griflet confided.

"I see. So you're going to go do deeds in her name, then?"

"Yes!"

"Does Ywain have a lady he wants to impress, too?"

"No, not yet," Griflet said, preening a little. "I am ahead of him."

"I see," Britt said, a fond half smile twitching on her lips. "Very well. Yes, I give my leave for both of you to go questing. Stick to the Forest of Arroy, though. Do not venture far from it," Britt warned, privately resolving to pay Nymue a visit to ask her to keep an eye on the two young knights. "And you have to convince Ywain to go with you before I will publicly send you off," she added as an afterthought.

"Thank you, My Lord! I shall do many great deeds in my lady's name, and in yours!" Griflet said, giving Britt another bow before he hurried off through the mostly empty feasting hall. A few knights were starting to trickle in and take their seats. Griflet almost ran two over in his enthusiasm to find Ywain.

"Young love," Britt said, shaking her head and smiling before she sipped her drink again.

"My Lord?" Sir Gawain cautiously asked.

"Sir Gawain, I'm glad to see you're not at all worse for the wear. I still apologize for yesterday morning," Britt said, taking a few steps closer to the younger knight.

"It was unexpected," Sir Gawain said, his voice was calm and guileless.

"It's kind of you to say it so nicely. Merlin was an idiot, but that's not the point. I suppose I was being an idiot, too," Britt said, turning to look out at the feasting hall.

"Were any additional discoveries made on the issue?" Sir Gawain asked, joining Britt to look out at the celebrators who were seeping into the hall for King Pellinore's celebration feast.

Britt shook her head and sipped her drink. "No," she said after swallowing. "Merlin's man took a look at the cider. He was able to conclude it was not a deadly poison and would only have made a drinker ill. It mostly would have given us all a case of stomach cramps since it was so diluted."

"It seems odd that a person would go through so much trouble only to give you *stomach cramps*," Sir Gawain said.

"That occurred to Sir Bedivere and Merlin as well. They are certain it was a set up," Britt said, glancing at Sir Gawain's wrinkled forehead before she amended her words. "A ploy. They think the culprit wanted to stir up distrust and never meant to kill me from the start."

Sir Gawain shook his head. "Strange and still dangerous."

"I agree. Whoever it is, they have a mean streak," Britt said.

"Is there no possible way to track the person down?"

"Not really," Britt said, her eyebrow twitching in irritation. She had suggested everything from finger printing to DNA, but none of the techniques she knew of from crime investigation shows were helpful in this age. "I guess the medieval times just had a lot of unsolved crimes," Britt muttered.

"What did you say, My Lord?"

"Nothing of importance. It seems that the troublemaker will go free. For now," Britt said.

"I don't think he will evade Merlin for long," Sir Gawain softly said.

"There is that, I suppose, if he decides to break out his magic," Britt agreed. "We'll see."

Sir Gawain nodded and exhaled. Britt smiled and tried to slap his back in a manly sort of camaraderie before she sipped her drink.

Britt grimaced when a great number of people entered the

hall—Guinevere and Lancelot among them—significantly raising the sound level.

Guinevere arrived with her three ladies in waiting, her eyes bright and a smile already flashing. When she saw Britt, she perked up even more—if that was possible. Behind her, Lancelot seemed to call her, for he smiled charmingly when she turned to face him. He said something to the princess, but Guinevere smiled and shook her head before she hurried towards the front of the room—towards Britt.

"My Lord, is this not exciting? I heard there was to be a *fire breather* tonight," Guinevere said, her eyes sparkling.

She makes me feel old, Britt thought before she said, "Yes, I believe there is. Pellinore is also sure to give us a good story—he better, anyway. He took so long, I'm surprised his wife didn't flay him alive."

"Quests seem to be exciting! I hope more knights go out on quests. It's so *romantic!*" Guinevere said, clasping her hands to her heart.

"I guess," Britt said, sipping her drink. "I've had a knight approach me about it. I expect after King Pellinore is celebrated tonight another knight or two will want to go out as well. That reminds me. Sir Gawain, do you have any idea what deer eat in the winter? The stables have informed me Rudolph doesn't eat hay."

Gawain frowned. "Rudolph, My Lord?"

"The white deer. Hart," Britt said.

"I'm not certain, My Lord. It isn't often a kingdom keeps a hart for a pet," Sir Gawain said. "You could try—"

"Oh my," Guinevere breathed. "Is that *Merlin?*"

Britt and Gawain looked in the direction Guinevere pointed, and Britt almost dropped her goblet.

It was Merlin alright, but unlike Britt had ever seen him. Gone was the stereotypical storm-gray cloak. Instead, he wore clothes of black and gold. The outer layer was a black robe with gold embroidery. The robe snugly fit his waist, back, and shoulders, but had wide, drooping sleeves. A hood lined with gold embroidery fell over his back, making his fine hair appear white rather than blonde. Under the robe, he wore a tunic that matched the brilliant blue of his eyes, black chausses, and—to Britt's shock —a pair of leather boots styled exactly like hers.

Britt took a deep sip of her drink to hide her shock.

"He looks…impressive," Sir Gawain finally said.

"I think he looks like a faerie lord—a good foil to your Elfking look, Arthur," Guinevere said. "Before he looked like a wise hermit. Now he's…"

"He's got a dangerous edge—like you do, My Lord, when you're fighting like a dragon," Sir Gawain said.

"I don't think I ever look quite like that," Britt said, jabbing a finger at the well-clothed wizard, who was slowly approaching them.

"Nay, My Lord. You do whenever you hold Excalibur at a man," Sir Gawain quietly said before Merlin edged into their conversation.

"Arthur, are you ready to begin the feast? Pellinore and Adelind just arrived," Merlin said, acting like nothing had changed.

It took Britt a few moments to reply. "Yeah, sure. There's enough people here. Why not?" she said before she turned to climb up the dais stairs, shaking her head. "Men," she muttered, "I'll never understand them."

10

THOUGHTS OF MEN

A few paces away, Lancelot du Lac watched King Arthur stop at the top of the dais when Merlin yanked on his doublet. The young king pushed his hair out of his face and retreated back down the stairs to offer his arm to Guinevere before climbing the stairs again.

"So, it didn't work. That's a shame," Sir Lionel said looking up and down the table—his eyes hinged on the various dishes and platters. "Seemed like it was working for a bit—something made him sour towards Merlin. But whatever damage was done has been repaired."

"Thankfully," Sir Bors frowned. "It would not be good for Camelot if the King and his Chief Counselor fought."

"You worry too much," Sir Lionel snorted.

"Enough," Lancelot growled.

"You're in a bad mood, are you?" Sir Lionel said. "You probably shouldn't have started by targeting Gawain. 'Specially after Arthur gave him the boon of mercy at Gawain's feast."

"That's why it *had* to be Gawain," Lancelot growled, briefly rearranging his handsome features to smile at a lady before he returned his attention to his cousins. "Their relationship makes me ill. What did Gawain do to afford such esteem? He is a green knight and has done nothing to expand Arthur's kingdom."

"Sounds like jealousy to me," Sir Lionel grinned.

"It's not jealousy. It's irritation at this incompetence. By all rights, *I* should be standing with Arthur. I am the best knight there is in these halls. He should place such trust in *me*," Lancelot said.

Sir Lionel shrugged. "He's seemed quite set against you since you first arrived," he said, brutally honest as usual.

"I heard the Lady of the Lake fancies him. Maybe she has told him tales of us?" Sir Bors suggested.

"Or perhaps old Morgause. Found out from a lovely lady that our King exchanges letters with her still," Sir Lionel said, winking at a lady who flounced past them.

"Whatever it is, I will right his thinking, or King Arthur will learn to regret the day he scorned my friendship," Lancelot said, glaring at the bright king and the mystic-looking wizard.

"Calling it friendship might be a bit much," Sir Lionel said before Sir Bors elbowed him hard.

You will call me your friend, Arthur, Lancelot promised himself. *You will recognize me, or I will ruin you.*

STANDING ON THE INNER WALLS, Merlin watched the bright spot on the outer walls that signaled where Britt was standing with her guards that evening. It was well after the midnight hour, but Britt was still up, battling her insomnia.

Merlin could see the flashes of Excalibur's blade as the girl swung her sword around her in a difficult, complex practice pattern.

Merlin curled his hands into firsts, squeezing them so tightly they shook. "It's ruined," he whispered.

Merlin thought apologizing to Britt would fix the upheaval of the courts. He thought renewing their friendship would fix the discomfort he encountered when they fought, and he was right. It did.

Britt was smiling at him again. Granted, her eyes were more guarded, but she no longer fled from him, and she was talking again.

But.

BUT.

Things had changed. It wasn't the fight, or even the silence that stretched between them during their quarrel. It was stupid Pellinore and his stupid, overheard plot.

Merlin knew that the way he reacted, the *terror* he felt—the loss of sense he had to shout her real name!—all of those were symptoms of a much bigger problem. The root of which was this: when Pellinore relayed the plot, Merlin feared not for Camelot, not for his scheme to have one king rule Britain, but for *Britt.*

The life of the time-traveling woman meant more to him than the whole of Camelot.

The thought terrified him because that wasn't how it was supposed to be! Merlin had to be dedicated, no, *obsessed* with King Arthur's reign. It was the only way his plans and ideals could be realized. He couldn't spare the room in his heart for a single girl, much less allow himself to put the *whole plan* at risk for her!

"She means more to me than I thought and far more than I ever wanted her to," Merlin grimly said as he pulled up his hood. "If she hadn't interrupted me...I don't know what I would have said."

So Merlin watched Britt as she practiced with her magical sword late into the night, resolving to stamp out all affection for the laughing girl-king.

But in the back of his mind, Merlin knew trouble was brewing. Britt was too well liked, and if *he* was struggling against such powerful feelings, what would the rest of her knights do if they discovered she was a woman?

THE END

A FATHER'S DAY FEAST

On a wet morning early in the summer season, Britt mulishly moved the heavens (Read: Merlin) and Earth (Read: Kay) as well as a number of pests (Lancelot being first and foremost) to schedule off a few hours to spend time with Sir Ector of Bonmaison—her foster-father.

She was highly pleased that her venture had come together successfully, but now that the appointed hour had arrived, Britt almost wished she hadn't followed through with her plan.

"Bless me, lass, you look splendid in that new armor," Sir Ector said, brushing raindrops from his fierce beard.

"Merlin ordered it." Britt peered down at her golden armor. "I think I own more suits of armor than any other man alive."

"It's only right, with you being the King 'n all," Sir Ector said, propping an arm up on a stall door. "I'm sorry to say, but it looks like we'll have to cancel our ride. I don't mind getting wet, but it's raining so hard the courtyard will soon be a lake."

"Yes," Britt said, shifting uncomfortably.

"Would you rather go inside and get a bite to eat? Merlin said we'll dine late tonight as you've called for a feast."

"Could we wait a bit?" Britt asked, hurrying to the stall that housed Roen—one of her two beloved horses.

"Certainly," Sir Ector boomed, his beard parting to reveal a toothy smile. "Something upsetting you?" he asked, joining her at Roen's stall. "You seem unsettled."

"No, I'm not mad. It's just—" Britt forcibly silenced herself to keep from saying anything stupid. *Get it together! I'm out of practice, but this isn't a big deal. Seriously.* She scolded, desperately trying to con herself into minimizing the effort she had gone through for today.

"Arthur?" Sir Ector asked, tilting his head like a puzzled dog. "Britt?" he dared to venture when she didn't respond.

"Happy Father's Day," Britt blurted out. She snatched up an elaborate sword belt that hung from a hook on Roen's stall door, presenting it to Sir Ector.

Sir Ector looked from the belt to Britt. "I beg yer pardon?"

"In America—in the time where I come from—we have a... custom," she said, forcing the words from her lips. "There's a special day every year when fathers—or men who inspired you— are celebrated. Kids thank their fathers for everything they've done, and recognize their hard work. I don't know exactly what the date was—I usually took pains to ignore it—but I'm sure it was sometime in early summer, and you've done a lot for me, and I wanted to thank you," Britt said, spitting out the last few sentences in a mad rush.

Since the day Britt's dad had left her family, Britt had been more than a little caustic about fathers. When she first met Sir Ector she brushed him off, and it had taken months for him to win her over.

And now, Britt couldn't imagine a future without the cheerful, sincere man backing her and gently leading her forward. Forget foster-father, Sir Ector had become the dad she always secretly hoped to have.

Unable to look the cheerful man in the face, Britt valiantly continued. "I know I was a brat when I first arrived, and you and Kay were still torn up about Arthur—the real one—but you've been incredibly kind to me, and I wouldn't be the king I am today if it weren't for you. You stood by me in the fight against King Lot and his cronies, and you've supported me when I've pushed back against Merlin. I'm thankful you're a part of my life. It's a little presumptuous of me, but thank you for being a father-figure." She dug her fingers into the leather of the sword belt, which she still held. "So...I got you this sword belt," she lamely finished.

Well, that couldn't have been more embarrassing, she thought, disgusted with herself. She rallied her courage enough to lift her head, and was shocked to see that Sir Ector had tears in his eyes. His face was blotchy and red, and he sniffed—his cheeks puffed in a joyful smile. "I would be proud, Britt, to call you my daughter," he said before drawing her into a bone-crushing hug.

Britt clung to her foster-father, unable to speak in the warmth of their hug. Words clogged her throat—the thanks she wanted to say, the things she admired about Sir Ector, and how much she cared about him—but she couldn't get them unstuck. Thankfully, Sir Ector seemed to sense what she was thinking, and he patted her on the head. "Me too, lass," he said, squeezing her one last time before letting her go. "Now, what's this business with the sword belt?"

"Oh, well usually kids give their dads—their fathers—gifts on Father's Day, and there's almost always a special meal involved. I wanted to get you something practical, so...the sword belt. Also, tonight's feast is in your honor."

"All that trouble, for me?"

Britt mutely nodded.

Sir Ector laughed and slapped his jiggling belly. "I'm the proudest father in Britain, with the best daughter and son any man could ask for. Thank you, lass. You've made an old man happy," he said, taking the belt and lifting it up so he could inspect it in the light with an admiring eye. "Ohhh, it's a pretty piece of work."

"I think I'm ready for some food now. We'll have to be quick about it, though. The kitchens are in an uproar, preparing for tonight."

Sir Ector shook his head as he made his way down the stable aisle. "You did too much."

"Not hardly. I didn't do enough!" Britt said, glee bubbling in the pit of her stomach.

She had lost many things when she was pulled into ancient Britain, but at least she had gained a father.

THE END

ENLIGHTEN:

KING ARTHUR AND HER KNIGHTS BOOK 5

1

THE LANCELOT HATECLUB

"This marks the opening of the tenth meeting of the *Lancelot Hateclub*. Attendance will now be taken. Morgan le Fay?"

"Present," the beautiful sorceress said, smoothing the skirts of her blue dress that set off her eyes perfectly.

"Nymue?"

"I still don't understand why you make us go through this. What is *attendance* anyway?" Nymue asked.

"Are you here or not?" Britt asked, ignoring the faerie lady's question.

"Clearly, I am."

"And I—the founding member—am present as well," Britt said, sliding the wooden stool she was seated on closer to the table. The three ladies were seated outside, in a garden that was barely starting to bloom now that the chill of winter was, for the most part, gone.

"What is the purpose of today's meeting, Founding Member?" Morgan asked. She more willingly played along with the required vocabulary Britt used to conduct *Lancelot Hateclub* meetings.

Britt tapped her fingers on the table surface. "Spring has come after a long, long winter," Britt said.

"It wasn't that long. This year's winter was actually quite mild," Nymue said.

"Yes, but you weren't cooped up in a castle with Lancelot dogging your every step," Britt said, her upper lip curling in dislike.

"Oh," Nymue blinked.

"It felt like a very long winter indeed," Morgan said.

"But now spring is here. Mostly," Britt said, conveniently forgetting the cooler temperatures that had plagued medieval England for the past week. "Which means my knights have begun to leave and go out on quests."

"So?" Nymue asked. "You designed that system. You said questing would 'expel their youthful energy, make the country think better of your courts through their good deeds, and get them out of your hair.'"

"I did," Britt acknowledged. "And it's a very good system. It's been working gloriously. There's just one problem."

"And that is?" Morgan asked.

Britt abruptly launched off her stool and leaned across the table to hiss, "*Lancelot isn't going out on quests!*"

"That is a problem," Morgan agreed.

Nymue frowned. "Can't you make him? You *are* King of Camelot."

"I could personally assign him to a quest. I *want* to, but we haven't really had anything quest-worthy pop up, and whenever I mention it, Merlin makes a squished face. He thinks it would be bad of me to boss around a prince."

Morgan chopped her hand through the air, disregarding Merlin's answer. "That is preposterous. Merlin orders the Orkney princes around as if they were stable boys."

"Yes, that's the catch, though," Britt agreed, sinking back onto her stool. "King Lot and King Urien are beholden to me since I have their sons in my courts. King Ban—Lancelot's father—and King Bors—Sir Lionel and Sir Bors' father—are my allies whom I owe a lot."

"I think Merlin allows you to be king only when it's convenient," Nymue said.

"Yeah. So, back to our topic: How do I get rid of that self-indulgent weasel?" Britt asked.

"Poison?" Morgan suggested.

"If you send him towards my lake, I will curse you with a perpetual itch," Nymue warned.

Although she was less-than thrilled with their answers, their clear dislike of Sir Lancelot du Lac warmed Britt's heart.

She hadn't discovered Morgan's great hatred of Lancelot until Camelot held a Christmas feast, and Lancelot—when sufficiently drunk—explained that he had previously made Morgan's acquaintance when courting a sorceress friend of hers. ("He broke her heart like a clay vessel," Morgan said. "I wish I could shatter his face in the same manner.")

It was no great secret that both Britt and Nymue couldn't stand the flowery knight, and with Nymue and Morgan living in the same area—both being avid Lancelot haters and both knowing that Britt (or King Arthur, as she was known in Camelot) was a girl—Britt couldn't deny herself the creation of the *Lancelot Hateclub*.

"Does anyone know of a damsel in need of saving?" Britt asked.

"You would inflict him on another female? You are treacherous," Nymue said.

"Not necessarily," Britt said. "Many of the ladies in Camelot enjoy his company."

"*Why?*" Morgan said.

"It is one of the mysterious of life. Many of the faerie ladies at my lake are also taken with the Debaucher and the Slobs," Nymue said, referring to Lancelot and the brothers Sir Lionel and Sir Bors.

"The bottom line is if I can locate a lady in distress, Lancelot will ride off to save her. The *only* quest he participated in last year was to save a damsel," Britt said.

"But if a lady is in distress, wouldn't it be Gawain who would have to ride out? He is the ladies' knight," Nymue said.

"My nephew is already out questing," Morgan said.

"Oh," Nymue said. "Well, if you can't find a damsel to save, why not encourage him to ride forth in the name of a lady? Isn't that another one of your finicky table rules?"

"It's the Round Table, and you have the right idea, but Lancelot is as loyal as a tom cat," Britt said.

"What?" Nymue frowned.

"I believe what King Arthur is trying to say is that Lancelot is not monogamous in his amorous attentions. He currently has no lady and instead simpers and preens with a flock of females at his beck," Morgan said.

"Exactly," Britt said.

"Truly? But I thought he was taking pains to show favor to Guinevere," Nymue said. "You stormed about that three or four meetings ago."

"He was. He *is*," Britt said. "But—and I can't believe I'm saying this—he doesn't appear to like her more than any of the other ladies he so arduously admires."

"You must be fair and also note that while Guinevere takes great pleasure in his admiration, she does not seem to devote herself solely to him. In the eyes of the court, she appears to be taken with you," Morgan said.

Britt shifted uncomfortably. As she came from the twenty-first century—she had been pulled back through time after touching an enchanted, rusty sword; then Merlin informed her she was to be King Arthur in place of the real Arthur, who had run off with a shepherdess—she *knew* all about them. Even though she knew she would obviously never marry Guinevere—which meant Guinevere would never be in a position of great power in Camelot—she could not forget that in modern times, everyone agreed that the legendary love affair between Lancelot and Guinevere brought the downfall of Camelot.

"I still want him gone," Britt finally said.

"Agreed," Morgan said. As long as she stayed at Camelot, she too was forced to listen to Lancelot boast about his supposed great deeds, so Britt had a feeling the sorceress had a vested interest in her proposal.

"Whom do you want gone?" asked a fourth female voice.

Britt winced and twisted around in time to see Guinevere step out of an inlet and into the small garden—the Queen's Garden—where Britt and her fellow Lancelot-haters were meeting.

"Lady Guinevere, good morning," Britt said.

Morgan smiled benevolently at the younger girl, but Nymue huffed in irritation and looked away.

"Good morning, My Lord," Guinevere said, elegantly curt-seying to Britt, although she looked at Nymue and Morgan with curiosity.

"What has you up and about at this early hour?" Britt asked.

Guinevere smiled and looked very pretty as she fussed with her reddish-blonde hair. "I am meeting with several ladies. We mean to listen to Sir Lanval—he will be performing music shortly. He said he recently wrote a ballad and dedicated it to my beauty."

"Isn't that nice," Britt said. When she first met the girl the previous summer, she struggled to be kind to Guinevere. Since discovering the girl was ruled by her cowardly, cheap father—King Leodegrance—Britt felt a little sympathy and could now tolerate the girl—even though she still considered her silly and shallow.

"If that is the case, though, you should probably leave. You wouldn't want to miss the ballad," Britt said. (Just because she could tolerate Guinevere's presence in Camelot didn't mean she was going to inflict herself with the girl's company too often.)

"Oh, but if you are having a party…" Guinevere said, looking past Britt to the little table she and her fellow Lancelot-haters were gathered around.

"We aren't," Britt emphatically said.

Morgan smiled. "It is only a meeting of *faerie* blood. We tend to wax on about our age and magic. You would be terribly bored, Lady Guinevere."

"Who are you calling old?" Nymue said, eyeing the sorceress.

"Oh," Guinevere said before her eyes lit in understanding. "*Ohhh,*" she repeated, giving Britt a significant look.

"Hah-hah," Britt said, her laughter wooden as she uneasily surveyed the garden.

Very few knew Britt—the ruler of Camelot and king of ancient Britain—was actually a girl. In fact, Nymue, Morgan and her two sisters, and Guinevere were the only ones outside of Merlin's men who knew her true gender. And no one besides Merlin's closest minions knew that Britt was actually from the twenty-first century.

"So, yes, you would be rather bored," Britt said, standing up and approaching Guinevere.

"But if you should like to talk…" Guinevere said.

"It's fine. You should go and enjoy yourself, Lady Guinevere," Britt said, placing an arm around Guinevere's shoulders to steer her away from the table.

"But—"

"I insist," Britt said, leading the younger girl to the edge of the garden.

"Very well," Guinevere said, her lower lip briefly puckering out in a pout.

"Have fun, and say hello to Lady Clarine and Lady

Blancheflor for me, please," Britt said, making sure to stand between Guinevere and the rest of the *Lancelot Hateclub*.

Guinevere's eyes widened. "How did you know I would be seeing them?"

Britt gave Guinevere a patient smile. "As the three of you are fast friends, I could not imagine you would attend a musical performance without them. Enjoy," Britt said.

"Oh, yes! I will! Take care, My Lord," Guinevere said before setting off, her hair gleaming in the morning light.

"Neatly done," Nymue said, clapping for a few moments. "I didn't know it was possible to get rid of a person so kindly."

"That one is rather like a kitten," Morgan observed. "Selfish and useless, but sweet. Take care with her. I suspect her loyalty to you is deeper than you would think."

"Why would that mean I should be careful with her?" Britt asked, seating herself at the table again.

"It means you could hurt her feelings and cause more pain than if she cared for you less," Morgan said.

Apprehension stirred in Britt, so she chose to distract herself by peering past a bush to locate her giant, apricot-colored mastiff, Cavall, who snoozed in the morning light. "Let's get back to topic, shall we?"

"I think you should give him a sleeping draught. While he snores away, have him carried outside of Camelot," Nymue said. "When he wakes up, bar the gates and tell him there is a threat, and Camelot will be closed for the foreseeable future. He'll get bored without ladies to preen to and move on. For a while, at least."

"And what do we tell him when he demands to know how he was mysteriously transported outside of the gates?" Britt asked.

"Say it must have been faeries. You don't have to think hard to come up with an explanation. Lancelot is not known for his intelligence," Nymue said, leaning against the table.

"I don't understand why you do not speak to Merlin about it," Morgan said.

"We've already established that Merlin is no help," Britt said.

"But have you explained to him *why* you wish for Lancelot to be gone so badly?" Morgan asked.

"Doesn't Merlin have eyes of his own? Can't he see how excessively *annoying* the Debaucher is?" Nymue demanded.

"He does, but Lancelot being a pest would not motivate Merlin to see the young knight out. But if he knew what a toad he is being…" Morgan trailed off and shrugged her shoulders.

"Wait, he is being something besides an irritant?" Nymue asked.

"It's nothing," Britt said.

"No," Nymue said, raising a long, slender finger and stabbing it in Britt's direction. "I refuse to be shrugged off as you just did to Guinevere. What is Morgan talking about?"

"It's nothing definite," Britt started. "But lately, Lancelot has been…persistent."

"What does that mean?" Nymue asked.

"He has been haunting her like a ghost," Morgan dryly said.

"It's difficult to point out. He's just…*there.* A lot," Britt said.

When she was first forced to allow the handsome knight into her courts, Lancelot seemed content to focus his attention on the ladies and knights who worshipped him. Lately, though, the knight seemed to follow Britt and her closer knights. He had formed a friendship with Sir Ywain and Sir Griflet—who were universally acknowledged to be some of her favorite knights. He had also tried—but horrifically failed—to befriend Sir Kay. Recently, the foreign prince had given up on Kay, though, and seemed to be gunning for Gawain before the younger knight left on a quest, taking his brother—Agravain—as his squire.

Britt ran a hand through her blonde hair. "It's like he's a weed and is slowly closing in."

"I agree with Morgan. If you are worried he is drawing too close to you, speak to Merlin. He will be motivated into action—if for no other reason than to protect his investment," Nymue said.

"Gee, thanks," Britt dryly said.

"You're welcome," Nymue said, looking down her nose.

"It would be the wise thing to do," Morgan said.

Britt heaved a great sigh. "Yeah, you guys are probably right. Okay, any other matters of business to discuss?"

"Yes!" Nymue said with great relish. "I wish to complain about Lancelot's dreaded cousin—Sir Lionel. Recently, one of his faerie loves stumbled into my lake and will not cease prattling about him. It is vexing!"

~

"THANK you for recounting your adventures, Sir Safir," Britt said as she shifted in her chair that was pushed up to the Round Table. "It is to your credit that you so swiftly slew the giant and finished your quest."

"Thank you, My Lord. I hope Camelot is honored by my acts," the knight said before he sat down.

"Yes, of course. Anything else?" Britt asked, leaning against her arm rest so she could twist and look up at Merlin—who hovered behind her shoulder.

"No. I believe we are finished here—although there will be feasting tonight in honor of Sir Safir," Merlin said.

"Excellent. I look forward to it," Britt said before she slipped from her chair, ending the meeting.

"My Lord, there will be a change in your guard rotation," Sir Kay—Britt's supposed foster brother—said, stepping closer to murmur the words.

Britt blinked. "Is there a problem?" she asked. She knew her guards quite well. They all were excellent men whom Kay trusted with her life—which was the highest honor the taciturn young man could give.

"No. Some of the men are swapping their shifts. That is all."

"Okay. Thanks for the head's up," Britt said.

Sir Kay accepted the strange word choice—for his time, anyway—and gathered up his papers.

Britt stretched her arms above her head and found Merlin not far from her. "Merlin, could I talk to you for a moment?" Britt asked, ambling up to the wizard and glancing at his clothes.

In the summer of the previous year, Merlin had ditched his usual gray, Gandalf-rip-off robe. He now mostly wore a fitted black cloak over a colored tunic—today it was a deep forest green. If he wanted to look particularly mystical and magical, he pulled up the hood, which gave his striking face an almost oracle-like air. Originally, Britt rejoiced in the lack of clichéd clothes, but after a few days, she realized the costume change made Merlin several degrees more handsome—an observation Britt was already battling.

"Is something wrong?" Merlin asked. He tilted his head as his eyes swept up and down her body, as if looking for obvious wounds.

"No—well, not anything serious. But there's something I want to discuss," Britt said.

Merlin frowned. "For the last time, you cannot skip out on tomorrow's court session. I don't care if Kay found a white bear that sings, dances, and matches that blasted hart of yours. You're the King of Camelot, and your butt will be on that throne if I have to tie you there myself."

"It's not that, and my deer's name is Rudolph," Britt said, referring to the white buck Sir Gawain had brought back to Camelot as a gift for Britt after completing his first quest.

Merlin's frown deepened to a scowl. "Must you name every animal you come across? It's not very kingly."

"Don't care. So, can we go to your study? I—"

"My Lord, My Lord! Are there any towns crying out for a savior or damsels in need of aid?" Sir Griflet, a young, exuberant knight asked, nearly crashing into Britt's chair as he skidded up to her.

"I'm sorry, what?" Britt said.

"Surely someone or someplace has signaled to you a need for a champion," Sir Griflet said.

Sir Ywain—Griflet's friend and supposedly Britt's nephew— rolled his eyes behind his friend's back. "He wants to go out on a quest, My Lord."

Britt's lips eased into a slight smile. "You're that eager to leave my courts, Griflet?"

"Not at all, My Lord. I am merely desirous of spreading news of your greatness!" Griflet said.

"Lady Blancheflor still doesn't know he exists," Sir Ywain said, naming the pretty girl Griflet had been calf-eyed over for nearly a year. "He wants to do great deeds to build up his reputation so she'll acknowledge him."

"Vagrant!" Griflet huffed.

"So, she still is a dedicated admirer of Lancelot, is she? That's tough," Britt said.

"The Lady Blancheflor knows my name," Sir Griflet insisted.

"Only because you've written her so much poetry she couldn't possibly make such a mistake," Sir Ywain said, earning a scowl from his friend.

"You recreant—"

"It is unfortunate, Griflet, but I have not received any requests for help or aid," Britt said, interrupting the friends before they could start insulting each other's honor. "You could always follow Sir Gawain's example and leave with the intent of *finding* wrongs and righting them."

Griflet frowned and looked at the ground.

"Nay, My Lord. He can't do that. Sir Lancelot du Lac has said that any knight that aimlessly wanders without a quest in his mind is foolish and without purpose," Sir Ywain supplied for his friend.

Britt gave the pair a flat look. "Sir Lancelot is an idiot who—before he came to my courts—wandered aimlessly without a quest in his mind."

"*Arthur*," Merlin hissed.

Britt half-expected Merlin to jab his elbow in her side, but he didn't. He hadn't elbowed her since awkwardness entered their relationship the previous summer when Britt admitted her feelings for the wizard, and the wizard rebuffed her. They had fought and ignored each other for a few days after, until they had The Talk—as Britt had come to call it—which cleared the air between them. Still, ever since The Talk, she felt the strain on their friendship. There was an extra barrier between her and Merlin that hadn't previously existed.

She ignored Merlin's hissed warning and smiled at her young knights. "If you are so eager to impress your lady, Griflet, I suggest you think it over. Why, I would go off on a quest myself if I didn't think Kay would make me drag twenty guards with me, and Merlin would follow behind with half of my court."

"*Arthur!*" Merlin repeated, this time his voice was a snarl.

"Think on it." Britt patted Griflet's shoulder in a clear dismissal before she turned to face Merlin with a bright smile. "Yes, Merlin?"

Merlin eyed her. "You need to work on holding your tongue in matters pertaining to Lancelot."

"Why bother?"

"Because he is a knight and a foreign prince who happens to be a member of your Round Table!" Merlin said.

"Whatever," Britt grumbled. "So, as I was saying, could we talk?"

"Certainly. Shall we—"

"My Lord?"

Britt turned to find herself face to face with Sir Bedivere—her marshal and one of the few knights in Merlin's close circle who had no knowledge of her gender or true identity. Even so, Britt considered him one of her most staunch supporters—he was the first knight besides Kay to truly believe in her.

"Sir Bedivere, how can I help you?" Britt asked.

"I am aware you already received the new knights who arrived in Camelot this morning, but I was hoping you would take a few additional minutes to speak to them," Sir Bedivere said, indicating to a group of young knights waiting several paces away.

"You don't usually have me directly address new recruits after my initial welcome," Britt carefully said.

"Indeed, because usually it is a waste of your time. But I agree with Sir Bedivere. You should speak with these knights," Merlin said.

Britt narrowed her eyes. "Who are they related to?"

Through unfortunate experience, Britt had learned just about every knight that came to her court had a cousin or sibling already in her service—which meant Britt had to treat them like glass, lest their cousin/sibling/powerful relative would be offended.

"Related to, My Lord?" Sir Bedivere asked, his forehead wrinkling.

Merlin impatiently waved a hand through the air, attempting to swat Britt's suspicions away. "They are renown knights who have already done a great deal of good."

"*Who* are they related to?" Britt demanded.

"Sir Percival, the oldest son of King Pellinore, is in their ranks," Sir Bedivere said.

Britt sighed. "I would complain about nepotism, but I actually *like* Pellinore. Fine, but can it wait? I need to speak to Merlin for a few minutes."

"Of course, My Lord," Sir Bedivere said in a reluctant way which made it clear that no, it couldn't really wait.

The clatter of children running across the stone floor caught Britt's attention, and she looked up to see Gareth and Gaheris—the youngest of the four Orkney princes—screech to a halt a stone's throw away from her. They looked like they wanted to throw themselves at her but were keeping themselves in check, having finally—after much tutoring from Gawain—grasped the fact that Britt was an important figure and was not only their beloved "uncle."

Since Gawain and Agravain's absence, the pair had become more affectionate with Britt. They were still little—perhaps ten or eleven-years-old—and they had yet to lose their adorable, baby possum looks with their big eyes and sweet expressions.

Britt groaned in the back of her throat.

Merlin moved, as if to pat Britt on her shoulder before he thought better of it and smiled at her. "I can talk to you later today, Arthur. Good luck."

"Right, thanks," Britt said. She offered Gareth and Gaheris a smile, motioning for them to draw closer. "Hello, nephews. How did your training go this morning?" Britt asked.

"My archery teacher says I have a natural eye," Gareth said.

"I rode a charger and hit the dummy in jousting practice," Gaheris said, almost jumping in place as Britt placed an affectionate hand on top of his head.

"Well done! I'm about to speak with a few new knights. Would you two like to accompany me?" Britt asked.

"Yes, please, My Lord," the boys chorused.

"Alright. Lead on, Sir Bedivere," Britt said, offering her marshal a smile.

MERLIN WATCHED the knight lead Britt and the boys away. When she greeted the knights, she flashed them her stunning smile—not the one she kept tucked on her face as King Arthur, but the smile she wore when she was genuinely pleased. The knight who caused the smile— Pellinore's son—gawked and lost his composure for a moment when faced with her radiant looks.

The wizard shook his head as he watched Britt lead the Orkney princes and the new arrivals from the room. They trailed around her with open expressions. Merlin knew that by the end of the walk, all of the knights would be completely, utterly loyal to her.

Britt won over men to her cause with pretty words and speeches like no ruler Merlin had ever heard of. In his heart of hearts, Merlin wondered if it was because she was a girl, but he also suspected that Britt knew how to appeal to the young knights' natures. They weren't that difficult to figure out—all they longed for was for someone to see something of worth in them.

I'm not one of her knights she can lead like a lamb, Merlin reminded himself. Over the previous summer, Merlin made the unfortunate discovery that he was fond of Britt. Far more fond than he had any right to be, and far more fond of her than he ever *wished* to be. "I like her no more than I like Sir Ector, or Sir Kay— well, more than Sir Kay," Merlin muttered.

He shook his head, smoothed his open, black robe, and made his exit from the hall. Whatever Britt wanted to discuss would wait, and dwelling on her would only borrow trouble.

2

BOONS AND FOOLS

Britt fiddled with a buckle that stabbed her in the armpit. She was—for once—dressed in a full set of armor instead of wearing her typical few pieces—the cuirass to cover her chest, a plackart to reinforce it, faulds to cover her thighs, and a gorget to shield her throat.

She would have preferred to wear the lighter armor set, but today had been declared a day of contests in the practice arena, and Sir Bodwain had all but blackmailed her into trying her hand at a few jousting matches.

So far, she had good luck. She'd ridden against three knights —all of them as green as grass—and tossed all three off their horses. After the three wins, Britt made herself scarce from the jousting field lest Sir Kay or Sir Bodwain decided to go up against her. (Both were nightmares to joust.)

"Got it. Thank you, Gareth. I'll take Roen back," Britt said, finally pushing the buckle into a comfortable position before she took the reins of her destrier. The black gelding swished his tail and nuzzled her when she affectionately patted his neck. "Are you two going to try your hand at archery?" Britt asked.

Gaheris shook his head. "We're not knights."

"So? Lem—Sir Tor's squire, that is—entered the archery competition," Britt said.

"We're not even squires, though," Gareth said.

"It doesn't matter. This isn't an official tournament. Go try—it will be fun," Britt said.

The Orkney princes exchanged looks before they nodded.

"As you wish, My Lord," Gaheris said.

"We'll make you proud, My Lord," Gareth added, remembering to bow at the last second before he ran after his brother.

The brothers disappeared in the swirl of knights and ladies attending to the various games being held. Britt laughed in affection before she noticed Sir Bodwain purposefully scanning the crowd. Britt lost her laugh and hurried to put a tent between the knight and Roen—who stuck out like a sore thumb as he wore tack and equipment emblazoned with Britt's personal symbol—a red dragon.

Britt peered around the tent, hoping to get a glimpse of the older knight to confirm he had moved on.

"Arthur, there you are. I was about to go look for you at the sword matches," Merlin said directly behind her, making Britt jump.

"Merlin," she said, holding a hand to her heart. "You haven't seen Kay, have you?" she asked, looking suspiciously past him for her foster-brother.

"I left him at the jousting ring, looking for you," Merlin wryly said. "I thought you would be hiding."

"It doesn't seem fair that he coddles me like a baby when it comes to my guards, but in jousting practice, he acts as if he *wants* to bash my head in," Britt complained.

"I'm sure he has his reasons. He probably believes he's making you tougher or some such nonsense. Raised by wolves, he was. What was it you wanted to talk to me about...two days ago, I think it was?"

"Right. I was wondering if we could fabricate some sort of quest for Lancelot," Britt said.

"Arthur," Merlin groaned, heaving his head back to look at the sky.

"It's not what you think," Britt was quick to say.

"I'm sure it's exactly what I think: you're still paranoid about Lancelot causing the downfall of Camelot. I thought my mentor's talk with you banished your obsession with your modern-day legend," Merlin said.

"It's not about Lancelot and Guinevere—at least not completely," Britt said.

"Then what is it?"

"I feel like he's...I don't want to say stalking me, but..." Britt trailed off as Merlin looked at her with disbelief written across his face. "I feel like I'm a deer that he's hunting," Britt said, finally finding a sufficient metaphor that Merlin would understand. "He's always near me—well, not always but most of the time. Whenever I turn around, he's there, asking for my opinion or boasting about one of his past quests. I would never be so deceived as to say he likes me; it's more like he's studying me so he can learn how to catch me."

When Britt looked at Merlin again, the wizard had changed his expression to one that was more thoughtful.

"It makes me really uncomfortable and uneasy. I mean, if he looks close enough he might...notice something," Britt said.

Merlin nodded and thoughtfully narrowed his eyes. "I see your point. I have not noticed his presence near you, but I will watch for it. *If* I see that he does roam around you, we will consider what sort of quest he could be sent on, but do not be deceived, Arthur. I will not dispatch King Ban's son without good reason if he is not inclined to leave Camelot on his own."

"Okay. Thanks, Merlin."

"Of course, lass," Merlin said, using the nickname he previously used frequently, but now hesitated to utter. Merlin opened his mouth to say something more, but his eyes focused on something behind Britt. "Sir Lancelot," he greeted, courteously bowing his head to the young knight.

"Good afternoon, Merlin, My Lord," the coal-haired knight said with a handsome smile. "I am here to see if My Lord would grant my request of seeking a jousting match against him."

"What—you don't want to try your luck with the sword, again?" Britt wryly asked.

In spite of her nettling words, Lancelot laughed. "No, My Lord. I have humbled myself enough to accept that you are a far better swordsman than I. I have hopes that my skill in jousting might redeem me, though."

Britt glanced at Merlin to look for his reaction, but the wizard wore nothing but a polite smile. "It seems unnecessary to me," Britt finally said. "I am fair at jousting but certainly not skilled. If redemption is what you seek, I suggest you try to face Sir Kay or Sir Bodwain. They are our champion jousters."

Lancelot laughed. "I don't think I could ever beat them, My Lord. Come, let's fight," Lancelot said, placing a hand on Britt's shoulder.

Britt shrugged Lancelot's hand off but reluctantly followed Lancelot to the jousting area—towing Roen behind her. Jousting against Lancelot was on the top of her list of things not to do, but if Merlin wanted proof of Lancelot's strange actions, Britt would provide it.

In a much shorter time than she wished, Britt found herself mounted and on one end of the jousting field.

Britt rested her lance on her saddle and shifted, aware that Roen was tense with excitement and power.

When a page stepped into place and lifted a flag, Britt reluctantly raised her lance, spurring Roen forward when the page dropped the flag.

Britt charged towards Lancelot—who was mounted on a beautiful horse with a gold body and white mane and tail. She tensed up as she narrowed in on Lancelot's shield, carefully aiming. When her lance hit his shield, Britt threw her weight into it. She gasped when Lancelot's lance hit her. It was a strong blow, but Britt's was clearly stronger; she threw the handsome knight against the back of his saddle but didn't manage to toss him from his horse.

"Good boy, Roen," Britt panted as her horse adjusted his stride and turned around to head back to their end of the jousting lane.

Britt heard the page shouting that there was to be another run as more knights and ladies gathered to watch. Britt's shield arm stung, but the pain was nothing compared to the numbing blows Sir Kay rained on her whenever they practiced.

"Maybe I can unseat him," Britt murmured. "That was not a good blow. He really is an idiot," Britt said, rolling her shoulder. When the page signaled to start, she forced her lance up and heeled Roen forward like a shot.

Again, Britt concentrated on Lancelot's shield. She felt Roen adjust his movements beneath her, his gait matching her balance.

Britt's lance hit Lancelot's shield, and she pushed into her lance and down in the stirrups. *I have him!*

And then Lancelot's blow hit her.

His lance hit her with such power, he knocked her shield aside, the blow making her arm scream with hot pain.

He was holding back, Britt realized in the moment she had before the force knocked her like a ragdoll. She slid off Roen—though the black gelding crow-hopped and tried to keep her on.

There was ringing in her ears as the crowd applauded for Lancelot's win, and several knights ran up to her.

"Arthur," Sir Kay said, plucking Britt's helm from her head.

"I'm fine, just a little stunned," Britt said, wincing as she tried to move her shield arm and found that she couldn't.

"Did you know Lancelot could hit like that?" Sir Bodwain asked Sir Kay.

"No," Sir Kay grimly said.

"I didn't know it either, or I wouldn't have let the match take place," Sir Bodwain said, his gaze fastened on Lancelot, who was circling his horse in their direction.

"Does anything feel broken?" Kay asked Britt.

"I don't think so. I feel like I was trampled by a bull, though. Help me up," Britt ordered, holding out her good arm.

Sir Kay grunted as he helped Britt stand, taking most of her weight. "One thing is for sure," Britt said, her teeth clenched with pain as she forced herself to smile for the audience's sake. "I'm not doing that again." She raised her arm in the air—making a few cheers break out of the crowd. The celebrators were mostly females—Britt could see—although some ladies shook their heads and watched with worry instead of applauding the hand-some knight.

"Well fought, My Lord. You almost had me at the first round. You are truly gifted. If I was not so experienced, you might have unhorsed me," Lancelot said, making his words loud enough for the crowd to hear him.

Reassured that their king had fought well, knights joined the ladies in clapping and cheering.

"I doubt that," Britt said, moving to stand on her own. "But now I have fulfilled your request, and you have found your redemption. It was a good match, Sir Lancelot," Britt said, turning to go.

"I have another request—if you will hear me out, My Lord," Sir Lancelot said.

Britt groaned in my throat, but Sir Bodwain shook his head. "Better hear him out, My Lord," he whispered.

"What," Britt finally said to the handsome knight, barely able to keep her tone even.

"As I have won a match against you, I ask for a boon."

Britt forced herself to laugh and appear lighthearted. "You seem to be getting ahead of yourself, my knight. This was nothing but a practice match—I only hand out boons for tournaments and special times of celebration."

"Yes, but we have not yet held a tournament since you were crowned," Lancelot said as his palomino mount stomped a hoof. "I have not had many chances to win a boon—and I do not intend to ask for much."

Britt held back a sigh. "What is your request?"

Lancelot smiled, making ladies in the crowd sigh. "I ask that you would grant me a morning of your time and go hunting with me."

Britt uneasily shifted at the odd request.

"It is not too much to ask for, is it?" Lancelot said. "You often ride out with your favorites—Sir Gawain, King Pellinore, Sir Kay, and a few others," he said, neatly trapping her.

"How noble—he wishes to ride with his King," a lady simpered.

"He is seeking a deep and honorable friendship," a knight—one of the useless men King Leodegrance had sent with the Round Table—said as he wisely nodded.

Sir Kay was tense—aware of the slippery slope on which Britt was standing—though Sir Bodwain seemed unbothered.

"I know you have little love of him, My Lord, but it would be best to agree. You can stand him for one ride, can't you? Just ask to disregard the hunting part," Sir Bodwain advised.

Britt stood up straighter and glanced at Sir Kay, hoping for additional guidance. The younger man shook his head and grimly looked at the hooves of Lancelot's horse.

"Alas, I cannot hunt with you, Sir Lancelot. That would take more time than I fear I have. But I would be...*delighted* to ride with you," Britt said, forcing the words from her mouth.

Lancelot smiled. "I look forward to it. Thank you for this honorable match and for granting my humble request."

"Certainly. If you'll excuse me," Britt said, turning her back to the handsome knight. She smiled and nodded at the audience as she forced herself to stride from the field. Sir Kay followed her like a shadow, and Sir Bodwain—leading Roen—trailed after.

"Let's see Merlin try to bluff his way out of this evidence," Britt growled as she headed for the stables.

~

"YOU HAVE to go through with it," Merlin said, tapping his fingertips together as he and Britt sat in the safety of his study.

"*What?*" Britt yelped.

"He asked you in front of a crowd of knights and ladies. You cannot back out of that," Merlin scowled. "The ladies are sure to ask him how the ride went, and when he tells them you took back the boon, they will be displeased."

"Why should I care what his fanclub thinks of me?" Britt asked, running a hand through her blonde hair.

"You should care because they will blab it to the rest of your court. In case you don't remember, Lancelot is the fashion icon you wanted so badly before he arrived. So far his popularity has worked for your cause. He has made clean-shaven faces the rage and has charmed most of your courts. The downside is that your court will be upset if things turn ugly between the two of you."

"You mean he can cause the downfall of Camelot—"

"I said no such thing," Merlin interrupted. "You read too deeply into it. I said your court would be upset, not that they would abandon you. He may be popular, but you are still undoubtedly the favorite. The point is his request isn't too costly. You take a turn around the surrounding meadow, and you've paid your dues. In the meantime, we'll concoct a quest that will take Sir Lancelot very far from these walls. If you ride with him, he will have no reason to refuse your 'small request' to dispatch him on a quest," Merlin said.

"That makes sense, I guess," Britt said. "So I will really have to ride with him?"

Merlin heaved his eyes to the ceiling. "You can stand his company for an hour, Arthur."

"Fine. But this quest better send him out for a *long* time," Britt grumbled.

"Of course," Merlin said. "You should have just said no to the boon before this got out of hand."

"How about next time you watch the match, and *you* can tell Lancelot to go throw himself off a bridge," Britt suggested.

~

TWO DAYS LATER, Britt deeply regretted agreeing to the ride.

"—And should a recreant knight appear before us and demand a joust, fear not! I will fight him to spare you any pain, My Lord—although I am sure you could defeat any recreant knight we find," Lancelot said.

"We're just taking a ride around the meadow, Sir Lancelot. I don't think we'll be meeting any knights," Britt said, tossing a treat to Cavall from the saddle.

Cavall caught the snack and gulped it down in a second before he wove around Llamrei—Britt's gray mare—and eyed the encroaching Forest of Arroy.

"But, My Lord! One never knows what sort of adventures there are to be had in the forest," Lancelot said.

"That may be so, but we're not going into the forest, *remember*? That's the only reason why we aren't dragging my guards with us," Britt said.

"Alas, I forgot of your agreement with your foster-brother," Lancelot sighed.

"Uh-huh, right," Britt said, scratching her nose. "So what was the real reason you wanted me out here with you, alone?"

"What do you mean, My Lord?" Lancelot said, fixing a mussed-up thatch of his palomino's hair.

"There's no way you kicked up all this fuss because you wanted to go *horseback-riding* with me."

"Why do you find that so difficult to believe, My Lord?" Lancelot asked, sounding as threatening as a baby fawn.

Britt was not deceived. "Because you are persistent only if it suits you. So what do you want?"

"You do not believe that I wish to be included in your inner circle?" Lancelot asked. His voice was soft and harmless, but his green eyes were dark and...*intense*.

"Quite frankly? No. My closest knights are the opposite of you in every way," Britt said, conveniently forgetting that Ywain and Griflet were rather prone to emotional outbursts—like Lancelot.

To her surprise, Lancelot laughed. It wasn't his usual laugh of cheer and good humor, but it sounded more...authentic, and it was several pitches lower than usual.

Britt was uncertain what to say next—and Lancelot was still laughing—but she was saved when Cavall growled and snapped, staring into the forest.

"Stand down, Cavall," Britt ordered as Llamrei pranced in place. She squinted, trying to peer in the forest without getting closer. "What set you off?"

"Let's take a look," Lancelot suggested, steering his beautiful gelding into the forest.

"What? No. Kay asked me to stay in the meadow," Britt said as Llamrei tossed her head.

"Come now, it will be an adventure. We won't go in deep," Lancelot laughed.

"No. I promised Kay," she said, as unmovable as stone.

Lancelot flashed Britt what looked like an amused smirk, but she suspected it had more rancor than mirth in it. "You're a grown man, Arthur, and you're King. You're not beholden to your brother."

"Maybe, but I love him enough that I will let him boss me around regardless. I've slipped away from him before, and it was my mistake and error. I won't hurt him by doing it again. Now are you coming out, or are you going to press on alone?" Britt said.

During her little speech, Lancelot lost all signs of humor. "I think I will press on alone. I was never one to back down from an exploit."

"In that case, I bid you farewell," Britt said wheeling her horse around. She nudged Llamrei forward, and the mare began trotting back to Camelot.

"As you wish, My Lord," Lancelot called after her before he pushed his horse farther into the foliage of the Forest of Arroy.

Britt was about halfway to Camelot when she heard Lancelot shout. There was the unmistakable clang of swords clashing and a few muffled yelps.

"Of all the stupid things—I really hate you, Lancelot," Britt muttered. She couldn't just leave him to be attacked, and if she returned to Camelot for help, they might arrive too late. She would have to get a head start. Certain that guards were watching from the walls of Camelot, Britt wildly waved her arms at the castle before wheeling Llamrei around and cantering for the forest.

She clung to the mare's back as she rammed into the woods, branches and twigs poking her and tangling in her hair. She expertly slipped Excalibur from its scabbard and raised it when Llamrei leapt into the small clearing where Lancelot's horse snorted. Britt swung her blade at what looked like a man-at-arms who was inspecting an unconscious Lancelot.

The man shouted and jumped away. Llamrei snorted and turned to go back to Camelot—she was trained to avoid conflict and carry her rider to safety, which is why she was Kay's favorite mount for Britt. Britt managed to slide from the tall mare, almost falling flat on her face in the process.

When she regained her balance, she lunged forward, moving

Excalibur in a sweeping arc. The blow hit the man's hauberk—keeping the blade from cutting through him, but pushing him back on his heels with the force.

A second man—dressed similarly to the first—joined the fray. He shouted as he jumped at Britt with a battle axe. She ducked, and the axe missed her and was instead lodged in a tree trunk behind her.

Britt could hear Cavall barking and snarling, but he wasn't in the clearing. Were there more men in the area?

Taking advantage of the situation, Britt sprang to her feet, slugging the man in the gut as she rose. An elbow to the back of his neck sent him sprawling, and she had just enough time to whirl Excalibur up to block a chop the original man attempted.

The man was strong, but thankfully slow compared to Britt's less forceful, but lightning-fast jabs. When the man drew his sword back for another strike, she struck his open side. She whirled in a half circle—gaining momentum—to strike his other side, tossing him like a ball in a pinball machine.

The man—unsteady as he was—was still on his feet. Britt grimly adjusted her grip on Excalibur and started to lunge at him.

Beyond the trees, Cavall yelped and Llamrei screamed. She saw something out of the corner of her eye before pain exploded in her skull. She toppled like a fallen bird, landing on top of the unconscious Lancelot. Her ears rang, and her vision grew cloudy before darkness set in.

Lancelot groaned and hefted himself onto his elbows. A raging headache throbbed in his temples. "Bandits, surely," he spat, taking inventory of his injuries and gear. Besides his aching head, he had no wounds, and strangely, he still possessed all his clothes and gear.

When Lancelot lurched to his feet, he brushed himself off,

squinting as he saw a squad of guards come galloping out of Camelot. "By all the saints, what has caused their fear?" Lancelot muttered. He frowned when he realized his horse was still with him, and King Arthur's Llamrei was tied up next to it. The giant dog that followed King Arthur around was there as well, muzzled and trussed up like a boar.

Lancelot looked back at the stoic guards and realized that something *was* missing—or rather someone. Lancelot growled, and his shoulders slumped with irritation and fury. "Sir Kay is going to slay me for losing Arthur—that prancing do-good-er."

～

BRITT STARTED to wake up once or twice, but either her kidnappers had a medieval version of chloroform on them, or they kept hitting her to keep her knocked out because she didn't gain complete consciousness for several hours.

When she opened up her blue eyes, she found herself splayed out on a dingy, moist, stone floor. Britt groaned and clutched her aching head. Something metal clanged a short distance away from her, ringing in her ears like cathedral bells located inches from her head.

Britt muttered several oaths—most of them involving Lancelot and a stick.

"So you've woken up, have you?" said a voice as rusty as the floor was dirty.

Britt blinked her eyes, hoping to make them work better in the dim light. "Where am I?" she asked.

Another voice laughed—coming from Britt's other side. "You are in the dungeons of Sir Damas. Welcome, knight, to a pit of Hades."

3

FUN IN A DUNGEON

"You truly have no idea who attacked you? They wore no livery or symbol of loyalty?" Sir Kay rumbled.

"If I hadn't been struck from behind—only a coward's move—I would know. But I wasn't! I have no idea who stole your precious king, our King," Lancelot snapped, his good humor worn thin.

For the past hour he had been questioned and badgered by King Arthur's inner circle about the few moments he remembered of the attack. The King's officials were there—Sir Bodwain, Sir Ulfius, Sir Ector, Sir Kay, and Sir Bedivere—as were his pet knights—Sir Ywain and Sir Griflet. Sir Tor was present as well—more because he happened to be in Merlin's study when Sir Kay dragged Lancelot inside than because of any great tie to the king.

"It's strange," Merlin said, his hands clasped behind his back.

"What is it, Merlin?" Sir Ector asked.

"Why would these mysterious attackers leave Sir Lancelot behind?" Merlin wondered. "Why not take him with—confounding us further? Even more odd—why would they carry him to the edge of the forest instead of fleeing right then and there?"

"Is it possible they don't know whom they've captured?" Sir Tor asked—his normally cheerful face was creased with worry.

"That's impossible," Sir Ywain scoffed. "Everyone knows King Arthur. We're wasting time. We should be out, tracking him!"

"Nay. Sir Tor may be right," Sir Bodwain rumbled, smoothing his beard. "King Arthur rode out in his plainest gear, yes?"

"Correct. Llamrei wore none of Arthur's usual trappings either," Sir Kay said, referring to the beautiful tack that was flourished with red dragons.

"It is best to hope, then, that whoever has King Arthur, does not know of the prize they have dragged off," Merlin said, his uncomfortably bright eyes fastened on Lancelot. "Otherwise, we may have to further pursue Sir Lancelot's involvement in the affair."

Aware of how bad it looked, Lancelot impatiently tilted his head. "I didn't mean to lure King Arthur there. I had no knowledge of the men. Indeed—it was King Arthur's dog that saw them, for he growled and snapped at the forest."

"Let us hope your words are trustworthy," Merlin said, his voice utterly without emotion.

The heavens laugh at me, Lancelot stewed. *The one time I do not seek to harm the king, he is taken—implicating me!*

The main cause of Lancelot's discomfort was Merlin's scrutiny. Lancelot was used to being admired and looked at—everything from his manners to the way he dressed was designed to draw notice. But men like Merlin—wise men—didn't often study Lancelot. In fact, they usually ignored him, writing him off as a silly but chivalrous knight. That is what Lancelot *wanted* them to do.

He did not like the way Merlin stared at him, as if he were studying a newfound threat.

"What are we waiting for?" Lancelot finally said, the words ripped from his throat. "We should be following those attackers, hunting them without mercy!"

"We will," Merlin said. "But first we must plan," he said, standing to retrieve a map from the wall. "We can attempt to follow the trail, but the guards already scouted the area and said it would be difficult, if not impossible to follow. Llamrei, Cavall, and Excalibur were left behind. As far as we know, Arthur has nothing with him. Whoever took Arthur carried him to a stream. Any tracks are lost there—although one might have more luck with a scent hound."

"If there is no trail, what do we do?" Sir Ector asked, nervously pacing.

"We divide our forces to cover the greatest distance," Merlin said. "Several knights should push north into the Forest of Arroy; some should travel due east, and several more should travel southeast," Merlin said, his finger tracing the cloud of trees. "We know they did not move west—we have open plains on that side of Camelot and would have seen any movement. Clearly they stayed in the forest. Most likely they will seek shelter in a radius close to Camelot. Based on Lancelot's description, I do not think we are dealing with men looking to ransom a king, which would infer they have no reason to believe they need to carry Arthur far away."

"We have to be intelligent about where we search," he continued. "To the north, there are small baronets. East takes one into more inhabited parts, but to reach them it is a much longer journey. Southeast, there are several baronets and a prince—though all are sworn to Arthur. The north is the least likely direction, for it is almost abandoned there. I recommend we send fewer knights, and no guards."

"Sir Ulfius and I will travel east," Sir Bodwain said after glancing at his longtime friend.

"I will go with you," Sir Ector said.

"No," Merlin said. "You will remain in Camelot to rule in Arthur's absence. It's what...he would have ordered," Merlin said, the words dispelling any argument Sir Ector would have posed.

Merlin turned his searing blue eyes on Lancelot again. "You said you and your cousins are acquainted with the Lady of the Lake?"

"Yes."

"Then Bors and Lionel will accompany Sir Tor and...Sir Percival and his companions there to speak to the Lady," Merlin said. "And you, Lancelot, you will ride north."

"What of the southeast direction?" Sir Griflet asked.

"Sir Kay and I will cover that direction. After our initial search parties set out, we will send out squads of guards," Merlin said.

"I request permission to accompany you, Merlin," Sir Ywain said.

"Your request is most emphatically *denied*," Merlin said. "I will be using all the powers I have to search for our king—I will not have the patience or ability to keep you from breaking your neck."

"I can help!" Sir Ywain argued.

"You will travel with Sir Lancelot," Merlin snapped.

Sir Ywain turned to look at Lancelot so fast, Lancelot could almost hear his neck snap.

"Truly?" Sir Ywain asked.

"Truly," Merlin wryly said, looking to Sir Bedivere. The knight gave an almost imperceptible nod, and Merlin continued, "You, Sir Griflet, and Sir Bedivere shall accompany Sir Lancelot in his northern search."

"What of the other knights?" Sir Kay asked.

"The rest of Arthur's inner circle is gone—off questing or, in King Pellinore's case, pursuing that rotten questing beast. If they happen to return while we are absent, Sir Ector will inform them. In the meantime, it will be up to Sir Ector to organize the guard search parties and the remaining knights of the Round Table— though I think it would be likely that if we do not find Arthur in our initial search, we will receive word of him," Merlin said. "It is to be hoped that we are overreacting. Perhaps it is nothing more than servants of a recreant knight seeking out an opponent, in which case, I am certain Arthur would return shortly. However, until we know for certain where he is, it is best to exercise caution. If you find Arthur, send word *immediately*," Merlin instructed. "Have I made myself clear?"

"Yes, Merlin," the knights chorused.

"Good. In that case, we must prepare for our departure. Good luck, men," Merlin said before he stood and opened the door to the study, clearly dismissing them.

To Lancelot's surprise, Morgan le Fay was standing out in the hallway, her hands clasped in front of her as she stared at the study door.

"Arthur has been taken?" Morgan asked Merlin as knights filed past.

"Yes," Merlin said.

Morgan nodded thoughtfully and turned to go—her skirts swishing around her as she walked up the hallway.

"Sorceresses," Merlin muttered, casting another intense look at Lancelot before shutting the study door.

Lancelot watched Morgan disappear down the hallway. *Merlin punishing me with Sir Ywain and Sir Griflet and sending me in the least likely direction is no shock—I have placed his precious king in danger, after all. But Morgan-the-man-hater's affection for Arthur is true? That seems suspicious, even if he is her half-brother...*

~

"So, let me see if I've got this straight," Britt said, folding her legs pretzel style when she sat on the filth-covered dungeon floor. "Sir Damas has taken me captive—just as he took all of you captive—in hopes that he can convince me to fight on his behalf and face his brother, Sir Outzlake, in combat."

"Yes," said the knight in the cell across from Britt.

"Sir Damas needs a champion because he is a rotten fighter—"

"He's more of a scholar, really," a dirty knight in a neighboring cell said.

"—and his brother, the previously mentioned Sir Outzlake, keeps challenging him because Sir Damas won't share his inheritance with him?" Brit said.

"Well, he's shared some. Sir Outzlake has a very fine, rich manor not far from here," one of the roughly ten captive knights begrudgingly admitted.

"Sir Damas must be going against his father's wishes then and is hogging the rest of the inheritance?" Britt asked, tapping her fingers on her knees.

"No," the knight across from Britt said. "Their father willed the majority of his wealth to Sir Damas."

Britt scrunched her eyes shut. "Then I don't get it. You all told me Sir Damas is rotten and evil, and that is why none of you have been willing to act as his champion."

"He is," a fellow captive said.

"But it sounds to me like Sir Outzlake is the one in the wrong. Sir Damas can't help what his father willed to him—although he's obviously no bleeding lamb either, or he wouldn't be kidnapping knights to fight for him," Britt said, rubbing the sore spot on her head.

"No, no. Sir Outzlake is very kind," a captive knight said.

"Then why is he challenging his brother?" Britt asked.

"Because it isn't fair that Sir Damas received so much, and Sir Outzlake received so little."

"The knight has a blooming *manor*. He can't have received that little!" Britt said, folding her arms across her chest.

"Yes, but he needs to provide for his sister," another knight said.

"Wait, Sir Damas and Sir Outzlake have a sister?" Britt asked.

"Yes, Lady Vivenne."

"And she's staying with Sir Outzlake?"

"No, she's with Sir Damas right now."

Britt loudly sighed. "That's it. I think they both could be considered recreant knights."

"Sir Damas is extremely selfish. He cares only for himself and his pursuit of knowledge," a captive knight protested.

"Yes, but at least he doesn't go around trying to attack his neighbors because he wants their things," Britt said.

"But he is cruel to Lady Vivenne," Britt's captive neighbor said. "She has been ignored since the day her father died two years ago. Although Sir Damas sees that she is fed and clothed, he keeps her locked up in his castle."

"Probably because otherwise Sir Outzlake would try and kidnap her," Britt said.

"Sir Outzlake would never!"

Britt rolled her eyes at the sea of protests. "Right, yeah. How long has this been going on?"

"Caradan, you were the first captive. When did it start?" a knight down the line shouted.

"Not a day over eight months," chirped a voice at the far end of the dungeon.

"And there you have it. Eight months," Britt's neighbor said.

"And none of you decided it was better to fight for Sir Damas because then—Oh, I don't know—maybe you could *get out*?" Britt asked.

The knight across from Britt piously shook his head. "It would never do to fight for Sir Damas' cause. It is unseemly to get involved in family matters."

"Besides, it's not that terrible here," another knight said. "Maybe a little chilly in the winter, and the food is questionable, but it's not a horror to sit around and sleep and do as I wish."

Britt stared at the knight before asking, "How many of you belong to King Leodegrance's court?"

Britt didn't get a reply—the great door to the dungeon swung open first. A huge, hulking man dressed in black filled the doorway. He was so muscular, he almost had to waddle down the tiny dungeon aisle. He stopped in front of Britt's cell and did a reasonable impersonation of Darth Vader as he breathed loudly in his black helm. Abruptly, he stepped aside, allowing a spindly man—who couldn't have been much over five feet and was as muscular as a scrawny boy—to peer at Britt.

"This is the new captive?" the stick-like man asked, glancing up at Muscular Darth Vader.

Muscular Darth Vader nodded.

Stick Man squinted. "He looks too pretty. Are you sure you did not snatch a faerie warrior? My brother may smash him like a butterfly."

Britt was simultaneously pleased and offended. Although she was forced to act like a man, her feminine pride always took a hit that the ploy seemed so easy to carry off. As such, she was always highly gratified whenever anyone thought her to be too beautiful to be a man. Still, the complete lack of faith in her physical abilities was a little much.

"I took out your men easily enough—they had to team up to capture me," Britt said, making a show of stretching her legs out in front of her and crossing them at the ankles—as if *she* was in a position to be confident, and not them.

"Good point. Very well, knight. What is your name?" Stick Man—who obviously had to be Sir Damas—asked.

"It's...Ywain. Sir Ywain," Britt said, providing the false name on a flash of inspiration.

"Sir Ywain, I find myself in need of a champion to defend my name against my black-hearted brother," Sir Damas said. "He continuously attacks me for no reason and harasses me worse than a recreant knight. My company is so pitiful that I have no men who can properly defend me against him."

Britt ignored the outraged shouts of her fellow captives and looked past Sir Damas to stare at Muscular Darth Vader. "I see," she said.

Sir Damas ignored her pointed look and continued—his voice was surprisingly deep and throaty despite his stick-ish body. "I have invited you into my castle with such hospitality in hopes that you would fight on my behalf."

"If I fight for you, will you release me—whether I win or lose?"

"I will release you only if you win. Naturally," Sir Damas said with a curdled smile.

Britt considered Sir Damas and tapped her kneecap. Although she didn't fancy the idea of helping him, she wasn't going to sit in the dungeons and rot either. *I can always come back and smite Sir Damas* and *Sir Outzlake once I'm freed.*

"Sure," Britt said, liquidly rising to her feet.

"Sir Ywain, you are about to commit a grave sin!"

"If you aid Sir Damas, you are a recreant knight!"

"Why would you agree to help *him*?"

"Silence!" Sir Damas shouted over the protesting knights. He was ignored. Sir Damas glared and took a key off his belt. He opened the door of Britt's cell with a great clank.

Britt followed the short man out of the dungeons and into an open air courtyard. Britt stretched her arms above her head and soaked up the fading sunlight.

"The contest will be tomorrow," Sir Damas said in his deep, throaty voice. "I suppose you need armor?" he grudgingly asked.

"Yes. Your men didn't happen to bring my sword with me, did they?" Britt asked.

"No. Markem will see you outfitted," Sir Damas said, nodding to Muscular Darth Vader. "See that he is given appropriate weapons and a room—have him guarded to make sure he doesn't run."

"Sir Damas, a moment, please," Britt said.

"What is it?" Sir Damas asked, impatience flashing across his face.

"Sir Outzlake is the challenger, yes?"

"Of course."

"Then that gives you the right to decide the contest. Request a battle by swords," Britt said.

Sir Damas frowned. "Such quarrels are traditionally decided by jousting."

"So I've heard, but I'm better at the sword. Ask for a contest of swords."

Sir Damas shrugged. "It makes no difference—so long as you win."

"Right, thank you," Britt said, adjusting her leather jerkin.

Sir Damas waved a hand in the air to acknowledge her and walked away.

Britt looked over at Muscular Darth Vader. "To the armory?" she asked.

Muscular Darth Vader nodded and led the way.

BRITT TOOK one of the three, two-handed swords Muscular Darth Vader had selected for her. She whirled it through the air and tried striking a dummy before stepping back. "Not quite balanced," she muttered, swapping the sword for a different one. Excalibur's empty scabbard was still strapped to her—there was no way she was taking the scabbard off, as it was imbedded with magic that would keep her from bleeding out if she was ever wounded.

Britt ran a finger down the scabbard, missing Excalibur like she would miss an old friend. She sighed and picked up the next sword, twirling it before testing it against the dummy.

"Better," she said.

"So you're the champion my brother finally found. Funny—I never thought you would be so comely."

Britt spun, her muscles tense as she found herself face to face with a teenage girl. She probably wasn't older than fourteen or fifteen, although she was dressed in a plain, undyed kirtle.

"Lady Vivenne?" Britt guessed.

Vivenne nodded and plopped down on a stone bench. "I thought only a recreant knight would be willing to help my brother. You don't look very recreant, though," she said, studying Britt.

Britt smiled. "Looks can be deceiving. You want your other brother, Sir Outzlake, to win, I suppose?"

"I don't care who wins. It's all the same to me," Lady Vivenne dully said.

"But the way everyone speaks, Sir Outzlake is a wronged saint," Britt said, trading swords again to test out her last option.

"Oh, he's nicer. But he's just as selfish as Damas. He doesn't give a berry for me—I'm just another thing Damas got put in charge of. Father always said Outzlake was less responsible—he's a bit of a warmonger. At least Damas will never get himself killed since he's hiding away in his study all the time."

"I see," Britt said, at a loss for the young lady's bluntness. She glanced up at the night sky and the four sputtering torches that had been lit for her benefit in the courtyard. "Isn't it a little late for you to be up?"

"Maybe. But I had to stay up. One of the servants was having her baby, and Damas won't hire an herb woman, so I'm the best the castle has," Lady Vivenne said.

"I see," Britt carefully said.

Lady Vivenne tilted her head. "Are you wondering why I'm telling you all of this?"

"You may say whatever you like, Lady Vivenne," Britt said, turning her back to the young lady to study the three swords.

"That's no fun. I thought I would whet your curiosity. I'll give you a hint—it's not because you are handsome."

"That is reassuring," Britt said, choosing the middle sword.

"It's because I've heard about you, Sir Ywain."

Britt almost dropped her sword. *"What?"*

"You're from King Arthur's court, and you went questing last summer and fall in the Forest of Arroy with your close companion, Sir Griflet. I heard about a few of your battles."

Britt stared at the girl in horror. She thought Ywain was a safe bet compared to Gawain, or Kay, or Pellinore. He wasn't as widely known. How had this girl heard of him?

"I want you to know that neither of my brothers are good knights—not really. They would never hurt their people, but they don't care for others like they should," Lady Vivenne said. "And if you beat Outzlake tomorrow, I know you're going to return to Camelot. If you speak to King Arthur, and if he decides to ride out to see both of my brothers removed from their knighthoods —as I would imagine would happen since Damas has *kidnapped* you—please ask him to be thoughtful when he decides what knight to give our lands to. Not for my brothers' sake—though I do love those silly men—but for the sake of our people. They deserve to serve a just knight—not one of King Leodegrance's men."

Britt had managed to regain her wits during Lady Vivenne's talk. "You have a compelling case. I will be sure to tell Arthur."

Lady Vivenne smiled brightly. "Thank you," she said before dropping a cloth bundle that contained food on the bench. "This is for you. If you'll excuse me, I really should retire."

Britt bowed. "As you wish, Lady Vivenne."

Lady Vivenne scampered out of the torchlight, leaving Britt alone with her insomnia and the night sky.

Britt rubbed her eyes. "This isn't what I bargained for. Why can't it be more clear-cut?" she muttered before she looked up at the stars. "One thing is for certain—Merlin and Kay must be *fuming.*"

4

A FIGHT BETWEEN CHAMPIONS

B ritt sneezed, spattering the inside of her helm with spit. "Gross," she said, making a face. The spring air was cool, but Britt was warm enough, bundled up in black armor as she was. The chest piece was a little uncomfortable since it lacked the extra padding Britt's armor was usually stuffed with to help camouflage her chest. As a result, the armor piece flattened her like an ironing board.

The morning sun beat down on Britt and her companions—Sir Damas, a number of his guards, and Lady Vivenne. Birds chirped and sang, and high in the sky a hawk wheeled overhead.

Britt tried to discreetly check her buckles—she had donned the bulk of the armor alone to preserve the illusion of her gender, and she wasn't certain she did everything right.

"Prepare yourself, Sir Ywain. Yonder comes my recreant brother, Sir Outzlake," Sir Damas said, indicating to the far end of the meadow, where a party of knights emerged from the forest.

"He looks…unwell," Britt said.

The man Sir Damas pointed to was, oddly enough, not wearing armor. He wore a plain tunic, and his arm was tied in a sling, even though he rode a spirited horse. He was a great hulk of a man—Sir Damas' opposite in every physical aspect.

"I thought I was going to fight him," Britt said, taking in his lack of armor.

"That was the plan," Sir Damas muttered. "What is the meaning of this, brother?" he shouted when the other party drew near enough to hear him over the jingling of horse tack. "Did you not agree to fight whatever champion I might find?"

"I did," Sir Outzlake said.

As soon as he spoke, Britt had to turn away to keep from laughing. While small, stick-like Damas had a voice of thunder, Outzlake the hulk sounded like a pre-pubescent boy.

"Unfortunately," Sir Outzlake continued in his almost soprano voice, "I have recently injured myself."

"This is suspicious timing. Perhaps you fear my champion?" Sir Damas asked.

Sir Outzlake puffed up like an angry cat. "Never!" he hissed. He cleared his throat and—with great difficulty—made himself relax. "I am pleased to say, however, that I too have found a champion to serve in my place."

"So two strangers are fighting each other for the sake of two brothers. Somehow this doesn't make sense," Britt muttered.

"Silence," Sir Damas snapped.

Britt rolled her eyes and adjusted her stance—her borrowed sword unsheathed and held at her side.

"If that is what you wish," Sir Damas said, directing his gaze to his brother. "As the challenged party, it is within my rights to declare the test."

Sir Outzlake frowned. "You mean our champions will not joust?"

"No," Sir Damas said. "I prefer a contest by swords."

Sir Outzlake turned in his saddle to face his followers.

At the far end of the meadow, an entourage of four knights was gathered. Britt squinted—trying to make out their coat of arms—but she couldn't see at such a great distance. They did appear to be arguing, though. One of the knights threw his hands in the air, and another emphatically pointed into the forest. The third knight launched for the fourth knight's reins but missed, and the fourth knight cued his horse into a trot, drawing towards Sir Outzlake.

Sir Outzlake spoke to the knight in an undertone before he shouted, "I agree. Let our champions settle the score through blades."

Britt rolled her shoulders—attempting to loosen them up—as she studied her opponent. He was tall—taller than Britt—and his shoulders were wider as well.

I'll have to compensate for his additional strength—and he very likely is a quick mover judging by the cut of his armor, Britt thought as she sashayed up to the open space between Damas and Outzlake.

Outzlake's champion met her there, an unreadable statue of armor and weapons. Britt wondered at the stance he took—she had seen it before.

"Champions! You may begin," Sir Damas shouted.

The words were barely out of his mouth when Britt struck—attempting a sweeping blow that would make a slash starting at her opponent's hip and ending at his opposite shoulder. He blocked—as she hoped he would—and Britt struck out with her left leg. The knight took the hit like a brick wall, but Britt slithered closer, attempting to use her sword like a lever to pop her opponent's sword out of his hands.

He unfortunately guessed her movements and sprang away. Britt followed at him with a gut thrust—crouching low before pushing forward.

The opposing champion blocked that, as well. Britt meant to rush him and carry through with the thrust, but the knight—using brute strength—pushed his blade up during the block, taking Britt's sword with his.

This left both of them wide open. The knight tried to hit her in the neck with the pommel of his sword.

Too flashy, Britt thought. She dodged by sinking to her knees and slamming her borrowed sword into her opponent's right knee with as much force as she could muster.

Finally, she had thrown the knight off guard. He muttered an oath inside his helm and took a step backwards. Britt pushed her advantage, leaping from the ground and throwing all of her weight into her opponent. He staggered again, and with a fancy twirl, Britt tangled her sword in the hilt of his, turning it at an unnatural angle so the knight was forced to break his wrist or let it go.

When the knight released his sword, it almost hit Britt in the face with the force he used to throw it, but Britt used her sword to direct it away.

The fight *should* have stopped there with the knight being unarmed and all, but the knight roared in rage and almost nailed Britt in the neck.

I was too careless, Britt grimly thought, dodging the worst of the blow—although her gorget dug into the skin of her neck from what pressure he managed to hit her with. *I have to end this, or my stamina is going to give out.*

Britt finished the knight off with a brutal chop to his helm, rattling his head and sending him to his knees. She kneed his shoulder, spilling him backwards so he landed on his back. Britt, brisk and business-like, kicked his arm away so she could wedge her blade in his unprotected armpit.

"Well done, champion," Sir Damas boomed, clapping his hands. "I believe this means you will give up all claims, brother?"

"Wait just a moment. I never agreed that I would stop fighting this injustice," Sir Outzlake said, puffing up again.

Britt sneezed again. "Ugh, I need a tissue," she muttered to the spitty inside of her helm. She removed her sword from her opponent's armpit and rested it on her shoulder as she strolled back to

Sir Damas' party, aiming for the chestnut gelding she had ridden to the meadow—lent to her by Damas.

Sir Damas and Sir Outzlake had stalked towards each other and were busy arguing in the middle of the meadow.

"So what if your champion beat mine? All that means is that you were able to pay a better man to fill your shoes—coward," Sir Outzlake said.

"I am a scholar—fighting was never my business. *You* are the warrior of the family, and yet *you* chose not to fight either!" Sir Damas said.

Britt tried unhooking her helm to get the spit out of her face but wasn't having much luck with it since she could only use one hand. When she finally got it so she could ease it off, something roared behind her—sounding like an enraged dragon.

Britt spun around—thinking Sir Outzlake had lost it and was going to kill his brother.

To her shock, she found the other champion lunging at her—his sword extended.

Britt didn't have enough time to react. She was stabbed—the tip of the champion's sword wedging through the armor pieces delicately arranged on her shoulder.

Britt fell to her knees with the force of the blow—her helm toppling from her head. Pain exploded in her shoulder, and her legs twitched as she tried to make them work—what if this maniac tried to finish her off?! Excalibur's scabbard would keep her from bleeding, but it couldn't keep her heart pumping!

There was the thundering of hooves as horses galloped across the field.

"Lancelot you dishonorable, blackguard. What are you *doing*?!"

"There! Your champion just laid an illegal blow upon my champion. Clearly I am in the right," Sir Damas shouted.

"Sir Ywain!" Lady Vivenne shouted.

"...What?"

There was a scuffle, and a knight appeared in Britt's line of vision.

"Lancelot, what have you *done*," the knight uttered. He tossed his helmet aside, revealing a face Britt knew well: Bedivere.

"Sir Bedivere," Britt said, licking her lips. "Fancy meeting you here."

"I could say the same, My Lord," Bedivere said, his expression tight as he started to remove pieces of Britt's armor.

"My what?...LANCELOT!"

"That sounds like Ywain. The real one," Britt said as Lady Vivenne knelt next to her, carrying a supply pack.

"It *is* Ywain—and Griflet," Sir Bedivere said fumbling with the buckles of Britt's borrowed breastplate.

"Then whom did I fight?" Britt asked.

There was a roar and a clang as Ywain tackled someone.

"None other than Sir Lancelot," Sir Bedivere said. "Though I'm not sure he'll live to see the end of the day."

Britt laughed and winced in pain.

"I have bandages and some herbs to staunch the blood flow," Lady Vivenne said, digging through her pack.

"Oh, where are my manners? Lady Vivenne, this is Sir Bedivere. Bedivere, this is Lady Vivenne. She's the little sister of the arguing idiots," Britt said, carefully exhaling in an attempt to master her pain.

"A pleasure," Sir Bedivere said, not paying attention.

"You know, you don't have to hurry. I'm not going to bleed out. Although my shoulder does feel odd. Did Lancelot dislocate it?" Britt frowned.

"How was I to know my opponent was Arthur? He was wearing a full suit of armor!"

"You shouldn't have been as dishonorable as to attack a man from behind after you clearly lost!" Sir Griflet shouted.

There was another clang as someone else—Griflet probably—tackled Lancelot again.

Britt gasped in pain when Sir Bedivere jostled her as he tried to slide her plackart off.

Lady Vivenne swore most colorfully. "I've forgotten my vial of ground ivy. I'll ride back to the castle—it's only a few minutes away. I shan't be long," the girl said before scrambling away, leaving a cloud of dust.

"Bon Voyage," Britt said, raising her good arm to swat the air away from her face. "I knew I was right to hate Lancelot. He's such a slug."

"I'm glad to see you haven't lost your tongue, My Lord," Sir Bedivere said, his face gray with anxiety.

"I'm not on my death bed, Sir Bedivere. This hurts about as badly as when I broke my arm as a kid. Ugh, stab wounds. Not fun," Britt grimaced. "Although it might be worth it. Kay is going to *murder* Lancelot."

∾

MILES AWAY, Sir Kay and Merlin rode together through the Forest of Arroy. Sir Kay abruptly straightened in the saddle and squinted, looking ahead.

"What's wrong?" Merlin asked, glancing at his taciturn companion.

"I have a bad feeling in my gut," Sir Kay said.

"About?"

"I feel as if Britt has been hurt."

Merlin uneasily shifted in his saddle, although he said, "That's not the worst that could happen. As long as she has Excalibur's scabbard, I expect she'll be fine. Besides, who is to say your gut is right?"

Sir Kay blinked. "I will track down whoever hurts her," he said.

"I wouldn't expect any less of you," Merlin said, urging his horse forward.

~

When Ywain's face popped into view, Britt could still hear Sir Damas and Sir Outzlake arguing.

"This is clearly my win, so trundle back to your little *manor* and cry off!" Sir Damas demanded.

"Never! You should have fought for your own honor!" Sir Outzlake said.

"*YOU* should have fought for your own honor as well!"

"Hello, Ywain," Britt said with a smile that showed more of her teeth than usual due to the pain.

"My Lord," Ywain said, his expression tight. "Are you, are you...will you make it?"

"Ywain! He stabbed me in the shoulder, and I'm fairly certain it didn't go in very deep. *Yes*, I'm going to make it!" Britt barked.

Ywain looked relieved.

"Help me remove the rest of his armor. We'll have to rip open the under-padding," Sir Bedivere said.

This brought Britt out of the ocean of pain with stark clarity. "Wait, what?" she said.

"We need to remove your armor and garments so your chest can be inspected," Sir Bedivere said, removing several pieces of armor on her arm.

Britt laughed. "That is a very nice thought, but no. No, that is unnecessary."

"My Lord, the wound must be cared for," Sir Bedivere said.

"Can't Merlin do it?" Britt asked.

"Merlin did not ride with our search party," Ywain said.

"Oh. In that case, how far away are we from Camelot?" Britt asked.

"We are not riding back to Camelot with you in this condition, My Lord," Sir Bedivere said.

"How is he?" Sir Griflet asked, skidding out and almost falling flat on his face when he joined his fellow knights in crowding around Britt.

"I don't know. I haven't gotten all of his blasted armor off. My Lord, please stop fighting us," Sir Bedivere said.

"You're all overreacting. I'm f-fine," Britt said, stammering when someone jarred her injured shoulder and pain hit her like a truck.

Ywain scowled. "This is all your fault. If you had just ignored Sir Outzlake's outrageous request to serve as his champion and not wasted our time, none of this would have happened!" he said as Lancelot knelt by Britt's head.

"If I had not served as Outzlake's champion, we wouldn't have found My Lord and would still be searching for him," Lancelot said.

"Maybe so, but if you weren't such a poor loser, he wouldn't be in this condition!" Griflet snapped.

Lancelot ignored the jab and rested his dreamy eyes on Britt's face. "I am sorry, My Lord. I don't know what came over me. If I had known it was you—"

"Your anger at being beaten got the best of you, eh, Lancelot? Temper, temper, temper. But you're lucky. I'm feeling magnanimous. I'll let you survive if you *stop* your cohorts from undressing me!" Britt said, real panic starting to build. "Where is Merlin?"

"We already told you, My Lord, he didn't ride with us," Ywain said.

"See—he is quite injured. His memory is slipping," Griflet hissed to Lancelot.

"It is not—I just didn't think you were serious. How can Merlin *not* be here?" Britt demanded.

"I'm afraid I don't understand, My Lord," Sir Lancelot said.

"I expect you wouldn't. Everyone, just *stop touching me*. I'm serious—in fact I order it!" Britt said, struggling to sit up.

One of the knights firmly pushed her down.

167

"You don't know what you're saying, My Lord. Finally, we can remove the cuirass," Sir Bedivere said.

"Don't—STOP!" Britt shouted, panic making her heart thunder in her ears.

The knights wouldn't need to strip her down to see she wasn't what she claimed to be. All they would need to do is take off her jerkin. Her body would betray the rest, and all would be lost.

How is Merlin not here? He's always here when I'm in trouble! Britt thought, panic making her breathe faster.

"Lift him up on three, Lancelot, so we can remove the cuirass. It's the least you can do," Sir Bedivere said.

"Don't you dare!" Britt said, starting to struggle in earnest. She thrashed, but Ywain and Griflet held her tight.

"One."

"Stop it!" Britt shouted.

"Two."

"I mean it! Merlin will kill you all!"

"Three."

When Lancelot lifted Britt up, her shoulder was wrenched. She gasped with the new wave of pain and, recognizing the feeling of disconnect from her shoulder, suspected that it really was dislocated.

I'm going to kill Lancelot. I was right—he DOES bring about my downfall, Britt thought before her vision grew hazy and pain claimed her, stealing her conscious.

STILL MANY MILES AWAY, it was Merlin's turn to straighten in his saddle.

Sir Kay raised his eyebrows at the wizard but said nothing.

"Maybe your gut isn't so far off," Merlin said, rubbing the back of his neck with a worried frown.

"What is it?"

"Apprehension. Some kind of magical foresight. I feel as if…"

"As if?"

Doom breathed down Merlin's neck like a murderous beast. "As if my life's work is about to come crashing down around my ears."

5

REVEALED

Britt groaned as she came to, consciousness easing into her like an ocean wave crawling up the beach. Her eyes fluttered open, and a moment passed before she remembered the precarious situation she was in. She snapped upright—her arm protesting with the sudden movement.

She still wore her jerkin, but there was no doubt in Britt's mind that her knights knew. Their faces said it all.

Sir Griflet paced back and forth, shaking his head. "It can't be," he muttered.

Ywain couldn't even look at Britt. His back was to her, and his hands were clenched in fists. Tension and anger lined his body, and although he was unmoving, Britt got the distinct feeling he was like a volcano, ready to erupt.

Lancelot—the knight Britt cared the least about—seemed to have the most control over himself. He leaned against his dapple-gray horse, his eyes narrowed.

Sir Bedivere sat about ten feet away, plopped on the ground as if his legs didn't have the strength to hold him upright. When he raised his head and met Britt's gaze, the look of betrayal in his eyes put a knife through Britt's heart.

They knew.

"Why?" Ywain said. His back was still to Britt, but he seemed to instinctively know she was awake.

Britt hesitated. "I had no choice," she said.

"You *lied* to us!" Ywain said, spinning around as if his body were yanked by puppet strings. The young knight's expression made Britt want to cry. He was angry, but his eyes looked lost and frightened. "Was any of it real? Any of the things you said—were they true?"

"Of course they are," Britt said, grimacing and holding her wound. It seemed that in their shock, the knights had done nothing with her shoulder wound—not that she blamed them. Besides, Excalibur's scabbard was keeping her blood in her. "I'm still the same person."

"No, you're not," Sir Bedivere said, his voice quiet.

"This is a nightmare—that's it! It has to be a nightmare," Sir Griflet muttered. "Does anyone care to stab me or some such thing? I wish to wake up now."

"You're not dreaming, Griflet," Ywain growled, his eyes narrowed in hatred as he stared at Britt. "This is real. Our *King* has done nothing but lie to us and laugh at our ignorance since the beginning."

"I have never laughed at you," Britt calmly stated.

"Impossible," Ywain said with a bark of laughter that was far too harsh for such a young man to utter. "I imagine this whole time you've been barely able to keep from splitting your gut with laughter. You called me your shield! You *lied!*"

"I lied about myself, but that doesn't mean the things I said to you were untrue," Britt said.

Ywain laughed again and turned his back to Britt.

The knights were silent.

Sir Damas and Sir Outzlake still argued in the background, completely oblivious to the drama taking place no more than thirty feet away from them.

Britt tried to move, the pain in her shoulder made her feel the throbbing of her heart in strange places. "I'm sorry, but I had no choice."

"Didn't you, My Lord?" Sir Bedivere quietly asked. The marshal looked as if Britt had stolen his reason to live with the reveal of her gender. Ywain's anger was easier to handle than Bedivere's look of betrayal and hurt. "You couldn't have told any of us?"

Britt hesitated.

Ywain laughed again. "Don't be foolish, Sir Bedivere. Of course someone knew. You can't tell me Merlin is oblivious, nor Sir Kay and Sir Ector. In fact, I bet most of those old codgers Merlin holes up with know about it. Know about *her*," Ywain scoffed, removing his armored gloves. He clenched them in his hand before throwing them at the ground.

"I was your marshal," Bedivere said, his voice barely above a whisper. "I would have done *anything* for you."

"I know!" Sir Griflet brightened. "This is a faerie trap! We've been caught in a faerie trap that plays games with our minds. We must find a way out of it—we have to continue our search for the real King Arthur. This one is obviously a farce," Sir Griflet said.

"We're not in a faerie trap, Griflet. We're just being played with by a conniving female," Ywain snarled.

Britt looked from the three unsteady knights to Lancelot—who still leaned against his horse. The shallow knight's face held traces of anger, but he was markedly less affected than the others. His dreamy, green eyes met Britt's, and he raised an eyebrow, looking down on her.

Everything has been ruined, Britt realized. *Once the rest of the Order of the Round Table knows, King Arthur's rule will be over. I'll be lucky if they don't hang me or burn me at the stake.*

It pained Britt to see the knights she knew, men she loved—with the exception of Lancelot—turn into enemies before her very eyes. Their anger, betrayal, and newly minted hatred were exposed in their eyes and the tight muscles of their faces.

Run.

"You're worse than my Aunt Morgause!" Ywain finally spat out. "At least a man *knows* when she's playing with him. But you whispered exactly what we wanted to hear and petted us and cooed over us like we were your *lapdogs*!"

"I never treated you—"

"LIAR! Everything you've told me is a lie—I cannot possibly believe you now!" Ywain said.

Britt's heart beat in her throat. *Run!* Her mind urged her, but her heart twisted to see the pain she caused her knights.

"I'm still Arthur. Just because I'm..." Britt trailed off and glanced at Sir Damas and Sir Outzlake, but they were busy poking each other in the chest. "I'm still the person you know me as."

Sir Bedivere shook his head. "No. The king I knew is dead," he said. The shadows in his eyes said he was mourning the loss of King Arthur—of Britt's charade.

There was the scrape of a sword sliding out of its scabbard. Britt snapped her head in the direction of the sound and found Ywain glowering at her, holding his unsheathed sword.

RUN!

Unable to leash her fear any longer, Britt lunged to her feet. To accomplish the feat, she had to use her injured arm—which made her stomach queasy. She pushed the nausea aside and snatched up her borrowed sword before scrambling to her temporary mount's side. She slid the sword in the scabbard attached to the horse and threw herself on the chestnut's back.

She wheeled the horse towards the woods and heeled it, making the animal launch into a canter.

"That's my horse!" Sir Damas shouted—finally distracted from his argument with his brother.

"Wait—My Lord!" Griflet shouted, running a few steps after Britt before he changed directions and ran towards his horse.

Lancelot caught him before he reached the charger. "Don't," Britt heard the handsome knight say. "Let her go."

Anything else he said was lost to Britt as she entered the thick forest, leaving broken dreams and broken knights in her wake.

～

WHEN SIR BEDIVERE, Sir Lancelot, Sir Ywain, and Sir Griflet returned to Camelot, they called a meeting of Arthur's core knights. These thirty or so knights were men that had served King Arthur loyally. Most of them stood with him—her, Lancelot supposed—since she was crowned, although there were some more recent additions, like Sir Tor, Lancelot himself, and his cousins—Lionel and Bors.

Normally, the numbers of King Arthur's loyal knights was much higher, but as it was spring, many of them—like Sir Gawain and King Pellinore—were absent from the courts and were out questing.

It's just as well, Lancelot mused. *If we had any more knights present, they might turn into a mob and rip Camelot apart*, he thought as he watched a knight throw a drinking goblet at the wall.

Sir Ywain was in a shouting match with Sir Ector, and Sir Bedivere was almost boneless in his seat—he had renounced his title of marshal shortly after the so-called meeting started. Sir Griflet was still in denial, spouting ridiculous ideas like the female King Arthur was a changeling from the faeries, and they needed to rescue the real Arthur; and Sir Percival was in the process of challenging Sir Bodwain since it had been revealed the older knight knew Arthur's gender. Chaos and shouting ruled the room.

The only knight that was taking Arthur's femininity in stride was Sir Tor. The good-humored knight was not enraged or at all shaken by the proclamation. Instead, he thought about it for a few minutes before shrugging and watching the "meeting" with the same good humor with which he did everything.

"Pay up, Lionel," Sir Bors said, holding out a hand.

Sir Lionel grumbled before slapping a few coins in Sir Bors' outstretched hand.

Sir Bors smiled in satisfaction and slipped the money into a money bag on his belt.

"What was that for?" Lancelot asked with a raised eyebrow.

"When we first heard about our pretty king, we made a bet," Sir Lionel grumbled.

"I said you wouldn't raise a fuss. Lionel bet otherwise," Sir Bors said in satisfaction.

"I see," Lancelot said, unperturbed by his cousin's behavior.

"So why *aren't* you raising a fuss?" Sir Lionel asked.

"There is nothing for me to be upset about," Lancelot said, leaning back in his chair to avoid a flying plate.

"You were set on worming into Arthur's inner circle," Sir Bors pointed out.

"Certainly, but not because I actually *liked* the man," Lancelot said. "It was more that I couldn't comprehend why he didn't want me in his circle. I am the best there is," Lancelot shrugged.

"Except at sword play. My Lord—or My Lady, I suppose—has you beat there," Sir Lionel said with a cheeky smile.

Lancelot gave Sir Lionel a look so dark and hateful, a lesser man would have begged for forgiveness. As it was, Lancelot's cousin was used to receiving such a look. "Ahh, see? You *are* angry. Give me my money back, Bors."

"Our bet was how he would openly react, not what emotions he harbored silently," Sir Bors said, folding his arms across his wide chest.

"Still, I'm surprised you're not more upset," Sir Lionel said, rubbing his chin.

"It's simple. I was not emotionally invested like the foolish sops around us were. They believed in him and in his cause. Now, everything they have known and fought for has been dashed," Lancelot said.

"I don't know that everything is dashed," Sir Bors said.

Lionel continued. "I know you were never Arthur's faithful little knight like most of the Round Table, but I thought you would be angry over his—her—deception. She had the wool pulled over our eyes."

"She was most assuredly not the one doing the tricking," Lancelot snorted. "King Arthur is a female. She hasn't the intelligence necessary to run this trick. Merlin is the one who played the courts."

"Merlin was the mastermind, no doubts there," Sir Lionel nodded.

"I don't think it would be right to say that King Arthur lacks intelligence," Sir Bors argued. "Yes, Merlin must have led the charge, but she would not have gone undiscovered so long if she didn't have some measure of cunning."

"She might be like Morgause or Morgan le Fay. That would be a chilling thought," Sir Lionel said, making a face as he watched Sir Ector and Sir Ywain come to blows.

"If anything, I find it reassuring," Lancelot said. "King Arthur being female explains why she was so easily able to manipulate the men and women of her courts. A few pretty words, that wretched smile of hers, and everyone wriggled like a puppy for the beautiful woman—even if they didn't know it."

Sir Lionel looked away from the fighting and gave Lancelot a strange look.

"What is it?" Lancelot asked.

"You're acting queer."

"In what way?" Lancelot scoffed.

"You're too easily accepting whatever ideas Bors and I toss out. Not a minute ago you were calling our pretty king stupid.

Now you're saying she's a conniving female," Sir Lionel said. "Normally someone has to bash your head against a rock to get you to change your mind."

"It is odd," Sir Bors agreed.

Lancelot shrugged. "The important bit is that I am not a vested party. I don't care about King Arthur or whatever happens to her. I'm only here for the fun of it."

"Fun?" Sir Bors asked, a frown forming on his square face.

"Fun," Lancelot said with a sparkling smile. "I cannot think of a more interesting situation than watching men who used to be faithful subjects turn against a king they idolized and adored."

"You're twisted," Sir Lionel said, taking a sip from his goblet. "But that's what I like about you."

Sir Bors was still frowning.

"What, did you love and adore King Arthur like the rest of his men?" Lancelot said with a mocking smile.

Sir Bors—who was unfortunately more observant than his brother—thinned his lips. He looked like he was going to say something before he changed his mind and looked out at the chaotic crowd.

"Still, I salute you, Sir Lancelot du Lac," Sir Lionel said.

"Why?"

"It takes a great amount of fortitude to brush off the knowledge that you were soundly beaten—thrashed even—by a girl every time you crossed swords with her," Sir Lionel grinned.

Lancelot darkly scowled at his cousin—who gave a great big belly laugh—before he returned his attention to the upset knights of the Round Table.

It is interesting now, but it will be absolutely entertaining when Merlin returns, he thought.

~

BY THE END of the day, Britt knew she would be in major trouble if she didn't get her shoulder looked at. She had ridden out of Sir Damas' lands hours ago, so she couldn't ask Lady Vivenne for help. Returning to Camelot wasn't an option—and it was even farther away than Sir Damas' home.

"Maybe I could get some faerie help. I'm still in the Forest of Arroy," Britt murmured, her body drooping with pain and heartache. "But how would I know where to find any? Night will soon fall. If I don't get help by then…"

Britt swallowed with difficulty. "I need to find Merlin," she said, swaying on the back of her borrowed horse.

"My Lord?"

Britt tried to turn, but she was too weak and fell off the horse, landing on her injured shoulder. Britt hissed in pain and tried to cling to consciousness. She almost lost it when she realized Morgan le Fay stood over her, worry etched into her face.

"Morgan, are you a sight for sore eyes," Britt groaned.

"What on earth did you do to yourself, My Lord?" Morgan asked.

"Lancelot stabbed me—that traitorous jerk," Britt hissed.

Morgan pressed her lips together. "Hold on. I have a healing draught in my pack—faerie made," she said, disappearing from Britt's view.

When she returned, she carried bandages, herbs, and a glass vial—which she gave to Britt.

"This tastes awful," Britt sputtered after taking a sip.

"You would find it worse should you learn the ingredients. Drink it," she ordered.

Britt swigged the rest of the drink down as Morgan slipped Britt's shoulder out of her jerkin and inspected the wound. "It's not deep, but I have no doubts your scabbard saved your life. This should have been bandaged hours ago," Morgan said.

"How did you know about the scabbard?"

"Nymue."

"Ah, should have guessed. Anyway, it's feeling better. I think my arm was dislocated earlier. Sir Bedivere and Lancelot must have set it before they...found out," Britt said.

"Before they found out about what?" Morgan prompted, pouring a liquid from a water skin on Britt's wound.

"What *is* that?" Britt hissed, her teeth clamped in pain.

"Another healing draught. What did they find out?"

The tale spilled from Britt's lips. She explained everything from getting kidnapped by Sir Damas, to facing Sir Lancelot, and finally being revealed as a girl.

"I *knew* Lancelot was going to cause trouble. Merlin should have let me kick him out the moment I knew who he was," Britt growled.

"Your knights were going to find out eventually, My Lord," Morgan said, wrapping Britt's shoulder. "It was only a matter of time."

"As long as Merlin was with me, no one would have learned," Britt said.

"Even Merlin cannot be with you every second of the day," Morgan said.

"I know," Britt groaned. "But I've only been ruling two years. Camelot is supposed to last much longer than that! Two years, and it's already over."

"Maybe it is not," Morgan said.

"Hah! Yeah, right. Unless Merlin can erase the memories of *all* my knights—because I'm sure Lancelot opened up his big yap and told everyone at Camelot—I'm sunk."

"You think your knights will no longer follow you?" Morgan asked.

"I *know* they won't."

"How can you know? You aren't giving them a chance," Morgan pointed out.

"I know because this is ancient England. They aren't going to be okay with a woman ruling over them," Britt said. She thought Morgan would question her about her strange choice of words, but the sorceress said nothing more and finished wrapping Britt's shoulder.

"Thank you for your help," Britt said, gingerly rolling her shoulders. "It's lucky you stumbled upon me. What are you doing here—if you don't mind my asking?"

"Not at all. I was searching for Gawain and Agravain to tell them you were kidnapped," Morgan said, gathering up her supplies. "It's just as well that I found you first. What will you do?"

"Ride to London, I think," Britt said, stripping off the remaining pieces of armor she had ridden off in. "I can easily blend in there, and I know a few knights who live near there and belong to Merlin. They'll let me stay with them."

"I believe I shall return to Camelot," Morgan said. "Perhaps my nephews have already returned."

"Would you tell Merlin where I am?" Britt asked.

"Certainly, if I see him. Merlin and Sir Kay set out to search for you when Sir Damas kidnapped you," Morgan said.

"Merlin will return to Camelot," Britt promised.

"Shall we spend the night together? I cannot ride back to Camelot tonight, and you have several days of travel before you will reach London," Morgan said.

"It would be a relief to camp with someone," Britt said, giving Morgan a weak smile. "Thank you."

"For?" Morgan asked as she started unhooking packs from the white donkey she rode.

"For helping me, for listening to me. I'm lucky to have you in this..." Britt trailed off, unable to think of a label for her nightmare.

"I believe you will see the situation with new eyes tomorrow,

My Lord. All is not lost. Your knights may be troubled, but their hearts still stand with you."

Britt exhaled deeply. "I'll start finding wood for our campfire. Is that alright?"

"Of course."

6

SHEEP WITHOUT A SHEPHERD

Britt slept very little that night. For the first time since her arrival in medieval Britain, she wasn't kept awake by thoughts and memories of the friends and family she left behind in the twenty-first century, but by the nightmarish events of the day. The expression of betrayal in Sir Bedivere's eyes and Ywain's barely contained rage seemed to set up a permanent base near the front of her mind.

In the morning, Morgan asked Britt to return to Camelot with her. Britt refused. The sorceress did not seem surprised by the refusal and packed up her camp.

"Take this—you'll need it if you are to survive the journey to London," Morgan said, offering out two stuffed saddle packs.

"What's in them?" Britt asked.

"Some provisions, a blanket, extra bandages, a hunting knife, and the like."

"I can't take all of that from you," Britt said.

"You can, and you will. I will reach Camelot this afternoon. You have several more days of travel before you," Morgan said, taking the packs from Britt and placing them on the back of Britt's horse. "I will not force you to return to Camelot with me, but I will *not* allow you to go gallivanting into the wild without any sort of equipment," she said, securing the packs to the saddle.

"Thanks, Morgan," Britt said.

"It is the least I can do," Morgan said before returning to her donkey. She nimbly lifted herself into her side-saddle and fixed her skirts. "I wish you would return. You underestimate your knights—and yourself."

Britt shook her head. "The rule of Arthur is over—unless Merlin can track the real one down. Thank you, Morgan. I hope I see you again," Britt said.

"So do I, My Lord," Morgan said before she nudged her donkey into a walk.

Britt watched the beautiful sorceress disappear through the trees before she turned and mounted her horse. She glanced around the abandoned camp and nudged her horse forward, heading for London.

She rode all morning long without meeting a soul. That didn't surprise her much—medieval England was far less inhabited than its modern-day counterpart. What Britt did find odd, though, was the lack of vagrants, bandits, and recreant knights.

Based on the stories her knights gave her, she thought the countryside was crawling with them. This did not seem to be so, based on the lack of contact.

Britt shrugged it off and plodded along, stopping several times to water her horse or to walk next to it and stretch her legs.

It was mid-afternoon when Britt finally heard another voice —although it was loud and angry.

Curious, Britt guided her horse through the trees, ducking low-hanging branches. She popped into a meadow, where two children stood with a flock of sheep.

A knight in dingy armor, mounted on a muscled stallion, held a razor-sharp spear at one of the kids—a dirty little girl—in a menacing manner.

The other child—a boy just a little older than the girl—held onto a squirming lamb.

Britt frowned and unsheathed her borrowed sword. Her shoulder protested at the use, and Britt checked to make sure Excalibur's empty scabbard was still strapped to her before she nudged her horse closer.

"Slaughter the lamb, boy. It is a proper tithe to a knight of great importance," the knight growled.

"I can't! They're not even our sheep," the boy cried, white faced and panicked.

The little girl started crying, and the knight swung his mount closer to her.

I can't leave them; I'll have to bluff. Britt heeled her horse so it shot into the meadow. She steered the horse with her legs and swung the sword up with her good arm—roaring like some of her knights did when they were about to attack.

The knight turned around and saw her coming. He raised his spear—as if to run her through.

"For Arthur!" Britt shouted in a moment of inspiration.

Surprisingly, the knight wheeled his horse around and, wildly kicking it, fled from the meadow.

Britt watched him go with wide eyes. "I can't believe that worked." She rested the sword on her saddle and stopped her gelding near the children. "Hello," she said, looking down to see the kids staring at her with adoring gazes.

"You're one of King Arthur's knights?" the boy asked, his voice worshipful.

"Do you sit at the Round Table?" the little girl asked, clapping her hands.

"Where is the rest of your armor?"

"Are Sir Ywain and Sir Griflet out questing again?"

"Children, I apologize. I'm not on a quest; I'm just trying to reach London," Britt said, interrupting the flow of questions.

"But are you from Camelot?" the boy urgently asked.

"Yeeees," Britt slowly admitted.

"Thank you for saving us," the girl said, doing her best to curtsey in her tattered skirts.

"It was good of you! Come back home with us," the boy said.

"I, err, I'm on my way to London," Britt repeated.

"But everyone will want to meet you," the boy said, crestfallen.

Britt was at a loss. Most of the peasants she met were awed by her—she thought they were awed by her knights as well. What gave these children such unrestrained enthusiasm? Typically, peasants were expected to bow and scrape before knights and noble ladies.

"Don't you need more provisions if you're goin' to London?" the girl asked.

"Our village will replenish you," the boy said.

"I suppose so," Britt reluctantly said.

"Great—we have to take the sheep back anyhow. This way," the little girl said, running to gather stray sheep.

"What's your name, Sir knight?" the boy asked, finally releasing the squirming lamb.

Britt thought for a moment, trying to invent a name. Last time she used one of her knights' names, it nearly blew up in her face, given that the *real* Ywain found her. "I'm...Sir Galla...Sir Galahad," Britt said, congratulating herself on the neat use of the word gallant.

"Sir Galahad, I ain't heard of you," the boy said.

"I'm a new addition to Arthur's court," Britt said.

"Oh."

"Caerl, get that sheep," the little girl shouted, pointing to a stray sheep as she herded the rest of the livestock along.

Britt reluctantly dismounted her horse and followed the children on foot. They walked for about twenty minutes before they left the forest and joined a dirt road. Britt could see a castle in the distance—it was crumbling and even smaller than Sir Damas'. Spread before the castle was a small village of cottages. Puffs of smoke trickled out of chimneys; chickens scratched in the dirt and grass; donkeys brayed, and several goats baaed.

"Arth! Arth!" the boy shouted, running ahead of the sheep. "We found another knight, Arth!"

A young man exited a barn, leading a donkey behind him. He couldn't have been older than Griflet or Ywain, but he wore a cheerful countenance and was built with broad shoulders and ripped arms. "Caerl, Isel—you're back already?"

The girl—Isel—burst away from the sheep—scattering them in her path—and skid to a stop in front of the young man. "Sir Rancor returned and was demanding a lamb—"

"One of Betta's lambs, the best one! I was going to run, but Isel threw a rock—" Caerl tried to add.

"I had to—he renounced Arthur as King! And he said Baron Marhaus was a stupid old codger!" Isel said, sounding scandalized.

"Sir Galahad saved us. He's not questing, though, just riding through. He wouldn't say if Sir Griflet and Sir Ywain are questing —do ya think they are? When will they come back?" Caerl said, gesturing to Britt—who was securing her horse to a wooden fence.

"Sir Galahad is going to London, but he doesn't have all his armor," Isel said.

"Children, enough," Arth said. He had to raise his voice to be heard over the chatter. "Go tell Edla your tale. She's out with the chickens."

Immediately Caerl and Isel turned on their heels and ran—hollering and screaming. "Edla! Edla!"

Britt saw a very pregnant girl waddle around a cottage and wave to the children.

"Wait—the sheep..." Arth trailed off with a sigh.

"They're charming children," Britt said as she started chasing sheep into the small, fenced-in area.

"They are *not* mine. Oh! Please, noble sir," Arth said, rushing to help when he realized what she was doing. "You need not lower yourself to this."

"It's fine," Britt said, feeling a little awkward from her sudden arrival and being abandoned by the kids.

"T'is not," Arth firmly said. "Caerl said you saved them?"

"It was much less glorious than it sounds. I stumbled up them and ran at the knight shouting at the top of my lungs," Britt said, wincing when a sheep ran over her feet.

"T'was honorable of you," Arth said.

Britt would have shrugged if not for her injured shoulder. "Am I in the lands of Baron Marhaus?"

"Aye, that's his fortress yonder," Arth said, nodding at the crumbling structure.

It took Britt a moment to remember all she knew about Baron Marhaus. The man was, if she recalled correctly, kind enough. He swore to her when she pulled the sword from the stone on Pentecost in London and had lent her a few troops in her fight against King Lot, King Urien, King Ryence, and their lackeys. He also didn't seem to mind that she sent her knights near his lands.

"I've heard he is a fair man. Is that true?" Britt carefully asked. (Last time she thought well of an ally, it turned out he was nothing but a greedy cheapskate.)

"Oh, yes," Arth said, shooing a sheep into the paddock. "He's quite nice. He comes riding through the village some days and says kind things to the children. He's gettin' a little up in the years and hasn't any heirs, I'm afraid to say. His court is small, too—that's why we're grateful to King Arthur."

Britt blinked. "I beg your pardon?"

"Before he sent his knights out questing, we used to get a lot of recreant knights demanding tithes and the like. Good ol' Marhaus couldn't take care of 'em, but you knights from Camelot do a smash-up job," Arth grunted.

"Who has been here before?" Britt asked.

"Sir Ywain and Sir Griflet hung around a bit last year. We saw Sir Gawain in the early fall, once. This spring, we even hosted King Pellinore for a night," Arth boasted with a broad smile.

Britt smiled fondly at the listed knights. All four of them were open men who didn't expect honors—no wonder the kids treated her more like a favorite uncle than a regent. "I know those men. They are very noble."

"Aye," Arth said when the last sheep ran into the paddock. He slapped his tunic, making a dust cloud puff up. "Isel and Caerl said you're going to London?"

"Yes."

"You can spend the night here, if you wish. We would be honored to have you, especially after you saved that pair," Arth said.

Britt thought about his offer for a moment. She wasn't in any great hurry to reach London—it wasn't like her knights would come galloping after her anyway—and she didn't relish the idea of sleeping outdoors without any company—or Excalibur.

"I will take you up on your offer, Master Arth. Thank you."

"Oh, no. Thank you," Arth smiled before he ran a hand through his dirty, strawberry-blonde hair. (He would have been handsome if he wasn't so grungy.) "I will speak to my wife, Edla, but I'm certain you can stay with us, if not Isel and Caerl's family."

"Thank you," Britt said, patting her horse.

"If you'd like, I can show you where you can stable that fine boy for the night."

"Yes, please. I would like to strip him of his tack and rub him down."

"Right, then. This way, Sir."

Britt unhitched her horse and followed the swarthy fellow, forcing a smile to her lips even though her heart still ached from the events of the previous day.

~

W‌HEN S‌IR G‌AWAIN AND K‌ING P‌ELLINORE returned to Camelot, everyone was still in an uproar. "What's going on?" Sir Gawain asked when he entered the hall of the Round Table. He expected to find King Arthur there. Instead, he found twenty or thirty knights who were in various stages of anger and drunkenness.

"You haven't heard? Have I got a shiner for you, cousin," Ywain said, struggling to stand upright as he held a goblet of mead. "King Arthur is a girl."

Agravain, who walked next to Gawain, tensed. "What?" Agravain growled.

"Yep," Ywain said. "A girl—complete with the looks and the-the—everything," Ywain said, vaguely motioning with his cup. He sloshed mead and frowned at his hand before giving his cousins a hiccupping laugh. "We've been had! He—*she*—lied to us, played with us, led us on. She strung us along like ducklings—worse than your mother. No offense."

Agravain's frown grew dark, and he narrowed his eyes.

"Agravain?" Gawain said, nudging his younger brother. He held his breath as Agravain processed the information.

When Agravain said nothing, Gawain returned to questioning Ywain. "How did you find out?"

"Lancelot stabbed her in the shoulder," Ywain said with a great deal of carelessness.

"*What?*" Gawain said.

Ywain was occupied drinking his mead, so Gawain grabbed him by the shoulders and shook him. "Is she alright? What happened? Why haven't you killed Lancelot for his act?"

Ywain snorted. "She's *fine*. She blacked out, and Bedivere started to strip her to get at the wound. That stopped him quick."

"You mean no one has seen to her shoulder, yet? Where is she?" Gawain asked, concern making his voice tight.

"Gone. Who knows where. Good riddance," Ywain said,

watching one knight take a chair to another knight. "You're taking this awfully calmly, you know?"

"I already knew," Gawain said, his mind racing. He had to find Arthur. Goodness knew what would happen or how badly she was hurt—and Excalibur was still here, at Camelot!

"You *what*?" Ywain squawked. "How?"

"Mother told me," Gawain said, already calculating what he would need to pack.

"And you didn't think to tell me?" Ywain scowled.

Gawain shrugged. "It was King Arthur's secret to reveal, not mine."

"You're so bloody noble, it sickens me. How could you not be mad about this deception? Who knows if she *ever* told the truth? I bet she laughed behind our backs. Aren't you mad, Agravain?" Ywain asked his younger cousin.

Agravain shifted. "A bit," he finally said.

"A bit? That's it? I thought you would blow your top," Ywain complained.

"That's because you smell like you crawled into a mead barrel a week ago and surfaced only recently," Agravain frowned.

"Why aren't you mad, brother?" Gawain asked.

"It doesn't make much of a difference if Arthur is a man or woman, does it? I mean, I would rather have Arthur rule than father," Agravain said.

This point was surprisingly well thought, considering Agravain was usually the most passionate of the four Orkney princes. Gawain was a little surprised, but not much. Agravain had blossomed in Arthur's courts, and his loyalty lay close to his bones. It would take all of hell to make him forfeit his loyalty to Arthur.

"Well said," Gawain said, resting a hand on his brother's shoulder and smiling. "I mean to leave and track her down. Do you wish to come with me?"

"What?" Ywain squawked again.

"Of course," Agravain said, ignoring his inebriated cousin. "When do we leave?"

"As soon as possible," Gawain said, leading the way back to the door. He was surprised when he opened it to find Morgan le Fay on the other side. "Aunt," he blinked.

"Arthur is fine," Morgan said, as if she could read his mind. "I met with her after Lancelot ran her through. The wound isn't terrible—though I would feel better if she was back here in Camelot under Merlin's care."

"She didn't return with you?" Gawain asked.

Morgan shook her head. "She wouldn't, stubborn thing. She means to travel to London and stay with one of Merlin's men. I suspect she's waiting to see what Merlin will do."

"That makes sense, I suppose," Gawain said.

"What do we do?" Agravain asked.

"I would advise you to wait for Merlin to make his move before you decide if you should attempt to retrieve Arthur," Morgan said.

"That sounds wise," Gawain said.

"*What?*" a deep voice boomed from in the hall.

"Looks like King Pellinore just found out," Morgan said looking past Gawain and Agravain.

Gawain winced, and Agravain scowled.

"I will wait for Merlin before I seek out King Arthur, but I will not stand by and let my fellow knights act like this," Gawain said, frowning as there was a crash when one knight pushed another knight to the ground.

"Good luck," Morgan said. "Take care, nephews," she said before sweeping away from the door.

Gawain grimly surveyed his fellow knights. King Pellinore was seated on a chair with a look of stupor hung on his face. Most of the other knights were wild with rage and disappointment. Only Sir Tor, Sir Lancelot, Sir Lionel, and Sir Bors looked to be of good cheer.

"What will you say to 'em?" Agravain asked.

"What do you think Arthur would say to them?" Gawain asked.

Agravain considered the question for a moment before replying, "He would probably make a grand speech about everyone still being the pride of his heart."

"Her heart," Gawain corrected his brother.

"Of course. I don't think it will work for you, though. She's the one they love and trust. Trusted," Agravain warned.

"I still have to try," Gawain grimly said before approaching the Round Table. "Enough! Knights of Camelot—enough of this foolishness!" he tried shouting.

Most of the knights couldn't hear him over the din, but Sir Tor did.

"PEACE!" the ex-cow-herder bellowed, his voice filling every space of the room.

"Thank you," Gawain said in the sudden silence.

"Of course," Sir Tor said with his ever-cheerful smile.

Gawain cleared his throat before he addressed his friends and companions. "Why do you act so...so disgracefully? We are knights of the Round Table. We are held to acts of honor and chivalry—not drunken displays of rage."

"Says you. You're the one who knew all along!" Ywain snorted.

"Why do you act like this?" Gawain asked.

"Because Arthur betrayed us!" Griflet shouted. He looked lost and frightened—as if someone had stolen his lady love from him.

"In what way? She is still the just and honorable leader we have known and served these past two years," Gawain said.

"Nay, I imagine this was all Merlin's doing," Sir Bedivere said, his expression was dead. "Every last bit. From whom appointed to those she favored."

"Do you really think that?" Gawain asked. "We have seen Arthur confront Merlin before—on our behalf!"

"And what if it's all for show?" another knight called off. "What if we're just tools?"

"We were always meant to be tools. That's why we swore loyalty to her," Gawain said.

"I would never swear an oath of fealty to a *woman*," another knight scoffed.

"Why not?" Sir Tor asked.

"Because she would be *inferior*," the knight said, giving Sir Tor a withering glare.

"That's not how I see it," Sir Tor said.

"What would you know? You sit in the King's pocket!"

Sir Tor grinned so nicely, the knight who scoffed at him couldn't help but soften his stance and sit down. "Now, that's an exaggeration. I'm not in the King's inner circle. Not like Sir Ywain and Sir Bedivere and the like. I think Arthur's been just, and I'm pleased to serve him—her—but that's as deep as our relationship goes."

"Then why defend her?" Ywain demanded. "If you weren't a lapdog like us, why stick up for her?"

"It's what she taught us, isn't it? That's what being a knight is about—righting wrongs and such. Besides, you forget. I was once a cow herder."

Griflet blinked. "So?"

"So if a cow herder can be a knight, why can't a girl be a ruling monarch?" Sir Tor pointed out.

"Those are completely different instances," a knight protested.

"You didn't disguise what you were, and mislead us and misdirect us," Ywain added.

"You all seem intent on thinking that My Lord, that *Our* Lord, is somehow a different person because of this," Gawain said. "Then I pose you a question: Why did Merlin use Arthur? He could have used any stupid sop he came across. Why would he dress up a girl and crown her King of Britain?"

No one had a response.

193

"You cannot believe that Merlin didn't know who she was," Gawain continued. "As that is the case, that must mean he saw something of worth in her. Something that made him believe that she could rule."

"Maybe so, but that doesn't account for the lies and false-hoods her rule is built on!"

"If King Arthur couldn't tell us the truth, how can we expect her to be just and true?"

"Hear, hear!"

"It is good if we wait to hear from Merlin before any brash actions are committed," King Pellinore finally said, his voice breaking through the anger that was starting to stir up again. "It does not sit well with me that I have been lied to, but I have seen King Arthur's heart in his actions, and it is good."

Gawain looked at Pellinore with an expression of thankful-ness. The King barely shrugged his shoulders. "We'll see," he rumbled to Gawain. "I'm not yet convinced. But I know Arthur well enough that I would like to hear the entire story."

"It's enough if we give her a chance," Gawain said, although his heart sank as he looked out over the Round Table. Although the men let Gawain speak, it was obvious he hadn't gotten through to any of them.

The knights sported clenched fists, angry expressions, and hearts filled with pain.

Where are you, My Lord? Gawain wondered when a knight shouted for more wine and mead. *Why won't you return to us? No one else can lead them.*

7

BACK TO CAMELOT

E arly the following morning, Britt was up to say farewell to Caerl and Isel—who were off to take the sheep to another grazing area.

"Come back and visit again, Sir Galahad!" Caerl shouted as he hurried after the livestock.

"Tell a minstrel about how you saved us!" Isel said, waving frantically.

"Isel, come on!" Caerl called. Shortly after, the two disappeared into the woods, the baas of the sheep meandering away with them.

Britt inhaled and looked to the sky—which was still dark with night. The sun wasn't even a sliver over the horizon yet, and it was extra cool and chilly. "Might as well get an early start for London," she murmured, turning to the stable her horse shared with two donkeys, several chickens, and a number of goats.

"Sir Galahad, come break your fast with us," Arth shouted, spying her in the yard.

"Your village has already given me plenty of hospitality, Master Arth. I cannot ask for more," Britt said.

Edla—Arth's outspoken and extremely pregnant wife—

snorted. "You stayed with Caerl and Isel's family last night. T'was hardly great hospitality."

"That may be so, but I saved their children. I have done nothing to aid either of you."

"Nay, that isn't so," Arth said. "Most of those sheep Caerl and little Isel watch are ours. With Edla due any day, I try to stay closer to home, so I watch their goats in exchange," Arth said, smiling at his wife.

"You had better let them out," Edla said, nodding her head at the stable. "I'll have food ready by the time you return."

"Yes, my heart," Arth said with a wide smile. He kissed Edla's cheek and was rewarded with a gentle smack before he left the cottage.

"I'll come, too. I would like to see how my horse is," Britt said, following the shepherd. They entered the stable and were greeted by a wave of animal noises. Britt slid into her horse's stall as Arth waded through the chickens to the small pen in which the goats were kept at the back of the stable.

"What takes you to London, Sir Galahad?" Arth asked, scratching the forehead of a caramel-colored goat.

"I'm seeking out a few friends there," Britt vaguely answered, running her hands up and down her mount's legs.

"I see. London is a great city," Arth said. "The jousting fields there are a sight of beauty."

"You've been to London?" Britt asked, surprised. It was unusual for commoners to travel great distances.

"Aye, my family traveled there a number of times. T'was dangerous then, but I imagine with King Arthur's knights out questing, your travels will be filled with less peril," Arth said.

"Do they really make such a big difference?" Britt asked.

"Aren't you a knight of Camelot? Don't you know?" Arth asked.

Britt picked up a brush and started briskly brushing the horse.

"I mostly stayed in the city limits. I wasn't often given a chance to quest."

"Ahh. Then I can testify to the difference. Arthur's knights quest through the Forest of Arroy and beyond. Usually they are seeking out adventures—damsels in distress, mythical beasts and the like. As they ride, though, they come across us common people. If we're plagued by recreant knights, they'll rid us of the problem. Some will take on bandits. I even heard a story from a village not far from here that Sir Tor rode through and met a farmer whose horse had thrown a shoe and couldn't pull a wagon load. Sir Tor hooked his own mount up and drove the farmer home," Arth said.

Britt leaned against her horse, longing stabbing her heart like a dagger. "So they really do perform good deeds," she said, her voice soft with affection.

"Aye, Sir Galahad. They're changing the country," Arth said, checking on a baby goat.

Britt was glad he was distracted, for her eyes stung with unshed tears. She hid behind her horse's neck and tried to brush her traitorous heart aside. *There's no use regretting it. I've lost them; I've lost my title. I can't change that. They'll never accept me as King Arthur again.*

"What has you seeking out your friends in London, if you don't mind my asking?" Arth asked.

Britt had ceased to be shocked by the villager's informality the previous night. She cleared her throat and petted her horse before she returned to brushing it. "I'm fighting with a number of my friends and acquaintances, truth be told."

"Has King Arthur exiled you?"

Britt couldn't hold back her snort of laughter. "No," she finally said. "King Arthur and I are on excellent terms. It's the rest of the Round Table that are...uneasy with me."

"What happened?"

"I lied to them. I made them believe things about me that

weren't true," Britt said. Merlin would likely rip her tongue out for even referring to the events of the Round Table, but he wasn't here, and it was comforting to tell an outside party of her problems. For too long Britt had carried the weight of her lie and everything it encompassed. It was freeing to cast it off like an old sweater—even if Britt's heart twisted as she remembered Griflet's denial or Sir Bedivere's look of betrayal.

"I find it difficult to think that King Arthur's knights would hold such a grudge," Arth said. "Why, Our Lord's closest knights are the offspring of his enemies. Misleading is hardly the stuff of traitors."

"No, I don't blame them for their anger. My lies hurt them more deeply than I imagined," Britt dully said, recalling Ywain's passionate anger.

"And they won't forgive you?"

"I'm sure they won't."

"You mean you haven't *asked*?" Arth said.

"If I did, there is a chance they might become...violent," Britt said.

"King Arthur's knights? The knights of the Round Table, of Camelot?" Arth shook his head. "I think you've misjudged them, Sir Galahad. Besides, if you still have favor with the King, can't he pardon you?"

Britt gurgled with laughter. "No, I'm afraid not. Not even Arthur could save me now."

Arth was silent, and the barn was filled with soft animal noises and the rustling of straw. When Britt looked up, she found the young man's eyes thoughtfully glued to her.

"You seem to know the knights well," Britt said, casting the brush aside.

"I hear many stories about them, and King Arthur," Arth vaguely said as he hopped over the goat pen and leaned up against a stall door. "You know, Sir Galahad, you are at a crossroad."

"A what?"

"A meeting point of roads. I went through one myself a short while ago," Arth said.

Britt cocked her head in curiosity. Arth looked barely seventeen or eighteen-years-old. What could he have possibly faced to be considered a crossroad? "What happened?"

"I met Edla. I loved her greatly, but if I married her, I would ruin my family's plans for me," Arth said. "I thought about what they wanted me to do, the person they wanted me to become, and I realized it wasn't for me. So Edla and I eloped and ran off."

"You must have been quite young," Britt said.

Arth laughed. "I was just a boy, but I've never regretted it. Edla and I belong here, in the village. We're happy. This is who I really am. But who are you, Sir Galahad?"

Britt shifted uncomfortably. "What do you mean?" she asked. He couldn't possibly have known that Galahad was a made-up name!

"I mean, who are you? Are you the person you led your friends to think you are, or was that entirely false?"

"Not all of it was," Britt was quick to say. Sure, she wasn't a teenage boy, but the things she said to her knights, her pursuit of honor and peace, all of those were true.

"It is who you are that matters—the way you act, the things you believe in, and the words you speak. If those are true, then who cares of your parentage? Who cares about your past or history? The knights of the Round Table don't follow King Arthur because he's good with the sword or as beautiful as a faerie. They follow him because they believe in his cause, and they believe in his heart. Do they believe in your heart, Sir Galahad?"

Britt was more than a little disconcerted that this young commoner was able to talk to her about the matter as if he knew what was wrong. But he was right.

Britt had lied about her gender and her origins, but that didn't change the heart of King Arthur. That didn't change her desire to see Britain changed or to see her knights righting wrongs and fighting for the weak and oppressed. She didn't have to be ashamed of being a woman. Although she lived in a time where female rulers weren't the usual thing, she also lived in a time where it was unheard of to have knights help those in need—and hadn't she changed that? Hadn't her knights changed that?

I have to go back, Britt grimly realized. *I have to apologize, and I have to remind them their oaths are worthwhile. They might not have me as their king again, but I can't let them throw away everything we've fought for.*

"Thank you for your wise words, Arth," Britt said as she threw a blanket on her horse's back. "You have helped me more than you know. Please give my apologies to Edla, but I won't be... um...breaking my fast with you," Britt said, placing the saddle on her gelding.

Arth watched Britt with a soft, pleased smile. "Aye, My Lord. I'll see if I can get you a few food items to take with on your return to Camelot."

"Thank you," Britt called over her shoulder as she slipped the girth around her horse's belly and tightened it—hearing but not necessarily taking in the shepherd's words.

When Britt finished readying her mount, the sun was over the horizon, casting streaks of warm, golden light into the sky.

"Thank you for...everything," Britt said, unable to put into words what the young couple had done.

"It was our pleasure, Sir Galahad. Thank you for saving Caerl, Isel, and our sheep," Edla said, leaning against Arth's chest with a smile.

"I wish you well, Sir Galahad. May the knights of Camelot hear you out," Arth said.

Britt swung up into the saddle. "Thank you. I hope they will. Even if they won't, I have to try."

"Godspeed," Edla said, waving to Britt.

"Thank you," Britt said before she nudged her horse into a trot, heading back to the Forest of Arroy.

Edla and Arth watched her go until Edla yelped, "The soup!" and scurried back inside their cottage.

Arth stayed outside, watching the woman-King ride off. Sir Ector was right—she was beautiful with a spirit that was just as pure. Arth—Arthur—had toyed with the idea of telling her who he was, but he was glad he hadn't. A person like her would think it to be her responsibility to give up the throne for him, and he was happy with Edla, the village, and his sheep. "God bless you, King Arthur. No matter your gender, you're the rightful King of Britain."

~

"*YOU WHAT?*" Sir Kay thundered. His voice was raised in one of his very rare shouts—Merlin had known him for ages and could count on one hand how many times the taciturn knight had yelled.

"She's not who she said she is," Sir Ywain said, his eyes red and his hair greasy. Finding out who Britt really was had taken an obvious toll on the knight.

"That doesn't matter," Sir Kay hissed. "What *does* matter is that our king was wounded—by one of her own knights—and you set her off without seeing to her injury? You *FOOL!*"

"She's nothing but a liar," Sir Ywain spat.

"She is your *KING* to whom you owe your life—and you abandoned her in a time of need," Sir Kay snarled. "You're not a knight. You're nothing but a child playing pretend."

"You—! I will challenge you if you do not take back your words," Sir Ywain said.

"Please, *do* challenge me. I will gladly break your bones on the jousting field," Sir Kay said, looming over the younger knight.

Griflet rubbed his eyes. "Will this nightmare never end? Can't we put this behind us?" he asked.

Merlin barely heard the argument. His mind was spinning. This was worse than he imagined. Most of the order of the Round Table knew the truth about Britt—or at least about her gender. He thought this would happen eventually, but he didn't think she would get ousted this soon. What should his first move be? Which part of his network should he notify first? And most important of all, how was Britt managing with her injury?

"Excuse me, Merlin," Sir Gawain said, his voice barely audible over Sir Kay's roars and Sir Ywain's shouts.

"What?" Merlin said, his voice tight with tension.

"If I might speak to you for a moment?"

"Time is rather precious right now, Prince Gawain. What is it?"

"It's about King Arthur. My aunt Morgan saw him—her."

"Ywain, Griflet. Both of you; get out," Merlin said.

"No, I demand to know why you did this," Sir Ywain said.

"I did it because Britt Arthurs is the best monarch in all of history that we could hope for. Now get out," Merlin said.

"Come, Ywain," Sir Griflet sighed.

Sir Ywain glowered at Merlin and then Sir Kay before he strode from the room, the muscles of his shoulders tight with anger. Griflet followed him out, closing the door behind them.

"Now, what did Morgan have to say about Arthur?" Merlin asked, turning every ounce of his attention to Sir Gawain.

"She saw to her shoulder wound. She said it wasn't too bad—as long as My Lord keeps it bandaged and doesn't involve herself in any fights, it should heal fine. King Arthur charged my aunt with passing a message on to you," Gawain said.

Merlin eyed the younger knight. "And you are playing messenger boy?"

"My aunt is traveling today to see the Lady of the Lake," Gawain said.

Some of Merlin's tension eased. Morgan and Nymue were Britt's staunch allies. If Morgan was seeking out Nymue, it was likely for help. "What is the message?"

"King Arthur is traveling to London. She said she knew several knights who are allied with you. She plans to seek them out and wait for instructions there," Gawain said.

"That is all?" Merlin asked.

Sir Gawain nodded.

Merlin threw himself into a chair. "Thank you for the information, Sir Gawain."

Sensing the dismissal, Sir Gawain bowed and left Merlin's study.

"She's been seen to," Sir Kay said, leaning against one of Merlin's workbenches in his relief.

"It doesn't mean she hasn't come to additional harm," Merlin said, earning a dark look from Sir Kay. "But I think it is unlikely she will be attacked. If she is riding to London, she will be in the Forest of Arroy for a long time. Her knights have cleaned it up so well, I wonder if there are more than eight or nine recreant knights in the whole place."

Before Sir Kay could reply, the door swung open to admit Sir Bodwain and Sir Ector into Merlin's study.

"You've heard, I take it?" Sir Bodwain asked after looking from Merlin to Sir Kay.

"We've heard that Britt was wounded and discovered—though Morgan le Fay later treated her wounds and set her on the path to London," Merlin said.

"That is the whole of it," Sir Ector wearily sighed. "I'm worried about her, Merlin."

"She's wise beyond her years. She will make it to London," Merlin said.

"What do we do about the knights? They've been in an uproar since Sir Lancelot, Sir Ywain, Sir Griflet, and Sir Bedivere returned. It's a miracle they haven't spread the news through the whole castle—although everyone knows they are unhappy with Arthur," Sir Bodwain said.

Merlin closed his eyes and thought. Or he tried to think. Instead, his mind was filled with images of Britt, scared and hurt by her knight's anger.

This is what affection for another person does, Merlin grimly thought. *It ruins your ability to reason and think clearly.* Merlin was not pleased with this realization, but he also recognized he was incapable of dealing with the consequence at this moment. He needed to concentrate. *England* needed him to concentrate.

"We do nothing," Merlin finally said.

Sir Bodwain stared at him. "I beg your pardon, *what* did you just say?"

"We do nothing," Merlin repeated.

"*Nothing*? But—can't you use magic? Or talk to the knights? They still trust you—I am certain of it. King Pellinore got them to hold off judgment until you arrived. And you will do *nothing*?" Sir Bodwain gaped.

"I cannot alter the memories of so many men—not to mention all of Camelot. My magic is not that plentiful," Merlin said.

"Couldn't you at least talk to them? Make them see it's not all bad?" Sir Ector said.

"I could, but I won't," Merlin said.

"Why not?" Sir Kay asked.

Merlin drummed his fingers on the arm of his chair. "Because if I meddle, Arthur's knights—Britt's knights—will never trust her again. I will become the person they hinge their hopes on."

"What of it?" Sir Bodwain said. "Have you not noticed, Merlin? If this does not end soon, our plans are doomed. Camelot will not survive this upheaval, and the knights will trust *no one*. All of our work will be destroyed, and once again, Britain will fracture into thousands of tiny fiefdoms and kingdoms.

Rome will sense we are weak, and they will attack," Sir Bodwain grimly predicted.

"I know that," Merlin said, "but I won't act."

"Merlin," Sir Bodwain said, shaking his head.

"Those knights belong to Britt Arthurs," Merlin said. "I will not take them from her. She is *fully* the King of Britain. If Camelot is to be saved, it will be by her hand."

"But Merlin, you could do it," Sir Ector said, his brow puckered with confusion. "You could reclaim it."

"And Britt will lose them forever," Merlin said.

"But if you don't act, *we* will lose everything," Sir Bodwain said.

"It doesn't matter," Merlin said. "I have faith in Britt. She will return. And when she does, she deserves a chance to rally her men again. Even if it means our plans might fail."

Sir Bodwain and Sir Ector gaped at each other.

Sir Bodwain spent a few more minutes trying to convince Merlin otherwise, but Merlin stood firm. Finally, Sir Bodwain left—saying he would pass Merlin's decree on to Sir Ulfius.

Sir Ector shook his head. "I never thought I would see this day."

"What?" Merlin asked. "The ruin of Camelot?"

"No," Sir Ector said. "The day you would allow affection to put all your schemes and plans in possible jeopardy." The older knight smiled wanly. "You've changed, Merlin. For the better, I think."

Sir Ector's observation chilled Merlin.

It's true. It is riskier to put my hopes in Britt instead of taking care of this matter myself. So why don't I? Even with his vast experience, great intelligence, and superior knowledge, Merlin could not answer his own question.

8

REDEFINED

It took Britt two days to ride back to Camelot. When she arrived, the guards at the gatehouse greeted her with relief. "Welcome home, My Lord," they said with broad smiles.

"Thank you," Britt smiled, nudging her horse forward. Any of the townsfolk or guards Britt ran across smiled at her, as if the mere sight of her could ease their tension.

"I guess they didn't tell everyone," Britt murmured as she rode the path that led to the keep. She passed the inner walls and directed her horse to the stables. She dismounted and led the horse into the barn.

She passed the chestnut off to a groom when she heard someone from the stable yard shout, "Arthur's here? Arthur!"

Sir Ector—with Sir Kay on his heels—waddled into the stable, a bright smile on his face.

"Dad," Britt said, her eyes momentarily clouding with emotion before she ran across the stable and hugged her foster-father.

Sir Ector squeezed her tight. It made her shoulder wound protest, but Britt didn't care. Hugging Sir Ector made her feel like a child again, and like everything would work out.

Sir Ector finally released her and anxiously looked at her shoulder. "How's your wound?"

"Stiff, but manageable."

"We should have gutted Lancelot," Sir Kay muttered.

Britt laughed and threw her arms around a surprised Kay. "You're a man after my own heart, Kay," Britt said, happy and amused for the first time since her parting with Lancelot, Ywain, Griflet, and Bedivere.

Sir Kay awkwardly patted her back. "I am glad you are safe, My Lord," he said.

"I would never dare to return to you in any state besides complete health. Or, mostly healthy I guess," she said, stepping back to give Sir Kay some space.

"We heard you meant to go to London. What good fortune brought you back to us?" Sir Ector asked.

"Kind people. I met a nice shepherd in a little village on Baron Marhaus' lands," Britt said.

Sir Ector seemed to suddenly have a great fascination with the ceiling. "Oh?" he politely asked.

"Father has traveled there a number of times in the past year or so. Baron Marhaus is a personal friend of yours, is he not?" Sir Kay said, turning to look at his father.

"I've been there a time or two," Sir Ector said.

His cagey reply made both Britt and Kay frown.

Britt was about to press the matter further when her thoughts were interrupted.

"Britt."

She looked past Ector and Kay to see Merlin standing at the stable entrance.

"Ah," Sir Ector said, casting a glance over his shoulder before grabbing his much taller son. "Come along, Kay."

"I'm not leaving."

"Yes, you are. Come along," Sir Ector said, yanking Kay out of the stable.

Kay suspiciously eyed Merlin but followed his father into the stable yard.

Britt wished they hadn't left. She would now be forced to tell Merlin about her failure alone. They were silent for a minute. Britt stared at Merlin's brown boots—a copy cat pair of her own boots she had personally designed and badgered a cobbler into making for her. Merlin, however, stared at her without embarrassment.

When Britt could stand it no longer, she finally spoke. "I'm sorry."

"For?"

"For ruining your plans. They found me out. I tried to stop them, but I passed out. I know—"

"Britt," Merlin said, interrupting her stream of apologies. "It's not your fault."

"Well, yeah. Lancelot was the one who stabbed me. But I shouldn't have—"

"Britt. It's not your fault," Merlin repeated.

With those few words, the careful control Britt had built up fell in shambles. Britt bit her lip to keep from crying and reached out—steadying herself on a stall door. Her shoulders shook, but she held it in...until Merlin pulled her flush against his chest.

"You did well, lass," Merlin whispered.

The awkwardness of the past year was peeled away, and it was like coming home again.

In spite of the somewhat public setting, Merlin embraced Britt—who was trying to keep from bawling her eyes out.

Merlin held her until the tsunami of emotions passed, leaving Britt bone-weary, but more controlled.

"You have to speak to them," Merlin said.

"I know. But can I?" Britt asked.

"I have absolute faith in you, lass."

"No, I mean...*can* I? Hasn't all of this ruined your plans and visions for the future?" Britt asked, pulling back from Merlin so she could look him in the eye.

"If you succeed, this incident will only make your relationship with them stronger," Merlin said.

"Perhaps, but it is more likely to fail than succeed, in which case we lose everything," Britt practically pointed out.

"It's a risk I'm willing to run," Merlin said.

"How many know?"

"Most of your inner circle. The knights Leodegrance sent with the Round Table are unaware, but the rest of your old court knows. The only ones that don't are those out adventuring, but most of them have returned over the past few days."

"Who is the angriest?" Britt asked.

"Ywain, still. He's a hothead—he'll have to learn to control his passion someday," Merlin said.

"What about Gawain?"

"It appears that he took it in stride—I would ask him about that if I were you. King Pellinore is...not pleased. But he's not angry."

"And Bedivere?"

Merlin sighed. "I won't lie to you, lass. He walks around as if he's lost his soul. He took it the worst—even more than Ywain."

Britt wearily rubbed her eyes. "I thought as much. And has Lancelot been busy hissing in everyone's ears?"

"He's quiet—unnaturally so for him. It's been reported that he hasn't told a story about his past exploits since they returned to Camelot after parting with you."

"He worries me," Britt said.

"Still?" Merlin groaned.

"He *stabbed* me! I think I have a right to be leery."

"You made him mad. What did you expect?"

"An ounce of chivalry, maybe? I swear I will give my knights a painfully detailed lesson about sportsmanship if we make it through this. Stabbing me after the match was over—what a jerk!" Britt grumbled.

"He should have his ears boxed," Merlin admitted. "But at another time. You need to prepare to speak to your men. When they find out you've returned, I'm sure their reaction will not be to mewl like hungry kittens."

"How much time do you think I have?" Britt asked.

"Not long. The guards were already singing of your arrival. If we hurry, we can hustle up to my study and help prepare you for what you'll face," Merlin said. "I'm sure you would like some refreshments?"

"That would be nice," Britt said, slapping dust from her clothes. "I think my shoulder needs to be rebandaged. Where is Cavall?"

"He's been staying with Sir Ector. We'll have a squad of guards wait in the hallways while you talk—lest your knights act...unseemly."

"That won't be necessary," Britt said.

"I *hope* it won't be necessary," Merlin said. "There's no telling—"

"My Lord," a stiff voice said.

Merlin and Britt whirled to face the front of the stable, where Sir Ywain stood with Sir Griflet and a cheerful Sir Tor.

"We request your presence at the Round Table, My Lord," Sir Tor said, his smile was as good natured and genuine as ever.

"Immediately," Sir Griflet said with a bone-weary sigh.

"She just returned," Merlin said, tilting his head and half smiling. "Couldn't you let her enjoy some refreshments and have her shoulder dressed again?"

"We will not give her the time you need to tell her what she should say to us. We will see her. *Now*," Sir Ywain said.

This is too soon. I'm not ready! Britt thought, her heart beating in her chest like a throbbing drum.

"Very well," Merlin said. He shrugged as if this change in plans was nothing to be bothered with. "I assume you do not mean to allow me to accompany her?"

"That is correct," Ywain said, his voice icy.

"In that case, good luck. I have confidence in you," Merlin said, smiling at Britt.

Panicked, Britt took in his expression, searching for hidden hints and clues. To her surprise, the wizard turned on his heels and left the stable.

Britt watched him go as her heart sank into her gut.

"If you'll come with us, My Lord," Sir Tor said, leading the way from the stables. Britt had no choice but to follow.

~

BRITT WAS LED ALL the way to the hall where the Round Table was located. They had stopped only at Britt's room so she could change into a clean tunic. When she entered the hall, the chambers were eerily silent. Everyone was seated, watching her with dubious looks—or narrowed eyes.

Britt was led all the way to the space where her usual seat was —although the chair was pulled back, far away from the table. Excalibur lay across the seat, and Britt longed to reclaim it. Her side felt bare without the magic sword strapped to her side. She wasn't given the chance to grab it, though. Sir Tor neatly maneuvered her so she stood in the blank space—visible to everyone gathered around the table.

Sir Kay and Sir Ector were there—as were the rest of Merlin's minions. Britt had no doubt Merlin was listening in somehow. The thought made her square her shoulders and raise her chin.

This is my one shot, Britt thought. *If I ruin it, it's over. If there was ever a time I needed to speak well, this is it.*

When Sir Tor sat down, the knights turned their gaze to King Pellinore.

The older king leaned back in his chair, his eyes fixed on

Britt. After several long moments of silence, he gestured with his hand. "Explain yourself."

Britt looked down at her hands. *How do I begin? How do I assure them that I'm still me?*

"My name is Britt Arthurs," she began. "I am a foreigner. I come from a different place—a different world. I was summoned here by the sword in the stone—which judged me to be the kind of person needed to rule Britain. And I resented that."

Whatever her knights were expecting, this wasn't it. Britt watched them exchange glances and shift in their chairs.

"I longed for the family and friends I left behind, and I wanted to leave this place so badly it hurt. But I couldn't. No one has the magic needed to send me back. So, Merlin popped me on his throne as his puppet king. I intended to sit there like a lump and do nothing—mourning my lost life for the rest of time—but something happened."

Britt waited until all of the knights looked up at her. "I met you," she said, her gaze sweeping the circle so she could meet their eyes. "I met knights who were good and just, and I fell in love with Camelot. You put your trust and faith in me, and together we were able to mold Britain. There are fewer recreant knights now than ever before. We have stopped the petty wars that used to devour time, resources, and precious lives. *You* ride forth and right wrongs, helping the weak and the oppressed."

"You will not sway us with your speeches this time, My Lord," a knight warned. "No matter how you flatter us, we will not fall for your schemes."

"What schemes?" Britt asked. "What have I made you do that you are morally opposed to? I have pushed you hard, yes. I have asked for your best and demanded much of you...but for purposes and for things you believe in."

"Lies!" Ywain shouted, standing up so fast he sent his chair flying. "Nothing but drabble falls from your lips."

Sir Kay put a hand to his sword, and Sir Ector said "What?"

and tried to roll to his feet. Both he and Kay froze when Britt signaled for them to remain still.

Time to play rough, Britt grimly thought as she gathered all her courage.

"You speak lies and manipulate us to accomplish your own goals!" Ywain spat.

"How can I lie and manipulate when the only thing I have ever done is accomplished what I promised!" Britt shouted, her voice was loud like thunder in the hall. "When I met you, Ywain, I told you I dreamed of a place where my knights could be equals, and *here* we stand," Britt said, slapping her open hand on her table with a crack. "I have said since I was crowned that I wanted Camelot to be known for its justice—not for military strength and campaigns. *How* did I lie, exactly? Give me one example!" Britt demanded.

"You cannot be angry," Ywain said, his voice rising in volume. "You were the one who proved to be a traitor—"

"NOT TELLING YOU MY GENDER DOES NOT MAKE ME A TRAITOR!" Britt roared.

Some knights leaned back in their chairs, recognizing the rage and anger Britt faced them with, as the temper she had briefly shown against King Urien in the battle for her throne.

The dragon king was *enraged*.

"I was upfront with everything I wanted to accomplish! I haven't made any of you follow me. You chose it because you wanted the same things I did. Guess what—we accomplished them! I won't let you color them as the acts of a traitor because you're too prideful to admit you can't believe it took A WOMAN to get these things done!" Britt shouted, her voice ringing in the hall.

The silence was suffocating. After several heart beats, Britt added—in a more controlled but still angry voice, "I am sorry I had to lie to you. It was wrong, I know. But if I had even *hoped* that you would listen to me, knowing who I was, I would have told you!"

"So, it is true. You didn't tell us because you didn't trust us," Sir Bedivere said. His voice was heavy with heartbreak as he stared at Britt. "You hid from us and never felt the way we felt about you."

Britt was silent. She leaned forward and placed both of her palms on the table, as if drawing strength from it. "I didn't tell you because I was afraid. I didn't want to lose you."

"You didn't trust us to stand with you," Sir Bedivere said.

"Yes," Britt said.

Sir Bedivere lowered his gaze.

"So now you want us to stand with you, even when you didn't believe in us?" Griflet asked. His voice quavered twice.

"Do you really think I don't believe in you, Griflet?" Britt asked, her voice soft. She stared at the young knight, trying to push every ounce of affection she had into her eyes. "Do you really think I don't believe in your abilities, in your goodness?" she asked. She paused before addressing the Round Table. "I made a mistake because I was worried you would think that *I'm* not good enough. I have trusted you with my life and with my kingdom. In this one area I have held back, but no more."

Sir Ector made a noise of distress as Britt stripped off her jerkin so she stood before her knights in a blue tunic that set off her eyes.

What made the men stare at her—as if she had grown a second head—was that she had removed the extra underclothes that flattened her chest when she had visited her room to change. Her chest, wider hips, and more slender waist were made obvious by the tunic.

Some of the knights averted their eyes; others stared at Britt with dropped jaws.

"I regret my actions," Britt said. "And if I had a choice, I'm not certain I would have it known that I am a female. Not because of you, but because of what will happen when all of Britain finds out. I apologize, and I recognize I have wronged you. So, I will step down from the throne."

"What!" Sir Percival said, his face turning pale.

"My Lord, you can't!" Agravain—who stood behind Gawain's chair—shouted.

Britt sadly smiled. "But I must. I don't deserve your loyalty, and I can't ask for it. Camelot is great not just because of me but because of its knights. So, I leave Camelot, its court, and Excalibur for the one whom *you* believe to be worthy," Britt said. She unstrapped Excalibur's scabbard from her side, walked the few paces to what used to be her chair, and set it next to the sword.

When she turned around to face the shocked knights, she bowed. "Thank you for hearing out my apology," she said before turning to go to the doors.

She walked quickly—she didn't want to hear the discussion that was about to take place, *and* she could feel that a corner of her wound was starting to bleed now that she lacked the magic-infused scabbard.

Whispers raced around the table, and Britt heard one chair push back before someone ran to catch up with her.

A hand caught her by the elbow and stopped her. "My Lord."

When Britt turned around, she was shocked—and slightly appalled—to find herself face-to-face with *Lancelot* of all people.

The handsome, coal-haired knight thoughtfully studied her. He had an odd expression fixed on his face—as if Britt was a puzzle he had nearly worked through, only to discover the picture was facing the wrong direction.

His look made Britt more uneasy than when had he stabbed her at Sir Damas' lands.

"If I may have a moment more of your time, My Lord," Lancelot finally said. He gave her a warm smile that lit up the depths of his green eyes.

Britt allowed him to pull her back to the Round Table but suspiciously eyed him as they walked.

When they reached the table, Lancelot waited until the knights quieted down to speak. "I know you all love King Arthur. I knew that the day I entered these courts, and I knew that even during our recent uproar. This woman—" Lancelot said, directing Britt so she stood slightly in front of him, "is the king you adore. She is still the king for whom you would put down your lives, and she is the king who has made Camelot a place of greatness. Do not allow your pride—or your pain—to set her aside. If you do that, our king will be justified in her fears, for we will have proved to her that we are temporary, unfaithful men. Think not of your pain, but hers. Look at her. *Remember* her. Remember the things she has said to you, remember the things she has done. She has shed sweat and blood for you, just as you have for her. Do not forsake her now."

Britt was struck dumb by Lancelot's kind words on her behalf, but her heart leaped when Gawain stood.

"I will always stand with you, My Lord," he said.

"As do I," Agravain was quick to add.

"It doesn't seem right," King Pellinore said as he rolled to his feet. "But you're an excellent King, Arthur. No matter *what* you are. I'll stand with you, too."

"Of course I stand with my girl," Sir Ector rumbled as he and Kay stood.

"So do we," Sir Lionel and Sir Bors said.

"My Lord has rescued us in the past," Sir Bedivere said, drawing Britt's attention. Hurt still echoed in his eyes, but the knight raised his shoulders and chin. "You are the same king to whom I swore allegiance. I will continue to serve you, no matter how long it takes me to earn your trust."

Griflet stood as well, with a number of other knights. He nudged Ywain, but the outspoken knight was staring at Britt.

"Tell me one thing, My Lord," Ywain said. "Was the Round Table your idea or Merlin's?"

"Mine," Britt said.

Ywain nodded rubbed his eyes. "Mother will thrash me when she learns how I acted," he muttered before rocketing out of his chair. "Woman or not, king or queen, My Lord has set out what he promised to long ago. I will stand with you, My Lord. Just... please don't wear dresses," Ywain winced.

Britt outright laughed at Ywain's statement, and the rest of the knights stood as well. The hall was a flood of noise as the knights tried to sort out what to call her.

"Hail, King...Queen Arthur?"

"Er...My Lady?"

"Empress...what was her name again?"

"Why did she have two names?"

"Someone ought to tell Guinevere."

The doors slammed open, and Merlin strode inside. "Congratulations, knights of the Round Table—men of Camelot. You have made an excellent decision, for none can rule as Britt Arthurs does," Merlin said.

"Hail, King Britt!"

"Lady Arthurs?"

"Queen Arthurs?"

Britt started to sag with the relief that flooded her system. They would still have her. Her knights weren't lost. Camelot wasn't lost. They would get past this.

"Hold this," Merlin said, shoving Excalibur—after he sheathed it in its scabbard—into her hands. "It would be a silly thing if you passed out from blood loss with your sword so close at hand."

"Thank you, Merlin," Britt smiled.

"Thank yourself, lass. You were the one who won them back."

"No, thank you for bringing me here."

Merlin gave her a look of surprise before he smiled. "Aye. T'was a blessed day when you came to us," he said before turning

217

to address the table. "Now that you have reaffirmed your loyalty, there are decisions to be made."

Merlin and the knights of the Round Table spent hours talking about Britt's position as king. They discussed everything from what to call her to how far they should spread the news of her gender. Britt was there for only a portion. She was shooed out when the meeting was halfway over and Pellinore happened to see a spot of blood that had dripped through the bandages from the brief time she didn't hold Excalibur.

"You're still to be King Arthur—though I wouldn't be surprised if some of them called you Britt in private. Sir Kay is already skulking around, looking at everyone with suspicion. This is his worst nightmare realized—men knowing who you really are," Merlin said, his hands folded across his chest as he sat in his study with Britt.

"I don't get it."

"I didn't think you would. Anyway, they've decided to keep this news confidential, for now. It won't spread any farther than the men you just addressed, and they decided that in order for a knight to be informed, he has to prove himself first."

"It sounds to me like they're making my identity a sort of… order. Like the Order of the Round Table," Britt said.

"That sounds fairly accurate," Merlin said. "Anyway, it's done. Ywain is now hounding Lancelot for injuring you in the first place, and Griflet is back to mooning over his Lady Blancheflor. Many of the knights are now eyeing Guinevere in interest, since she's obviously not meant to be your intended. All has ended well, for now."

"Not quite," Britt said. "There's one more thing I would like to do before we put this behind us."

Merlin frowned. "What?"

9

QUARRELS ADDRESSED

When Britt—with her company of forty knights and forty or so guards and soldiers—rode up to Sir Damas' castle, the scholarly knight and Lady Vivenne practically flew from the castle to greet them.

"M-my Lord," Sir Damas babbled, taking in the flags and standards that flapped in the breeze—they were all decorated with red dragons. "What brings you h-here?"

Britt—dressed in a full suit of armor, the fancy stuff with the red dragons etched into the surface—turned Roen to look at the horizon. Ten soldiers headed by Sir Griflet, Sir Ywain, Sir Lancelot, and Sir Bedivere marched into sight, Sir Outzlake pushed in front of them.

Britt waited until the sister and two brothers were standing together before she removed her helm. Lady Vivenne gasped; Sir Damas turned pale and grasped his throat, and Sir Outzlake looked curiously at both of them.

"Sir Damas and Sir Outzlake. I come to you as your rightful *king*—Arthur of Camelot," Britt said as the siblings hastily bowed. "I have seen with my own eyes your terrible behavior. You, Sir Damas, kidnap knights in hopes that they will fight for you. You,

Sir Outzlake, spend most of your time challenging your brother and the will your father left instead of managing your own lands. In light of these short comings, I exercise my right as monarch, and I remove the title of knight from both of you and claim your lands and all that you own. Due to your disregard and poor actions, your homes now belong to *me*."

Britt pinned the two brothers down with narrowed eyes. Sir Damas shook in his shoes, and Sir Outzlake looked hardly any better. "I will appoint a ruler to your lands, as is my right. I choose—as the ruler and owner of both your properties—Lady Vivenne."

Lady Vivenne yelped. "*What!*" as she stared at Britt.

"But—" Sir Outzlake started.

"During my interactions, Lady Vivenne displayed a greater concern for your lands and people than either of you. As such, I make her the heir of the holdings and give her the title of Lady and owner. As Lady Vivenne is not yet of age, you two—Damas and Outzlake—will share custody of her and serve as advisors until she is. If I hear that you have attempted to force your will upon her, I will see to it that you are permanently exiled from Britain. I am giving you this chance to prove yourselves. Should you become useful, I will restore your titles to you. Until then, I suggest you learn to work together," Britt said.

"Y-yes, My Lord," Damas sputtered, relief and irritation pinching his face.

"Yes, My Lord," Sir Outzlake squeaked with a scowl.

Britt turned her gaze to the shell-shocked Vivenne. "I suggest you empty the dungeons of kidnapped knights, Lady Vivenne."

"Of course, My Lord," Lady Vivenne said.

Britt smiled, significantly softening the moment. "I have great confidence in you, Vivenne. I'm certain you can handle this. Good luck. If you need anything and your brothers prove to be useless, send word."

"If you'll pardon me, My Lord, but why?" Lady Vivenne said.

"Why what?"

"Why bother yourself with this—why give me the lands? I'm nobody," Lady Vivenne said.

Britt smiled. The setting sun made her gold hair shine and all her knights—also dressed in full armor—dazzle and glint. "It has been my experience, Lady Vivenne, that it's often the nobodies who become the greatest somebodies," she said. Roen snorted and reared, impatiently rising up on his back legs.

Britt kept her seat and spun the big destrier to face her company. "We return to Camelot. Move out!" she shouted.

The knights and soldiers shouted, and as they returned in the direction from which they had come—armor glinting, horse tack jingling, and the flags still flapping—Lady Vivenne could only shake her head.

"Hail, King Arthur," she whispered. "Long live the King."

~

"So, Gawain, do I have your mother to thank for your calm reaction to my...identity," Britt asked as she rode next to the young knight the following morning on the ride back to Camelot.

"What do you mean, My Lord?"

"You didn't seem much shaken with my reveal. I assumed it was because of your mother that you knew women could be good rulers," Britt said.

"Oh. While it is true that my mother has taught me that women can be as...competent as men, that's not why I reacted calmly."

"Then why?"

"Because I already knew you were a woman."

"You *what?*" Britt yelped. Roen tossed his head, sensing her heightened emotions. "You knew?"

"Mother told me," Sir Gawain nodded.

"You knew this *whole time?*" Britt said, a hint of an accusation lining her voice.

"Yes," Sir Gawain said.

Britt groaned.

"Is that bad?" Sir Gawain asked.

"No, but my life would have been easier if *I* knew *you* knew," Britt grumbled, thinking of all the times she could have been more open with the eldest Orkney prince.

"I did my best to help you," Gawain said.

"That's why you always offer to help me with my armor," Britt realized. "I just thought it was sheer luck that you helped me put on my armor without making any observations."

Sir Gawain bowed his head in acknowledgement.

Britt was silent for a few minutes—contemplating Gawain's actions as Roen's smooth gait rocked her in the saddle. "Thank you," she finally said. "I appreciate what you did for me."

"It was, and continues to be, my pleasure, My Lord," Gawain said.

"My Lord, could you spare a moment of your time?" Sir Bedivere asked, holding back his charger for a moment so he could fall in line with Britt.

Sir Gawain nodded to the older knight and nudged his horse forward, trotting to catch up with Sir Percival and Agravain.

"Of course, Sir Bedivere," Britt said after a moment's hesitation.

"There are a few small matters at Camelot that must be addressed," Sir Bedivere said, launching into the topic. He didn't look at Britt as he spoke.

"Do you think, Sir Bedivere, that you'll ever be able to forgive me?" Britt asked.

Sir Bedivere blinked. "My Lord?"

"My deception. I didn't mean to hurt you. I'm sorry, and I regret it more than you realize," Britt said with a sad smile.

Sir Bedivere finally looked at Britt. "It is not a matter of forgiveness, My Lord. I remain your faithful subject."

"I know. But I miss our camaraderie," Britt said. "And it's not just you. I can see the consequences of being female already. My knights don't approach me like they used to."

"With time, we will adjust, My Lord," Sir Bedivere said. "If I might venture to say, for many of the younger knights, it must be somewhat awkward to be told the man you wanted to emulate is actually a woman."

Britt laughed. "I didn't think of it that way."

"Once your knights see that you are still the same king we've always had, they will settle in," Sir Bedivere said.

"Will we settle in, too, Sir Bedivere?" Britt asked.

"I should hope so, My Lord," Sir Bedivere said, giving Britt a small but warm smile.

Britt returned the smile, some of her tension easing. She had always counted on Sir Bedivere—whether it be to take her side against Merlin or to be a voice of reason for the younger knights. She was afraid she was going to lose that—even if he stayed loyal to her. Her heart lifted with joy because *maybe* everything was going to be okay.

"My Lord!"

Britt almost fell off Roen when Sir Griflet came crashing through the procession.

"My Lord!" Sir Griflet repeated, his eyes wide as he stared at Britt. "I have prayed, and God has answered me!" he said, his horse prancing in place.

Britt exchanged looks with Sir Bedivere. "And how did he answer you?" Britt asked.

Sir Griflet stabbed a finger in Britt's direction. "With *you*, My Lord."

"...What?"

Seconds later, Ywain also came crashing through the procession. "Griflet! You can't just—don't!" he hissed.

"Don't what?" Britt asked.

"You, My Lord, are my answer to all my prayers. Because *you* are a female," Griflet said, brandishing his finger in the air as if this was a new revelation.

Britt and Sir Bedivere stared at the self-awed Griflet.

"Ignore him, My Lord. He is sick in the head. Griflet, *come*," Sir Ywain hissed.

"No! This is a wonderful idea, even if you don't think it is," Griflet told his friend before turning to Britt. "My Lord, as you are a woman, could you cast your pearls of wisdom before me regarding the state of ambience and heart of the fairer sex?"

"…What?" Britt repeated, staring at the starry-eyed knight.

Sir Ywain scowled. "He means he needs help with Lady Blancheflor, and he's hoping that you will have a greater understanding of her heart than him because…well…you're a girl."

"That is precisely what I said," Griflet frowned.

"Oh," Britt said after a few moments of shocked silence. "I could try. But I'm terribly out of practice."

"You see, My Lord? Give them time," Sir Bedivere murmured. He gave Britt another smile before falling back to ride with King Pellinore.

Reinvigorated, Britt rolled her shoulders back. "So tell me, Sir Griflet, what are you doing to try and impress your fair lady?"

"Mostly he writes her horrible poetry and sighs at her like an over-fed mongrel," Sir Ywain said.

"I beg your pardon—you take that back!" Sir Griflet said, puffing up like a cat.

"It's true, My Lord," Sir Ywain said, finally looking at Britt. "I think Lady Blancheflor is starting to dread the sight of him. Last time she saw him, she ran away."

"She did not!"

Britt smiled as she listened to the friends quarrel. There was still a slight hesitation for Ywain, but Sir Bedivere was right. She needed to let her knights adjust. Things likely would never be the same, but that didn't mean it wouldn't be better than it was before.

10

OVER?

"I'm so glad that's over," Britt said, falling back in her bed with a sigh.

"Truly, My Lord, I think it has just begun," Morgan le Fay said.

Britt frowned. "What do you mean?"

"There will be plenty of new problems now that your knights know you to be a woman," Nymue said, plopping down on the edge of Britt's bed. She kicked off her thin slippers and joined Britt on her bed.

"What problems?" Britt cautiously asked.

"To begin with, you are a beautiful woman who spends most of her time surrounded by men whose current goal is to find a lady to whom they can pledge themselves," Morgan said.

Britt laughed. "Is that all? I don't think there will be any troubles there. I have to be five years older than most of my knights."

"Don't be so quick to brush it off," Morgan warned.

"Indeed. I bet that foster-brother of yours will soon run himself into exhaustion with worry," Nymue pertly said.

"Kay worries over all kinds of things," Britt argued.

"Perhaps, but one of his fears has certainly become more pressing," Morgan said.

"What?" Britt asked.

"Lancelot," Nymue said.

Britt shifted uncomfortably. "Merlin doesn't think he'll be a problem."

"As I recall, you thought differently. Did his little speech on your behalf change your mind?" Nymue asked.

"No," Britt shook her head. "He feels…"

"Deep," Morgan said.

"Exactly," Britt said.

"Lancelot is a fathomless character. One can never get a full measure of him," Morgan said.

"What Morgan le Fay is being too sweet to say is that Lancelot might ruin you yet," Nymue said, "because you've gone from a threat to overshadow his greatness to a possible target."

Nymue's words struck Britt like a truck. "So, that's a possible complication from being revealed as a girl," Britt sighed.

"He is ruthless," Morgan said.

"I haven't seen that yet. It's there, but he keeps it leashed most of the time. Except when he stabs people," Britt scowled.

"It doesn't mean it isn't there," Morgan said.

"Mark my words: he'll stir up more trouble—just a different sort now that he knows who you are."

"He'll have to tangle with Kay," Britt said, brightening at the thought.

"And Merlin," Morgan added.

"What? Merlin won't care," Britt said, laughing at the idea.

"I disagree. Merlin will care very much," Morgan said.

"No way. Now that my core group of knights knows, he's floating around without a care in the world. He won't give a rip if Lancelot tries seducing me," Britt said.

Nymue and Morgan exchanged looks.

"Anyway, besides that, things should quiet down. *Finally*! I'll have to do something about Guinevere, but that's easy compared to everything else. This is a load off my shoulders; I feel amazing!"

"I'm glad, for your sake," Morgan said.

"Now you can only hope that no new problems show up at your gatehouse," Nymue said.

Britt snorted. "Who else is left? No one. I'm safe! I'm going to enjoy this summer. Maybe we'll even throw one of those tournament things."

"That would be fun," Nymue said, clasping her hands together. "I've always wanted to see someone toss Lancelot from his horse. I have heard both Sir Bodwain *and* Sir Kay can best him."

"It's true," Britt grinned. "It's a sight I never grow tired of."

"I imagine so!"

$\approx$

As Britt spoke with Morgan and Nymue, a knight mounted on a coal black charger rode up to the gatehouse of Camelot.

"Who goes there?" a guard shouted down to the man.

"I am a knight, seeking to join King Arthur's court," the knight said.

"What is your name?"

"Mordred."

THE END

THE CONTINUED OBSERVATIONS OF
SIR KAY

Kay stood in the shadows, quiet and unobtrusive, and watched Britt Arthurs—King of England, known to most of the Knights of the Round Table to be a girl—with two of her knights.

Britt was smiling—her controlled one, not her brilliant and lethal grin—and attempting to engage her quiet knights. "She *still* hasn't acknowledged you? Are you sure she's not playing hard to get?"

"I beg your pardon, My Lord?" Griflet said, his forehead wrinkling in confusion.

"Er...do you think she is ignoring you on purpose?" Britt asked.

Griflet blinked in confusion. "Why would she do that?"

"To drive you mad with passion," Britt suggested. "What do you think, Ywain?"

"I would not presume to understand the mind of a lady, My Lord," Ywain said, his words chosen with an unusual amount of care.

Britt's smile dimmed for a moment, and Kay saw the flicker of pain in her eyes.

It was only four days ago that the knights had reaffirmed their loyalty to her, even though she was a woman. Their new relationship with their monarch was as shaky as a newborn fawn—which was to be expected. Still, the new degree of uncertainty brought much pain to Britt, and it seemed her men suffered nearly as much.

It is better if the knights keep a distance, but I wish their reaction would not cause her grief. Kay thought.

"I apologize, I wish I could be of more use to you, Sir Griflet, but I don't know Lady Blanchflor well enough to guess if she would do something like that." Britt turned her attention back to the flowery and loquacious knight. "Tonight, when we dine, I could watch your interactions with her."

"If you would not mind terribly, My Lord," Sir Griflet said with an eager smile.

"Of course not." Britt walked up the garden path, her knights trailing her.

"I think the lady finds Griflet an utter fop and is too kind to tell him to leave her be," Ywain muttered under his breath.

A hearty laugh burst from Britt's lips, drawing a smile from everyone present, and softening the moment. Griflet beamed, and Ywain relaxed, tension leaving his shoulders and neck as he ducked his head and smiled in pleasure.

Kay narrowed his eyes and leaned forward, watching Ywain and Griflet with careful scrutiny. Griflet looked both offended and pleased, and wore a silly grin. His eyes were lit with happiness as he watched Britt laugh. There was not a trace of anything besides pleasure in his eyes—which was not surprising considering his devotion to his temperamental Lady Blancheflor.

Ywain, however, was Kay's foremost concern.

Kay watched with a hawk-like focus, looking for any hint of love. There was—there was so much that Ywain's eyes were practically wells of love. Thankfully, it was the sort of love a man had for his King, and for a highly esteemed mentor, not the romantic love Griflet had for Lady Blancheflor.

Kay rocked back on his heels—assured for the moment. *As long as they continue like this, she will be safe.* Most of Britt's close knights were older, married men, who posed no threat. However, three young knights were known to be Britt's favorites: Gawain, Griflet, and Ywain. Gawain had always known of Britt's feminine nature and seemed to view his King as not only his ruler, but almost like a stand-in-parent. Griflet's admiration was the deeply rooted respect a soldier has for his leader—which made sense as Britt had won him over with her battle prowess. Ywain, however, was the dangerous one. He had parents who loved him, and in his first meeting with Britt, she had proven to him she was superior in the ways of the sword and his loyalties hadn't budged. It was with words that Britt had won Ywain to her side, words that pulled at the young knight's heartstrings. Thankfully, the young prince did not look upon Britt Arthurs with admiration.

Good.

Still, Kay needed to remain on his guard. The Knights of the Round Table were cautious and formal with their woman-king, but he doubted it would remain that way for long. *My Lord Britt Arthurs is too charismatic to allow formalities for long. And that **smile**.*

Britt's true smile—her lethal one that could steal a man's breath—was going to become the bane of Kay's existence.

As if God was aware of Kay's sour thoughts and sought to play a joke on him, Sir Percival entered the gardens. Sir Percival was the oldest son of King Pellinore—a man Britt called her friend. "Forgive me, My Lord, for my intrusion?"

"Don't be silly, Sir Percival, join us! The more the merrier," Britt said, offering the knight a smile.

Sir Percival looked down at his feet, which sent another bolt of regret through Britt's eyes.

Kay was glad Britt couldn't see what he could—that Sir Percival was smiling at the ground like an idiot.

Kay scowled, his mustache bristling.

"What brings you to the gardens?" Britt asked Sir Percival.

"I was seeking you out," Sir Percival admitted.

"Did you need something?"

"No," Sir Percival said.

"Oh. Say, Percival, what is your impression of Lady Blancheflor?" Britt asked.

"Lady Blancheflor?" Percival said, finally wiping his shy smile from his face and looking up. "Isn't she one of Sir Lancelot's admirers—or not," he quickly amended when he caught sight of Britt shaking her head behind a downtrodden Griflet.

"She isn't really. She does not fawn over him like many females," Britt said, soothing him.

"But she still admires him, and I am not yet on the same level as Sir Lancelot," Sir Griflet said, his voice heavy with sadness.

Sir Ywain snorted. "I'll say."

"You could concentrate on training—though he is the second best swordsman after My Lord, and he is equally as skilled at jousting," Sir Percival said.

"No, if Blancheflor ends up liking you only because you're strong, she's not the right lady for you. Why don't you try speaking to her—*without* reciting poetry?" Britt suggested.

"But she is so beautiful! I cannot help but speak verses of praises whenever I see her," Griflet said, gaping at Britt in bafflement.

"You would," Britt said, drawing a snort of laughter from Sir Ywain. "You could try getting a puppy. It seems the ladies of Camelot are much less impressed with a dog than they are where I come from, but you could borrow Cavall and see if Lady Blancheflor shows any interest at all."

The idea made Kay scowl. Cavall was Brit Arthur's meticulously trained guard dog. He was supposed to be with her at all times—not being lent out to knights with poor romantic judgment.

He wouldn't dare agree to it. Kay thought as he fixed his gaze on the younger knight.

"Hahah, I believe that will be unnecessary," Griflet said, quaking under Kay's scrutiny.

"Very well. I'm starved. I'm going to plunder the kitchens for some lunch. Does anyone wish to join me?" Britt asked, rubbing her injured shoulder.

"I'm always in the mood for a spot of food," Griflet said, leading the way.

Ywain swaggered after him. "Perhaps that is why Blancheflor won't speak to you—you're worse than a dog begging for scraps."

Britt moved to trail after her men when she realized Sir Percival was hesitating. "Are you coming, Sir Percival?"

Sir Percival scratched the back of his neck. "Oh, I don't wish to interrupt your conversation."

"Nonsense, we would love to have you with us," Britt said. She threw her good arm over Percival's shoulders and towed him towards the exit.

Sir Percival smiled...until he caught sight of Kay glowering at him. "Ah, yes, thank you, My Lord," Sir Percival said, bowing to Britt to squirm away from her.

Britt winked at the knight before calling out. "Kay—are you coming with, or will you keep lurking there?"

Kay's scowl cleared from his face and he pushed away from the wall he was tucked against. "I suppose I shall join you."

"Great. Come on!"

Kay smoothed his mustache and trailed after Britt. *I recognize this is a painful time for her. All the same, I am glad for it. It gives me time to assure that no one begins entertaining...ideas.*

"My Lord!"

"Lancelot," Britt said, sounding less-than-thrilled. "Greetings, Sir Mordred."

"My Lord."

Although I may already be too late.

The End

ENDEAVOR:

KING ARTHUR AND HER KNIGHTS BOOK 6

1

A MAGIC FOUNTAIN?

"We should muster your armies."

Britt frowned and looked to Merlin—her sharp-minded advisor. "What?"

"We should muster your armies," the handsome man repeated. He leaned against the Round Table, his arms folded across his chest, and watched Ywain throw Cavall's beanbag.

"I heard you the first time," Britt said, watching her apricot-colored mastiff pad around the table to get the beanbag. "What I meant was what do we need the armies for?"

"Ah. You really should have stated your entire question, if that is the case."

Britt leaned back in her chair. "Merlin, stop dancing around the subject and tell me."

Merlin's pale blonde hair looked more colorful in the orange glow of the crackling torches, but his handsome face was devoid of expression. "It is time we look to expand your kingdom into Ireland."

"No," Britt said.

Merlin sighed. "At least think it over before giving your refusal."

"I don't have to think over it, because there isn't one good reason in this ancient world to attack Ireland. They haven't attacked us—they don't even plot against us. If you were suggesting we finally tweak that weasel King Ryence, I *might* consider it; but until we face a direct threat, I will not ask my knights and subjects to throw away their lives for me—for your desire of a unified Britain."

"There *is* a threat," Merlin said.

"You've mentioned Rome, but they have yet to make a move of any kind," Britt objected.

"That's because they are planners—like us."

Britt tucked her chin, prepared to argue, when Sir Ector—her foster father—spoke. "He's right, Britt." His stout belly jiggled, and his eyes glowed with the simple pleasure of openly calling Britt by her real name. Only a few weeks ago, Sir Ector had no choice but to call her by her alias: King Arthur.

Britt was an American girl from the twenty-first century. When touring England with friends, an ancient magic pulled her through time, plopping her in medieval London where Merlin explained that the real Arthur had run off with a shepherdess, and Britt was going to be the replacement. Her gender was a carefully guarded secret for over two years until a few short weeks ago when she had been accidentally outed by the less-than-chivalrous actions of her least-favorite knight, Sir Lancelot du Lac.

"What is Merlin right about, Father?" Britt asked, her lips curling into an indulgent smile. She loved all of her knights (well, except Lancelot), but Sir Ector and Sir Kay were special. They had taken up the role of her family when her life had been abruptly wrenched from her.

"Rome is a terrible threat," Sir Ector said. "And with all your best knights out questing with your blessing, it's risky not to prepare."

"Not *all* of My Lord's best knights are out questing," Sir Ywain objected. He had grown again—in the shoulders and arms this time—and moved more like a noble lion than the spider-limbed youth he had been when Britt first met him. The young knight glanced at Britt before bowing in reverence to her. "I beg your pardon, My Lord. I did not mean to presume."

The realization that Britt—Arthur—was female had shaken the confidence of the knights of Camelot. They had accepted her and reaffirmed their vows to her, but things were still...tense. The close sense of camaraderie was gone, but both Britt and her knights were trying to bridge this new gap.

"Ywain is right. To say all her best knights are out is dramatic," Merlin said. "Sir Lancelot remains here, after all."

"Lancelot doesn't count," Britt snarled. She smoothed her face and smiled in Ywain's direction. "But Ywain is right. All of those present in this room are among the greatest of my knights."

Ywain smiled shyly and busied himself with petting Cavall to hide his blush.

Merlin openly rolled his eyes and shook his head in disgust.

"We're honored by your words, My Lord," Sir Ector said.

Sir Kay, paging through a logbook next to his father, paused in his work to bow to Britt in acknowledgement.

Britt shook her finger at her foster-father. "*Britt*."

Sir Ector smiled again and stroked his bushy beard. "As you wish, Britt. Though I'm afraid I must ask you for a boon."

"What is it?" Britt asked, leaning forward in her chair with interest.

"I wish for your permission to return home for a lengthy time."

"Of course," Britt said, disappointed the request wasn't something grander. As Sir Ector held the lands of Bonmaison, he often left her courts to check on his holdings—and his much beloved wife.

"Thank you, My Lord," Sir Ector said, bowing.

"How long will you be gone?" Merlin asked before Britt could launch an argument over her title.

"The rest of the summer at least, possibly the fall—unless you call for my return sooner, of course," Sir Ector said.

Britt tapped her fingers on the Round Table—which was a misleading name as it was more oval and was pieced together like a train track. Sir Ector had never been gone so long before. "Is everything well with Bonmaison?"

"Of course, of course!" Sir Ector laughed, making his belly jiggle. "It is only that I have been gone so long, and I miss my lands."

"I see." Britt's heart twisted oddly in her chest. She could sympathize with Sir Ector, as she had been torn from her home and family to live in medieval England, but she was still sad to know that he would be gone for so long. She shook her head to rid herself of the selfish thought. "Enjoy your return home. You won't leave until after tomorrow's tournament, won't you?"

"Aye," Sir Ector said. "I wouldn't miss your first tournament for all the riches in England!"

"It's not *my* tournament," Britt said, shooting Merlin a glare. "I can't even enter it."

Any reply Merlin would have made was cut off when someone banged on the large doors.

"Who would want to see me at this hour?" Britt wondered. She started to stand, but Ywain was already halfway to the door.

Merlin frowned. "It must be trouble."

Ywain hauled a door open to reveal Sir Tor.

"Oh, good. I thought you might be here," Sir Tor said, his usual good nature was a little subdued. "There's a knight here to see you, My Lord."

Out of all the knights of Camelot, Sir Gawain and Sir Tor were the most at ease with Britt's gender reveal. Gawain wasn't much of a shock—he had known all along Britt was a girl and kept his silence—but Tor's quick acceptance was a testimony of his good nature rather than a show of the esteem in which he held her.

"Who is it?" Britt asked, pushing back from the Round Table.

"Sir Lanval," Sir Tor said, stepping aside.

The knight—younger than Britt but older than Ywain and Gawain—stiffly entered the room. The normally handsome knight—who was a member of the Order of the Round Table— looked haggard and pale. His torso and right shoulder was swaddled in bandages that were rust-red with dried blood, and he walked with a limp.

"What happened, fair knight? Who did this to you?" Ywain gaped.

"Never mind that." Britt hurried to her wounded knight. "Call for a medic, er, healer. Send a servant to fetch new bandages— and hot water."

Sir Tor bowed. "As you wish, My Lord."

"Thank you, Sir Tor," Britt said, distracted as she studied the wounded knight. "Sword thrust to the shoulder?"

Sir Lanval inhaled slowly. "Yes."

"And the belly wound?" Britt asked with less worry. The fact that he could stand and walk assured her—it meant the belly-blow must not have pierced deeply—a fortunate thing as abdomen and belly wounds were the worst.

"A glancing blow," Sir Lanval said.

Britt frowned and leaned closer to look at his wrapped shoulder. "How did he get through your armor?"

"I wasn't wearing any, My Lord."

"*What?*"

Sir Lanval's face was downcast. "It was an unexpected encounter."

"Sir Lanval," Britt said.

"Yes, my Lord?"

Britt sighed when he wouldn't meet her eyes—a common occurrence since her big reveal. "Come, sit down. Standing around isn't going to do your injuries any favors," she said, leading the way back to the table.

Sir Lanval mulishly took up his assigned seat at the table, letting Britt, Sir Ector, Sir Ywain, and Merlin crowd around him. Sir Kay hung back and, to all appearances, took notes.

"Why have you come before the King, Sir Lanval?" Merlin asked, tilting his head back.

"Because of my strange encounter with the man who gave me these." Sir Lanval motioned to his wounds with his good arm.

"Who did it? Where were you?" Ywain—always eager for an adventure—drew closer to the knight.

"I was riding in the Forest of Arroy, searching for a new adventure or quest to set out upon, when I came across a magical fountain," Sir Lanval started. "I stopped to drink from it when a knight who called himself Sir Esclados the Red attacked me. He said he was the lord of a nearby castle and the protector of the spring."

"Spring?" Britt asked. "I thought you said it was a magical fountain."

"It is," Sir Lanval said, his eyes still downcast.

"But you just called it a spring."

"I did."

Britt looked to Merlin. "I don't understand. Does fountain mean something different, here?"

"Describe the fountain, Sir Lanval," Merlin instructed.

"It is a clear spring, and beside it stands a large block of marble and a gold basin."

"In what way is that supposed to be a fountain?" Britt grumbled. She sat down in one of the chairs next to Sir Lanval and petted Cavall when the mastiff placed his giant head on her lap.

"The knight said he guarded the fountain because if someone poured water on the marble, a fierce storm would suddenly break out," Sir Lanval continued. "He feared I was there to do just that, and attacked me, driving me from his lands."

"If he was so concerned about someone pouring water on the marble, why doesn't he remove the gold basin?" Britt asked.

"Hush," Merlin ordered.

"It's a fair question," Britt argued. "After all, how often do you go pouring water on chunks of marble?"

Merlin glared at Britt and pointedly turned his attention back to Sir Lanval.

"Well. I think it is a good point," Britt muttered, caressing Cavall's ears. When she looked up, she found Sir Ywain watching her.

"There is not much else to tell," Sir Lanval said, wincing when he tried to lift his injured arm. "Though I do not enjoy admitting my shameful defeat, I thought it would be wisest to inform you, My Lord, so you would know such a device exists."

Britt set aside her attitude to give the knight a smile. "You have my thanks, Sir Lanval, for bringing your knowledge forward. It is certainly a strange tale."

Sir Lanval still did not look up.

"What shall you do about it, Arthur?" Sir Ector asked, returning to her alias out of habit.

Britt shifted her eyes to the wizard. "Merlin?"

"We must address it. If such an artifact can be moved, it may be troublesome in the future."

"I agree," Britt said.

Merlin drew back in shock. "You do?"

She nodded. "At the very least, this Sir Esclados must be taught he cannot attack an unarmed man who has done him no harm."

Sir Lanval shook his head. "'Tis my shame that I lost, My Lord. I brought dishonor upon you by losing. As a knight of the Round Table, I am expected to be better."

"There is no shame in losing, Sir Lanval," Britt said.

Sir Lanval tucked his chin.

Britt stifled a sigh. "Look at me," she told the young man. She

243

was shocked when he complied, raising his eyes to meet her gaze. "I have lost more jousting matches to Sir Bodwain and Sir Kay than I can count. Does that make me ignoble?"

"Of course not, My Lord." Sir Lanval's lips morphed into a sharp frown.

"Winning all your fights is great and wonderful, but there will always be a knight who can match you in one area or another. It is not losing that brings shame, but how you react to it. Did you happen to stab Sir Esclados in the shoulder when he had his back to you?"

"Sir Lancelot has apologized for that—numerous times," Merlin reminded Britt.

"Did you?" Britt repeated, ignoring the wizard.

"No, My Lord."

"Then you did well, and you can be proud. If you learn from your fights—the ones you win and lose—I can ask for nothing more. Do you understand?"

"Yes, My Lord," Sir Lanval said.

Britt smiled in delight and reached out to clasp Sir Lanval on his (good) shoulder—a move she had performed a thousand times before while under the guise of King Arthur. It was the only manly expression of affection she could come up with. "You are a good knight, Sir Lanval."

Sir Lanval swallowed and gave Britt a shaky smile. He paled a little when he looked past Britt and saw Sir Kay staring at him.

Moments later, two manservants and a woman who carried a basket of herbs bustled into the room.

"Ah, here is your help, I believe, Sir Lanval." Merlin gestured to the servants. "I imagine you wish for them to attend to you in your chamber?"

"Yes," Sir Lanval said, standing with some assistance from Sir Ector. "Thank you, My Lord." He bowed once (as best he could) to Britt, nodded to the rest of the knights, and followed the servants out of the room. One of the servants closed the door behind them, breaking the silence.

"My Lord!" Ywain said, his voice echoing loudly in the large chamber. "I ask your permission to avenge Sir Lanval and seek out this magical fountain."

Britt shifted in her chair and thought for a moment. "No."

Ywain looked crestfallen. "But Sir Esclados must be corrected!"

"Yes," she agreed.

"Then why shouldn't I go? You don't trust me, is that it?"

"I trust you a great deal, Ywain," she said.

"It is because you think I'm not skilled enough."

Britt patted Cavall. "You have trained hard these past two years. You are quite skilled."

"Then why? You cannot keep me tied—you might be a woman, but you are not my mother!" the moment Ywain shouted these words his eyes bulged, and he almost strangled himself when he clasped his hands around his own throat.

The room was silent. Not even Merlin moved as they awaited Britt's reaction like the silence before a storm.

Britt took a moment to close her eyes and settle her emotions. As hurtful as her knights' outbursts—that, like this one, threw her gender in her face and their assumption that it made her weaker —were...she needed to bear it. For now. She was still winning her knights back after betraying their trust with her lies. She probably deserved the occasional comment.

"A thousand apologies, My Lord." Ywain's voice was tight as he bowed low. "That was reprehensible of me. I am shamed, and I have no excuse."

"My reason for you to not go, Sir Ywain, which you did not give me the chance to explain, is that a company of knights shall go to this Sir Esclados," Britt said. "I suspected you would want to go, and I planned to include you in their ranks."

Ywain did not move from his deep bow.

Merlin narrowed his eyes as he studied her. "Why a company of knights?"

"For several reasons. First of all, because of your point. If the marble block can be moved, we should bring it back—a task that is impossible for a lone knight," she said.

"Well thought. But a dozen knights could easily accomplish this. Why a company?"

"Because I will not send my knights and subjects to war. If you so badly want them to see action, then I will handle their activities myself."

"Taking your knights out on this excursion will only delay the inevitable," Merlin warned her.

"Perhaps, but it will give me more time to think. Ywain—please, stand up straight. I'm not angry."

"Yes, you are," Ywain said, his face red from all the blood rushing to it.

"Maybe a little, but I'm not *that* angry," Britt assured the young knight. "We're still settling in. There're going to be some tense moments. Although, if this becomes a habit—"

"It won't," Sir Ywain said. He hesitated and asked with a voice painfully raw with hope. "Then I am forgiven?"

"Of course. You're one of my closest knights, Ywain. I trust you," Britt said, offering him a smile.

Ywain inhaled deeply and nodded, the light of his eyes softening.

"We had best decide who else is to be included in this company of yours. We cannot leave Camelot undefended, and all will clamor to go," Merlin said.

Britt stared at the roughly 120 chairs gathered around the Round Table, remembering the men who sat there. "Sure. Merlin, that empty spot near mine," Britt said, pointing to a chair.

It had opened up some months ago when the knights first started questing. Many of the knights the incompetent King

Leodegrance had sent had slowly returned to Camelgrance over the past year. The men were "honorably" released as they claimed their own lands and dominions needed them, but in reality it was that these knights—used to an inactive king and an equally inactive life—were not happy with the questing and rigorous practicing Britt and the Round Table encouraged. As such, chairs and spots had opened up, and some of the knights rearranged themselves.

"Ah, yes. The seedy Sir Vaince used to sit there—he was one of King Leodegrance's closest knights. Probably left after spying on you long enough to learn you weren't going to marry Guinevere. What of it?"

"Are you saving it for Sir Mordred?"

Merlin rubbed his chin. "Not particularly."

"I don't know what to do about him," Britt said.

Merlin scowled. "Why? I thought the two of you would become instant companions of the heart."

"Why?" Sir Ector asked.

"When I inquired after his parentage so I would know what degree of care I should afford him, he refused to answer."

"Why?" Sir Ector repeated, baffled.

"Said he wanted to be respected for his own merits and conduct, not his lineage," Merlin said, sounding disgusted. "If I didn't know any better, I would say he is a spy who has studied you closely, lass."

Britt tried to laugh, but it fell flat. She was conflicted over Mordred. She vaguely remembered his name from the tirades that Lyssa, one of her lost modern-day friends, used to go off on. Mordred was no friend to King Arthur, but she couldn't recall much beyond that. She had always saved her hatred for the scumbag Sir Lancelot and the adulterous Guinevere.

Even more thought-provoking, Merlin was right. Mordred was Britt's perfect vision of a Knight of Camelot. Still, Britt wasn't certain how close she wanted to bring him, and Merlin agreed that until he joined the Round Table, he was to remain ignorant of her gender.

Someone knocked on the door.

"Yes?" Britt shouted.

Sir Ulfius—her chamberlain and one of Merlin's companions —stepped inside. "My Lord, there are a few decisions that must be made for tomorrow's tournament—like the champion's boon, the distance for the archery targets, and so forth."

"Right." She sighed. "Come in, Sir Ulfius, and take a seat. But Merlin, don't think I've forgotten. After the tournament, I want to organize a company to go to that marble block."

"It was a fountain, lass," Merlin said.

"I refuse to call it that," she said.

"Of course you would," Merlin grunted. "I shall begin drawing up the plans. Good evening, Britt."

"'Night, Merlin."

2

THE TOURNAMENT

King Arthur is a legendary British king and hero. His historical existence and role is widely debated, but he is said to have been crowned at age fifteen on the day of Pentecost. The day of his crowning ceremony, he selected Merlin as his counselor, Sir Ulfius as his chamberlain, Sir Bodwain as his constable, his foster brother Sir Kay as seneschal, and Sir Bedivere as marshal.

"I know! But what about Mordred?" Britt murmured as she poured over her Britain Travel Guide—one of the very few mementos she had left from her twenty-first century life.

...The only story as famous, or perhaps even more famous, than Arthur is the romantic relationship between Guinevere and Sir Lancelot —Arthur's best knight. It is said that Guinevere's affair with Lancelot destroyed Camelot and King Arthur's Court.

"Somewhere in this book, Mordred's historical significance must be referenced." She grumbled as she flipped to the back to peruse the index, again. She missed Google. And smart phones. She glanced up from the book and shifted in her seat—a cushioned chair positioned under a red tent. The comfy chair and the tent were thoughtful gestures, but they were positioned not for her comfort, but to keep her out of the way as the grounds swarmed with people making last-minute adjustments for the tournament.

Ill at ease, Britt stared out at the knights in shining armor accented with their colors. They led their prancing chargers, and their squires trailed behind them. Commoners were already claiming patches of grass to sit on, and court ladies filed into rows of chairs.

"Is everything well, My Lord?"

Surprised by the voice, Britt set her guidebook aside and smiled. "Sir Bedivere, what a pleasant surprise. Yes, I'm fine. I was merely thinking."

Sir Bedivere nodded, though his expression was not convinced. "Is there anything I can do to aid you?"

Britt stood and adjusted her gold-leafed curiass—which covered her chest. "Maybe...tell me, what do you think of Sir Mordred?"

"Mordred?" Sir Bedivere's eyebrows went up in surprise.

Britt nodded.

Sir Bedivere turned to look out of the tent, his eyes settling on the young knight.

Mordred was a comely young man with coffee-colored hair that was closely cropped to his head—an oddity in Britt's courts. He had deep dimples that made him absolutely charming when he smiled, and his facial structure was almost fine enough to rival Lancelot. His eyes, just like Lancelot's, were even green. However, while Lancelot's had a dreamy look to them, Mordred's were dark, and glittered with chips the color of obsidian.

"He's not quite like anyone in Camelot," Sir Bedivere said.

"He is not passionate and brash—like Griflet and Ywain—nor does he sport a perpetual good mood—like Sir Tor. He hasn't Sir Bodwain's wisdom, Kay's seriousness, Gawain's quiet thoughtfulness, or your loyalty," Britt said, standing shoulder-to-shoulder with her marshal.

"Your words are too kind, My Lord," Sir Bedivere said.

"I am no flatterer, Sir Bedivere. I call it as I see it. Unfortunately, I cannot seem to call Mordred."

"You will," Sir Bedivere said. "No one can hide from you very long."

Her lips curved into a small smile, and she retreated deeper into her tent. "I'm not so sure about that, but I apologize. Did you need me?"

Sir Bedivere trailed after her. "Yes, I wish to inform you of something."

"Oh?"

"One of your knights left in the middle of the night."

"Was it Lancelot—please let it be Lancelot." Britt twisted to look out at the tournament grounds again.

"Nay, Sir Lancelot is still present. He is preparing for the tournament as we speak."

Britt sighed and poured herself a tankard of water. "Just my luck."

"Don't you care who it is?"

She threw herself in her cushioned chair. "If it's not Lancelot, then not particularly. Almost all my other favorite knights are gone questing, or they are tied to their jobs here in Camelot, so it can't be them."

"I do not think you are recalling all of your closest knights."

Britt ran her free hand through her blonde hair—the top half of which was pulled back in a "manly" half-pony tail and tied off with a leather chord. "Really? Who am I forgetting?"

"Sir Ywain."

"Ywain—I should have known he would run off after that knight and fake fountain." Britt sighed.

"Are you angry?"

"No, but I am disappointed."

"In his conduct?"

"Not at all. It's just that without him, I don't have a buffer for Lancelot," Britt wryly said.

Sir Bedivere coughed to cover a snort.

Britt sipped her water. "It's selfish of me, I know."

"No, I believe I can understand your feelings. The past few weeks, Sir Lancelot has been especially…vocal."

"He's been a royal pain, braying all sorts of stupid declarations at the top of his lungs. I'm surprised Merlin hasn't lectured him yet."

"He has."

"And I *missed* it?"

"I believe Merlin conducted the chastisements in secret for that very purpose."

"Blast. Well, no harm is done by Ywain leaving. With luck, I'll still be able to talk Merlin into taking a company to the fake-fountain. Although I'm truly sorry he's going to miss entering the tournament. I thought he would stand a chance at winning the jousting portion."

"There will be more tournaments in the future."

"I guess."

"If you'll excuse me, My Lord." Sir Bedivere bowed and left the tent.

Britt watched him go, feeling a little lightened. Sir Bedivere had been quite stiff for days after Britt's reveal. As one of her most loyal—and emotionally invested—knights, he felt particularly betrayed by Britt's secret. His slight emotional thaw encouraged her.

"My Lord—you-hoo! King Arthur!" Guinevere called, cupping her hands around her mouth. When she caught Britt's attention, she waved and motioned for her to join her at the royal stand.

"The tournament is ready to begin—are you really certain I can sit with you?" she anxiously asked when Britt joined her on the platform—which also had a canopy pitched over it to shade

Britt's makeshift throne, as well as Guinevere's and Merlin's chairs.

"Yes, of course," Britt smiled at the younger girl. Guinevere was the daughter of King Leodegrance and was a semi-permanent guest at Camelot. When Britt visited Camelgrance—her father's castle—Guinevere had begged Britt to allow her to go to Camelot with her in order to escape her father—who was not unkind, but planned to use Guinevere's marriage as a bargaining tool and would not hesitate to tie her to a less-than-savory character.

Her presence was beneficial for both of them. As long as Guinevere was rumored to be Britt's—Arthur's—favorite, her father wouldn't dream of bringing her home; and as long as Guinevere—who knew Britt's real gender—sat at Britt's sides for events like today's tournament, women were much less pushy and flirtatious with Britt.

"Any knights in particular you are cheering for?" Britt asked.

"Sir Lancelot—*of course*—and Sir Percival. Sir Agravain got back early this morning, and he intends to fight as well. He won't be as impressive as his brother, of course, but few can beat Sir Gawain," the young lady rattled off.

"He's been a knight for two weeks; I should think Gawain wouldn't be trounced by such a green knight," Britt said.

"I suppose so," Guinevere shrugged. "There's also Sir Lionel—he is *such* fun…"

Guinevere chattered on until the knights gathered for the tournament opening. "I would cheer the most for you if you were fighting," she finished. Although loyalty was not a trait Guinevere often possessed, Britt had been surprised on more than one occasion with her faithfulness.

"Thank you," Britt said, thinking—with some guilt—of all the times she complained to Merlin about hosting the bird-brained (but kind) girl.

Merlin climbed onto the dais. "Arthur, it's time."

Guinevere bobbed a curtsy and scampered to her chair.

"Any idea what I should say?" Britt asked as she and Merlin walked to the edge of the platform.

"Good luck, and don't kill each other," Merlin said, squinting out at the crowds. "Bloody-minded ruffians."

"You were the one who suggested a tournament."

"It is a good way to judge the skills of your men yourself, so you are not forced to rely on their assurances. That doesn't mean it is at all refined," Merlin said. "Besides, they have long desired this, and you *need* to boost their opinion of you as much as possible right now."

Britt shook her head at her advisor and turned to her knights, her courts, and her people. "Thank you for attending this joyous occasion. It is a day worth remembering, for these courageous, honorable knights who stand before us shall do battle to find the man who is the most skilled and the most capable—the best knight in all of Camelot!"

The spectators cheered and clapped, drowning Britt out.

She waited until the noise subsided before directly addressing her knights. "You have worked hard for today, and I am eager to see how the sweat and blood you have shed have shaped and prepared you. No matter the outcome of today's tournament, I am proud to call you my knights and to have you stand at my side! Good luck—may the *best* knight win!"

The crowds roared again, and the knights bowed to Britt from horseback. Britt smiled, but it was a shallow, fragile gesture. Usually her knights would be overflowing with mirth and joy, but there was still that strained air...

It's been only a few weeks. I need to give them more time. Things will get better, I hope.

Britt held her fist above her head and moved to take her seat.

"You still have it, even after all your trials," Merlin said.

"What?" Britt twitched her chair a smidge before sitting down.

Merlin smirked. "The charisma and pretty words charming enough to make a lion eat from your hand."

"Of course. What, with all the practice I've been getting, did you actually think I would get worse?"

"You get worse? Never. So, Lady Guinevere, King Arthur. Who do you hope will win?"

3
THE QUEEN'S CHAMPION

The tournament lasted for hours. There were jousting matches, archery competitions, sword battles, and more.

Colors, coat of arms, and personal symbols paraded past Britt and her dais as the matches progressed. Predictably, Lancelot was at the front of the pack, although Sir Mordred—in a surprise move—trailed closely behind him.

"'Tis a pity Sir Lanval is too injured to fight," Guinevere sighed in longing. "He is ever so handsome."

"Yes, although I am more regretful that Sir Kay nor Sir Bodwain were allowed to enter," Britt said.

"For the last time: you, nor any of your men—like Sir Ulfius and Sir Bedivere—can enter. The point of the tournament is to find the best *knight*, not the best vassal," Merlin said.

"Sir Kay is an excellent knight."

"Sir Kay is your seneschal and does not go questing and adventuring as your knights do. And you cannot fool me; the only reason you wanted Kay or Bodwain to enter is because they would be guaranteed to beat Lancelot in jousting."

Britt grew misty-eyed. "It would have been a glorious thing, to watch one of them tossing Lancelot from his horse like a ragdoll."

"You are just as savage as the rest of your subjects," Merlin muttered.

"I think they are about to begin the last match. Only the brave Sir Lancelot and Sir Mordred remain." Guinevere leaned forward in glee. "Look how Sir Lancelot's clear brow gleams in the sun."

"Because he's sweating," Britt said.

Guinevere heaved a sappy sigh. "It's so heroic."

Britt was admittedly out of touch with girl-talk—her closest female friends in this time period were the mouthy Lady of the Lake, Nymue, and the war-like enchantress, Morgan. Neither of them took the time to notice Britt's knights, much less admire them, but Britt couldn't help but think how bizarre medieval girl-talk was. "Unless, was it always this silly, and I just never noticed?" she muttered as Lancelot—in silver and blue—and Mordred—in black and red—directed their horses to opposite ends of the jousting field.

A herald blew a horn, and the men spurred their horses, driving them forward in a flood of blue and a storm of black. There was a massive crack when they met, but both men stayed in the saddle.

Britt winced in sympathy for Mordred. Lancelot had once unhorsed her with a bone-crunching blow. Mordred had to have a significant amount of strength to ride out the blow and return for a second pass.

The crowd murmured with excitement as the knights lined up at opposite ends of the jousting field, again. The herald sounded his horn a second time, and the horses burst forward. When they met this time, there was a tremendous crack as Lancelot's lance shattered.

The men returned to their posts, and a squire ran out to deliver a new weapon to Lancelot. The young, charismatic knight flipped up his the visor of his helm to smile at the squire. He took a moment to wave to his supporters—drawing cheers—then flipped his visor back down. In the split second before his face disappeared, Britt could have sworn she saw him frown.

"He's actually taking this seriously," Britt said.

"Who, Lancelot? Of course he is. He wouldn't miss the chance to be titled the best knight of Camelot for all the riches in your courts," Merlin said.

Guinevere twisted the end of her braid. "Sir Lancelot du Lac is serious in all of his ventures."

Britt was unconvinced. She had never before seen the knight wear a look of such grim determination. "What is he up to?"

She didn't wonder long, for the knights spurred their horses forward into another run. There was the familiar crack of the lances hitting shields, and Mordred was thrown from his black steed.

The crowd roared.

"Brave Sir Lancelot!"

"The Greatest Knight of Camelot!"

"Hurrah for Sir Lancelot!"

The field monitors ran to Mordred to see if he was still alive, but he was already peeling himself off the ground. He pulled his helm off and smiled, wincing a bit when a young page helped him stand.

"Well fought, Sir Lancelot. It was an honor to cross lances with you. You, indeed, are the best," he said, bowing.

Lancelot wrenched his helm off. "You have such valiance, Sir Mordred. The honor was all mine," he said before undoing the humbleness of his words by riding up and down the field with his right arm raised, gathering cheers and squeals.

"Sir Lancelot!"

"Knight of the Lac!"

"Peerless among knights!"

As Lancelot's win was not unexpected, Britt had spent hours

preparing herself so she could smile at the knight she detested. Watching him, she was glad she had.

When he finally finished bathing in the praise of the crowds, Lancelot approached Britt's dais and bowed on the back of his horse. "My Lord, King Arthur!"

"Well done, Sir Lancelot du Lac," Britt said in a voice falsely filled with wonder. "You have proven yourself today, out of those *present*, to be the best knight of Camelot. In honor of your feat, I bequeath you that title."

"Thank you, My Lord." Lancelot's green eyes shone with exuberance.

"He certainly lives for the crowds," Britt muttered. She cast her eyes to the side and smiled with a little more realness when Mordred, leading his horse, limped up to the podium. "Sir Mordred, well done. You also fought valiantly today. Though you cannot share the title, I must say I am proud and awed by your performance." Merlin cleared his throat and Britt quickly amended, "*Both* of your performances."

Mordred bowed. "Thank you, My Lord. It was my honor."

"I was especially impressed with your swordsmanship, Mordred," Britt continued, warming up to the subject she was most passionate about. "Your matches were splendid to watch."

"I thank you for the compliment, My Lord, but I fear I am yet unskilled." Sir Mordred stroked his horse's muscled neck.

Merlin shifted closer to Britt—probably so he could be within elbowing range—and frowned. "The boon," he whispered.

"I'm getting to it," she hissed. She cleared her throat before continuing, "As Lancelot is the winner of today's contest of arms, I will—as I promised—grant him a boon. What is it you wish for, Sir Lancelot?"

Lancelot studied Britt for a moment before he smiled—his slick smile that was dangerously close to being a smirk. "I request permission to be the Queen's Champion."

Spectators gasped and cheered at the "kindness" of

Lancelot's request. As King Arthur, Britt couldn't serve as the Queen's Champion—she didn't have the time, and it would have opened up political battles. If Lancelot did not know of Britt's real gender, the action would have only been pompous and politically motivated as there was no queen. But, as he knew Britt was a girl, there was only one way she could interpret his actions.

He was openly asking to be declared *HER* champion, as she was secretly a queen.

"Accept his request, lass," Merlin whispered.

"You cannot be serious," Britt hissed.

"You cannot easily deny his request. Accept it, and I will speak with him. In *private*."

"Why not publically? He deserves to be humiliated," Britt snarled.

"My Lord?" Lancelot said, his eyes falsely innocent and artless. "Is my request inappropriate?"

"Accept it," Merlin said.

Britt squared her shoulders and stood. "No, it is only unusual as I don't even *have* a queen, yet. Trying to get ahead of the competition, Sir Lancelot?" she asked, making a show of smiling at the man—as if she was teasing him.

Lancelot laughed back. "Perhaps, My Lord."

"Very well. If that is the boon you wish for, you shall have it— though I warn you it will be a *long* wait before your services are ever needed," Britt said. She hopped off the platform and unsheathed Excalibur as Lancelot slid off his horse. He knelt before her, and she touched Excalibur to his shoulders. "I call you, Sir Lancelot du Lac, the Queen's Champion!"

As she hoped, the spectators went wild and crazy, so as Britt leaned in—Excalibur weighing heavily on Lancelot's shoulders— no one heard her whisper, "Step carefully, or the *Queen* will eat you alive."

Britt made a show of pulling Lancelot into a standing position. "Camelot, I give you your victor!" she said before "playfully" pushing the knight at the roaring crowd.

Ladies squealed and fanned themselves, and children strained on their tip-toes to see the famed knight.

"They do love him," Sir Mordred said, his words mirroring Britt's earlier utterances.

"Yeah. You fought well, though, Sir Mordred. I thought you almost had him," Britt said, turning to the dark-armored knight.

Sir Mordred chuckled. "It was never that close. He hits like a dragon."

"I was impressed you lasted three rounds. He unhorsed me at two—and he was gentle for the first pass," Britt said.

"You've jousted Sir Lancelot?"

"Yes. He moved to jousting after learning not to test my sword." She twirled Excalibur then slid it back in its magical scabbard. "It's a shame King Pellinore couldn't make it—although I appreciate Percival's presence. I think Pellinore would have beaten him. Sir Kay and Sir Bodwain, though, could have thrashed him while blindfolded."

"I have heard of their great prowess on the jousting field. Perhaps I should ask them for pointers." Sir Mordred's dimples flashed when he smiled.

Britt—who took great pride in her foster-brother's abilities, felt highly gratified. "If you can catch Kay when he's not buried in work, he's an excellent teacher. He made me into a passable jouster, which I thought was beyond my grasp."

"Never, My Lord," Sir Mordred protested. "You are too hard on yourself!"

"You didn't see what I was like when I first started. I think he would enjoy helping you, particularly as you are already quite skilled." Britt noticed Merlin staring at her—and Mordred—and gave the wizard a questioning look. He averted his eyes and turned his back to her. She mentally frowned at his odd behavior, but kept her expression pleasant.

"Perhaps, then, I might win next time," Sir Mordred said. "That is, of course, assuming there will *be* a next time?"

"Count on it," she emphatically said, wrinkling her nose as she watched Lancelot smile at a court lady, making her swoon. "In fact, if you can take the title of Best Knight at the next tournament, I will forever hold you in high esteem." As far as Britt was concerned, the sooner Lancelot was pushed from his throne of "Best Knight," the better.

~

"L et the mead run thick and the wine spill over—the Knights of the Round Table have proved their valor!" Lancelot shouted.

"Hear, Hear!" Sir Percival, King Pellinore's oldest son, said.

"Drink up!" Lionel—Lancelot's boisterous cousin—yelled.

Two tables down, a knight tipsily stood on top of a table and recited terrible poetry about Guinevere. Just past Bors, the injured Sir Lanval was already passed out and lay snoozing on the ground.

"I always thought the King made brief appearances at our celebration before leaving because he was too busy." Bors contemplated his goblet of wine. "Now I know better."

"This drunken display is enough to make anyone hiding a secret as she did nervous," Lancelot said. "There's no telling what drunkards would do."

In spite of his words, it had not escaped Lancelot's notice that barely a word was uttered over their King, and whenever someone mentioned her, they were careful to use her title only—never her name or gender.

"It seems I am not the only one with their eye on our little King," Lancelot said.

"Little?" Lionel snorted. "Our King may be slight, but she's as little as Kay is talkative. Speaking of which, what was this afternoon about? The Queen's Champion? *You*? You're as faithful as a stallion!"

Lancelot frowned. "I am loyal to those I choose to serve."

Lionel swatted the air. "Of course—until you change your mind."

Lancelot smiled so hard his teeth ached. "Naturally. Here, have some more wine, cousin."

"Thank you." Lionel chugged the drink after Lancelot topped off his goblet.

Lancelot glanced at his younger cousin, surprised by his narrowed eyes. "What is it?" he asked, fixing a look of good will upon his features.

"Nothing. Just thinking," Bors said.

"That's no good. We're not supposed to think tonight. Instead, *we drink!*" Lancelot shouted, emptying a pitcher of wine into Bors' goblet.

The rest of the knights roared their approval.

An hour later, all of the men—even stuffy Bors—were completely drunk. "My Lord is going to *kill* us," Bors said, barely able to keep his head upright.

"Let 'er try. I ain't afraid of no woman," Lionel slurred.

"Then you don't know our Dragon King," Sir Safir—who showed a surprisingly high tolerance level for a man who commonly played the harp—snorted.

"Killing us would be a kindness. My head already aches," another knight bemoaned.

"Here's an idea," Lancelot said, standing. He made a show of tottering for a few steps. "Why don't we make an *order*, the Order of Queen's Knights?"

"Eh? What?"

"Why would we do a *stupid* thing like that?" another knight said, his voice unnaturally high from the abundance of alcohol. "Our King...Queen? Eh, that woman's first act would be to slaughter us all and have us buried."

"Only if she got to us afore Merlin found out," another knight added. "If we make an order for a queen the public don't know we have…it'll raise a few questions. Merlin *hates* questions."

Lancelot stepped in before the knights could out-logic themselves of the idea. "Even if we call her our King and serve her as we would serve a King, she is still a woman," he said. "She delights our souls the way only a woman can. She knows the best and worst of us, and she still sees worth in us. No man could do that—least, I don't for all of you," Lancelot said, getting the desired laughter.

"She makes enormous demands," Sir Agravain said, slumped on a bench. "But she is loyal and looks at a person like, like…"

"Like she believes in you, like she can see straight into your heart and knows that you're strong and valiant."

Lancelot froze for a moment—the voice sounded too terribly much like Sir Mordred's, whom he had worked hard to lead out of the gathering so he could prod this conversation. Thankfully, it seemed Sir Percival was the one who said such a surprisingly astute observation.

"That's what makes her great," Sir Bedivere said—the only one of Britt's officials present, thank goodness. Kay would kill him before the King would. "She's not like other women, who lose faith in you the moment you lose a match or commit a sin. She trusts in your goodness and strength."

Lancelot moved in for the kill. "And she would have us think —no—*Merlin* would have us think her strength is boundless. Yet, she is but one person, and times have changed. We ride out and leave her, for the good of the kingdom. But what about *her*? Can't we be knights errant *and* our sovereign's protectors?"

"Yeah!"

"Can't we?"

"Hear, hear!"

"Then let those of us present take a vow to protect our King," Lancelot declared.

"Hurrah!"

In minutes, the Queen's Knights were formed, the oaths—predetermined by Lancelot—were taken, and the celebration was back in full swing. Not all the knights present took the oath, and there were a few that *had* taken the oath that he intended to expel. But there was no need to worry about it tonight. The order was just another way to try and move the King.

She is so untrusting! Lancelot thought. Ever since King Arthur revealed she was really Queen Britt, Lancelot had shifted goals. After all, how much fun would it be to have the *High King of Britain* calf-eyed over him! There were a few problems with this plan. Foremost, the disgustingly honorable girl appeared to like him the least out of all her knights, even though he was the greatest. Secondly, Lancelot was starting to suspect that King *Britt* was not the type of woman to get calf-eyed and stupid when she was in love. Which was quite unfortunate.

"I wonder what she *would* look like, if she were to fall in love," Lancelot murmured.

Lionel dragged his attention from his cup. "What's that?"

"Nothing," Lancelot said. He leaned back in his chair, mulling over the idea. Though she looked at each of her knights as if he was a dragon-slayer, no one would be so stupid as to think she actually fancied any of them. She was warm to all of her men—exceedingly so to her pets like Gawain and Ywain—but she didn't look like a woman in love, just as her knights did not look at her with any unholy thoughts.

What about Merlin? She does not look at him the way she looks at any of us. The thought wiggled in the back of Lancelot's mind, and though his first impulse was to mercilessly crush it—who, after all, would pass *him* by in exchange for Merlin, the crackpot wizard?—he thought it over.

It was no secret Britt and Merlin had a big fight in the summer of the previous year. Although they were on good terms, things had been stilted between them for months. *But.* There was the way she looked at him. Her soul—vulnerable and fragile—glimmered in her eyes. She was hesitant to reach out and touch her advisor, and while their smiles were frequent, shared laughter was not often present.

Britt, our High King, is in love with Merlin.

Lancelot narrowed his eyes as he considered the idea, and decided it was the most realistic. *He must have rejected her, for he knows it as well.*

Neither observation afforded Lancelot pleasure. What the King saw in Merlin was a mystery to Lancelot, but the bigger mystery was Merlin's rejection. One would think he would encourage her feelings—if only to make her more malleable. But looking past plots and politics, Britt had her knights and relationships. Merlin had...Britt. Although he had the loyalty of thousands, he had the heart of none. *None except for Britt's, that is.*

"Why the gloomy face, Sir Lancelot?" Sir Percival—one of the milder drinkers—sat down next to him. "It is your night! You are the Best Knight of Camelot, the Queen's Champion—sly move, by the by—and the founder of the Queen's Knights. You have done well! I especially admired your match against Sir Mordred."

"Yes, Sir Mordred is a jouster of high caliber," Lancelot said, absent-mindedly rubbing his aching shoulder. The knight had hit him with the force of a rampaging boar. "I saw your match against Sir Agravain. Your stance was impeccable."

"Thank you—though I must admit, Agravain was much better than I thought he would be, given he is a knight of but a few weeks," Sir Percival said.

"I expect you have his teachers to thank. Before he served as Gawain's squire, he spent hours on the jousting fields with King Arthur, watching her, Sir Kay, and Sir Bodwain. Or so I've been told."

"Trains like a madman."

"Agravain?"

"No, our King." Sir Percival paused to take a drink and licked his lips. "Have you seen her—practicing with Excalibur on the walls of Camelot in the late night hours?"

"Yes," Lancelot said, keeping his expression hooded.

"I've talked with Sir Gawain in between his quests and defense as the Ladies' Knight. He said it's when her demons plague her."

"I see," Lancelot said, employing all of his strength to keep a smile off his face. He often wondered what kept the King up at the late hours. Her emotional scars, was it? *Perhaps I have been going about this all wrong...*

4

REASSURANCES & ARRIVALS

E arly the next morning, Britt sat on her cushioned throne in the beautiful throne room of Camelot. The morning sunlight trickled in through the windows, making her armored—bowing—knights glitter. Birds sang outside, and the blue sky seemed especially brilliant and glorious.

Britt, however, was so enraged she couldn't speak. She had a stranglehold on her tankard of juice, and dug the nails of her other hand into the arms of her wooden throne. She was so furious, she shook.

Cavall, sitting at her side, whined and leaned away.

"You did *what?*" Britt hissed.

Lancelot puffed his chest up with pride. "We founded the Order of the Queen's Knights."

"We?" Britt inquired, her tone mild.

"Well, it was *my* idea," he preened.

Someone banged on the shut doors. "Arthur—I know who you've got in there. Open these doors!" Merlin shouted.

The guards stationed at the door moved to let the wizard in.

"DON'T!" Britt thundered. She rocketed out of her chair, and jabbed her finger at the door while giving the one-word order.

The guards shifted back into place, their mouths grim lines.

Britt rested her hand on Excalibur's pommel as she went down the few stairs of the dais on which her throne was perched. "Merlin's attempts to rein you in obviously have not worked. It is now my turn," she said. Her gold armor clanked, and her red cloak swirled behind her.

The knights swapped worried looks—Britt was surprised to see Sir Percival and Sir Agravain among them—but Britt made a beeline for the smug Lancelot.

"In case you have forgotten, *Champion*, my identity is still a secret. Only my valiant Knights of the Round Table and my hand-picked personal guards know that I am really a woman. No one else in Camelot knows, nor do the rest of my subjects, allies, vassals, or enemies. When I was placed back on the throne, you— along with every man in this room—took a vow to protect my secret with your *life*." Britt glared into Lancelot's green eyes.

"Arthur, stop this at once and open the door!" Merlin shouted again.

"As it stands, you have done a *horrible* job of standing true to your vow." Britt spoke in a tone of frosted fire.

"*Arthur!* If you kill him, I will make your life a misery! Guards, open this blasted door!"

"I apologize if you find my conduct worrisome, My Lord. I only have your best interests in mind," Lancelot said.

Britt opened her mouth to reply, but she was shocked when someone released a happy sigh. She twisted on her heels, her lips slightly downturned as she looked—with eyes as hard as granite —at Sir Bedivere. "What."

"T'is nothing, My Lord, I apologize for interrupting you," Sir Bedivere said.

"No. You sighed. In happiness. What is it?"

"It's only that, even though you are a woman, you are still our Dragon King."

"Our Elf King," another knight added.

269

She turned, sweeping her eyes across her gathered knights. "I don't understand."

Agravain bowed. "I believe the idea, My Lord, is that although you are a woman, you are still the fierce being we know you to be."

"Aye," Sir Safir said. "I saw that enraged look in your eyes when you faced down Urien with the wrath of an ageless elf."

"ARTHUR!" Merlin howled and banged on the door some more.

"I see. Thank you, I think," Britt awkwardly said. She turned back to Lancelot with renewed vengeance. "But *you*—"

"While I do not regret creating the Queen's Knights—for you are worthy of such honor, My Lord—I will say in the...state I was in, I perhaps was not at my clearest," Lancelot said.

"You were drunk," Britt said. It wasn't a guess, but a fact. The knights' haggard appearances were a big enough tip-off, but she had known last night that *Lancelot* had plans for a party that would put a twenty-first century fraternity house to shame.

"I was," Lancelot said, sounding pious as he tipped his head. "I apologize for my excessive indulgence, but I shall endeavor to make amends and regain your favor."

"You never *had* my favor to begin with."

"Arthur, if you do not open this door, I will blast it to bits!" Merlin shouted.

"Steady," Britt said to her guards.

"If that is so, then I have an even greater vested interest in my mission," Lancelot said.

"You expect me to believe that sending you out questing is a *punishment* to you?" She asked, raising one eyebrow.

Lancelot bowed his head.

"I don't buy it," Britt said.

"My Lord?" Lancelot forehead wrinkled.

"On the count of three!" Merlin warned.

Britt smiled—a barely-there curve of her lips. "Here is my

judgment. If your actions and attitude haven't altered by the time you return to Camelot after an appropriate amount of questing, you will forfeit the title of Queen's Champion."

Several knights gasped, but Lancelot did not look surprised.

"One!" Merlin shouted.

"As you wish, My King." Lancelot accented his words with a polished bow.

"Two!"

Britt pointed to the door. "Guards," she said.

"Three!"

With great relief, the guards hauled the doors open, revealing Merlin, holding a ball of fire in his palm.

"I shall begin my journey immediately," Lancelot said. He bowed to her, then strode from the room, smiling at a confused Merlin as he passed him in the doorway.

Merlin frowned and watched the handsome knight leave. "He's not maimed. What did you do to him?"

"Nothing...yet." Britt turned her attention to the rest of her knights. "I release you from my presence, though you should know I am still angry with this development. I suggest you all see the cook in the kitchens. She has a draught to help cure hangovers."

"You do not wish to punish us, My Lord?" Agravain asked.

Britt wanted to shout and lecture them, but she knew they would react poorly to such a chastisement, so instead she gave them her best verbal punch. "No." She smiled with all the tranquility she could muster. "I am filled with grave disappointment over your conduct, but I *trust* you—as I always have. I do hope you will act with greater wisdom next time, wisdom I *know* you possess."

The knights winced and exchanged guilty glances. "My Lord," they murmured before they left the room in a massive herd.

"What did you do to them?" Merlin asked when they all left. "I haven't seen them so at ease in your presence since the reveal."

Britt shrugged. "I was furious. It seemed to make them feel better."

"Ahhh, I think I understand. It assured them you are the same person." Merlin folded his arms across his chest and nodded.

"So they said, but I still don't get it. No matter; the issue has been resolved, and Lancelot is going to go questing for a while—months, I hope. It has been a good morning." She slapped her thighs. "Cavall, come!"

"Where do you think you're going?" Merlin trailed after her with her guard dog.

"Riding with Sir Ector."

"We have Ireland to think of."

"And my foster-father leaves tomorrow for the rest of the summer. I'm spending time with him."

The wizard sighed. "It is understandable, I suppose. But I want to see you in my study this evening."

"As you wish," Britt said. When she left Merlin in the corridor, she was already planning ways she could derail the inevitable conversation of invading Ireland.

~

"RUDOLPH, come on. There's better grazing up ahead." Britt tugged on the rope tied to the white stag's red halter. Rudolph followed behind her like a dog, wiggling his white tail. They stopped at a patch of wildflowers—the deer's favorite food—and Britt settled in, patting her giant pet's back with an absent-minded fondness.

Behind her, Camelot rose up—a picture-perfect fortification of stone walls and towers, surrounded by forest. The Forest of Arroy circled around the castle in a horseshoe shape, and Britt and her companions were picking their way to the open plains at Camelot's flank—where there was rich farmland and, most importantly, an abundance of wildflowers.

The sky was heavy with smoke-gray clouds, but Merlin insisted it wouldn't rain. His faith in his weather-telling skills was obvious, as he carried rolls of parchment. At the moment, he brandished a rolled-up map and muttered under his breath as he poked around the grassland. He squinted out at the farmland, compared it to his map, and muttered incessantly.

Past him, Kay strolled with Morgan. It was a surprising pair, but as the grave seneschal and the beautiful sorceress strolled, Morgan laughed, and Kay's mustache twitched—which was his equivalent of a smile.

Are they friends? Morgan has never seemed particularly close with Kay...have they united under their mutual distaste for Merlin?

"Do you graze your white hart often, My Lord?" Mordred asked, drawing Britt's attention from the unlikely pair.

"No, there's a stable boy who is assigned the duty. But as Gawain went through a great deal of trouble to procure Rudolph for me, I feel I need to be a halfway decent pet owner," Britt said, scratching the animal's shoulders.

Rudolph rewarded her by smearing a plant across her golden curiass. "Not that he seems to care," She muttered as she wiped plant residue off her chest.

"I had heard much of you before I arrived in Camelot." Mordred seated himself on a large boulder and offered her a smile charming enough to spatter on a magazine cover in modern America. "I must confess, you are not what I expected."

Britt tilted her head, trying to get a gauge on him. "Oh? What did you think I would be—a noble man with great bearings?" She asked, jealously thinking of King Pellinore, who oozed nobility from every pore.

"You *are* a noble man, and your presence cannot be summarized with the mere word 'great,'" Mordred said.

She snorted in disbelief and followed Rudolph as he moved closer to Mordred.

"It's not just you, but your court and subjects as well. You rule over the cleanest castle-folk I have ever set eyes on."

"It's the public baths," Britt said.

"I heard the Romans had such things. It's a brilliant plan," he said. "Especially for one so young."

"What?" Britt frowned.

"I thought you were only seventeen or eighteen—am I mistaken?"

"Nooo," Britt said, dragging out the o. Although she had graduated college, Merlin insisted Britt say she was fifteen when she was crowned King of England.

"Fascinating," Mordred said.

"In what way is my age fascinating?"

Mordred leaned forward and rested his forearms on his knees. "Your age was not particularly what I was thinking of. It is more the air in which you carry yourself. I heard much about you from a dear friend. He boasted in particular that you were able to win the hearts and loyalty of your knights. I doubted him, but I must confess he spoke the truth."

"What is the name of this friend of yours?" Britt asked, wondering if she would for once be able to out maneuver Merlin and find out Mordred's political connections before the wizard did.

Mordred smiled—it was small, as if he knew a good joke but couldn't find the right moment to share it. "He does not know you well, but he has spoken often with Sir Ector, who is very vocal—and rightly so—of your praises."

"If your friend's source is Sir Ector, I'm afraid I will be a bitter disappointment," Britt laughed. "Sir Ector has a parent's pride."

"Perhaps, but I came here to weigh your character. I have found Sir Ector's portrayal of you to be perhaps not entirely accurate, but faithful."

Britt would have questioned him further, but at that moment someone called out, "My Lord!"

Britt swung around to see Sir Ulfius striding across the field, a beautiful girl gliding behind him.

She couldn't have been more than fifteen or sixteen. She was beautiful with blonde hair and hazel eyes, but had a self-conscious, mean-spirited presence that reminded Britt of the catty, popular girls in high school.

"My Lord, King Arthur, and the great Merlin. I ask that you would allow me to announce the presence of Lady Vivien, daughter of the King of Northumberland," Sir Ulfius said, his bow short and choppy.

Britt tucked a stray strand of hair behind her ear and looked to her advisor, a frown threatening to tug at the corners of her lips.

Typically Sir Ulfius never bothered to introduce *any* girls to Britt and Merlin—princess or not. As much as it chafed Britt to witness it, women—young girls in particular—were unimportant, politically speaking, in the era. There were exceptions, like Queen Morgause, wife to King Lot and mother of Gawain, Agravain, Gareth, and Gaheris; and her sister, Morgan. But women like them were mournfully few.

Merlin stared at Sir Ulfius, who was scratching at his throat. It seemed to be a kind of wordless communication, for Merlin abandoned his map-checking and joined Britt, Rudolph, and Mordred.

"Welcome to Camelot, Lady Vivien," Merlin said. His voice was neither warm nor cold.

Following his cue, Britt added, "We hope you enjoy your stay."

"Thank you. I am delighted to be here," Vivien said in a whispery, simpering voice.

"Sir Ulfius and I will show you to your chambers, if you will wait for a moment," Merlin said.

"Of course. I do not mean to intrude upon you, My Lord," Vivien said. She waited until Britt met her gaze and smiled.

Merlin stepped between them—his back to the girl—and

275

hooked his arm around Britt's shoulders. "Come along, Arthur," Merlin said, towing her away.

Mordred reached out and took Rudolph's rope with a smile.

"Thank you," Britt said before Merlin yanked her out of hearing range.

"Listen to me." Merlin spoke in a soft whisper as he gripped her shoulder with surprising strength. "At any public event, I want Guinevere with you."

"*What*? Please tell me you are joking."

"Morgan will do in a pinch, but keep that silly-headed princess by you whenever possible."

"Why?" Britt asked. Conversing with Guinevere wasn't the punishment it used to be, but that didn't mean she was Britt's first choice—or even in the top ten—as a dinner companion.

"I can't explain it right now, but it is *essential* that you do as I ask. Do you understand?" It wasn't his words that convinced Britt the situation was serious, but his dazzlingly blue eyes. They had a faint cast of desperation to them that seemed to highlight the gloomy sky and heavy air.

"You'll tell me soon?" she asked.

Merlin mutely pressed his lips together and his forehead wrinkled with worry.

Britt nodded. "Fine. I'll sit with Guinevere."

"Thank you, lass," Merlin said. He studied Britt for a moment, looking her up and down, then squeezed her shoulder and stepped away. "Shall we be off, Sir Ulfius?" he asked.

"Of course," the older knight said, turning back to Camelot. "This way, Lady Vivien."

"Goodbye, King Arthur. I hope to see you tonight," the girl said.

Britt raised her hand in a wordless farewell as she rejoined Mordred with Kay and Morgan. "That was odd. Do any of you know her, or the King of Northumberland?"

"No," Mordred said.

"I'll find out," Kay said as the first raindrop fell.

"Better get inside before this storm wages war. Wouldn't want to frighten…Rue…?" Mordred started, turning to Britt.

"Rudolph. And that is a wise plan." Britt took her pet's leadline back and marched towards the castle.

Morgan joined her as the sky opened up in a steady trickle. "That was not, I take it, the Lady Vivenne you crowned lady over her brothers' lands a few short week ago?"

"No. She's about as opposite as you can imagine. I gave Vivenne her brothers' lands because she is responsible and kind. This Vivien reminded me of a high school mean-girl."

"I do not know exactly what you refer to, but I believe the title of 'mean-girl' might accurately reflect this new arrival," Morgan said. "Though I hope we are wrong."

"Me, too."

5

TRUE COLORS

"You seem to be in good spirits, My Lord," Sir Percival said, joining Britt. She was tucked against a wall of the feast hall, surveying her friends and subjects as the evening feast progressed. Dinner with Guinevere as her "date," so to speak, was progressing well, but she needed the break or she would soon go cross-eyed from listening to the younger girl categorize the knights by their pleasing manners and questing feats.

"Indeed. I was just thinking how *nice* it is with Sir Lancelot gone," Britt said.

"You do not miss his tales that highlight his prowess?"

"No," Britt said sourly.

Sir Percival laughed. "Father said you didn't care much for him. I find it surprising—you're so similar, after all."

Britt gave the knight a look of horror. "You think so little of me?"

"Not at all, My Lord. I think the very best of you, just as I think the best of Sir Lancelot. He is a skilled man."

Britt made a noise of disgust in the back of her throat. "He's talented. But I prefer my knights more chivalrous—like Gawain, and your father—although he's a king, not a knight," she said, referring to King Pellinore.

Sir Percival shook his head. "Father is proud to be called your knight."

Britt thought for a moment to arrange the appropriately courtly words in her mind before she spoke. "It is a testimony to his character that he is so." She watched Vivien the vixen stroll up to Britt's table—which was located on a dais. (Merlin seemed to have a thing for daises and putting Britt several feet above everyone else.) Guinevere sat there, nibbling on her food and smiling at the knights who approached her. "I am proud to say, however, that many of my knights more closely resemble your father's character than Lancelot's. Even those new to the table."

"Such as myself?"

"Yes. And Mordred, I think," Britt said, frowning as Vivien clasped her arms behind her back and climbed the dais stairs to speak to Guinevere.

"He fought well and lost honorably to Sir Lancelot," Sir Percival said.

"Yes…Tell me, do *you* think he is a good knight?" Britt asked, tearing her eyes away from the girls to directly address the tall knight at her side.

"I do," Sir Percival said, his manners open and his expression honest. "Just as I think Sir Lancelot is a good knight."

"What do you mean?"

Sir Percival shifted and placed a little space between them as he cleared his throat. "Forgive me for my impertinence, My Lord, for I have been a Knight of the Round Table for only a short time. I should have said nothing."

"I value your opinion. What is it?"

Sir Percival hesitated.

"Percival?"

"It is only that, well, you seem unusually suspicious of Sir Lancelot and Sir Mordred."

Britt tried to think of a response that wouldn't involve the word "huh?" but came up short. Thankfully, Sir Percival didn't seem to notice and pushed on.

"You invited Sir Tor, the son of a cowherd, to the Round Table when any other King would have beaten him for his request. You welcomed my father—who waged *war* against you—when by rights you could have killed him and taken his lands. Yet with Sir Lancelot and Sir Mordred—two of the most talented knights in Camelot—you withhold your affection. You are more polite with Mordred, but it is obvious to all that you keep him at arm's length."

"He doesn't know who I am," Britt said, gesturing up and down her body.

"A scant month ago, *no one* knew who you were," Sir Percival quietly replied.

Britt considered the knight's words. Was she unfairly prejudice of Mordred and Lancelot? She had always struggled with the responsibility to either fulfill or destroy the legends of King Arthur that she knew. While she no longer put herself under pressure to be a replica of the original Arthur, she still held Lancelot and Guinevere's affair responsible for the downfall of Camelot, when that wasn't even possible—*especially* as her knights now knew who she was.

"You've given me much to think over, Sir Percival."

He drew his shoulders back. "I hope I did not overstep my place, My Lord."

"Not at all. You are as wise and insightful as Pellinore. He has helped me puzzle through the difficulties of being a king on more than one occasion." Britt smiled. "Thank you."

The faintest hint of a blush bloomed in Percival's cheeks. "You exaggerate, My Lord."

Britt chuckled and opened her mouth to respond as she flicked her gaze back to her table. "If you'll excuse me, Percival," she said, distracted by the sight before she pushed away from the wall.

She barely heard Percival's "Of course, My Lord," before she edged into the crowds and made her way to the table.

Vivien stood in front of Britt's table—the King's table—her face morphed into a beautiful smile as she spoke to Guinevere. Her blonde hair glimmered in the torchlight, and she laughed. Guinevere, however, had tears in her eyes, and her lower lip trembled.

Britt narrowed her eyes and made her way through the diners, but she couldn't hear Vivien's words until she reached the dais.

"...You, on the other hand, are nothing but a tool for your father —a fattened calf he will sell to the highest bidder. He doesn't even care about you. He considers *anyone* with a fat purse or a large army, and you're just as stupid and foolish as he is. Your beauty will fade, and then *no one* will want you!" the vile girl hissed through her smile.

Guinevere trembled, and her tears still fell, but she squared her shoulders.

"You have nothing to say? I should have known," Vivien laughed, looking lovely.

"I do not reply because, because Arthur would want me to rise above your cruel words," Guinevere said, a hiccup popping at the end of her words.

"You bring the High King into this conversation? You think he *likes* you? I haven't been here a day, and even I can see he only tolerates you. He *pities* you," Vivien said.

Brit moved to start up the stairs, but Guinevere's next words made her freeze and broke her heart.

"I know, but he is kind to me anyway, and I will not embarrass him," Guinevere said.

Britt shut her eyes with regret. Sir Percival was right. Britt— who did her best to instill honor and justice in her knights—was terribly unfair with Guinevere—just as she had been with Mordred. Kind? She was nothing of the sort. But no more.

"You won't, will you? I apologize, for I will drive you from these halls," Vivien said.

"I find that interesting," Britt said as she glided up the stairs. "For it is *I* who rules Camelot. How do you intend to carry out your decree?"

Vivien looked simultaneously horrified and angry enough to spit nails. "My Lord! I apologize; you misunderstand the situation."

"Do I? I arrive at my personal table—a place of honor—to find Lady Guinevere—a companion of my heart and a lady under my personal protection—in tears, whilst you hiss poison in her ear like a snake. Tell me, Lady Vivien, what part have I misunderstood?" Britt asked as she walked around the table to stand just behind Guinevere's chair.

Although Britt did not shout, her words were loud enough that some of the feasters sitting at the tables closest heard and gaped at the speech.

Lady Vivien gasped and recoiled, her face shaped in a look of hurt. "I'm sorry if my words caused Lady Guinevere pain, but I am shocked by your conduct, My Lord. I was told the courts of Camelot were unrivaled in the respect and honor they bestowed upon the fairer sex."

Lady Vivien's dramatic reaction garnered more attention, drawing notice from additional guests.

Britt smiled darkly. "You are right. I have made great strides to bring the Ladies of Camelot honor. However, that also means the Ladies of Camelot must be more considerate of their positions. Insults of the degree to which you were delivering would never be accepted among my knights, nor will I allow them among my subjects—no matter their gender. Step carefully, Lady Vivien. Increased status and honor does not give you a free-pass to act in an ugly manner. If I ever hear you speaking to another person as you have to Guinevere—whether they be man, woman, or child—I will not hesitate to send you from my courts."

"You wouldn't," Vivien sputtered.

"He would, and he is being generous. I would have tossed you from these hallowed halls the moment you uttered your first insult," Morgan said, quickly climbing the dais. She joined Britt and laid her hand on Britt's shoulder, murmuring "Brother."

The feasting hall was mostly silent now. Almost everyone stared at the drama with wide eyes.

"This is dishonorable," Vivien said. "Are you so unfeeling, King Arthur?"

"No. My Lord holds us to the same degree of conduct he holds the knights of his Round Table. It is an honor," a lady at a table said, standing up.

"We must conduct ourselves with nobility so we can be found worthy of the honor and favors the knights win for us," another lady—Blancheflor, one of Guinevere's close friends and the apple of Sir Griflet's eye—said.

Vivien gave a muffled cry. "I apologize, I did not know—I wasn't aware. Forgive me, My Lord."

Britt raised an eyebrow. "It is not I to whom you owe an apology," she said, pointedly looking down at Guinevere, who had wiped away her tears—although her eyes were still red.

Vivien's façade cracked for a moment as she looked at Guinevere with hatred. "I apologize, Lady Guinevere, for my harsh words."

"You are forgiven." Guinevere sniffled and raised her chin.

Vivien cast a glance at Britt and Morgan before she fled the dais, hurrying through the feasting hall. In mere seconds she was out a door, disappearing from view.

"You conducted yourself well, Guinevere," Morgan said.

"Thank you," Guinevere said in a small voice.

"If that brat ever comes at you again, let me know. Okay?" Britt asked, her anger making her slip.

"W-what?"

"If Vivien speaks to you again like that, I want to hear about it," Britt rephrased.

Guinevere bobbed her head. "Yes, My Lord."

"Do you need to freshen up?" Morgan asked, an unusual amount of sympathy warming her voice. (Usually, she didn't have much patience for Guinevere either.)

"That would be nice."

"Let's go then," Britt said.

"No. You, Arthur, must remain here. I shall accompany Lady Guinevere," Morgan said.

"Oh, right. Thanks, Morgan. Take all the time you need."

Guinevere rose and curtsied. "My Lord," she said before she and Morgan also left the dais.

Britt sighed and drummed her fingers on the back of Guinevere's large, wooden chair. Just as everyone started returning their attention to their food, Britt was yanked back by her armor. "Arthur, a moment," Merlin said.

"Merlin, ah, hi," Britt said, letting Merlin turn her around so their backs face the feasters. "Sorry, I know I should have stayed with Guinevere. How did you know Vivien would target her?"

"I didn't tell you to stay with Guinevere for her sake, but yours."

"What?"

"Guinevere isn't Vivien's target. You are," Merlin said.

"So? She's not going to charm me," Britt snorted.

"I know. However, this is more complex than you know. You need to trust me. Stay *away* from Vivien, and don't confront her again."

"I'm not going to let her get away with mocking people in my courts," she said, her voice sharp.

"I know, but I don't think she'll try it again. Just avoid her at all costs, and make sure Guinevere is often seen with you,"

Merlin said. His forehead was wrinkled, a sure sign he was worrying.

"Is there anything else I can do to help?" Britt asked.

Looking tired, Merlin shook his head. "No. This, unfortunately, is something I must take care of alone."

"Alright. Thank you for taking it on," Britt said.

Merlin's spirits lifted, and he offered her a smile. "Of course." His eyes lingered on Britt for an abnormal amount of time, a hint of his smile still lurking. "Whatever it takes, I will see you safe. Now, mind my instructions," he said. He darted down the dais, leaving her alone, before Britt could say anything in response.

~

THE FEAST CONTINUED ON, but it wasn't until after the food had been cleared that the next bit of excitement arrived.

"Do you intend to practice with Excalibur on the castle walls this night, Milord?" a guard—one of the ones Kay had selected to be part of Britt's elite guards/babysitters—asked.

"Yes. I'm hoping to slip out soon—the noise is getting to be too much." Britt rubbed her temples as she stared out at the hall.

The feast doors opened, and Britt straightened with a smile when she saw who stood in the doorway. "Griflet!"

Knights crowded around the young man to welcome him back, but they cleared out when Britt reached him.

"My Lord," Griflet said, bowing to Britt. He offered her a boyish smile. "I've returned home!"

"How were your travels? What feats did you manage?" Britt asked, performing a manly back-slap for appearance's sake. She noticed Griflet winced under the lighthearted blow. "Are you alright?"

"As good as can be expected. My travels were magnificent until their end. I was helplessly trounced by a white knight."

"Come, eat and rest at my table, and tell me your story," Britt said.

Griflet—and several knights of the Round Table—followed Britt to her place on the dais and filled the abandoned table.

Griflet ate with gusto, which quickly restored his energy and spirits. He spoke of the quests he conducted and the services he rendered for the poor and champion-less. He looked at Blancheflor with great longing as he recited his actions, but the beautiful lady didn't seem to be aware he even existed.

Griflet's stories progressed like the typical recitation of a knight's feats, until the end.

"That was where I found the abbey with the shield." Griflet paused to take a swig of his drink.

"Shield?" Britt asked.

"Yes. T'was a great white shield emblazoned with a red cross. One could see, just by looking at it, that it is blessed and is surely a holy talisman."

"I see," Britt said.

"I was filled with great desire to own it. It is a noble-looking thing, and all who saw it would admire it," Griflet said, staring at the lady Blancheflor again.

"Did you take it?" Sir Percival asked.

Griflet winced. "Ah, well. The hermit who lived at the abbey told me off. He said the only one worthy of the shield was to have it, and anyone who took it would face the White Knight."

"But you took it anyway?" Britt guessed. She would never understand why, but the men of Camelot were like ravens—obsessed with shiny things.

"Yes," Griflet was slow to admit.

"Then where is it?" Sir Agravain demanded.

"I met the White Knight."

"And?"

"I lost."

"Ah," all the knights around the table said, their voices heavy with sympathy.

"Where was the abbey?" Sir Agravain asked, eagerly leaning forward.

"A ride a day and a half south of here," Griflet said.

Britt glared and tapped her fingers on the table. "Pellinore," she muttered.

"Did you say something, My Lord?" Griflet asked.

"You say this was all over a shield?"

"Yes."

"He trounced you badly?"

"That is not to say that—"

"Griflet."

"Yes."

Britt's glare sharpened into a scowl.

"Is something wrong, My Lord?" Sir Percival asked.

"Yes. This has your father's fingerprints all over it."

Sir Percival blinked. "I beg your pardon?"

"Twice he's set up camp and swiped shields from knights. I wouldn't be surprised if this is his newest modus operandi."

"His what?"

"Nothing," Britt said, shaking her head.

"Is the abbey due south or southeast?" Agravain asked.

"You're not thinking of going, are you?" Sir Safir asked.

"Why not? Wouldn't you like to have a go at this knight?" Agravain asked.

"No, because I have a correct notion of my level of skill," Sir Safir said.

"You are too modest, my friend," Sir Percival said.

"The White Knight is dreadfully skilled. It will take someone great to defeat him," Griflet said.

"Wasn't it King Pellinore who pounded you the last time you went after a shield?" Agravain asked.

"I am much more skilled now," Griflet huffed. "Besides, you haven't done a tenth of the quests I have."

"He's got you there, Sir Agravain," Sir Lanval said.

Britt affectionately shook her head and pushed away from the table. Her knights didn't even notice when she slipped away.

"Wasn't it you, My Lord, who defeated King Pellinore?" Mordred asked. He stood directly behind her, making her jump.

"I apologize, Mordred. I didn't know you followed me. What was that?" Britt asked, resting one hand on her sword belt.

"I couldn't help but overhear what Griflet and his friends were saying. The time he faced King Pellinore, right after he was knighted; didn't you ride out and defeat King Pellinore in return?"

"He was dressed as a black knight at the time, and Merlin clubbed him in the helm first to get him off his horse so it would be a sword fight, but yes."

"It is remarkable," Mordred said, strolling after Britt as she walked the perimeter of the room.

"What?"

"You. I cannot recall ever hearing of a king who fought for his knights and subjects on such a personal basis. Most stay in their castles and fight only in wars."

"Oh, well, it was early in my reign. We didn't even have a peace treaty with King Lot of Orkney at the time. My life was a lot less valuable then." She grinned. "Merlin let me off my leash more often. The last time I rode out on a real adventure was last year when I accompanied Sir Tor for part of his first quest."

"Do you wish you could quest more?" Mordred asked, tilting his head like a curious dog.

"Of course. It's refreshing to get away from the politics and weight of being king, but it is also nearly impossible to leave because of those same reasons."

"Would you like to go to the abbey with me and face this White Knight of Griflet's?" Mordred asked.

Britt was so surprised, she stopped walking. "You're serious?"

"Yes."

Britt carefully considered Mordred. It would be a dream to leave Camelot for a few days, but was it wise to go with *Mordred*? "Perhaps...but only if you convince Sir Kay to agree to it," she said.

"Why, if I may inquire."

"I made Sir Kay a promise last year that I would never venture forth without informing him—or without his blessing. If he does not accept your proposed idea, I'm sorry, but I will be forced to refuse it."

"I see," Mordred said, scratching his cheek as he thought. "Very well, I shall speak to him."

"Honestly, I don't think you'll ever get him to agree," Britt said, thinking it was only fair to warn him.

"I can be most persuasive, My Lord."

Britt shrugged. "Give it all you've got, then. I look forward to hearing the results. If you'll excuse me," Britt said, making her way to a door.

"Of course, My Lord," Mordred bowed, and Britt slipped from the feasting hall.

He has no idea how badly he is about to fail, Britt thought, shaking her head.

6

THE HOLY SHIELD

wo days later, Britt, baffled and shocked, found herself
mounted on Roen, geared up in plain, silver armor, and
holding the rope of a packhorse.

"How did this happen?" she asked.

Mordred checked the girth of his saddle. "You said to get Sir
Kay's permission, so I did." he mounted up.

"Are you secretly a *wizard*?" Britt asked, turning in her saddle
to face the handsome knight.

"No," Mordred chuckled. "I'm afraid magic is not one of my
talents. But I believe I did tell you I am very persuasive."

"Forget persuasive. You would need to have the powers of
mind control to convince Kay to let me quest with only you and
no bodyguards," Britt said.

"I'm not sure I follow your meaning, My Lord."

Britt frowned and looked around the nearly empty stable-
yard. Only three other knights were present: Kay, Sir Bedivere,
and Sir Bodwain.

Britt nudged Roen, her black courser, to the trio. "Are you
sure he didn't magic you into agreeing, Kay?"

Mordred laughed. "I can hear you, My Lord."

"I know. I genuinely want to know," Britt called back to him.

"Both Merlin and I believe it would be wise for you to leave Camelot for a while, My Lord," Kay said.

Britt sighed. "This has something to do with Vivien, doesn't it?"

Sir Bodwain and Sir Bedivere avoided Britt's gaze, but Kay nodded.

"And *why* does Merlin insist on keeping me in the dark?" Britt asked, her voice frosty.

Sir Bodwain gave her a sympathetic smile. "It's because he cares for you, My Lord."

"More like he's afraid I'll do something stupid." Britt snorted and secured the packhorse's tether to Roen's saddle.

"No," Sir Bedivere shook his head. "Not this time."

Sir Bodwain pitched his voice low. "He's afraid for you, Arthur. He's protecting you as best he can. Ignorance is part of it."

Britt looked to Kay for confirmation. Her seneschal nodded, easing some of the tightness in her chest.

"Well then. I may as well enjoy myself."

"Remember, you agreed to travel as Sir Galahad," Kay said, naming the alter ego Britt had created when her position as king was shaky at best.

"For safety—I know. Thank you for seeing me off, gentlemen. Although I must say I'm surprised you are the only ones," Britt said, leaning forward in her saddle. She gave the stable-yard another quick inspection, looking for Merlin. He did not appear.

"We won't announce your quest until tonight," Sir Bedivere said. "We thought it would be the wisest course of action—or young knights like Agravain might chase after you."

"That sounds about right," Britt chuckled.

"Are you ready, My Lord?" Mordred asked, fussing with his war-horse's black mane.

She patted Roen. "Yes."

"Shall we be on our way?"

"I guess." She turned Roen for the gates.

"Arthur, be safe," Kay said, his voice gruff.

"You too, brother." Britt smiled and winked. "Until I return—most likely with King Pellinore. Makes you wonder how he got a hermit to agree to help him," she muttered. She waved to her seneschal, constable, and marshal before losing sight of them when she followed Mordred through the inner gates.

"So, do you have any idea where we are going?" She nudged Roen closer to Mordred and his horse.

"Of course. Sir Griflet gave me directions, and Sir Kay has lent me a map," Sir Mordred said with a shy smile that nicely complemented his dimples.

"I see. When we get back, can I ask for your help, Sir Mordred?"

"Of course, My Lord. I would aid you with anything. What is it that you need?"

"Your golden tongue to crack Merlin's plans for Ireland."

Mordred laughed and directed his horse around a cart of straw. "I'm afraid not even my skills of persuasion are powerful enough to move Merlin, My Lord. That is a skill only you possess."

"Falsehoods. I could move Camelot more easily than I can move Merlin." Britt said, waving at an awed blacksmith.

"I must risk your royal wrath to say that you are gravely mistaken, My Lord."

Britt removed her focus from Roen's ears and raised her eyes to stare at Sir Mordred. The knight did not react to the sudden scrutiny and guided his horse toward the outer walls of Camelot with ease.

ALTHOUGH IT WAS MIDDAY, the windows in Merlin's study were

closed, and a fire was lit in the fireplace to illuminate the stuffy room.

"Are you *certain* Sir Bedivere has that witch distracted?" Sir Ulfius asked, his hand grasping the hilt of his sword.

"Yes," Sir Bodwain said. When he sat down on a wooden chair, it groaned under his large frame. "He lured her outside of Camelot. The guards will send notice of their return."

"I don't like it," Sir Ulfius said. "When I took my oaths to our King, I knew I would have to protect her from much. But a user of black magic?"

"Has it been confirmed, then?" Sir Kay asked. His eyes flickered between the older knights and then settled on Merlin.

The young wizard was hunched over one of his worktables, his colorful eyes crinkled with worry. "It's undeniable. Vivien reeks of death and destruction."

"How could a mere *girl* have such power in dark magic?" Sir Bodwain asked.

"Careful, Sir Bodwain." Merlin straightened his posture like a pained, elderly man. "You underestimate the female gender. Remember, our King is also a woman—her allegiances merely lie on the other end of the spectrum."

"But Vivien is fifteen if she's a day. King Arthur is some years ahead of her and underwent an extensive education," Sir Ulfius said. "How did Vivien acquire such power? Morgause and Morgan are the most powerful sorceresses, and they will not touch black magic. Who taught her?"

"Sometimes darkness itself will draw a man into its embrace," Merlin said, his voice tight. "But in this case, I suspect she was led. She's not working alone."

"It cannot be Orkney. King Lot still sulks, but he is fully under Arthur's power," Sir Bodwain said.

"Correct. Orkney is no longer a threat," Merlin said.

"Rome?" Kay guessed.

Merlin braced himself on his worktable. "I believe so."

293

"The traitorous witch," Sir Ulfius muttered.

"Ulfius, such language," Merlin said. A wan smile passed across his lips.

"Can we drive her from Camelot?" Sir Bodwain asked.

Merlin shook his head. "It will only stoke her fury. She already made one magical attack against Arthur after being publically corrected. I managed to intercept it, but I might not manage it a second time."

"Then we should slay her." Kay's voice was hard and unforgiving.

Ulfius and Bodwain looked at the younger knight with shock.

"If there is a threat against my King, I will not rest until I see it eliminated," Kay said.

"Touching, but sadly there is very little you can do." Merlin flopped down in a chair. "Politics is still an issue—killing the daughter of a king will bring our enemies out of the woods."

"We would win," Sir Ulfius said.

"Undoubtedly, but it would break Britt to send her men to that battle, followed by a conquest for Ireland, and the inevitable war against Rome."

"Kings must sometimes do ugly things—if it is for their people," Sir Ulfius said.

"Not Arthur," Merlin said.

"She is strong. Too many times I have underestimated her," Sir Bodwain said.

Merlin snarled. "Allow me to put it plainly, men: War is not an option. Britt has already bourn more than her share of sorrow for our vision. I will not make her shoulder more!"

The room was silent as Merlin took a moment to recollect himself. "War aside, I'm not certain Vivien *can* be slain. She is filled with great darkness."

"What magic has she been using?" Sir Bodwain asked.

"Seduction, mostly."

"But only a few knights have fallen at her feet. Indeed, since

Arthur's vocal disapproval, many take pains to avoid her," Sir Ulfius said, smiling broadly.

"Her spells are not aimed at the knights, but at Arthur," Merlin said. "Arthur being a female means the specific spell Vivien is using will not work on her, and it is making her angry... and suspicious."

"That was why you sent Arthur from Camelot, then." Sir Bodwain rubbed his forehead. "To get her out of Vivien's grasp."

"It was a last resort," Sir Kay said. "I would have preferred to send guards with her, but it would have been conspicuous. Mordred is a trustworthy knight; he'll keep an eye on her."

"Even though he does not know Arthur should, by all rights, be *queen*?" Sir Ulfius doubtfully asked, raising his shaggy eyebrows.

"At this moment, Arthur is safer at any location besides Camelot," Merlin said.

"So, what choices do we have?" Sir Bodwain asked. "How do we react to this?"

"She cannot be forced out or slain. Do we send word to her father to call her back?" Sir Kay asked, smoothing his mustache.

"The King of Northumberland is in his dotage. He will do nothing to contain his offspring," Merlin said.

"Then what can we do?" Sir Ulfius asked.

Merlin shook his head.

"There must be *something*," Sir Kay said.

"With luck, we might be able to distract her if we tempt her with a different kind of power," Merlin said, staring into the fire.

"What do you have in mind?" Sir Ulfius asked.

"I would rather not say." Merlin raised his gaze to study the men. "However, I would like to affirm that we all believe Britt is the highest priority. Any sacrifice required of us is worthy if it will see her through this time."

"She is a good King," Sir Bodwain gruffly said.

"Even if we were not her advisors?" Merlin asked.

Sir Ulfius pondered the question. "She would find new men to lean on. She's intelligent, so much so that she knows she cannot rule without help. But none of this matters. She'll always have you, won't she, Merlin?"

"Yes," Merlin said carefully. "Always."

~

IT WASN'T until the following day that Britt and Mordred reached the fabled abbey. Considering it was in the middle of the forest, Britt had been expecting a small, square hovel. Instead, the abbey was a beautiful, stone structure, complete with archways, a bell tower, and airy corridors.

Mordred motioned to the bell tower. "This is it. Griflet mentioned the carving of the Virgin Mary."

"A hermit lives *here*?" Britt asked, sliding off her horse. "Sheesh, if this is what the building is like, no wonder Griflet wanted the shield."

"Who is Sheesh?" Mordred asked.

"No one. It's an expression of surprise where I come from."

Mordred tied his mount and the pack horse to a hitching post. "Bonmaison has such a colloquialism? How interesting."

"Er, right. Shall we find the shield?" Britt asked, picking a leaf from Roen's mane.

"Yes, this way. I suspect we will find the shield—and the hermit—in the abbey sanctuary." Mordred led the way into the abbey.

They passed through the entrance—Britt gawked like a child —and made their way into the sanctuary, their footsteps shattering the reverent quiet of the place.

The sanctuary was similar to the cathedral Merlin had built in Camelot. Windows lit the room and the vaulted ceiling, and wooden pews filled the floor, leading the way straight up to a stone altar.

After seeing the splendid abbey, Britt had high hopes. These high hopes were dashed when she set eyes on the shield propped against the altar. "I'm pretty sure an assistant blacksmith at Camelot can make a better shield," she murmured to Mordred.

The shield was too big to use with the sword or lance, and while the red cross on the white background was striking, it was all too clear that it was cheaply made, for some of the paint had been scratched off—most likely from previous skirmishes with the White Knight (a.k.a. King Pellinore).

"Perhaps it is supposed to be symbolic rather than useful," Mordred suggested.

"You're being generous. I like my red dragon shield Merlin has bolted to the walls of Camelot much more," Britt said. "But it doesn't matter. We're only here to grab the shield so we can summon Pellinore."

"You are so certain it is your ally?" Mordred asked as Britt approached the altar.

"Oh, yes. Believe me, if there is any kind of knight attacking people with or for shields, it's Pellinore," Britt snorted. She picked up the shield and whirled around, her muscles tensed.

"I think we have to take the shield from the abbey before the white knight will attack," Mordred said after several moments of silence.

Britt awkwardly laughed. "Ah, yes. I think you're right— Griflet said something about that, too. Let's go, then." She hefted the shield and started down the aisle, pushing the doors open when she reached the entrance. She was so intent, she almost walked straight into a tall, sturdy man.

"Careful, there," the man said, reaching out to steady her. Instead of wearing brown robes—like the stereotypical hermit— he wore a bright blue tunic, and his hair and beard were trimmed and combed. "Why, if it isn't—"

"Arthur!" Britt was quick to say when she realized she knew him. "Blaise, I'm glad to see you again!"

Blaise was Merlin's mentor—who happened to have a great sense of humor and possessed hundreds of stories about Merlin's unruly childhood.

"My Lord, Sir Kay gave me specific instructions that you were to use the name of Sir Galahad," Mordred said, one corner of his lips tightening with worry.

"It's fine, Sir Mordred; he already knows me. This man is Blaise—Merlin's mentor. Blaise, this is Sir Mordred—one of my knights."

Sir Mordred bowed. "It is an honor to meet you, sir."

Blaise whistled. "Nice manners—I hope Merlin spends time with you. You could teach him a thing or two. That boy has the etiquette of a giant."

"He can be welcoming when he sees a direct benefit," Britt dryly said.

"Ah, there is that."

"Forgive my nosiness, but why are you here, Blaise? Have you moved?" Britt asked.

"Goodness, no. I love my home too much. No, a friend of mine is the keeper of this place, but he set out on a pilgrimage in spring. I promised him I would look after it for him. Speaking of which, Welcome to the Abbey of the Crimson Cross. I see you have already encountered the Abbey's holy treasure."

"Yes, sorry. We've got to borrow it." Britt awkwardly shifted in place.

"We're looking for the White Knight," Mordred added.

"You'll find him, then. I have no idea who the man is or where he stays, but he's never failed to bring the shield back. I expect that will change with you two here." Blaise smiled.

"We're not interested in keeping the shield. It's...nothing against the shield; it is just the knight we want. Whether or not we beat him, we'll bring it back," Britt said.

"It is a fairly useless thing," Blaise said, cheerfully cutting to the truth. "But I'm sorry to say, if you beat the man you've got to keep the shield."

"Even if we don't desire it?" Sir Mordred asked.

"It's the reason why the abbey has the shield—to find someone worthy of it," Blaise said. "Either way, the knight won't attack you until you leave abbey lands—be sure to strap on your helm, Arthur. Merlin would foam at the mouth if you went into battle ill-prepared."

"I know. Thank you for your help, Blaise."

"Of course. But Arthur, could we speak for a moment?"

"I'll attach the shield to Roen." Mordred gently took the shield from Britt's grasp.

"Are you sure you don't want to carry it?" Britt asked.

"I am certain." Mordred smiled and strode out to the court-yard where their horses waited.

"So, what's on your mind, Blaise?" she asked.

"How is your relationship with Merlin?" Blaise asked.

Britt nodded as she listened to his words and paused to let the meaning sink in before she said, "*What?*"

"Your relationship with Merlin. He said you fought last year over your feelings."

Britt groaned and covered her face with her hands. "Did the idiot tell you *everything*? I'll have him stabbed!"

"Try to see it from his point of view—he's lost. He's never encountered something like this before," Blaise said, his voice soothing.

Britt glared at the hermit, unmoved.

"He also," Blaise said in a nonchalant, conversational tone, "is quite stupid when it comes to relationships."

Britt cracked a smile. "What are you getting at, Blaise?"

"Nothing. I was merely wondering if you two had returned to normal."

Britt sighed and turned so she could watch Mordred prepare

their mounts. "It has gotten better," she said. "Things aren't quite so...tense."

"I see. That's disappointing of him," Blaise said.

"Excuse me?"

"Nothing. I will let you set out on your quest, but, Britt...?"

"Yes?"

"Merlin has never been good at discussing matters of the heart, and while he may be a prodigy at magic and among the most clever and learned men alive, in the realm of the heart he is as apt as Sir Lancelot is humble."

"Now you're speaking my language. But I want to cut you off before you get any strange ideas: Merlin has no romantic intentions towards me."

Blaise tapped his chin. "I don't think he knows what romantic intentions look like—the Good Lord knows I never modeled it for him. But please, don't give up on him. I must tell you that he has great affection for you."

His words made her brighten for a moment, but she savagely silenced the hope. *No. Affection could mean anything, and Merlin doesn't look at me that way.* She forced a look of peace upon her face. "Why are we discussing this?"

"Because Merlin and I might not be related by blood, but he is still my son, and I love him dearly—even when he's acting like a thick-headed dunce who doesn't know what he wants, what he *needs*. Now, I had best send you on your way. Your companion looks ready to leave."

"Yes. Thank you, Blaise." She was eager to abandon the conversation, which was swiftly becoming uncomfortable. She waved to Blaise as she strode into the courtyard, then mounted Roen and nodded to the hermit. "I hope to see you again, soon."

"As do I. Godspeed, Arthur, Sir Mordred."

Mordred inclined his head in acknowledgement and wheeled his horse around. "We thank you, sir."

"Goodbye, Blaise," Britt called over her shoulder. She cast a look at the shield—which hung over Roen's rump—and sighed. "Let's go find Pellinore, shall we?"

"As you wish, My Lord."

~

BRITT AND MORDRED rode in companionable silence for twenty minutes before a knight in white armor crashed onto the path in front of them. His horse was dapple gray with white tack.

"Hail, Sir Knight," the white knight said, using his horse to block their way. "Was it you who tooketh the shield—though the hermit at the abbey said not to?"

Britt—her helm already secured in place—scowled at the knight through the slits of her visor. "You're the White Knight?"

"I have been called that."

"*Pellinore*! You have got to get over your obsession of using shields to incite fights!" Britt seethed as she climbed down from Roen.

"I beg your pardon?" the White Knight said.

Britt stalked up to the White Knight, ignoring the unsheathed sword he held. "Get down, or so help me, I will drag you off that horse myself. Does your wife know you're doing this?"

"I am not this Pellinore you speak of," the White Knight said. His horse snapped at her, but she ignored it. Pellinore wouldn't let her get hurt.

"Likely story." She grabbed the knight's arm and yanked, hard. He fell down with a clatter.

"You, Sir Knight, have acted without honor," the knight wheezed, his tinny voice echoing in his helm.

"So you still want to fight?" Britt asked. She would have placed her hands on her hips if Mordred hadn't been there.

"Of course. You have dishonored me! I must punish you," the White Knight said.

"Fine. Let's fight," she said, unsurprised by his stubbornness.

301

Pellinore loved a good fight—regardless of whether he won or lost.

The White Knight stood in a basic defense stance. Britt gave him a moment before she descended upon him, moving like lightning.

She opened with a thrust to his left shoulder—which he blocked—and struck his right side with her knee. As he was protected by padding, the knee didn't hurt him, but it made him stagger back. This surprised her—Pellinore always had a great stance and usually wouldn't be moved so easily.

The knight managed to shove her away from him, but he barely had enough time to block her strike against his right side —leaving his left side completely open, which Britt kneed. Again, the knight staggered backwards.

Britt pulled back in temporary confusion. What was going on? King Pellinore was an excellent swordsman, but now he was fighting closer to Ywain's level—good, but sloppy.

"You really aren't Pellinore, are you?" she asked.

The White Knight raised his sword to chop at Britt's neck— the stupidest attack you could level against someone *waiting* for you to strike. Britt parried—their swords clashing between them —before she angled her sword down, turning her parry into a strike at the knight's open stomach.

The knight jumped backwards, but he still didn't learn his lesson. This time, he chopped his sword at Britt's left side. Britt used Excalibur's hilt to block the blow. She placed her palm on the back of her sword and—using Excalibur like a lever and a bat —slammed the blade into her opponent's helm.

He staggered backwards, and Britt followed up this time, braining him in the same spot with Excalibur's hilt, and then slamming him with her shoulder.

He went down like a tree, and Britt kicked his sword away. She leaned over, flicked the visor of his helm up, and declared, "I have *no* idea who you are."

Mordred, still mounted on his horse, politely looked away and tried to muffle his laughter.

The White Knight was young—perhaps a little older than Griflet—and bore no resemblance to King Pellinore. Now that she studied him, he was much more slender in the shoulders, and not nearly as tall. He stared up at Britt with wide eyes. "You are the chosen-one, the knight destined to own the shield," he said, his voice awed.

"No, I'm not." Britt backed up and sheathed Excalibur. "I apologize; I attacked you on false terms. I thought you were someone else. Here, let me get the shield for you."

"Oh, no! You must keep it! My family has guarded it for three generations, waiting for the day a worthy knight would arrive." the knight shook his head. "May I ask who you are?"

"Sir Galahad," Britt said. "Look, I don't think you get it. I'm not really after the shield. I only grabbed it because I thought you were a friend of mine—although in my defense, I've never heard of anyone besides Pellinore fighting a man over a shield."

"You must take it," the white knight said, easing himself off the ground. "My grandfather will flay me if I tell him I met the proper owner and kept the shield."

"Your grandfather?" Sir Mordred asked.

"He is the hermit who cares for the abbey—though he is gone right now on a pilgrimage. He'll be so disappointed he missed meeting you," the White Knight said, walking over to his horse.

"He's a hermit, but he's your grandfather? How does that work? I thought hermits were supposed to be celibate," Britt said. She popped off her helm so she could breathe in fresh air.

"Oh, he is, now."

"I wonder if that's what Merlin is aiming for—old age as a hermit," Britt muttered.

"My Lord—your chance to return the shield is ending," Sir Mordred said, nodding to the mounted White Knight, who nudged his horse to the trees.

"Wait, take the shield!" Britt shouted. She hurriedly unhooked it from Roen's rump and ran after the knight.

The White Knight shook his head. "Nay, I cannot. It has long been foretold that a worthy knight should receive the shield."

"I pulled you off your horse. Wouldn't that imply I'm a black-guard knight who is *unworthy*?"

"My Lord," Mordred said, his voice strangled with stifled laughter.

"Not at all," the White Knight said gravely.

"Fine, then we'll take it back to the abbey ourselves," she said, turning for Roen.

"Don't do that!" the White Knight yelped.

"Why not?" Britt demanded.

The White Knight remained mute.

"Fine. Mordred, let us turn around and return to the abbey."

"Please don't take it back! I am so *tired* of fighting men for that useless shield."

"Ah, so you also see its deficiencies," Mordred said.

"Of course," the knight snorted. "It's obvious. And...I may have used it once or twice for practice when my grandfather was away."

"Tisk, tisk," Britt said.

"I want to be free—free to leave this abbey, free to sleep *indoors* instead of camping outside, waiting for someone to try to take the shield. I beg of you, Sir Galahad. If there is any mercy in your blood, *take* that wretched thing."

"He sounds desperate, My Lord," Mordred said.

"I can't say I blame him," Britt said. "Alright, I'll take the shield."

"Bless you, Sir Galahad!"

"Yeah, you're welcome. All I'm going to do with it, though, is toss it in my armory."

"It matters not what you do with it. You won, fair and square.

Godspeed, Sir Galahad." The White Knight kicked his horse, fleeing into the forest.

Britt returned to Roen and hooked the shield back on his rump. "You *do* think I won fairly, don't you, Mordred?"

"You did nothing that could be frowned upon, My Lord."

"That's not what I meant. Do you think he purposely fought at a lower skill level?" Britt asked, putting her helm back on.

"Perhaps a little, but you clearly were the better swordsman."

"Good. Well, that was not at all what I was expecting. Shall we return home?"

"Whatever you wish, My Lord."

"Don't tempt me," Britt grinned and flipped her visor up so he could see it. "Now on to Camelot—lest Kay send out a search party after us!"

7

SIR LANCELOT'S DEEDS

A week later, Britt—with Cavall and a squad of guards trailing her—walked the familiar route to her throne room. As she navigated her way, she gnawed on a very green, unripe apple and complained to her guards. "Sir Ulfius said I have a *line* of vanquished knights waiting to swear loyalty to me, compliments of Sir Lancelot. I'm beginning to think I should have bells sewn into his horse's tack."

"Think of all the recreant knights he's clearing from your lands, lassie," Britt's guard—the one with the Scottish brogue—chuckled. "That's the point o' questing, isn't it?"

"Yes, but—just like the rest of his life—Lancelot takes it to excessive measures." Britt chewed her acidic apple as they walked past a garden. She paused and retreated, her forehead puckering. "Merlin?"

The handsome wizard was standing in the middle of the castle herb garden, staring at the plants. His hair was messy and unkempt, and he had bags under his eyes—like he hadn't gotten much sleep. "Yes?" he asked, still staring at the herbs.

"Are you alright?" Britt asked.

"Of course I am. Why?"

"You look terrible."

"You never choose to be charming and use your pretty words when you can bludgeon a person with the truth," Merlin said, looking to her with a wry quirk in his brow.

Britt entered the garden. "Is it that thing you still won't tell me about?"

"Perhaps."

"And there's still nothing I can do?"

"Goodness, no."

Britt ate another chunk of her unripe apple. Merlin stared back at her, forbidding her to inquire further. "Is it really worth it to push yourself like this?" she asked.

Merlin drew his shoulders up. "I thought I told you this was for *your* sake."

"I know. I remember, but that's why I'm asking. Is putting yourself through *this* worth sparing me?" Britt asked.

Merlin sighed. "It is."

"So it must be something about uniting Britain?" she guessed.

Merlin scowled. "My dream has nothing to do with this mess."

His response surprised Britt. She thought he moved only to benefit Britain. Although he had in the past occasionally shown acts of kindness to her, he hadn't been so gentle or thoughtful since he learned she...well...loved him. She awkwardly cleared her throat and guiltily realized she had assumed the worst of him. Feeling at fault, she decided it was her duty to lighten the moment. "So you must be brooding over your weak magic, huh?"

The jest had the desired result of bringing fire back to Merlin's eyes. "You!" he declared. "I suggest you turn on your tail and run, puppy, before I light your blasted cape on fire!"

"*Someone* is sensitive. Do you need to talk about it? Admitting your limitations can make you feel better—or so I've been told. I wouldn't know, of course."

"How humble of you. Have you become the new Lancelot in his absence?"

"Okay, now, *that* was below the belt," Britt said.

"And insulting my magic was not?"

"No. If I compared your magic to Morgan's or Morgause's and noted how you lacked skill in contrast to them, *that* would be below the belt."

"You would," Merlin muttered, rubbing the side of his head. He abruptly broke into a laugh. "It's been months since you've mocked my magic."

"I only needed to learn that lesson once," Britt snorted.

"Oh?"

"Bringing it up for comedic effect is a different matter," Britt said when she noticed his look of disbelief.

"I see. You are on your way to the throne room?"

"Yes. Lancelot has defeated more foes."

"See to them as quick as you can—Kay always complains about feeding recreant knights."

"Of course. See you later, Merlin," Britt called over her shoulder before she resumed her march, tossing her apple into a compost pile as she left.

"Cheeky brat," Merlin muttered as she left.

"At least I didn't destroy Stonehenge."

"Blaise fixed it!"

Britt waved farewell and retorted, "Doesn't matter!"

"Mind your cape, you cave troll!"

"Again, you resort to insults. Yes, you're clearly more mature than I am."

"LEAVE!"

"We're going!"

≈

For the next two hours, Britt sat on her throne and listened to recreant knight after recreant knight report Lancelot's activities and wins.

"The man has been gone for only two and a half, almost three weeks. Does he not sleep? Thank you," Britt said, taking the tankard of water Kay offered her.

"He did say he would attempt to win your favor," Kay said.

"I wish he would 'attempt' a little less. We're going to run out of roles to put these guys in."

"Lady Morgan suggested we use them as farmhands."

"That's a good idea—though I'm not certain they'll appreciate that, being knights and then demoted to farmers."

Kay shrugged. "They chose for mercy to be extended to them as opposed to dying by the sword. I believe they will be thankful to be alive and have a chance to redeem themselves."

"Perhaps. Wait, *Morgan* thought that up? Not that I doubt it, it sounds like her, but you were talking to Morgan, voluntarily?"

"She clubbed Merlin while you were gone with Sir Mordred."

"And I missed it? Dang it! Everything fun keeps happening whenever I'm gone. What did he say to her?"

"He suggested she was getting to be too old to have younger knights enamored with her."

"Hooo, and she only hit him once? She was feeling kind."

"I thought her restraint was admirable," Kay said.

"*Admirable*? I mean, admirable? Yes, for sure," Britt said, scrambling to check her shock. Kay was shy and spoke to the ladies of Camelot only under dire need. For him to actually converse with Morgan was huge. Although, now that she thought of it, when Sir Ulfius first came to tell Merlin about Vivien, he was speaking with Morgan. She was about to question her brother further about this interesting personal development, but her thoughts were interrupted.

"My Lord?"

Britt shook her head to clear it and smiled at the knight standing in the doorway. "Yes, Sir Bedivere?"

"King Pellinore is here to see you."

309

"Pellinore? Marvelous, send him in!" Britt said. She stood and trotted down the dais stairs, rolling her shoulders to loosen them.

King Pellinore entered the throne room with his typical noble bearing. "Arthur." A smile creased his face when the two met just past the line of recreant knights still waiting for review.

The two kings paused awkwardly before Britt slapped him on the back. "Come, pull up a chair and suffer with me." She beckoned for him to follow her to her throne.

"Are you expanding the Round Table?"

"No. These are some of the knights Lancelot has beaten during his summer holiday," Britt said wryly. "What brings you to Camelot? Percival? You just missed him; he left yesterday on a quest."

"No, although I did hope to hear he is conducting himself in an honorable manner. How did he do in the tournament?" King Pellinore asked, taking a seat on a padded bench a servant placed near Britt's throne.

"Quite well! I was impressed, although I think he wished he had done better. He did justice to your family, though."

"I am glad you think that is so," Pellinore said. "I heard Lancelot won the tournament and asked to be called the Queen's Champion?"

"Yes." Britt's voice was as hard as stone.

"Ah. Is that why he's out questing?"

"No, he did something even more stupid. If only Gawain wasn't gone for the tournament—he might have beaten Lancelot."

"I thought a lady requested his help, and as the Ladies' Knight, he had to aid her?"

"Yes," Britt admitted, her shoulders slumping. "It was a chivalrous action. I'm just missing my knights—although Griflet is back for a bit."

"Ah, yes. I meant to tell you I met a knight in the Forest of Arroy. He said Sir Ywain had been captured by a knight who guards a magic fountain."

"What? The knight must have been better than he thought. I guess I'll be taking that company to the fountain after all."

"You know of what he speaks?"

"Yes. One of my other knights—Sir Lanval—stumbled upon it and was roughed up by a knight after inspecting it. Ywain wanted to avenge Sir Lanval's injuries—though I think he was just sick of sitting around the castle, waiting for Griflet or Gawain to come back and release him from babysitting duty."

"From *what*?" King Pellinore asked.

"Guard duty, I guess you could say. Ever since...Lancelot injured me, one of that trio has been in Camelot."

"How loyal."

"And stifling. However, it sounds like it is my turn to return the favor," Britt said before raising her voice. "Sir Bedivere, would you please dismiss the rest of the defeated parties? Kay—Ywain has been captured. You know what knights to take?"

"Yes, My Lord," Kay answered.

"Excellent. Pellinore, come tell Merlin with me—we ride at dawn."

~

"HE'S TRAPPED in the gatehouse of the castle?" Sir Bedivere asked, turning his horse in a tight circle.

"That's what the knight said," King Pellinore said.

"Ywain *would* chase a knight straight into a stronghold," Griflet said, shaking his head.

"So would you," Sir Lionel—Lancelot's cousin—said with a mischievous smile.

"I would," Griflet admitted. "But I haven't, yet, so I will use this opportunity to gloat."

"Are we to assume it is likely that the knight is holding Sir Ywain in a dungeon?" Sir Bors asked.

"Most likely. He must have been captured—Sir Ywain could

not defend a gatehouse on his own," Sir Kay said. "Are you ready to leave, My Lord?"

"Yes, but where is Merlin?"

"Here. I apologize; Sir Ulfius and Sir Bodwain required last-minute instructions." Merlin rode out of the stable on his spindly-limbed horse. "Has everyone assembled? Good, let's go save that foolish youth."

The company of fifty knights clattered from Camelot. The sound of horse hooves on stone was deafening and almost muted the jingle of armor and equipment. Britt led the line with Merlin and Kay directly behind her.

"No—you can't be serious," Britt said in horror when they left the castle for the meadow that surrounded Camelot. A knight with blue embellishments on his armor and tack rode a palomino —a horse with gold-colored fur and a white mane and tail—in their direction.

"I say, that's Lancelot, isn't it?" Merlin asked, shielding his eyes from the sun with his hand.

"Merlin," Britt started.

"He may as well come with us, Arthur," Merlin said.

"Why?"

"He will make our company one person stronger," Merlin said mildly.

"Shouldn't he stay behind to see to the defense of the castle?"

"Nonsense. This is much better than setting your cape on fire. *Lancelot!*" Merlin shouted.

"I *hate* you."

Merlin waved an arm in the air. "Lancelot! Come, join our company!"

"*Seriously* hate you," Britt said as the palomino pranced closer.

Lancelot pulled off his helm so he could subject them to his full-wattage smile. "Good morn to you, My Lord and Merlin the Wise. What trouble has befallen the lands to require such a grand company?" He peered past Britt and gestured to the spread of knights flowing out of the castle.

"We ride to the rescue of one of the companions of the Round Table—Sir Ywain," Merlin said. "He's gotten himself in a bit of a scrape and has apparently been taken captive."

"A rescue of this level? It is sure to be inspiring. Might I intrude upon this company and join you?" Lancelot asked.

"Actually—" Britt started.

"Absolutely, yes!" Merlin said. "We will be highly appreciative to have you in our ranks, Sir Lancelot. Now if you'll excuse me, I believe I shall check with the tail of our procession. Arthur —lead on."

Roen took a few steps forward, impatiently flicking his tail. Lancelot moved to pull his horse next to Britt, so they would ride shoulder to shoulder. Britt twisted in her saddle to give a pleading look to Sir Kay.

The taciturn knight shook his head, his mustache twitching, and looked to the sky when she made a face at him.

"If Sir Ywain is being held in a castle, does that mean you intend to lay a siege upon it?" Lancelot chattered as he and Britt led the company to the forest road.

"No. We're hoping if we show enough of our power, hopefully they'll just hand him over."

"That's a well-thought plan, though it seems a little lack-luster. I would prefer a full-frontal attack; though, then you would need armies instead of a company of knights."

"Tell me, Sir Lancelot, why are you back so soon?" Britt asked, distracting the knight. The temperature dropped as they moved farther into the forest and the trees blocked out the sky. "I thought you intended to do quests to earn favor and return your-self to my good graces. It's only been two or three weeks."

"Indeed, but I hoped your anger might have cooled by now."

"My anger over your public request to be called the Queen's

Champion, or my fury over the formation of the Queen's Knights?"

"Both, My Lord."

"And you thought a mere two weeks was a long enough period for my emotions to subside?"

"You haven't taken Excalibur to my throat, so I would say it was," Lancelot mildly observed.

Behind them, Kay suspiciously cleared his throat several times.

Britt twisted in her saddle to scowl at her foster-brother, but Kay was busy, innocently looking at the sky—though his mustache still quivered.

"Did my vanquished foes arrive in Camelot to give their vows to you?" Lancelot asked.

"Yes. Though I must ask if it was really necessary to defeat them *all*."

"I defeated an impressive number of men, did I not?" Lancelot preened.

"It was *excessive*."

"You are a difficult person to understand, My Lord," Lancelot said.

In spite of herself, Britt's curiosity was piqued. "What?" She ducked a branch and cast the boastful knight a questioning glance.

"When any of your younger knights defeat a foe, you congratulate them and throw them feasts. When I defeat foes, you say I used excessive force."

"That's because you *do* use excessive force."

"I deeply apologized for stabbing you."

"In the *back*. After our match had already *finished!*" Britt stressed.

"Mayhap you would better receive me if I captured an animal to join your menagerie. Do you fancy owning a lion?" Lancelot asked.

"No. No more animals," Britt firmly said.

"Jewels?"

"If you start asking about chocolates and flowers, I will have you tossed from this company," Britt warned him.

"Chocolates? What is that?"

"A food. Forget about it. Just—why don't you go talk to Sir Bedivere?"

"Why would I?"

"He has all the details of Sir Ywain's capture."

"Does he?"

"Indeed."

"Very well, I shall seek him out and speak to him. Good day, My Lord."

"Cheerio." Her shoulders slumped when he left her.

"You failed to mention that Sir Bedivere knows all the details only because you told him," Sir Kay said, joining Britt at the front of the procession.

Britt smirked. "You think that wasn't on purpose? And thanks for helping me out of that, by the way, *brother.*"

Sir Kay smoothed his mustache and said nothing more on the subject, although his eyes glittered with their shared humor.

8

SIR YWAIN'S FATE

"It's almost evening. Perhaps we should consider camping soon, My Lord?" Sir Bedivere suggested. He rode at Britt's left.

"Maybe, but aren't we almost there?" Britt looked to her companions for confirmation.

"I could go ask Sir Lanval," Griflet offered.

"Do you think it would be more intimidating if we arrived just before dark—so they worry about us the entire night?" Britt asked.

Merlin scrunched his handsome face. "Sometimes your deviousness surprises me."

"Only sometimes?" Britt asked.

"Look yonder—your courageous scouts return," Kay said, pointing to Sir Lancelot, Sir Lionel, and Sir Bors, whose mounts cantered down the road. Starting around noon, Britt had ordered her "champion" to ride ahead of them on scouting duty. Everyone —from Kay to Merlin—complimented her military thinking, when in truth she just wanted something to occupy the charismatic knight so he would stop prattling.

"Good, perhaps they will have news for us," Merlin said.

"My Lord, we have returned from scouting." Lancelot pulled his horse to a halt a few feet away from Britt, Merlin, Griflet, and Bedivere. His cousins narrowly avoided him.

"So I see," Britt said. "Anything to report?"

"The castle—which we believe belongs to the knight who guards the magical fountain—lies but a short distance from here. At a brisk pace, one could reach it in a fraction of an hour," Sir Lancelot said.

"Excellent." Britt turned Roen in a tight circle. "So, men, do we press on, or camp and catch them by surprise in the morning?"

"That is not all we have to report," Sir Lancelot added.

"Oh?" Merlin asked.

"There is a strange sight waiting at the castle," said Sir Lionel —who sounded deep and guttural like a bear.

"What is it?" Britt asked.

"I don't think you would believe us if we told you," Sir Lancelot said. "It is better if you see it yourselves."

Britt exchanged looks with Merlin.

"It's quite surprising," Sir Bors added in the silence. "I do not think any sort of combat will be exchanged."

Wrinkles spread across Merlin's forehead like a spider web. "Oh?"

"Shall we press on, then?" Britt asked.

"I'll alert the rest of the company," Griflet said, his voice tight with excitement.

"Alright, let us set off." Merlin sighed. "If we do fight, and this move forces us to give up a tactical advantage, I will string the three of you up by your thumbs," Merlin warned the scouts.

"We're moving out!" Griflet shouted. He spurred his horse down the column in which the knights were arranged.

They picked up their pace, moving at a controlled trot. Metal jingled, and knights checked their weapons as Griflet rode the perimeter of the company, shouting instructions.

"How much farther in?" Britt asked after several minutes of riding. Lancelot's palomino pranced next to her, flicking its white tail at Roen.

"Not far, My Lord. It lies just beyond that break in the woods." Lancelot pointed to a bright spot on the dirt road where the trees thinned out.

The trees opened up into a vast meadow—the center of which was pressed down in a dimple. The castle stood at the center of the dimple. It was fairly standard with its stone walls and two towers. However, as it was in the low part of the meadow, it had (Britt was jealous to see) a moat.

It was the flags that hung from the taller of the two towers that caught Britt's attention. One of them was stitched with the outline of a lioness.

"What—how did—what?" Sir Griflet gabbed.

"That boy." Merlin's voice was heavy with disgust.

Britt halted Roen at the crust of the dimple. Her knights poured from the forest and spilled out from behind her so they too stood at the edge, lining half of the meadow.

A drawbridge lowered from the castle, and out rode a single knight. He had unembellished, simple armor, but his horse had a lioness painted on its crupper armor—the armor that covered its hindquarters.

"Ywain." Britt squeezed Roen. He leaped into a canter, carrying her across the meadow with the speed of the wind.

Britt would have recognized Ywain anywhere, for he credited her with the choice of his lion symbol, claiming they had discussed it when she was first getting to know him as he was a captive—the son of her enemy—held in her army's camp.

She was barely aware that a small brood of horses thundered after her, trying valiantly to catch her.

Ywain halted his horse and dismounted. He wrestled his helm off and was waiting with a huge smile when Britt pulled Roen to a stop just a few feet away.

"You brash idiot." Britt laughed as she slid off Roen.

"I knew you would come, Arthur! I have so much to tell you!" Ywain gave Britt a bear hug that almost pulled her off her feet.

"Yes, you do! What possessed you to ride *into* another knight's castle, chasing him?" Britt patted his back a few times before he released her.

"Ywain—you sly fox!" Griflet leaped from his horse. He landed on the ground with a splat, but he dog-piled on his friend, who staggered under his weight. "Leaving on a quest in the middle of the night!"

"Get off—you giant git!" Ywain laughed.

"I heard you got caught in a gatehouse—for shame." Griflet slid off his friend.

Ywain threw an arm on Griflet's shoulders and an arm over Britt's. "That's not even the best part—oh, greetings, Sir Kay," he said when Kay removed Ywain's arm from Britt's shoulders.

"Congratulations on your conquest, Sir Ywain," Lancelot said. "I don't think I have ever met a knight who has accomplished such a thing on his own."

"Thank you," Ywain grinned.

"You mean to tell me you actually took the entire *castle?*" Merlin said, his voice crusted with disbelief.

"You were the one who told me I was destined for grand things, Merlin." Ywain grinned like an exuberant puppy.

"I can't say castle-conquering was a part of my vision," Merlin said dryly.

"Wait, so you're the lord of this castle?" Britt asked.

"Partially…"

Sir Bedivere furrowed his brow. "How can you partially be a lord?"

"Well, really I'm just the new guardian of the Fountain. My wife, Laudine, she's the real ruler of our household."

"*Wife?*" Britt yelped.

"*Guardian?*" Griflet yipped.

"I am not surprised you should marry what sounds like a strong-minded female. Like father like son," Merlin muttered.

"How can you be married? You're like, seventeen!" Britt said, her eyes big with shock.

"I'm nearly twenty," Ywain frowned.

"No, you can't be," Britt shook her head.

"I'm older than you are—er, older than you're supposed to be," Ywain said.

Britt still gaped at him, and Ywain shifted uncomfortably.

"It is common to marry at what you presume to be a young age," Merlin muttered into Britt's ear.

"I thought you would be happy for me," Ywain said, his voice subdued.

Britt recovered, flashing him a brilliant smile. "I am. I absolutely am. It just...surprised me. Did you know your lady...before?"

"No, she was married to Esclados the Red—whom I mortally wounded," Ywain said. "Here, let me call her down. LAUDINE! LAUDINE—COME AND MEET KING ARTHUR!" he bellowed at the walls of the castle.

"You forced the wife of the man you killed to marry you?" Sir Kay asked when Ywain stopped shouting.

Griflet clasped Ywain's shoulder. "You're a brave man— stupid, but brave."

"It's not like that." Ywain swatted his friend away. "The fountain has to be protected, or the storms will rage over these lands. Laudine knew she needed to remarry quickly to protect her lands; I volunteered."

"So you don't love her?" Britt asked, still struggling with the line of the story.

"Of course I do!" Ywain said, looking horrified. "I fell in love with her when she held me captive in her dungeons."

Griflet nodded knowingly. "Love at first sight—'tis quite romantic."

"It sounds rushed." Britt was shocked that *Lancelot* of all people spoke those words, his usually joyous face blank as one of his eyebrows rose in suspicion.

"One cannot deny love," Ywain said with a boyish smile.

Britt took a moment to carefully plan her wording and then asked, "So you married her, and you're now the protector of this magical fountain?"

"Yes. Oh—Merlin, it cannot be moved. I checked," Ywain said.

"I did not think it could be countered quite so easily, but one must always thoroughly investigate," Merlin said.

Britt barely heard his reply, she was mulling over Ywain's situation. *He said the fountain had to be guarded.* "So am I to assume you will not be returning to Camelot?"

Ywain shook his head. "I will still do deeds in your name, My Lord. I'll just be like King Pellinore—not a permanent resident, but a common visitor!"

"I see," Britt said.

Ywain's smile faded, and he grew still. "You're not pleased with me, are you, My Lord?"

"I," Britt hesitated. It was all going so *fast*. She could have sworn Ywain was barely past sixteen, and now he was *married*? To a lady he had known for only a few days? Had he gone *mad*?

"Not here, lass," Merlin whispered in her ear.

Britt clamped down on the unhappy words threatening to escape her mouth and instead shook her head, making a show of looking dismayed. "It's only that your father is going to *kill* me! Setting you up as a married man was never part of our treaty."

It was the right thing to say. Ywain and Griflet roared with laughter, and even Sir Bedivere chuckled.

"I don't think he would expect anything less from me. Oh! Here she is!" Ywain was all smiles as a lady on a white donkey rode across the drawbridge.

Laudine—as Ywain had called her—was quite beautiful, with silken blonde hair and wondrous blue eyes. She was a few years older than Ywain, but those extra years gave her a grace and poise that other pretty girls—like Guinevere—lacked.

Ywain threw an arm across Britt's shoulders and dragged her over to the lady when she halted her donkey. "Laudine, this is King Arthur—my lord, my liege, and my life. My Lord, this is Laudine—the most beautiful lady in the world and the love of my soul," Ywain said. He leaned over and whispered in Britt's ear. "Please don't give her your best smile—I don't think I can compete with it."

Laudine curtsied. "My Lord, King Arthur," she murmured.

"It is a pleasure to meet you, Lady Laudine," Britt said as Sir Kay grabbed Ywain by the neck and yanked him a foot away from her. "Sir Ywain is one of my dearest companions and bravest knights. I know he will love you with a faithfulness and loyalty that are rare."

"Thank you, My Lord," Laudine said.

Britt and Laudine studied each other for a few moments—gauging each other. Britt still wasn't sure what to think of her, but it was out of her hands at the moment.

"Oh, and here is my greatest companion—Sir Griflet." Ywain paraded his best friend before his wife.

Griflet treated her to a sweeping bow. "A pleasure, Lady Laudine. You must be among the most patient creatures in these lands if you married—ack!" He yelped when Ywain kicked the back of his knee.

Britt watched Ywain introduce his new wife to the small group of knights one by one.

Mordred drifted out of the crowd so he could stand at Britt's side. "You don't look at ease, My Lord."

Britt allowed herself to deeply exhale. "I'm not."

Mordred briefly rested a hand on her shoulder and then returned to his horse. "What shall I tell the other knights, My Lord?"

"We'll camp here for tonight. Is that acceptable, Merlin?" Britt asked.

"Yes. We will begin our journey home in the morning," Merlin said.

"Oh, but you must feast with us tonight," Ywain said eagerly. "Can't they, Laudine?"

"Of course, husband." the beautiful lady smiled faintly at her company. "We would be honored to have you as our guests this evening."

"Then it's settled. Stake your horses, and come in! I wish to show you the castle!"

~

THE FEAST WAS a strange cocktail of emotions. Laudine's guards and men at arms were polite but tense, and Britt thought she could detect a trace of fear among them. Most of the knights of Camelot were in high spirits, but there were a few surprises.

Lancelot was quiet and introverted—he didn't even look at any of Laudine's ladies in waiting—Merlin acted unusually exuberant, and Griflet was thoughtful.

Britt walked the perimeter of the room, sipping drinks and observing her knights. She watched Sir Ywain and other Round Table knights laugh and shout. Sir Mordred had set up court at another table and was doing his best to charm Laudine's quiet ladies. Sir Bedivere seemed to genuinely enjoy himself, and Kay —Britt could tell—was reveling in the knowledge that this was one feast Camelot was not paying for.

"Ahem."

Britt pulled her attention away from her knights and pushed a smile onto her lips. "Lady Laudine—you look beautiful this evening."

Laudine moved to join Britt on her stroll. "I thank you. I hope everything is to your liking, My Lord."

"Indeed, it is. You are a generous and pleasing hostess," Britt said, feeling a little awkward. Previously, the only married knight in the Round Table was King Pellinore, and his wife, Adelind— Queen of Anglesey—was much older and gave off a motherly-vibe. It had been easy to interact with her. As Laudine was roughly her age, she was at a bit of a loss in knowing how to act —and the lady's stiff demeanor certainly wasn't helping her.

Laudine knit her fingers together. "I am glad to hear you think so. My husband greatly esteems you and your opinion."

"Please allow me to extend my congratulations on your nuptials. I am sorry I was not present for the happy occasion," Britt said.

"It was a sudden thing—although Ywain has stated his desire for you to visit ever since."

Britt smiled and, lacking anything to say, sipped her drink.

"Are you pleased to have Sir Ywain as a lord under your command?" Laudine asked.

"Of course. Sir Ywain has a loyal and true heart. He can be brash, but you have won him for life, Lady Laudine."

"Yes, just as you have," Laudine said.

"Yes," Britt acknowledged.

"Which is why I wanted to speak to you, My Lord. Because of the location of our lands, and the proximity of the fountain, it is absolutely necessary that a strong and able man rules as lord protector."

"I am confident Ywain will properly protect you," Britt said.

"Of this I am aware," Laudine said. Her voice held a hint of frost. "What I seek, My Lord, and what I ask of you, is that you would not call my husband from these halls."

"I beg your pardon?" Britt said.

"I have heard much of Camelot—indeed, I acknowledge you as my King, and my lands enjoy your protection. But while I have heard what a just and worthy King you are, I have mostly heard of your knights and their conduct. I have heard of your Round

Table and how you bind your knights to you as lord and comrade."

"It is true that my knights are my closest companions," Britt said.

"And Sir Ywain is one of them."

"Of course."

"But, My Lord, you have enough other knights. Please, do not lure my husband from these lands."

An ungracious part of Britt wanted to pull Laudine's hair. The lady was basically trying to sever their friendship. But as poorly delivered as the request was, Britt could see how much it mattered to the lady. It was probably why everyone from her castle was on edge. As a knight, Ywain was easily the best trained and best equipped in a castle of guards. If he left, they would be without his protection.

Still, Laudine didn't have to be such a hag about it.

"I understand the position you are in, Lady Laudine," Britt said. "Please allow me to assure you that I understand Ywain has responsibilities here. Yet, I cannot promise that I will not call him —for Ywain is a knight of the Round Table, and as a knight, he is concerned not only with his lands, but the country. However, I am confident that if you and Ywain are as deeply in love as you appear to be, he will not stray to me without purpose." Britt smiled to ease her thinly veiled threat.

Laudine did not return the smile. "I see."

"You have married an honorable man, Lady Laudine. I suggest you worry a little less on what he *might* do and concentrate, instead, on your relationship," Britt added.

"I sense you are used to your subjects' endless trust in you, My Lord," Laudine said.

Britt smiled fondly. "Perhaps."

"Do not let such pride rule you. If you'll excuse me, My Lord," Lady Laudine said.

Britt watched her leave with a frown. "Good riddance," she muttered into her cup.

"Had a spat with Lady Laudine, did you?" Merlin asked, making Britt jump at his sudden arrival.

"Yes, and I have no idea why. Are you sure Ywain *wanted* to marry that nag? Maybe she enchanted him."

"She did no such thing. The two of you are bucking heads because you are selfish, and she is needy and untrusting," Merlin said.

"Gee, thanks," Britt said.

"You're welcome. She presents an issue we must discuss."

"Now?"

"No, on our ride tomorrow."

"Great. That means it's going to be a *long* lecture."

"No, it will merely require some introspection on your end."

"Hmph."

"Britt," Merlin said, drawing her attention—he didn't often use her true name, and he *never* used it where they might be overheard. "I'm sorry. I know this is troubling to you and rather unexpected."

"I think *everyone* finds it unexpected," Britt said.

"Perhaps, but you are Ywain's king. This change was sure to hit you—and perhaps Griflet—the hardest, but there are certain factors that make it even more difficult for you to accept."

Britt tilted her head. "Like?"

Merlin opened his mouth, hesitated, and looked around. "Tomorrow," he promised. Britt would have protested, but the soft look in his blue eyes made her heart twist.

"Tomorrow," she agreed.

Merlin cleared his throat and straightened his blue tunic. "Now. I'm going to mingle—as should you. You don't want to give off the impression you disapprove of this union."

"But I *do*."

"It is not your call to make. This is your knight's personal life;

he may decide whom to love." Merlin scowled, as if angry with his own words. When Britt raised an eyebrow at him, he swapped the frown for his charming court grin. "Now smile, or you can go sit with Lancelot. His presence will serve as an explanation for your grim look."

"Hah-hah, you're so funny." Britt turned on her heels and descended upon a cloud of ladies. "Mordred—you scoundrel. Introduce me to your companions."

9

THE TALK

"Alright, Merlin. Hit me. What did you want to talk about?" Britt asked the following day as she and the wizard rode side by side, leading the way back to Camelot.

(The farewells that morning had been joyful and stilted. Ywain was all smiles, but the night seemed to have done little to improve Laudine's possessive mood. As such, Britt was both sad and grateful to be leaving Ywain so soon.)

"The passage of time," Merlin said.

"What, are you looking into inventing quantum physics—or is this the start of a poem? I don't do poetry, just an FYI."

"FYI? You speak almost normal now, but you have retained some of the oddest sayings from your home," Merlin said, shaking his head. "No, I wish to explain something to you. Your knights are growing up."

"Why do you sound like a teacher preparing to speak to his students' parents?" Britt asked.

"Because you haven't noticed this issue yourself. When Ywain first came to you, he was seventeen. Two years have passed since then, making him nineteen. You must have noticed the changes his maturation has produced, for the lad no longer resembles a gangly spider. Nineteen is a perfectly acceptable age for a knight to marry."

"Has it really been two years?" Britt adjusted her hold on Roen's reins. "It feels like it's only been months."

"Gawain is even older than Ywain. You can expect he also will marry soon, as will your other young knights."

Britt uneasily glanced at the wizard, who wore a deceivingly placid expression and stared at the road. "What are you getting at, Merlin?"

Merlin was quiet for a few moments as their horses plodded along. He nodded, as if pumping himself up, and settled his gaze on her. "Your knights are mature, lass. You have taught them well, and they have flourished under your principles. It is time to release them."

"Release them? Do you want me to dissolve the Round Table?" Ice spread in her heart. These men were her friends—her brothers!

Merlin drew back in horror. "No, no, absolutely not! You think I would go through all that trouble to get you a circular table to use for a mere year and give up one of the most genius methods of ruling I have ever seen? *No.*" He glared at Britt like a chicken with ruffled feathers.

"You said you wanted me to release them," Britt said. "Besides their oaths as knights, I have no other hold over them."

"But you do," Merlin said. "You have in your hands your knights' loyalty and love—not the kind Ywain has for Laudine, but the deep affection of comrades. If you don't set them free, they will stay bound only to you until the day they die. You must know that would be a disservice to them."

Britt looked to the sky and tried to swallow the lump in her throat. *They will leave me, and I will be alone. Again.* She knew it was a selfish worry, but she couldn't help it. Men like Gawain and Ywain made her new life enjoyable. This wasn't like the twenty-first century. She couldn't zip over to meet Ywain in his new castle for lunch.

When the knights started having families of their own, she would be alone in Camelot.

"No," Merlin said, as if he could read her thoughts. "You have men who will always stand with you, and your knights already leave you now to go on quests. But even so, you will still see your knights after they have married."

"I guess."

"No, there are no guesses, Britt. Pellinore is married, and you see him often enough that you still consider him a close comrade. It will be the same with Ywain and the others. You have instilled chivalry and honor into them, lass, so they don't *have* to be at your beck and call to accomplish good deeds. You must trust them, and let them make lives for themselves."

Britt was silent.

"Some of them will not stray very far. Young Griflet and Sir Tor, I doubt, will ever move from your halls. I imagine they will wed Camelot girls and remain in your court. But those who inherit land…it is different for them. They must take up their roles as landowners."

"Like Sir Ector," Britt said. "I need to let him spend more time at Bonmaison instead of Camelot."

"Exactly," Merlin nodded. "It is not that you are cutting off contact; rather, you are letting them be knights in their own right. They cannot be known only as 'King Arthur's Knights.' They must establish identities of their own."

"It's hard," Britt said, glancing over her shoulder. Kay, Griflet, Lancelot, and Mordred were riding in a row—arguing about ladies from the sound of it. "It feels like I'm saying goodbye."

"Perhaps a little, but it's not forever. And you have to know their loyalties will *always* lie with you. Just as a portion of your heart belongs to them, so will a part of their soul belong to you. Isn't that what friendship is?"

Britt sighed. "You're right. I am being selfish."

"I knew you would come to your senses."

"Just because I understand doesn't mean I have accepted it yet."

"It can only be expected. You have poured much into these men; it is hard to let them go. If it's any consolation, Laudine spoke to you last night because she's terrified you have a deeper hold over Ywain than she does."

"Whatever. She's the most important lady in his life now," Britt sighed.

"She is, but do not underestimate the power you still have over him," Merlin warned. "You are his King. I said it before, but the love he has given you was never the romantic kind. That means Laudine's entrance into his life has not taken away any bit of the love he has for you. It is the same for all of your knights."

Britt turned around to look at her men. Sir Bedivere had arrived and was laughing with Sir Griflet—his relative—about Ywain's newly married status.

"I can't believe so much time has passed already," Britt said. She smiled at Mordred and Kay—who was discussing jousting techniques.

Merlin frowned and swatted at a fly. "Yes, I believe that is a common affliction with those who are like you."

"Like me? You mean kings?"

"Hm? Oh, certainly," Merlin said, going evasive. "Back to young Ywain. You seem afraid he will never come to Camelot."

"Unless we are in deep need, I don't think it's likely," Britt said.

"Pish posh," Merlin snorted. "You are forgetting one very important thing."

"What is that?"

"During the winter, water freezes."

"So?"

"That magical fountain Lady Laudine is so concerned with will freeze, leaving Ywain free during the winter months."

Britt blinked. "Oh…I hadn't thought of that."

"Every knight you set loose will have a similar time when they will yearly return to you. Fret not, lass. Just as they are important to you, you are important to them," Merlin said. He flashed a smile at her before scowling. "This stupid fly!"

Britt relaxed, lulled by Roen's rocking walk and the singing of birds. Although she was still conflicted about Ywain and his sudden marriage, the event had significantly cheered her… because things were finally returning to normal with Merlin. She still loved him, and she knew Blaise's kindly-meant prompts were misinformed, but it didn't matter. Life in Camelot was much more fun if she and Merlin were laughing and chattering rather than living with the silent tension that had plagued their conversations and actions for nearly a year. If Merlin didn't want anything more, she could force herself to be content with friendship. She would rather do that than lose the relationship they had.

She lazily yawned. "Who else do you think will stay?"

"What?" Merlin asked as both he and his horse gave the fly the stink-eye.

"You said earlier some—like Tor and Griflet—would stay at Camelot. Who else?"

"Gawain will, if he can," Merlin said. "And so, I imagine, would Lancelot."

Britt's expression turned sour. "What."

"Lancelot loves the female gender too much to tie himself to one, and he thrives in a place like Camelot."

Britt made a noise of disgust. "He's a prince. Doesn't he have lands to rule?"

"Yes, but his father is young and healthy. I imagine it will be decades before he is needed," Merlin said.

"Great. Thank you for ruining my hopes and dreams," Britt complained.

"Percival might. I would think it is likely his father will encourage him to marry a lady from your court. All of your vassals will stay—like Bedivere, Kay, Bodwain, and Ulfius." Merlin hesitated. "As will I."

Merlin offered his presence casually, drawing Britt's attention. She would have taken his presence for granted—uniting Britain was *his* dream, after all. But Merlin didn't—wouldn't—look at her, and fussed over his horse. He was almost *bashful*.

No. I just decided I would be fine with friendship. I'm not going to look for something that isn't there. "Good," Britt said. "There's no way I'm going to suffer Lancelot's presence alone."

"Mordred might stay as well," Merlin continued.

Britt patted Roen on the neck. "Mordred? He's not even a Knight of the Round Table."

"Yes, but I expect you'll receive his oath any day now," Merlin said. "You will treat him with proper respect when he does. I saw you whispering assumedly vile things to Lancelot when you dubbed him the Queen's Champion. You cannot do that with Mordred—we still do not know whom we would anger by doing so."

"It doesn't matter; I wouldn't do that to Mordred."

"Why not?"

"For starters, he hasn't stabbed me in the back."

"You hold grudges the way squirrels hoard food."

"And you are more concerned with politics and relations than a father looking to marry off his daughter."

Merlin gave her a slanted grin. "You artless piece of baggage."

"Washed up hack," Britt returned.

"Ho-ho, what's this? Did you not learn your lesson last time, or are you that eager to while away the long hours of this ride in Lancelot's company?"

Britt tried to glare at him, but couldn't help the peal of laughter that escaped her. *Yes, I have missed this.*

~

"MY BUTT," Britt moaned as she slid from Roen's saddle. "I haven't done a cross-country ride in ages."

Merlin unbuckled a saddlebag. "What of your holiday with Mordred?"

"We took a lot of breaks. And you can't fool me—I saw you wince when you touched the ground."

"That's because I'm getting old, and my joints hurt," Merlin groused.

"Nonsense. You're not much older than I am," Britt snorted.

Merlin pressed his lips together and said nothing in response.

"May I take your horse, My Lord?" a stable boy asked.

Britt rolled her shoulders back with a groan. "Please, and thank you."

"My Lord!" Lady Guinevere gushed. The pretty lady ran into the inner courtyard—her dress floating around her like a flower. Morgan was on her heels. Together, the two came and embraced her.

"Guinevere, and my dearest sister." Britt hugged Morgan first.

"Lady Vivien is right behind us," Morgan whispered in Britt's ear.

"It's so good to see you," Lady Guinevere squealed, playing her part perfectly.

I really must thank her some day for her help in this, Britt thought as she hugged her. "Indeed, I am glad to be home." She winked at Guinevere. Morgan gave Merlin a haughty look before she approached Kay.

"King Arthur, how glad I am that you have returned to us," Lady Vivien said with a beautiful smile as she glided across the courtyard.

334

"Take my arm," Britt whispered to Guinevere, who claimed it as if she and Britt were commonly entwined. "Lady Vivien, I hope Camelot continued to warmly receive you in my absence."

"Of course," Lady Vivien said.

Sir Ulfius hurried out from the castle. "Welcome home, My Lord. If you don't mind, I have several important documents for you to see."

"Yes, yes. I'll come now—thank you, Sir Ulfius. If you'll excuse us, Lady Vivien," Britt said.

"Us?" Lady Vivien asked, tilting her head.

"Shall we, Guinevere?" Britt asked, smiling at the younger girl.

Guinevere glowed with happiness. "Yes!"

Britt nodded to Vivien, then headed for the castle keep, Guinevere still holding her arm and gliding along beside her.

"I have so much to tell you, Arthur," Guinevere started as they drew closer to the castle doors. "Blancheflor, Clarine, and I went to the lake where the Lady of the Lake calls home. We, we didn't see her..."

"Yes?" Britt patiently asked.

"But, but..." Guinevere said, stumbling.

"Guinevere, are you alright?" Britt asked, pausing when she realized the girl was gasping oddly.

"I don't feel very well," Guinevere said before dropping like a rock.

"Guinevere! Merlin, Morgan, help!" Britt shouted. She caught the younger girl before she hit the stone ground and gently laid her down. Guinevere's eyes were shut, and her chest heaved oddly.

"Move," Morgan ordered, crouching at Guinevere's side.

"What happened?" Merlin demanded.

"I don't know. We were going inside, and she collapsed," Britt said, panic beating in her heart.

"You, get ground horseradish—the kitchens have it. Hurry!" Morgan barked at Sir Lionel.

"Yes, lady," Sir Bors—who was standing next to his brother—said before he ran for the herb gardens.

"Can you tell what's wrong with her?" Britt asked with wide eyes. She barely noticed when Merlin strode away from her.

"She's having trouble breathing," Morgan said.

Britt hadn't felt so helpless in a long time. Since arriving in medieval England she had been, for the most part, able to physically beat down her opponents. But this? *We need modern medicine.*

Brit knelt next to Morgan. "Is there anything I can do?"

"No. There's nothing *I* can do either," Morgan said, sounding panicked.

"She has to pull through," Britt said, a numb feeling spreading through her body. "The little idiot *has* to make it."

Morgan said nothing as Guinevere turned white.

"Here, horseradish," Bors said, passing a wooden bowl to Morgan, his body heaving with the effort of sprinting.

Morgan smeared the horseradish on Guinevere's neck and chest. The plant smelled strongly, but it did nothing to ease the young lady's gasps.

Britt's heart thundered in her ears. "It's not helping,"

"I know!" Morgan said, her voice tight.

All of a sudden, Guinevere gave a deep gasp—as if a hand had been clutching her lungs and had finally let go. She coughed and breathed more easily when Britt strong-armed her so she was sitting up. She took heaving breaths for a few seconds before saying, "I smell horrid—no one will want to sit by me for dinner, now."

Britt laughed as she hugged Guinevere. Morgan gave them a tired smile and pushed some of her hair out of her face. "I think you'll manage," she wryly said.

"My dress is filthy, too," Guinevere frowned as she started to stand. "This is embarrassing."

Sir Lionel lunged forward to help Guinevere rise. "You look lovely, Lady Guinevere," he said, earning himself a bright smile.

Britt also stood—taking care to dust herself off—and looked around. Merlin was standing in the middle of the courtyard, a grim look fastened upon his face. *I'll talk to him about this. He knows something.*

"Are you coming, My Lord?" Guinevere asked.

"Yes—I know, the papers await me." Britt turned on her heels and entered her castle. *Later.*

A STORM OF FEELINGS

Excalibur flashed as Britt moved through her warm-up practice pattern. Torches crackled, but they weren't entirely necessary as the full moon lit up the sky so brightly it gave her a shadow.

Britt moved down the castle wall, stretching her muscles and wielding Excalibur with deadly precision. When she finished the exercise, she turned, intending to walk back up the wall to begin the pattern all over again.

"If I could have a moment, My Lord."

Britt almost dropped Excalibur in surprise when she saw who addressed her. "Of course, Sir Mordred."

He climbed two stairs to join her on the castle wall and looked up and down the pathway. "You practice here every night?"

"Nearly," Britt said as she sheathed Excalibur.

"Do you never sleep?" he asked, tilting his head like a dog.

Britt laughed. "Not often. How can I help you?"

"This might be uncalled for, My Lord," Mordred began, "but I wished to speak to you about my loyalties." His face was unusually somber, and his green eyes glittered.

"Oh?" Britt asked, glancing at the knight. Merlin was right. Mordred was probably going to swear his loyalties to her. She had been planning to extend him an invitation to the Round Table, but she was surprised he was swearing service to her in the middle of the night, when none would see. Usually knights chose public settings so all would know.

"Yes," Mordred said. "I see what is happening."

Britt turned to look out over the patchwork of farmland that covered the plains behind Camelot. "And what *is* happening?

"The Knights of Camelot are departing."

His observation made Britt's heart go still, but he continued.

"Your kingship has been established, and your enemies are beaten. The knights no longer remain cloistered in Camelot, but they go questing and return home to manage their lands. Most notably, your favorites—your best knights—are gone," Mordred said. "Gawain is out questing most of the year; Ywain will now be tied to his lands, and Griflet comes and goes like the wind."

"Are you trying to convince me I'm alone?" Britt frowned.

"No, quite the opposite," Mordred said. "I wish to offer you my loyalty."

"You wish to take the oath to become my knight?" Britt turned from the beautiful view to face him.

"Yes. I vow to protect you and serve you," Mordred said. "But, if you would have it, I would give you more than that."

Britt rested a hand on Excalibur's hilt. "Yes?"

"I wish to be your sword and shield," Mordred said. "Instead of traveling, I would rather remain in Camelot—like Kay and Bedivere—and help you in any way I can."

Britt stared at him, and tried to think of something to say.

"I do not seek a position in your court. The men who serve you are trustworthy, and I have nothing beside my own word to recommend me. I ask only that you would allow me to support you."

"Why?" Britt asked.

Mordred scratched his chin and gave her a thoughtful look. "It is difficult to be a leader. And I imagine it is very lonely. I do not know this from experience, but from what I have seen when visiting other courts. I wish to serve in Camelot because I believe *you* need knights you can trust in your own castle as well as in the field."

Other courts? He must have powerful connections. Britt studied him, trying to detect any shard of dishonesty in his features. He looked intent and earnest.

"I know it will take time to prove my loyalties, and I do not seek to replace those who are gone," he continued. "I don't have to be first in your affections, My Lord. I just want to be a support to you."

Words entirely failed Britt. She wanted to laugh and cry at the same time. As her knights were growing older, and those she most cherished grew up and left her, Mordred—the knight she suspected had a hand eventually in Arthur's death—was the one who offered such loyalty?

He was right. She could use another close friend. Gawain was gone most of the time, as was Griflet, and Britt had noticed the way Kay and Morgan interacted more these days. Britt wouldn't have it any other way—she *wanted* Kay, Griflet, Gawain, Ywain, and everyone to achieve happiness. But it felt like time was moving for everyone except for her.

There was a catch, though. He didn't know she was a woman. She sighed and ran a hand through her hair. "I appreciate your loyalty, Mordred, and I do not doubt it, but there are things about me…"

"It doesn't matter," Mordred said.

I should talk to Merlin about this first. Even now he still doesn't want me spouting off my secret to anyone. Britt fiddled with Excalibur and tried to buy herself some thinking time.

Mordred, apparently sensing her hesitation, smiled. "Perhaps it would be best if there were a trial period," he said. "Allow me to serve you, and if you cannot stand me, you are free to send me on a year-long quest." He smiled.

Britt laughed in relief—a "trial period" would let her push the issue off and bring it before Merlin. "I'm more worried that you will be disappointed when you see more of me."

"Never, My Lord," Mordred said, shaking his head.

"As you say. Very well—we may begin a trial," Britt agreed.

"Excellent. Let us begin now," Mordred said. "I was recently informed you practice swordsmanship here until the early hours of the morning. Please allow me to serve as your practicing partner."

Britt grinned. "That would be great. I've been looking to face off against someone—it's been hard trying to find opponents."

"I am hurt, My Lord," Lancelot's lofty voice came out of nowhere as he climbed the last few stairs and joined them. "If I had known you longed to cross swords, I would have offered my services."

"Lancelot," Britt said, her tone flat.

"Indeed, it is I! If Sir Mordred does not mind, could I claim a practice match against you as well?"

Mordred grinned. "Our King hardly needs *my* permission to enter a fight—particularly one he is assured of winning."

Lancelot's sour look made Britt laugh. "Fine, I'll fight you, Lancelot—but no stabbing this time."

"My Lord, if I live to be a hundred, I will never regret enough losing my temper that day," Lancelot said, sighing with a great deal of dramatized sorrow.

Britt ignored him and retreated down the wall with Mordred.

"You will not lament this trial, My Lord," Mordred said. "I will do my best to fill in the gaps—especially when Merlin leaves."

Britt stopped and stared at the young man. "When he *what?*"

"When he leaves. He has been shadowing Lady Vivien quite a

lot—" Mordred fell like a sack of flour when Lancelot casually grabbed him by the pauldrons and threw him down.

Britt scowled. "Lancelot!"

"Sorry, Mordred. I can be so clumsy," Lancelot said, helping the knight stand.

Mordred watched Lancelot for a moment, his hand hovering near his sword. He shook off the moment of seriousness and smiled. "Of course, no harm done."

Not so easily pacified, Britt clenched her hands into fists to keep herself from placing them on her hips as she glared Lancelot down. The flirtatious knight returned Mordred's smile and then pinned his green eyes on Britt.

"Never mind Merlin, My Lord. Are you ready for a match?" he asked.

In that instant, Britt realized...*he knows.* Lancelot knew of the affection she harbored for Merlin. She had no idea how he had figured it out, or how he would use it, but it was unnerving that he was aware of the situation. *He's going to try to use it to his advantage...but how? What merit was there in silencing Mordred's thoughts about Merlin?*

"Are you alright, My Lord?" Mordred asked.

"Of course. Come, Lancelot. Give me your best—*chivalrous* shot."

"When will you cease reciting my sins, My Lord?"

"Probably never. Here we go!"

MERLIN WAS MORE than a little irritated that Vivien—an upstart with a bit of black magic to help her—was able to perform a black spell no less than two horse lengths away from him, nearly killing Guinevere. It was inexcusable.

"I don't care if Sir Bodwain and Sir Ulfius disagree. I'm going to dislodge her. Of course, it will take some footwork, but this is no good. At this rate, she's going to kill someone in her anger, and with the knights still renewing their feelings of loyalty for Britt, it's a dangerous time to take a tumble."

Merlin sighed and sat down in a chair. Britt was the real root of the issue. Vivien was a danger to her, yes, but there were a few other ways the witch could be eliminated. All of them, however, required a sacrifice from Britt.

"She has sacrificed enough," Merlin said firmly as he reached for his goblet of wine. "She doesn't know the cost she has paid..."

Guilt wedged a nail in Merlin's heart. He knew he had ruined Britt Arthurs' life. He had stolen her home and family from her, required her to put forth enormous effort as King, and perhaps worst of all, he had stolen her mortality. Several conversations with Blaise had proved it. When Britt Arthurs traveled back to their era, her time started to stand still because of the faerie spell Merlin had employed to accomplish the task.

"I sound like a lunatic," Merlin snorted into his drink. "People dream of immortality...but not Britt."

To Britt, her friendships and relationships were her life. He realized that when he saw her panic over Guinevere—a girl she didn't even like all that much. And he had effectively sentenced her to make friends and watch them die again and again, for thousands of years.

"It's already affecting her. Time is starting to blur," Merlin almost threw his wine cup when his thoughts lingered on Britt's laughter and enchanting smile.

She was the best person he had ever known and the only friend he had let past his emotional defenses, and he had *ruined her life.* He tapped his goblet as he thought. "Yes, distracting Vivien is the least I can do. I can handle a puffed-up *girl*. And when Britt has Ireland secured, I will eliminate Vivien."

Merlin abandoned his chair and peered outside to watch the

sun rise. "Yes. I better start wooing her today." That was his plan, to make Vivien think he had fallen for her seduction spell. All he had to do was behave like an empty-headed fool, and she would never think he was acting. *But Britt...* "She'll know I'm faking it," Merlin said, trying to make himself feel better. "But...maybe I should tell her. While I'm acting, I'll have to stay away from her, after all. Yes, I'll tell her. It's dawn. She will have just gotten to bed only two or three hours ago," Merlin said, rubbing the rim of his cup and feeling surprisingly chirper considering his all-nighter. "I shall go wake her. She'll be so furious—it will be fun!" he decided. He banged out of his study and strolled through the quiet castle.

A few minutes later, he stopped outside Britt's door. "Arthur," he said, banging on the door with his free fist. "Arthur, wake up!" he shouted before downing the rest of the wine in his cup.

"I'm going to kill you."

"Ahh, that is Britain's High King. Rise."

"We don't have mass today. Go away."

"True, but we have much to discuss."

"Like your death?"

"You don't sound like you're getting out of bed."

"I'm not. Get lost."

"Are you dressed?"

"No, I spent the night dancing naked on the castle walls," she hissed.

Merlin chuckled and threw her double doors open. Cavall growled at him, but he paid the huge dog no mind as he shut the doors behind himself and padded across the room.

Britt was a lump buried under blankets.

"Wake up. I have important news to share," Merlin said.

Britt poked her head out of her blanket roll—her blonde hair ruffled and her eyes bleary. To Merlin's liquored eyes—good heavens, he *hoped* it was the wine, or his situation was direr than he thought—she looked adorably disheveled.

"Are you *drunk?*" she demanded.

"No! Maybe. Just a little. I needed it. Just thinking about Vivien infuriates me," Merlin placed his empty goblet on a chest.

"Is that what has had you so grouchy? Vivien?" Britt rubbed her eyes with one hand.

"Indeed. She has black magic, which I've been trying to contain as she has her sights set on you. Probably wants to be made Queen of Britain and then kill you. The lunatic. I haven't been able to counter her very well, so I'll be employing a new tactic." Merlin inched towards her bed, drawing as close to her as he dared.

"What's that? Waking her at dawn and being a pain in the—"

"Language, Britt. And no. I'm going to woo her so she thinks *I* am in love with her. Though I'm no King of Britain, she knows I am a powerful wizard."

"Who can't counter or contain her spells."

"*Shush.* This took a lot of thinking, and it's a big sacrifice for me," Merlin complained.

"Fine, I get it. Thanks—although I don't believe you could possibly be convincing at pretending to fall in love," Britt snorted.

"You'd be surprised," Merlin said, the buzz of wine leaving him for the moment. "Anyway, I am here to bid you farewell."

"What, you're going on vacation together?" Britt said. Merlin could hear the jealousy that colored her voice.

"No, I will remain in the castle. I just won't be able to meet as freely with you—I can't let her suspect anything." Merlin reached out and twined a piece of Britt's gold hair around his finger. She raised her eyebrow at him, but he didn't care. If he was going to be separated from her for a while, he would savor this moment.

"Fine. Thanks for the warning. Good luck, womanizer," Britt grunted and sounded even more irritated.

"I'll also be acting out of character, so I apologize for my future conduct," Merlin said. He tried to tug his finger out of her hair, but it was caught.

Britt reached up and eased his finger out of her wild mane with warm hands. "Great. Thank you for getting me up at dawn to tell me this. I'm sure it couldn't wait even another hour."

"No, I intend to put my plan into practice immediately," Merlin said.

"Well, then." Britt sucked her head back into her blankets. "Good night."

"Britt...I'm doing this because I care for you, and because I'm sorry."

"If you're sorry, why did you wake me up at *dawn?*" Britt snarled, throwing her blankets off and sitting up in bed. She was wearing, Merlin was interested to see, linen pants and a tunic, but without her usual bindings. He was spellbound for a moment —staring wide-eyed at her—until Britt snapped. "*Merlin!*"

"Because I don't know what else to say," he said. He felt lost. He was in uncharted territory, and thus far it had not been very pleasurable.

"There's a saying from my time: actions speak louder than words. You should try it some time," Britt grunted.

Merlin vaguely recalled Blaise railing a similar statement at him over the past few months. Funny how such an irritating but logical piece of advice could last for centuries. *If it's that logical, maybe I should try it. She practically told me to...*

Merlin mulled the thought over for a moment. "Very well, I will." He sat down on Britt's bed, grabbed her by the shoulders and pulled her close.

"What are you—" she was silenced when Merlin pressed his lips against hers.

At first, kissing Britt was like kissing a soft and warm statue. Her shock made her unmovable. He was afraid she would pull back, or possibly even slap him.

Worried, but highly motivated to make it work—this was Britt, after all—Merlin inched one hand around her waist to tug her closer, and slipped his other hand under the blanket of her hair and rested it on the back of her neck. Britt moved the tiniest bit forward so she leaned into him, and the change was immediate.

The kiss went from one-sided to a song of senses. Her lips were soft like silk, and his heart almost leaped from his body when she placed a warm hand on his chest. Heat, like a crackling fire on a winter day, flooded him, and it felt like even his blood sang with joy. It was astounding how *natural* it felt to have her nestled against him, her silken hair caressing his skin. It was enchanting. *She* was enchanting.

Sadly, below the warmth and the delight, was a hint of bittersweetness. He knew what he had done to her—intentionally or not—and he knew that while he had her now, there was no telling what would happen after he left her room. For a brief moment, he considered slaying Vivien and ignoring the consequences, but he couldn't let Britt suffer more than she already had—more than she would.

Yes, he realized he loved Britt, but he—more than anyone else —did not deserve her.

He pulled back before Britt had time to think. "I'm sorry, for what I've done and for what will happen next." he bolted from the room, closing the doors behind him.

Britt sat upright on her bed for several minutes. "Was that a *dream?*" she wondered, pushing her hair from her face. She had been kissed before but had never experienced one so...*right.* Plus, that was *Merlin. Merlin* had kissed her!

What is going on? He can't possibly... She contemplated chasing after him, but decided against it after recalling the haunted light in his blue eyes. She flopped back in her bed and grabbed a pillow, pressing it to her face to muffle her scream. *He's so infuri-*

ating! In spite of her unkind thoughts, she spent the rest of the dawn hours staring into space, trying to piece together what Merlin—and that kiss—meant.

THE END

THANKSGIVING

Britt shivered and fluffed her fur cloak so it covered her throat. Her breath turned into silvery puffs of mist in the crisp night air as she peered from the inner walls of Camelot, looking out at the dark countryside. She could hear the rustle of dry leaves—during the day the forest surrounding Camelot was a beautiful explosion of colors—and the wind tugged on her hair.

She sniffed. "Not much longer and I'll have to start pacing indoors."

"Aye, Milord," one of Britt's guards said. He was already swaddled in furs, and his nose was red with the cold.

Britt leaned against a wall and rubbed her hands together. "Right, might as well try to warm up." She slid Excalibur out of its magical scabbard and twirled it once.

"Couldn't you practice inside, Milord?" a guard asked. The cold temperatures had brought frost—which made the walkways slick.

"No, I need to be prepared to fight on any terrain," Britt said. She lunge forward, whirling Excalibur in a step pattern she had drilled so thoroughly she could do it blindfolded. Her right boot slid only once—not bad for such a slippery surface.

349

The guards shifted and looked disgruntled, but they didn't try to stop her.

Britt got through three patterns before she heard feet stomping up the stairs and a familiar voice grumble. "That churlish coxcomb!" There was more stomping. "Wayward lout!"

Britt leaned over the side of the wall. "Merlin?"

The wizard's pale blonde hair and brilliant blue eyes—that were narrowed due to his bad temper—appeared over the wall first. "You!" he glowered.

Britt raised both of her eyebrows. "Yes?"

"What are you doing?" He climbed the last few stairs and adjusted his blue tunic while glaring at Britt like a moody chicken.

Confused, Britt tilted her head. "What I always do?"

"No, no. Not the insomnia, Excalibur! Why must you run, swinging that pig-stickler around on an icy castle wall? Excalibur's scabbard will keep you from bleeding out, but it won't stop you from cracking your silly head should you take a spill!"

Britt rolled her eyes and slipped Excalibur back in its scabbard. "Fine. Starting tomorrow I will pace indoors. Will that pacify you?"

"I suppose," Merlin said.

"Then I'll do that. Now go be crabby elsewhere." She turned to look back out over Camelot, her eyes watering from the stinging wind.

Behind her, Merlin shifted. "It's still bad, isn't it?" His voice had lost its edge, and was soft with a little hint of sadness.

The change in his voice made Britt twist around to look at him. The flickering torches made his blue eyes look almost sorrowful, as did the upward slant of his eyebrows. Britt pushed off the wall and smiled. "It's better. I have made many friends and gained a family that I love."

Merlin looked away from her. "But you still miss your old life."

"Yes," Britt acknowledged. She had lived in ancient Britain for a short time compared to her life in modern America. It would be stupid not to admit that she missed her mother, her sister, and her friends.

She rubbed her hands together again. "But I can think of them with less pain, now."

Merlin looked at her with a furrowed brow.

"It's true," she continued. "Homesickness keeps me up late into the night still, but I don't feel so alone now. In fact, I think I can actually be thankful."

"*Thankful?*"

"Yes. There's a holiday in Ameri—er, where I come from," Britt said, casting a glance at her guards who were carefully not paying attention. They idly shifted backwards, shuffling out of hearing-range. "It's in the fall—right around now, actually. Families get together and feast for an entire day until you are so stuffed, you make yourself sick."

"Gluttony is a sin," Merlin tisked.

Britt laughed. "Maybe, but it's still fun. My mom always made my sister and I list the things we were thankful for." She hesitated. "I'm thankful for my life here. I never would have chosen it, but having Sir Ector as a foster-father has changed me, and I'm so lucky to have Kay as my foster-brother. But even outside of my foster-family, there are so many people I'm grateful for."

"Young Gawain, I imagine, is near the top of the list?" Merlin asked.

"Yep! As are his brothers: Agravain, Gareth, and Gaheris. There's also Sir Ywain, Sir Bedivere, Sir Griflet, and Sir Bodwain and Sir Ulfius. King Pellinore and his family make the list, of course. Oh, and Morgan and Nymue—I would have gone crazy ages ago if not for them."

"I am surprised you have included none of your animal menagerie," Merlin said.

"Of *course* I'm thankful for them too! Cavall, Roen, Llamrei,

Rudolph—the whole bunch!" Britt said, warming up to the topic. "I'm also super thankful the cook has stopped trying to get me to drink soup for breakfast, and I'm *really* glad Guinevere has made some female friends."

"I notice a certain handsome knight is missing from your list."

"Sir Tor?" Britt asked, deliberately being obtuse.

"No. Lancelot."

"I can assure you there will *never* be a day I am thankful for that idiot."

"To *never* be thankful for him seems a bit much. After all, because of him clean-shaven faces are now the fashion," Merlin said, rubbing his chin.

"I'm also thankful for you!" Britt blurted out, anxious to derail Merlin's thoughts. She cringed. *That was a dumb thing to say. He's going to have a cow.* Britt cautiously looked to the young wizard, who was thoughtfully staring at the sky.

"I am also thankful for you," he said.

Britt relaxed and gave him a half-grin. "Of course you have to be thankful for King Arthurs. How else would you—"

"No, not Arthur, but *you*, Britt," Merlin said.

Britt would have thought it was a joke, but Merlin's blue eyes were serious and his expression was solemn.

"I'm thankful it was you who pulled the sword from the stone, and I'm thankful you are here—though I am sorry for your loss."

Britt looked down at her feet. "I miss them horribly. Sometimes I wake up and reach for my phone to call my sister or mom, but..."

"But?" Merlin prodded.

She hesitated. "But...I'm thankful I'm here."

A smile bloomed on Merlin's face. "Good," he said. "Remember that next time I make you preside over your subjects."

"Merlin," Britt groaned.

"Now, let us climb down from this wretched wall. Why must

you stand out here like a fop when you can call for a fire in a study or the feasting hall? Are you a bird that you must get as close to the sky as possible?"

"It's soothing to look at the stars," Britt said.

"I see."

"Though I am half frozen, and I suspect my guards would support the change in locations," Britt admitted.

"Wonderful. Then let us move—if you get yourself killed while practicing I won't let you hear the end of it."

"It's great to see where your priorities are," Britt said.

"Of course," Merlin said as he shuffled towards the stairs.

"Merlin?"

"Hm?" he turned around to suspiciously eye her.

Britt smiled. "Thank you."

He quickly looked away and stormed down the stairs, but not before Britt heard him say, "Of course."

THE END

ACKNOWLEDGMENTS

Around the time I wrote King Arthur and Her Knights book 3, *Embittered*, the Timeless Fairy Tales really started to take off. Within months of writing *Beauty and the Beast*, I was able to become a fulltime author—my ultimate dream job.

I poured most of my time and energies into the Timeless Fairy Tale series, but every so often I would release a new King Arthur book because of the devoted Champions who would determinedly ask for/request/beg for the next book.

I love all my Champions, but right now I want to specifically thank those loyal King Arthurs Champions. Thank you for patiently awaiting each book. Thank you for persisting and asking me to finish the series. And most importantly, thank you for reading it.

For the longest time I viewed the King Arthur series as a time sucker because I knew it wouldn't pay my bills the way the Timeless Fairy Tale series would. But you guys opened my world and showed me that the King Arthur series was rich in the way it inspired courage and laughter—something I will always find important.

Thanks, guys, for sticking with me and for remaining proud Britt Arthurs' Fans.

OTHER BOOKS BY K. M. SHEA

The Snow Queen:

Heart of Ice

Sacrifice

Snowflakes: A Snow Queen Short Story Collection

Timeless Fairy Tales:

Beauty and the Beast

The Wild Swans

Cinderella and the Colonel

Rumpelstiltskin

The Little Selkie

Puss in Boots

Swan Lake

Sleeping Beauty

Frog Prince

12 Dancing Princesses

Snow White

Three pack (Beauty and the Beast, The Wild Swans, Cinderella and the Colonel)

The Fairy Tale Enchantress:

Apprentice of Magic

Curse of Magic

The Elves of Lessa:

Red Rope of Fate

Royal Magic

King Arthur and Her Knights:

Enthroned

Enchanted

Embittered

Embark

Enlighten

Endeavor

Endings

Three pack 1 (Enthroned, Enchanted, Embittered)

Three pack 2 (Embark, Enlighten, Endeavor)

Robyn Hood:

A Girl's Tale

Fight for Freedom

The Magical Beings' Rehabilitation Center:

Vampires Drink Tomato Juice

Goblins Wear Suits

The Lost Files of the MBRC

Other Novels

Life Reader

Princess Ahira

A Goose Girl

Second Age of Retha: Written under pen name A. M. Sohma

The Luckless

The Desperate Quest

The Revived

ABOUT THE AUTHOR

K. M. Shea is a fantasy-romance author who never quite grew out of adventure books or fairy tales, and still searches closets in hopes of stumbling into Narnia. She is addicted to sweet romances, witty characters, and happy endings. She also writes LitRPG and GameLit under the pen name, A. M. Sohma.

Printed in Great Britain
by Amazon

60197078R00220